To Shirley & Sons

Enjoy!

THE ADVENTURES OF
THADEUS BURKE

Terry Minahan lived from an early age in London then for the last twenty years has lived with his wife Lydia in Newmarket; this has suited his work with bloodstock insurance and her work as an artist.

He left school at sixteen years of age and went straight to a firm of Lloyds' Brokers, starting in accounts then spent many years wandering around the Underwriting Room as a broker, gathering friends and enemies in consideration of a modest monetary reward.

Always an avid reader of detective fiction along with a love of Shakespeare and Plato; he has recently expanded his interests beyond listening to classic and baroque music to the study of music theory and attempts at playing the clarinet - do not expect to hear a public performance, but look out for the next instalment of the adventures of Thadeus Burke which is progressing well.

THE ADVENTURES OF THADEUS BURKE

Terry Minahan

The Adventures Of Thadeus Burke

Olympia Publishers
London

www.olympiapublishers.com
OLYMPIA PAPERBACK EDITION

Copyright © Terry Minahan 2008

The right of Terry Minahan to be identified as author of
this work has been asserted in accordance with sections 77 and 78 of the
Copyright, Designs and Patents Act 1988.

All Rights Reserved

No reproduction, copy or transmission of this publication
may be made without written permission.
No paragraph of this publication may be reproduced,
copied or transmitted save with the written permission of the publisher, or in
accordance with the provisions
of the Copyright Act 1956 (as amended).

Any person who does any unauthorized act in relation to
this publication may be liable to criminal
prosecution and civil claims for damage.

A CIP catalogue record for this title is
available from the British Library.

ISBN: 978-1-905513-39-0

This is a work of fiction.
Although some characters in this publication are drawn
from history, they have been treated respectfully and any precise
resemblance to any real person, living or dead, is purely coincidental.

First Published in 2008

**Olympia Publishers
60 Cannon Street
London
EC4N 6NP**

Printed in Great Britain

This book is dedicated to my wife Lydia

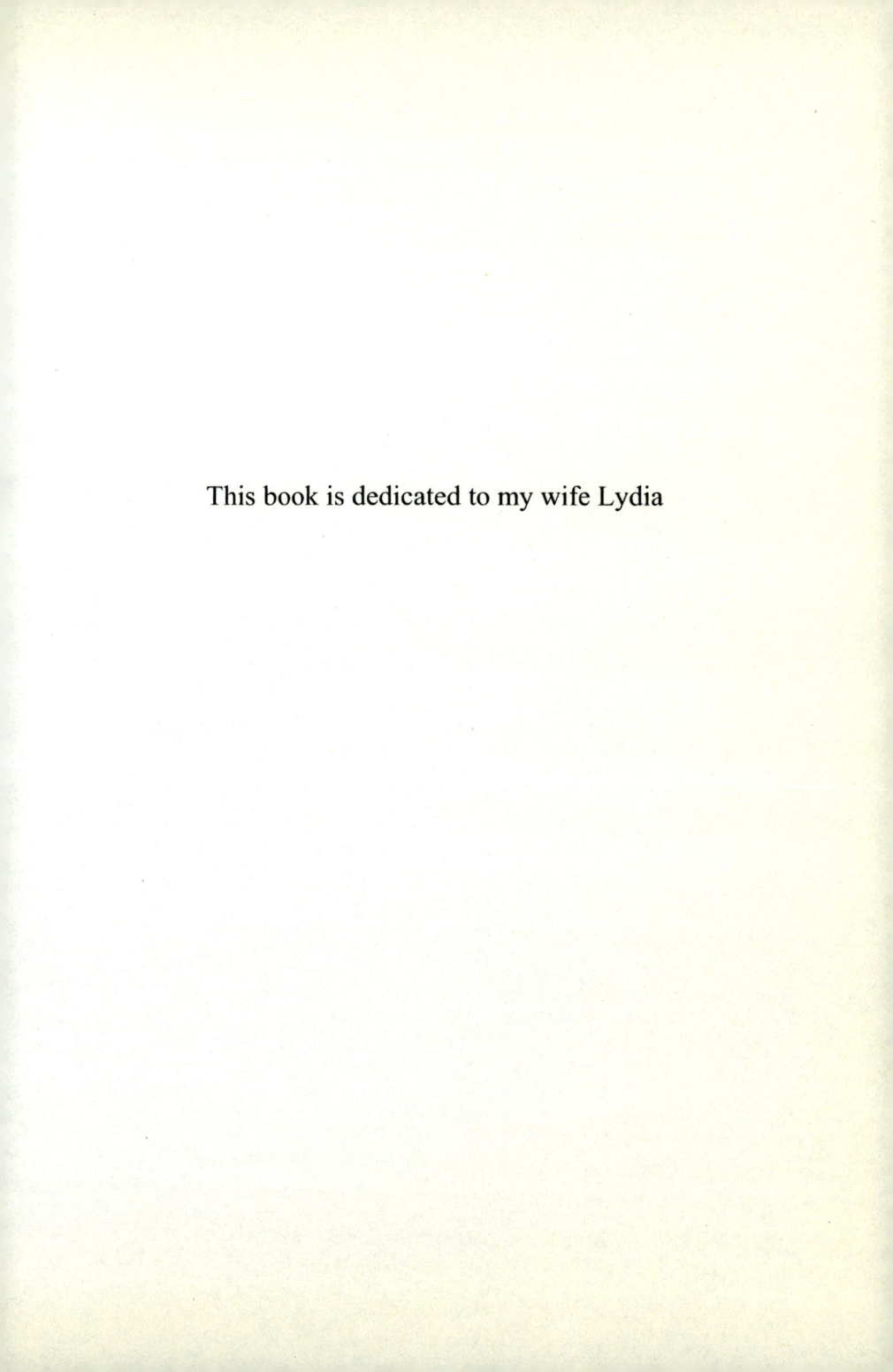

Acknowledgement

Artwork for the cover:
Lydia Minahan

Contents

1.	THE NEW OFFICE	17
2.	ASSASSINATION IN THE ROOM	33
3.	A DOG FIGHT IN ESSEX	51
4.	A DAY AT THE RACES	69
5.	NOUGHTS AND CROSSES	85
6.	WHO WANTS TO BUY A DEAD FOAL?	101
7.	A PARADOX FOR LUNCH	118
8.	CHRISTMAS WITH THE FAMILY	135
9.	A NEW YEAR	153
10.	A FAREWELL CONCERT	172
11.	A VISIT TO THE WHIRLING DERVISHES	189
12.	THE CHELTENHAM GOLD CUP	206
13.	THE DOCTOR'S GRADUATION	222
14.	THE MINING DISASTER	239
15.	THE END AND A NEW BEGINNING	256

CHAPTER 1

THE NEW OFFICE

The Honourable Thadeus Burke met the Chairman of Lloyd's of London, Mr P G Mackinnon, for the second time on Tuesday the first day of September 1925. Two years earlier they had met when Thadeus became an underwriting member or 'name' as they are known on the floor of the famous international insurance market. Several sheets of paper were signed regarding the relationship between the 'name' and Lloyd's and the 'name's' agent. The chairman of Lloyd's, at that time a Mr A L Sturge, was a personal friend of Thadeus' father and his eldest brother. His father was a proper lord coming from a long line of aristocracy and land ownership; his brother's peerage had been bought from the Liberal Party just for the fun of it. Thadeus was the third son and might have been destined for the church had not his mother totally opposed what she termed 'such a stupid idea'. Fortunately Thadeus had proved far too intelligent for the Church of Ireland and even the Church of England, graduating at Trinity College Dublin and having a year at St John's College Cambridge. Mathematics and music were his subjects.

He might have become a professional pianist or cellist, but his older brother Jonathan, the middle one, died in an air accident in 1920 and Thadeus moved up the aristocratic ladder, his father quickly deciding that he should become 'something in the city', in particular something within the golden financial square mile. This suited Thadeus for he was keen to engage in the cut and thrust, duck and dive, of the business world – he could play numbers with anyone!

Thadeus was introduced to Lloyd's in 1923 as a 'working name', a device that allowed those who worked within the Lloyd's community to become underwriting members with lower deposits than the outside names. This saved money for his father and enabled Thadeus to get into the action as a broker. He joined the company of Crawford & Amos, established marine brokers but with a newly formed non-marine department to which Thadeus was attached.

The brokers at that time were mostly gentlemen of breeding and good schooling, though not necessarily well educated. They arrived in the office at about 10.30 am wearing their black top hats and sticks, read the newspapers for an hour, picked up a nominal amount of broking from the clerks and went off to coffee. For the next four hours – including two hours for lunch at the George & Vulture or Simpson's – they obtained initials on simple endorsements to current policies, or maybe placed a piece of new business. At about 4.30, after tea, they returned to the office, dumped a heap of paper and slips on the clerks and went home to prepare for dinner.

Although equipped with his hat and stick Thadeus shunned this dilettante life and spent a lot of time with the clerks, taking on the servicing of some clients himself and thoroughly learned his trade. However, with regard to appearance Thadeus was strictly conservative, one might even say 'high church'. He wore his fair hair rather longer than the current fashion; he found this mode a better mount for his top hat, or occasionally his bowler. He tended to model himself on Mr Stevens the underwriter at Syndicate 116; each partnership of underwriting names was styled a syndicate and allocated a trading number by the Committee of Lloyds; this was a gentleman in the finest city tradition – fine habiliment and a fresh rose in his buttonhole every day. Like Mr Stevens, Thadeus always wore a frock coat in the Room at Lloyd's. Most brokers at the time wore lounge suits. Thadeus did permit the use of a folded collar, wearing his wings not more than once a week, unless he felt that the business in hand demanded the 'full regalia'.

Which brings us on to 1st September 1925 when Thadeus was applying to establish his own broking company, Burke & Company. The 'company' being twenty per cent his mother and twenty per cent his sister – silent partners, well fairly silent partners. Again family connections worked well and everything went through on the nod.

A few days later Thadeus was looking for premises. He had seen an advertising board outside an office at 3 Gracechurch Street, just round the corner from the Lloyd's Underwriting Room at the Royal Exchange and right opposite the entrance to Leadenhall Market, where a new Lloyd's building was proposed on the corner of Leadenhall Street and Lime Street. The new building should be up and running within three years. The Burke family did not need any lessons on choosing locations!

The lease was being handled by solicitors Hargreaves & Simpkin. Thadeus viewed the premises during lunchtime when the present tenant had arranged for the office to be empty. Mr Hargreaves accompanied him. It was a single large office on the second floor, serviced by a lift. Within the room a separate mini office had been built, obviously for the boss, mainly of glass windows so that he had seclusion but a good view of the staff. There were desks for three workers. The tenant, a Mr Whelan, also a Lloyd's broker, was retiring and Thadeus was able to complete reasonable terms for the lease and the office furniture.

Mr Whelan was due to leave the following Friday and Thadeus made arrangements to take over the keys and occupation on the Saturday morning. He was to meet a Mr James Pooley, an employee of Mr Whelan.

Thadeus arranged to meet James at The Stray Dog Café in Cullum Street, a scruffy little establishment run by a Russian émigré, but probably the best breakfast in the city.

He had been impressed with James when they spoke on the telephone and had in mind interviewing him for a post with the new firm. He already had a shorthand typist, Ethel, a very efficient young lady – and he needed a bright right hand man. Perhaps James could fill the post.

'Tell me about yourself,' Thadeus ventured as they sat in front of a huge plate of eggs, bacon and tomatoes. Within minutes he had a complete curriculum vitae recited to him. James was nineteen, courting a young lady named Eddie, living with his parents in a house in a place called Nunhead, in South London near Peckham Rye. James and Eddie intended to buy a house in the area. He had attended St Olave's Grammar School in Tooley Street just across Tower Bridge, passed his Cambridge University entrance exams, but with no intention of going to university he had had an introduction to a company in the city where he intended to build his career. His father was a motor mechanic, started as a bus driver, horses then autobuses, now had his own business under a railway arch in Peckham. James's forte was bookkeeping; he walked around the city 'ticking up' the ledgers between broker and underwriters. He handled the bank account and completed trial balances at the end of every month. He owned a motorcycle, a Royal Enfield 350cc, but also held a full driving licence. This information put them on a slight detour, Thadeus providing details of his Bentley 3-litre short chassis in British racing green, a colour that almost matched James's face, until it was suggested that he might like to try it out one of these days, at which an eager smile filled his face.

He earned £78 a year from Mr Whelan. He was clean, well dressed, had a bowler hat, was six years younger than Thadeus and stood at five feet ten inches, three inches shorter than Thadeus – an ideal relationship. Thadeus engaged him on the spot, at £104 a year and suggested that he start straight away with a visit to the new office where they could make plans regarding stationery, telephones and the like. They set off for 3 Gracechurch Street. James had three sets of keys: street door, office door and the little office – apparently known to Mr Whelan's staff as 'the shed' – and the wall safe.

Unfortunately they found Mr Whelan still in his office, sitting at his desk, dead from a gunshot to the head.

Within an hour the tiny office was full of policemen and various members of the medical fraternity. The body was removed and Thadeus and James were questioned by an Inspector Jackson, a tall impressive individual about the same height as Thadeus, with dark brown hair cut very neatly in an almost military style. Thadeus noticed that his suit and shoes were of bespoke manufacture. He looked very healthy, physically fit and his face had an outdoors or country hue.

Thadeus knew nothing, never having had the pleasure of Mr Whelan's company during his lifetime. James supplied full details of Mr Henry James Whelan of an address in Norwood, south of London, with a family of wife and two daughters, and a Morris Oxford Drophead Coupe 1550cc. James could think of no reason why Mr Whelan would commit suicide, he had just sold his business for a substantial sum and planned to retire to Ireland. He had never known him to be involved in any sort of Irish politics, indeed he had shown no interest in politics at all. He did read *The Times* every day, very thoroughly, over his morning coffee. James had last seen him the previous evening when he had left him in the office and went home at 5.45 pm. Thadeus thought it odd that a man would commit suicide at his desk, equipped with pens, pencils and paper and yet leave no note of explanation. It did not seem to worry Inspector Jackson, however, who appeared to be happy with the medical evidence. Thadeus and James made some brief notes of what needed to be done in the office, but generally decided to make a new start on Monday morning.

On Saturday evening Thadeus was visited for dinner by an old chum from Cambridge, Augustus Downing, no relation to the college or its eminent founder who had also built Downing Street, the home of the prime minister, Mr Stanley Baldwin. This Downing was a wealthy young man from a family in Norfolk who had studied law at St John's College and was now a practising barrister-at-law at Middle Temple. He was known to his friends as 'Gussie'; Thadeus and he had roomed on the same staircase. The dinner was a longstanding engagement, honoured by Thadeus without much enthusiasm as he would rather have been planning his new company.

Gussie had recently become a communist and was at Thadeus' mews house – actually two mews houses knocked into one – near Sloane Square in order to convert Thadeus to the cause. Hilton, Thadeus' manservant, butler and general dogsbody to 'his master's voice', had prepared a shepherd's pie with salad. Thadeus always told diners that this dish was made with real shepherds. It was good student grub and the two young men enjoyed it immensely.

The Burke family had long been supporters of the Liberal Party and Gussie attacked them with vigour.

'Asquith and Lloyd George act as if they were still a power in the land; they do not have enough Members of Parliament to set up a decent rugby team. They think they will be back in government within twelve months, it will just not happen.' Thadeus added that they might just make a rugby team, but they would not all be wearing the same colour shirts.

Gussie was amused by this reference to the open hostility between the Asquithians and the Lloyd Georgeites and made a note of the quip in his little notebook.

Gussie's economic arguments rested on the prime factors of production, capital, land and work. Thadeus pointed out to him, on several occasions, that as capital was a result of production it could not be a prime factor in the creation of wealth. Thadeus preached from the gospel of Henry George, the American economist that had influenced the Liberal Party from the turn of the century.

Gussie had no answer to Thadeus' clear principles, except to say that they were 'old hat'. 'We need new ideas, even Lloyd George is thinking about the nationalization of land. With Lenin dead and this new man Stalin starting to organize a true workers' state in Russia, the world is going to change forever.'

They both agreed that the current crisis in the coal mining industry was not going to be resolved easily or amicably. Mr Baldwin's subsidy of the miners' reduced wages could not continue long, and the Trades Union Congress had made it clear that they anticipated full support from other workers. There was talk of a general strike; Gussie anticipated this leading to a full-scale revolution. This was not the sort of scenario that Thadeus wanted for his activities in the city.

Over a glass of port Thadeus threw in the towel, advising Gussie that the problem with politics was that nobody was interested in the truth, the only goal for politicians and public alike was 'success'. Promise to give the people what they want and get elected. Even the electorate were not interested in economic justice, far from it, they wanted to be better off than their neighbour without working harder.

Gussie thought that this was 'head-in-the-sand' stuff; get out there and do something he advised.

'I do,' replied Thadeus. 'Myself and my family invest regularly in land; we collect rent and put it in our pockets. The nation does not appear to want it. I shall probably become very rich.'

Strangely this did not appear to worry Gussie, who was beginning to wilt under the weight of consumed claret, and at about 11.15 pm set out for his own house, up the road in Chelsea.

Thadeus, thoroughly depressed by all the politics, prepared for bed.

His mood was changed dramatically by a telephone call from his sister. She was in a hospital just west of London with a broken leg, having driven her car into a ditch. Would Thadeus come and get her in the morning? Her left leg was in plaster from the knee to the ankle, a simple fracture of the fibula. She was equipped with a pair of crutches and thought that she might stay with him in London for a few days: 'At least until I get the hang of the crutches!' She gave him the directions and he promised to be there at 10.30 am. 'Good heavens! What a day!' thought Thadeus, as he went to sleep. Sunday had to be better.

Thadeus was up studying his AA road map when the telephone rang at five minutes past nine in the morning. It was James Pooley in a call box. Sunday was *not* going to be any better than Saturday. Thadeus phoned James back at his call box. James had been working on some data in the evening and wondered if it would be possible for them to meet during the day, then he could continue developing the ideas this evening ready for Monday. You can't keep a good man down – or something like that, thought Thadeus. 'Yes. Come over at about 1.30, we can have lunch. My sister Freddie will be here. You should meet her. She owns part of the company and is a director. She has had a motor accident and is staying with me for a few days.'

'Nothing serious I hope,' said a worried James.

'No, it was only a bull-nose Morris,' chuckled Thadeus.

'I meant your sister...' started James.

'I know,' interrupted Thadeus. 'She has a broken leg, but as she is a medical student I imagine she is looking forward to the experience.' He paused. 'Do you want to bring Eddie?'

'No, she is away with her mother visiting a sick uncle in Essex.'

They said their goodbyes and Thadeus set off for the Great West Road. By 12.45 pm they were back. Freddie was set up in a sort of throne that Hilton had erected during the morning. The nucleus of the construction was a leather wingback chair, to which had been added several rugs and cushions. It faced an ottoman similarly attired. Hilton always treated 'Miss Freddie' as a queen and was therefore in his element; books, magazines, cakes and sweets were all within easy reach. Game pie with mashed potatoes had been organized for lunch together with a decent bottle of Chateau Latour.

James's Royal Enfield roared up at exactly 1.30. Introductions were made. James had great difficulty referring to Hilton simply as 'Hilton' and perhaps more difficulty with the reciprocal 'Mr James'.

He made a huge mistake addressing Freddie as 'Ma'am', a title she felt should be reserved for the old queen alone. He settled for Miss Freddie. He was clearly impressed with Thadeus' sister; indeed she was a stunning young lady, with strawberry blonde hair, cut short in the modern 'bob' cut, possibly a little taller than James.

Thadeus showed James round the house; Hilton did not think that Miss Freddie should be left unattended. James had only seen a kitchen like this one in a hotel where he had worked during school holidays. Apart from the Bentley in the garage, his greatest admiration was reserved for the bathroom, which had a stand-up shower. He explained to Freddie later that at home their bath was a large galvanized contraption that hung on a nail outside the back door and was dragged into the scullery on bath nights.

'God, how primitive James,' exclaimed Freddie. 'I do hope you're planning better facilities for the new Mrs Pooley?'

'I had not anticipated a shower, but I think now that it will be essential. Actually I don't use the tin bath nowadays; we go to the public baths at Goose Green. The facilities there are excellent.'

James commented on the extravagant amount of plaster on Freddie's left leg. Freddie explained the rudiments of fracture repair requiring that the broken bone be held still in order that it may grow back to normal and, as in the nature of things, bones were connected to each other, it was necessary to keep practically all the leg still. She also added that the hospital where she had been taken following the accident was the same hospital at which she was completing her final year as a medical student and that her colleagues did get somewhat over-exuberant. Thadeus and James inspected the graffiti that adorned the plaster.

'Some of this is disgusting!' exclaimed James.

'The Latin is even worse,' offered Freddie

'It was the Latin that I was reading,' explained James.

'Oh God!' exclaimed Freddie. 'I've got to spend the next three or four weeks with uneducated males.'

Lunch passed uneventfully with Freddie and James exchanging brief life histories. Thadeus was quiet, his sister being twenty-three months older than him, his mind drifted back to his teenage years when Freddie's friends used to use him for their early sexual experiments. Happy days.

After lunch was cleared away, Thadeus and James engaged in some serious paperwork. Notes were made. Telephone pads for messages, a date stamp for incoming mail. The policy register required lengthy discussion, new column headings being added every minute; it would be the hub of office information. Rough ideas for a renewal system were drafted and a double entry bookkeeping system agreed. They were making a half-hearted attempt at organizing a claims department, when Hilton suggested cocktails. James was of the opinion that motorcycling and drinking were incongruous activities and, as it was time for him to set off to an appointment with Eddie, he said his farewells and rode off in the opposite direction to the sunset.

Freddie had bought her flute with her and during the evening Thadeus accompanied her on the piano, suffering much good-natured abuse.

'Thadeus, you play very well, but "accompanying" is quite beyond you. Your rallentando waits for no man, and irrespective of where I am in the music, your hands hover like a couple of sea eagles for hours before crashing down on a final cadence.'

It was a pleasant evening and Thadeus retired for the night well contented.

Monday morning, 9.00 am. Thadeus, James and Ethel were sorting out their desks. Ethel was instructed to arrange for the telephone to be switched to the new company and carefully check the telephone number before the letter heading and other documents were printed. James gave Ethel the drafted letter heading and the slip for use at Lloyd's to be typed up. Their first post that morning confirmed their Lloyd's broker number: 502. Ethel advised that their telephone number would be Gracechurch 4949.

Thadeus' office had a large cupboard, which was half full of back-copies of *The Times*. James informed him that it had been Mr Whelan's habit to keep at least the last six months' copies for reference.

'What for?' enquired Thadeus.

'He was a Justice of the Peace, so I assume that he referred to the law reports. He was also quite active on the Stock Exchange, buying and selling stocks and shares. He dabbled in the commodity market as well, metals and coal.'

'A man of many parts,' commented Thadeus.

'Oh yes, he had several little money making enterprises, apart from the Lloyd's broking. One of his little earners was witnessing documents. Hargreaves & Simpkin used to send people round for him to witness their signatures on leases, or official company documents, because he was a JP, I think. He witnessed wills as well, charged one guinea every time. There were three or four witness sessions every week.'

'Maybe that is why he was shot,' ventured Thadeus adding, 'where is Friday's copy of *The Times*? It is not in the cupboard and it was not on Mr Whelan's desk on Saturday morning. Would you mind going up to Fleet Street and getting a copy in your lunch hour, James?'

James nodded. 'Certainly, sir.'

During the afternoon James was busy at the stationers buying ledgers, a couple of very smart leather-bound ones for private accounts, and several red leatherette ones that opened out with a key so that new pages could be inserted. One of these latter types, a short but very wide one, was to be used as the company's policy register. It was so big that it needed its own desk. Ethel was supplied with a card index system for names, addresses and telephone numbers. After consulting with Thadeus, James began heading up the policy register's several columns, in his best copperplate writing. Thadeus proposed that when they were alone together they would be 'Thadeus' and 'James'; in the company of any third party, they would be 'Mr Burke' and 'Mr Pooley'.

James felt that in private he would be happier calling Thadeus 'sir'.

'If you must!' agreed Thadeus. 'Yes, sir!' responded James.

The telephone was working and Thadeus spent most of the afternoon ringing potential clients and advising them of the new arrangements, telling them that a letter setting out the details of the new firm would be posted to them when they had paper back from the printers. Many of these contacts had already been warned over the previous couple of months of Thadeus' plans, and were pleased to have his new telephone number ready when needed. Nobody actually wanted to insure anything that day, which was just as well as Thadeus did not want to go out into the Lloyd's market until he was equipped with his own 'slips'. Blank sheets of paper or phone calls would have worked, but Thadeus wanted everything right.

At 4.00 pm Ethel produced three cups of tea. Thadeus took a break and had a look at last Friday's *Times*. The obituaries page revealed that a Colonel Bennet had died in a shotgun accident. Although a distinguished and much decorated soldier Colonel Bennet had been a disaster with shotguns. Some years ago he had shot himself in the leg, and within the last twelve months had managed to shoot a fellow gun in the elbow and a beater in the shoulder. It seemed only a matter of time before he blew his own head off; this final mismatch of man and weapon had occurred last Wednesday. His only remaining relative was a Major Bennet, also with an address in Berkshire.

Thadeus telephoned Inspector Jackson. 'I think that you will find that our Mr Whelan was shot by a Major Bennet. If you would care to pop round to my office, either this afternoon or tomorrow morning, I will give you the full details.'

'Do you have any evidence?' enquired the inspector.

'No, no, that will be your job. It shouldn't take long,' advised Thadeus.

'I'll be round in about fifteen minutes,' said the CID man.

Thadeus pretended to take an interest in the work that James was doing; had a look round Ethel's desk; asked about post, and generally wasted fifteen minutes. Thadeus had returned to his desk and was trying to look busy. Inspector Jackson appeared right on time.

'Good afternoon, inspector,' said Thadeus.

The inspector responded with, 'I think this is where I say, "Perhaps you would like to start at the beginning". Does that sound like a good idea?'

'Right!' said Thadeus, continuing. 'Firstly, I am privileged to hold three pieces of information that you do not have. One, Mr Whelan was a Justice of the Peace and quite often acted in that role as a witness to various documents. I understand that these were usually company documents presented by company secretaries, or leases for offices, but occasionally wills. He had his own contacts for this work but often it was referrals made to him by Mr Hargreaves, a solicitor in St Clement's Lane. Secondly, Mr Whelan took *The Times* every day and kept the back-copies, for at least about six months, in that cupboard behind you. In there at present are copies going back to May of this year.'

The inspector turned and glanced briefly at the cupboard in question.

'And, thirdly and most interestingly,' continued Thadeus, 'is that in that cupboard there is no copy of *The Times* for last Friday. And, being the observant policeman that you are you will have seen that there was no copy of Friday's *Times* on his desk when we found him on Saturday morning.' Thadeus paused momentarily, awaiting the inspector's comments but none were forthcoming.

Inspector Jackson never interrupted a witness in full flow – it was foolish to risk losing potentially vital information. Experience told him there was more to come.

'I can confirm that there was no copy of the said newspaper anywhere in this office.'

The inspector stalled for a couple of seconds. 'So you went out this morning, up to Fleet Street, and obtained the missing evidence,' he said simply.

'Actually my assistant James obtained a copy at lunchtime and this is what I found on the obituaries page.' Thadeus handed the relevant page to Inspector Jackson.

The inspector read through the writing, unhurried and carefully. 'I think we can say that your accusations made over the telephone are, to say the least, a rather imaginative hypothesis.'

'True!' responded Thadeus. 'But a few simple telephone conversations by you will either dissolve the affair, or lead to a prompt arrest. Here is Mr Hargreaves' telephone number.' He handed over a piece of paper, pushing his own telephone across to the inspector's side of the desk.

A few minutes later and the inspector was put through. 'Good afternoon Mr Hargreaves, my name is Jackson, I am a police inspector with the Criminal Investigation Department at Scotland Yard.'

This opening gambit made Thadeus sit up.

The CID man continued. 'I am investigating the death of a Mr Whelan, a man that I think you know and may have done business with.'

There was silence in the office while Mr Hargreaves spoke and the inspector listened.

'Yes that is exactly the situation as I understand it. The question that I particularly want to put to you at the moment is are you aware whether or not Mr Whelan witnessed a will for a Colonel Bennett at any time?'

There was more silence with occasional remarks by Inspector Jackson.

'I see... Royal Ascot week... Would it be possible for me to speak to the solicitor in Newbury, if I came round to your office straight away? I can be there within three minutes... Fine, thanks.' Jackson rang off and got to his feet.

'Jackson!' almost screamed Thadeus. 'You cannot just walk out of the office leaving me in limbo!'

The inspector's voice was calm and controlled. 'The hour is late and I must speak to another solicitor this evening. I'll return as soon as possible, probably in about half an hour, and give you all the details. Your hypothesis is looking good.' And with this remark he left.

It was nearly six o'clock when the inspector returned. Ethel and James had departed for their homes; Thadeus had been genuinely busy checking carefully through James's draft letter heading and cover note.

'I suggest we retire to The Lamb for a glass of refreshing ale,' was all that Jackson said. Thadeus put on his coat, locked the office and followed the inspector into the street and the fifty yards or so to the public house. Not yet a well known watering hole for the Lloyd's fraternity who were due to arrive virtually next door within three years, but a popular city pub both with the Leadenhall market boys and the business gentlemen.

Thadeus had not yet established himself as a regular, but the inspector was clearly well known to the landlord and they were both escorted to a quiet booth upstairs, equipped with two pints of Young's bitter.

The inspector supped the first mouthful of his beer. 'My name is John, known to friends – and enemies – as Johnny, Johnny Jackson. Do you mind if I call you Thadeus?'

'By all means,' replied Thadeus.

'Well, Thadeus, I should disclose that I have two clues to which you are not privilege. The pistol had been the property of a German officer in the war, not what you would expect to find in the position of a confirmed Irish neutral. Also routine enquiries have unearthed a witness who saw a man leave the premises at 3 Gracechurch Street some time about a quarter past six on Friday evening. Apparently the unknown man was "short and of a dapper military appearance". Also he shut the street door, I quote again, "as if he were the last to leave".'

'Nothing like the photograph of the Colonel Bennett that appeared in Friday's *Times*,' observed Thadeus.

'Indeed not,' replied Johnny Jackson emphatically. He continued his story. 'Mr Hargreaves remembers being approached, by telephone, by a solicitor in Newbury about some documents that needed witnessing for a Colonel Bennett. It was during Royal Ascot week and the work had to be done quite late, between six and six-thirty in the evening, as apparently the colonel would be at the races, returning to stay in London at about that time. Mr Hargreaves did not want to get involved and gave the telephone number and address of Mr Whelan to the solicitor and suggested that he try him. Mr Hargreaves had no other involvement in the matter, apart from using his excellent memory.'

Thadeus said nothing.

Johnny Jackson supped his beer, and continued. 'From Mr Hargreaves' office I spoke to his friend in Newbury, a Mr Pearson, solicitor to both the colonel and his brother the major. He confirmed Mr Hargreaves' evidence, adding the he had not actually spoken to the colonel about the appointment in London, it had been handled by, I quote, "the colonel's office". Mr Pearson played no further part in the drama, except he does remember asking the colonel some weeks later if he got his documents signed in London. The colonel looked a bit puzzled but replied "yes".' Jackson supped more beer.

'You asked him about the colonel's will?'

Jackson smiled, 'Yes, indeed!' Apparently the colonel's recent will enacted during Royal Ascot week this year, and witnessed by Mr Whelan and a Lady Frances Downing, with an address in Norfolk, left his entire fortune to his brother the major. The will was discovered in the desk of the colonel after his death. His previous will had bequeathed only 2,000 guineas to his brother and the remainder of the estate to his regiment to establish a fund to assist young officers. The war had apparently left the regiment a bit short of young officers and the colonel had been anxious that the regiment did not get absorbed or amalgamated into another group. His total estate at the time of death is estimated at about 90,000 guineas.'

Thadeus smiled broadly and even more so when Jackson continued.

'I asked Mr Pearson for a brief description of the major, he said he was a little shorter, and slightly heavier than his brother, and, entirely unprompted by me, I quote again, "a rather dapper little man".'

'Gotchyer!' cried the two men clicking glasses.

'Actually I know Lady Frances. I had lunch with her son yesterday. If you send someone to interview her, he will need to be on horseback; I have never seen her out of the saddle! She may well have been at Royal Ascot, but I know that she hates London and never goes near the place,' added Thadeus usefully.

The two men left the pub and went their separate ways home.

It was 10.30 pm when Jackson phoned Thadeus at home. The story was a simple one. The Norfolk Constabulary had interviewed Lady Frances Downing that evening; she had been in the stables. She had not visited London for many years, and had no intention of revisiting the noisy and smelly place again. She had never witnessed a will, as far as she could remember. She had attended all four days at Royal Ascot; on the first day she had backed a young jockey named Gordon Richards riding his first winner at the Royal meeting. She insisted that the Norfolk Constabulary make a note of his name, actually watched carefully as the sergeant wrote the name into his book. On the Wednesday before racing started Lady Frances had attended, and chaired, a meeting of a charity concerned with the welfare of retired cavalry horses. The secretary at the meeting had been a Mrs Bennett, the wife of a Major Bennett, a cavalry officer. Yes, Mrs Bennett had collected up all the papers for the minutes, including documents signed by Lady Frances.

The Norfolk Constabulary had done a very good, low profile job. Now it was time for a slightly heavier and more aggressive visit to the home of Major and Mrs Bennet by the Berkshire Constabulary. They arrived at just after ten o'clock in the evening; two motorcars, two detectives, an inspector and a sergeant, and two of the new WPCs. The end game was brief, confronted by such a mass of information Mrs Bennett quickly broke down and confessed to assisting her husband forge his brother's will. She knew nothing of any murders. The major tried valiantly to defend himself but eventually yielded to the overwhelming accusations and undeniable facts. He insisted that his brother's death had been an accident.

At the end of the bulletin Inspector Jackson added, 'There was a Lloyd's underwriter, Sir Percy Dennington, committed suicide about six months ago. I was never entirely happy with the result of the inquest. We adjourned it twice but eventually had to go to the jury. When you've got five or ten minutes to spare you might solve that one for me. I'll give you the details over lunch one of these days.'

'Right!' said Thadeus.

Within six weeks Mrs Bennett had been sentenced to twelve years in Holloway Prison, a period that suggested that the judge was not entirely happy with her pleas of ignorance about the deaths of Colonel Bennett and Mr Whelan.

Her husband was hanged.

CHAPTER 2

ASSASSINATION IN THE ROOM

It was just two weeks after Burke & Co had commenced operations that James Pooley had been introduced to the Lloyd's Underwriting Room. He was authorized to transact business as a 'substitute' to Thadeus. Working brokers, not themselves underwriting members, were allowed in the Room on a substitute's ticket, which James had begun to flourish proudly at the waiters who guarded to entrance to the Underwriting Room. His name appeared on the broker's list held by the Caller, who stood at the rostrum and called the names of brokers who were required to meet somebody, usually a colleague.

The 'call' consisted of the company name followed by the name of the individual required to respond to the call. Thadeus' was 'Burke–Burke', which came out of the caller's voice box rather akin to an attack of indigestion. James' call had a similar start followed by a 'Pooley' that appeared to include at least a dozen 'o's.

These exaggerations were necessary in order that the music, as it were, of the caller's voice attracted the attention of the required broker above the general hubbub of the Room.

For the most part James had accompanied Thadeus, watching his technique and being introduced to the underwriters that underwrote the Burke & Co account. Occasionally he was let loose with a simple endorsement for an underwriter with whom he was acquainted. On one such occasion he was strolling through the Room when a chap on one of the marine boxes, with which James was not familiar, shouted his name out.

'Jim Pooley!' the voice exclaimed.

'Jimmy Payne!' responded James, recognizing an old school friend. With red hair, freckles and large spectacles, it was not difficult. He had one of those 'young' faces and could have just walked out of the physics lab as a member of class 5A.

J Payne stood up and shook hands with J Pooley.

'I thought that you were up at Cambridge,' questioned Pooley.

'I've been up there and come back down,' responded James Payne. 'It's a long story, or a short story, whichever one you want. I'll tell you all about it over a beer some time.'

'Oh right!' said James Pooley, adding, 'So here you are working at Lloyd's?'

James Payne smiled. 'The underwriter is my uncle,' explaining everything, 'What are you up to?'

Pooley explained his position with Burke & Co, advising his school chum that the company did not appear to have any business with Payne & Others, as they seemed to be only marine business.

The young Payne challenged this immediately. 'We write a small incidental non-marine book and...' he paused for effect, '...I am underwriting a small motor account.'

The two young men had been keen motor vehicle buffs at STOGS – short for St Olave's Grammar School – following all the new makes and models with the enthusiasm of the train spotters that flood the railway stations.

'Crikey, that's exciting!' exclaimed Pooley.

'Do you have any motor business?' questioned Payne.

'We have only existed for four weeks, but we will have the boss's Bentley, and his sister's Morris Cowley when they come up for renewal. But I do have the boss's permission to try and establish a motor portfolio, and as you know, if you can remember, my dad has a small garage/workshop.'

'Oh right! How is he getting on? Because one of the things I am working on is setting up a register of motor repair agents whom we can trust for dealing with claims.'

'He is still underneath the arches in Peckham,' replied Pooley, 'but business is good, and he is looking at some new premises out in North Essex, an old aircraft field with some huts and hangers.'

'Crikey! That really is expansion.' exclaimed Payne

'It is because he may be working on some buses. Putting roofs on "Ks" and "NSs", fitting pneumatic tyres, and that sort of thing.' Jim did not need to explain to Jimmy the different types of omnibus. He was sure that the underwriter was familiar with the Bs, the Ks, the recent S-Type and the new NS as they had followed the development of the London General Omnibus Company, and their vehicles, from the time when Sydney Pooley, James's father, used to drive them to school on the Brown and Cream Special.

At that moment two young brokers arrived at the box to see Jimmy Payne.

'Crikey!' he exclaimed, 'I've got a queue. What about lunch later today – 1.00 pm at Simpson's?'

'Fine, see you there,' answered James, and he set off to find Thadeus.

James approached the rostrum, to call 'Burke–Burke' but before he reached the front of the queue of brokers seeking the caller's attention, he saw Thadeus' top hat held high above his head about six boxes away. A 'box' is a large desk with a set of benches down each side, rather like a luncheon booth, indeed they are a remnant of the old Lloyd's coffee room. At these desks sit the underwriter, his deputy – who usually sits opposite the underwriter – and some staff, quite often these are youngsters who enter the lines written by the underwriter or his deputy. At the other end of the box from the underwriter might sit a senior member of the syndicate staff engaged in claims settlement.

As Thadeus was probably the only person in the room wearing a top hat it was easy to spot him. On this occasion Thadeus had spotted James on his way to the rostrum and had simply raised his hat confident that eventually James would come over to him even though he continued his conversation with an underwriter.

As James approached Thadeus was leaving the box and saying goodbye to the underwriter.

'I am very grateful, sir, for the time that you have allowed me, and the careful attention that you have given to my proposals,' said Thadeus.

'No luck there then!' said James as they moved out of hearing range of the box.

'No. Damned man will not write any cotton mills.'

James enlightened Thadeus about his fortuitous meeting with young Payne.

Thadeus was delighted, advising James to get a policy wording and, if possible, a set of rates from the underwriter. 'I think they have different premium rates for each type of vehicle and I think they have different rates for different areas of the country.' Thadeus continued. 'I have a lunch date with that CID inspector. He is entertaining me at the George & Vulture, so I am only a few yards away if you should need me.'

They continued together with their broking work. By 12.50 pm the cotton mill had 70 per cent in written lines, 25 per cent from the leader and three lines of 15 per cent, and 12½ per cent in promised lines, a 7½ per cent and a 5 per cent – a total of 82½ per cent. Thadeus would need at least three or maybe four extra underwriters to finish his slip. It would not be easy and he might end up scrabbling around for 2½ per cent lines. As a last resort one of the 15 per cent lines might increase a bit.

They walked up Cornhill together to their luncheon dates.

Thadeus had not spoken to Inspector Johnny Jackson since the Whelan affair, other than accepting his invitation to lunch. At the George & Vulture the inspector was inside the doorway checking his table booking. They shook hands and said hello, took their seats and exchanged some general banter with Lucy, their waitress, a bright young thing, wearing the full ceremonial dress of her trade, including the strange, and useless, little white hat.

A decent bottle of red wine was already opened on the table. Both ordered a steak – the sirloin had been recommended by Lucy – with bubble and squeak and cabbage. No starter as they agreed that they would have spotted dick for afters.

'How is the world of crime?' asked Thadeus.

'Nothing serious in the city, but around the country there is much unrest following the strike compromise on "Red Friday". Many of the militant miners are already being cruelly victimized by the employers and that is leading to violence and theft; a very sad situation.'

'I agree,' replied Thadeus. 'I think that the TUC will just sell off the miners to help the Labour Party.'

'There certainly appears to be a lot of underhand political shenanigans,' posited the inspector and, sensing that Thadeus was about to launch himself into an economics debate, wisely changed the subject. 'So, how is the world of insurance?'

'Do I detect an unusual leaning towards the left-wing in a policeman?' asked Thadeus, refusing to be deflected by the new question.

'No, I would not regard myself as in any way a political animal, but I do have a passionate belief in justice, as I think every policeman should. And I feel that quite often privileged social groups within our country have held on to what they see as economic advantages which act as a catalyst for justifiable reaction. Whereas the greater social and economic justice to all people would be of the greater advantage to all classes of society. Look at the unnecessary suppression of Jews, Catholics and, more recently, women. And, before you comment, I am not going to discuss the Land Question,' harangued Jackson.

'You have certainly done your homework on me!' responded Thadeus with a smile. 'Burke & Co are progressing as well as can be expected, as one of the directors might say.'

'A doctor on the board?'

'Not quite, my sister is in her final year at Edinburgh, although at present she is working in a hospital down here.' Then, changing tack Thadeus went on. 'There are rumours in the Room of one, or maybe more, underwriters leaving some of their figures out of the audit. Are you involved in looking into that?'

'I have been shown evidence of substantial financial guarantee business that seems to be avoiding the watchful eye of the committee, but it is not a subject for general discussion,' said Jackson *sotto voce*.

'Well, if I can be of any help, let me know,' said Thadeus.

'I thought you were busy solving the Sir Percy Dennington case for me.'

'I've made a few enquiries,' defended Thadeus. 'I know nothing of the alleged crime, but I now know more about the deceased. The fourth son of Sir Henry Dennington, inherited the baronetcy following the death of all three of his elder brothers in the war. Perhaps there is a crime there? '

'One of the brothers was "missing, believed died in action",' corrected Jackson.

'If he appeared suddenly, he would be ahead of Percy in the title and money stakes anyway, so there is no motive for murder'. I had met Sir Percy in the course of business. He was not a very prominent member of the Manning's syndicate; 'third man' on the box, handling endorsements and some simple underwriting. I had shown him a piece of bloodstock business, and I was aware that he was interested in thoroughbred breeding. I think he personally owned a couple of horses. 'I understand that he drank a poison. Can you give me more details of that?'

'Arsenic,' came the simple reply. 'Drank it in a glass of Drambuie. Arsenic can taste quite sweet, so a glass of Drambuie would be ideal cover. But for a fatal dose you need quite a large amount. With a small amount you get sick, symptoms vary according to the dose, but generally there is vomiting and diarrhoea. The bottle carried a huge amount and the one, or possibly two, large glasses that he consumed was more than enough to finish him off.'

'Two large glasses of Drambuie is unusual,' said Thadeus

'Yes. Either two glasses or the one glass filled to the brim, according to the pathologist. Sir Percy was drinking from a small brandy balloon. That is what I think swung the verdict towards suicide,' replied Jackson.

'I quite often use a small brandy balloon for liqueurs. There is a cocktail drink, popular at the Savoy called a "rusty nail", Drambuie and Whisky. I drink it sometimes with a knob of ice,' informed Thadeus.

They had finished their steak and were awaiting the pudding, but when Lucy arrived at the table she advised Jackson that he was required urgently on the telephone.

Meanwhile the two James had been enjoying similar fare just round the corner. Steak and kidney pie, or Kate and Sydney as the South London lads called it, also with bubble and squeak. But it was to be followed by cheese and a glass of port.

Jim avoided any reference to Cambridge, which Jimmy clearly wanted forgotten, and they got down to some serious insurance work. The Payne syndicate would grant Burke & Co a binding authority, allowing them to issue certificates of insurance to motor vehicle owners. The syndicate would supply a pad of these certificates and a set of detailed rates for use all over the country. The commission was not high, just 15 per cent, but the underwriter handled all the claims direct with the insured, and so the broker had no work to do in that field, unless there was a problem of course.

'What excess do you have?' asked Jim.

'A standard £5 excess each and every loss for material damage, but no excess on the third party section in respect of bodily injury. That seems to be the market norm. However clients can reduce the premium by carrying an increased excess amount,' was the reply.

'Unlimited liability under the Road Traffic Act?'

'Yes.'

'What about motorcycles? I ride a Royal Enfield 350cc.'

'Yes, I write motorcycles, and can do a special deal for your one.'

'Do you have a bike, or a car?' enquired James Pooley of his friend.

'Nothing at the present time. But I have been promised a bonus at the end of the underwriting year, and I intend to get something sporty at that time,' informed James Payne.

Pooley returned to business. 'How about horse boxes? Mr Burke is particularly interested in establishing a book of bloodstock business and that might be useful as part of his presentations.'

'I do not see a problem with that. The only worry would be the loss of tack and rugs at shows or the racecourse, when the box is left unattended. More particularly they drive off and leave a bucket full of brushes, mane-combs and the like behind, or a horse-rug that they had been using to sit on the grass. Then later they report it as stolen.' Jimmy knew his underwriting!

'We could probably insert a large excess; say £25.'

'That would suffice, for a start, but I'll tell you now that I would keep a close eye on that section of the policy.'

'What about liability for horses, the property of a third party, killed or injured in an accident? Say a maximum of £500 any one horse.'

'We could try that. I would prefer half of that limit. And I will need to think about the premium required.'

They selected their cheese from the trolley and ordered two large glasses of the Warre.

'When could we start?' asked Jim

'This afternoon if you like. Uncle Charles will have no problem with Mr Burke; he is a name on our syndicate. It is a pity that you went to STOGS with me rather than Harrow or Eton, but I expect I'll swing that one,' Jimmy chuckled.

'Mr Burke will need to read all the papers and it will be his signature on the documents. Can I pick up a set of this paperwork when we get back to the Room?'

'No problem!' advised Jimmy Payne. 'Now, what about some paperwork for your dad to do some claims work for us?'

'I think that he will be very interest in the idea. He has had an apprentice working with him for about a year, but he has just recently taken on an experienced man. The new chap worked on bus engines at Camberwell Garage, so I expect that his expenditure has increased. He could probably use any extra income. I'll talk to Dad at the weekend,' said Jim Pooley.

Jackson came back to the table, but did not sit down. 'On your feet, sleuth,' he said, addressing Thadeus. 'A Lloyd's underwriter has just been shot dead in the Room.'

They hurried along the south side of Cornhill, crossed the road and went into the Royal Exchange building. As they bustled along Jackson explained that the dead man was Edward Thomas Thurlow, deputy underwriter to his brother George Thomas Thurlow, and Thadeus was just able to confirm that he knew both of the men and had placed bloodstock business with them.

'Shot by a communist apparently!' advised a sceptical Jackson.

'At what time?' questioned Thadeus

'Ten minutes past two – that's about five minutes ago,' was the reply.

'Odd,' said Thadeus

They walked into the building and up to the 'barrier', an archway manned by a waiter at the entrance to the Underwriting Room proper.

A group of people were gathered around the body. Two uniformed police officers, a man and a woman kneeling beside the dead man, two uniformed Lloyd's waiters in serious discussion with what looked like staff from the Superintendent of the Room's office, and a handful of curious watchers.

The police sergeant recognized Jackson and saluted, with a smart 'sir', Jackson nodded an acknowledgement. The two kneelers rose and the sergeant introduced Drs Bryce and Ellington. They had been at a meeting with an accident underwriter, who was there in the crowd somewhere, explained the lady.

'Two shots, both straight through the heart, by the look of it. Death would have been instantaneous,' she explained.

'Thanks,' said Jackson. 'We'll need a full statement from each of you, I am afraid. Perhaps you would be good enough to give the constable your names, addresses and telephone numbers. The police doctor will be here in a short time and I would be obliged if you could wait and have a quick word with him. You did not see the actual shooting?'

The younger male doctor spoke. 'No, we heard the shots as we came down the stairs, but when we reached the scene it was all over "bar the shoutin'" as they say, and there was a lot of that.' His voice tailed off under a withering look from his more senior colleague.

'We will wait over there,' she said, pointing to a column a few feet away. Just next to where Thadeus was standing writing something into a pocket notebook.

Jackson turned to the sergeant who had the waiter ready and waiting.

'This is Mr Malcolm, he was the waiter on duty at the time,' explained the sergeant efficiently.

'I would like the whole story, from the top,' instructed Jackson.

Thadeus came over and stood in an adjacent position.

Mr Malcolm started his tale. 'It was just after two o'clock, sir, when Mr Edward Thurlow came up to the barrier from inside the room. He stood for a moment or two deciding which direction he was going to take. Took a couple of steps towards the exit on the Bank of England side, then "Bang!" he was shot by the communist.'

'How do you know he was a communist?' asked Jackson.

'He shouted out, sir, if you will excuse the words used, "You capitalist bastard! Up the workers!" and he threw a red flag over the body.'

Jackson stuck his tongue into his cheek in order to hold back a smile, Thadeus needed to turn his face away. Definitely a communist, they both thought.

'Can you describe him?' questioned Jackson.

'He was an Orthodox Jew,' stated Malcolm. Jackson waited for more and Malcolm, realizing this, continued. 'He wore a long black coat, had a bushy black beard and a black hat,' he explained, adding, 'and he wore glasses.'

Again Jackson struggled to hold back a grin, and again Thadeus needed to turn his face away.

Definitely an Orthodox Jew, they both thought.

'How did he manage to escape?' Another question from Jackson.

'There were not many people in the corridor at that time of day and I rushed over to see if I could assist Mr Thurlow. The communist ran down the corridor towards the Bank exit. There were two chaps coming the other way carrying large bundles of papers and he pushed them both over, ran out of the doorway, and, as I have been told later, jumped on to the back of a motorcycle and rode off.'

'Excuse me a moment,' interrupted Jackson. 'I need to consult with my colleague. Please wait here, Mr Malcolm,' and with that he called the sergeant across and led the officer, and Thadeus, some distance from the scene. 'Before I hear any more evidence about this incident, I need an interval,' he explained. 'Is it a Jewish communist, a Jew disguised as a communist, a communist disguised as a Jew? Or a disgruntled Name who owns a theatrical costume shop?'

'It is certainly a bizarre affair,' commented the sergeant.

'There could be a more serious aspect to this incident,' warned Thadeus. 'There is quite an established group of fascists in London, interested in slandering both Jews and communists. The University of London has been a nucleus for their efforts over the past two or three years, and this affair has a student flavour to it! However, I am of the opinion that their activities would be more convincing.'

'True!' said Jackson, 'that should be taken into consideration.' He turned to the officer. 'Have you arranged for more men to come here?'

'Yes, sir,' came the response. 'There should be three extra chaps arriving any minute.'

'Good. Get the names and addresses of all concerned. You need to be quick about that as the building is beginning to fill up as people return from lunch. Allow those who work here in the building to return to their places; but make sure you know where that is. Ask the

Superintendent of the Room if he can find an office nearby for you to use. Then start taking written statements.'

The sergeant nodded and began to walk away but while he was still within earshot Jackson added, 'As soon as you have the extra men see if any witnesses can be found in the street. Not easy, but there might be someone hanging around expecting to be interviewed.' He nodded a 'get on with it' signal, and the sergeant strode purposely towards the constable.

'Well, Thadeus, what do you think?'

'If it had been George Thurlow I would definitely suspect a disgruntled Name; the syndicate has lost a lot of money recently. But it was Edward, it might be something personal. I will make a couple of telephone calls. Meanwhile keep a note of this name.' Thadeus handed Jackson a piece of paper, torn from his notebook. On it were written three words.

Jackson took the sheet of paper and walked across to the waiter, Mr Malcolm, who was looking strangely naked, having relinquished his red coat and been supplanted in his duties at the barrier by a colleague.

'Do you know a man named Alfred Tammis Austin?' he asked.

'No, sir,' was the response.

As Jackson turned to set off in the direction of Thadeus, a tall, dignified man wearing a plain dark grey suit and a bowler hat of the same colour confronted him. He carried a rolled umbrella, the handle of which he held up to attract Jackson's attention. The gentlemen introduced himself, 'George Thurlow, brother of the poor fellow lying there.'

'We need to talk,' said Jackson simply.

'Yes. Do you mind if we go to my office? It is just round the corner in Finch Lane. I appear to be the centre of attention here, understandable but disconcerting.'

'Certainly. One moment,' responded Jackson, then, turning to Thadeus, 'would you be good enough to tell the sergeant where I have gone?'

'Certainly,' replied Thadeus, then to George Thurlow, with a dignified bow of the head, 'Mr Thurlow.'

Thurlow responded similarly, 'Thadeus.'

The inspector and the underwriter set off towards the Cornhill exit.

Thadeus advised the police sergeant of Inspector Jackson's movements, giving him the address of the Thurlow office from memory and the telephone number from his pocket notebook. He decided to return to his own office, crossed Cornhill, looked into Simpson's – upstairs and down – but James and his lunch date had left. He then went into the George & Vulture, apologized to Lucy for the sudden departure from her table, settled the bill and walked through the alley to his office. 'Jackson now owes me two lunches,' he thought.

James was at his desk making notes about the new motor account, the subject that he would discuss with Thadeus at an early opportunity.

Ethel was typing a letter. There were no messages.

Thadeus telephoned his home. 'Hilton, is Freddie there?'

'Yes, sir, one moment.'

'Hello, Thady.'

'What are you doing?'

'Reading Fyodor Dostoyevsky's short stories. They are excellent, much better than his long books. Some of his characters are like oil paintings…'

'I thought that you were supposed to be swotting *Toxic Materials*,' Thadeus interrupted his sister.

'I have completed that task and am now engaged in well earned recreation,' she responded.

'Good,' he stated decisively. 'This evening I need a brief lecture on the subject of arsenic.'

'I thought that we were to attend the theatre to try out my new leg, the pale and slightly withered one, to be encased in trousers,' she complained.

Two days ago the plaster had been removed from Freddie's leg and she had taken to wearing trousers and carrying one of Thadeus' country sticks. The combination gave her the appearance of a music-hall performer. Thadeus feared a visit to the theatre might involve his elder sibling being dragged backstage and admonished for mixing with the clientele.

'We may be able to fit in a fleeting visit to Oscar Wilde, I suppose,' he admitted.

'Good. Arsenic is far too important to be taken seriously!' quipped the girl.

They said their goodbyes and Thadeus called James into his office.

He informed the young man of the events in the Underwriting Room at lunchtime. Adding that it was not a good afternoon to be insuring a cotton mill.

'Can we talk about motor insurance,' James leapt in.

'Why not,' said Thadeus, feeling that some light diversion was in order, 'but I need to make an important 'phone call first.'

He dialled from the instrument on his desk and spoke to an Algernon Tammis Austin at his home in Kensington. The gentleman was too distressed to hold a conversation and Thadeus found himself talking to a manservant and receiving a brief outline of the afternoon's tragic events at the house.

Thadeus and James discussed motor insurance until nearly 4.00 pm. The most important aspect being who would do what in the office?

'I am looking around for a man to handle the policy documentation, of which, hopefully, there will be a mountain soon,' disclosed Thadeus. 'You had better get over to the Room and pick up the promised paperwork from your friend Jimmy. I am attending the theatre this evening, so I will leave the office before 5.00 pm.'

'Shall I take the cotton mill with me?' asked James,

'Why not. See what you can do,' smiled Thadeus, 'and telephone me at home before you leave.'

'Yes, sir,' said James, gathering up his papers from the desk.

'I have arranged for Hilton to prepare us a small meal before we go to the theatre,' greeted Freddie. 'Arsenic granules with a hollandaise sauce.'

'I think I'll stick to the theory of poisoning rather than the practice,' responded Thadeus, pouring himself a glass of white wine from the open bottle.

They sat down to salmon fishcakes with new potatoes and a green salad.

'I expect you are working on a case with your man Watson, or is it Jackson.' smiled Freddie. 'Give me the facts!'

'Arsenic in a bottle of Drambuie,' said Thadeus simply.

'An excellent choice, arsenic can taste a little sweet. Almost certainly it would be arsenic trioxide crystals. They take a time to dissolve. Heating the liquid would speed things up, but you run the risk of over saturation which might lead to sediment forming as the liquid cooled. To be sure I would dose a room-temperature bottle the day before.'

'How much would you need?' asked Thadeus.

'To do the job properly I would recommend half of a gram for each mouthful. That is about double the fatal dose, but you do not want your victim throwing up all over the place and staggering out of the room shouting your name.'

'Our man drank several mouthfuls, possibly a couple of glasses,' informed Thadeus.

'That was extremely obliging of him. It means that you need less arsenic per bottle. But you would need to be sure that he has a good swig. Sitting back and sipping the drink would bring on nausea and warn the victim of danger. Was it a full bottle?'

'I do not know. Why do you ask that?' enquired Thadeus.

'Drambuie bottles are not large but you would still need quite a lot of arsenic to ensure a fatal dose for the victim. Half a bottle equals less arsenic! And if you stand in front of him and say, "Cheers. Down the hatch!" off he goes.'

'And, if it was suicide?' suggested Thadeus.

'Personally I would go for a quarter-full bottle. Ensure that my dose was equal to three quarters of an ounce per dram sit back and say "Goodbye".'

'That may well be what happened,' said Thadeus.

'That could be bad news. No crime, no free lunch,' commented the girl.

'That is no problem, I solved a murder for Inspector Johnny Jackson this afternoon!'

The rest of the meal was taken up with Thadeus' tale of the lunchtime epic.

It was nearly 6.00 pm when James telephoned. He had a lot to say. 'I have a complete Motor Department on my desk. I will take it home tonight and study the documents and start working out a system for handling them. Also I have finished the cotton mill!' He paused at this point.

Thadeus said, 'Well done you. Tell me all about it.'

James continued. 'I was introduced to Mr Charles Payne, Jimmy's uncle, and a formidable gentleman. We shook hands and discussed the motor business, and then he asked me if I had any other business to show him. So I produced the slip for the cotton mill. He studied it for a short while, asked me a couple of questions that, fortunately I was able to answer, then said, "Cotton. I can put it under my cargo account. Would a line of 15 per cent suit you?" Yes, I said, thank you very much, sir, and he put down his line and passed the slip over to Jimmy to enter. Then as I was leaving the Room I passed old Mr White, who was sitting quietly on his own at his box. I went up to him and said "I know you have seen this risk before Mr White, but I now only need 2½ per cent to finish and I thought that you might help." He glared at me, took the slip from my hand and said, "As I probably know more about this bloody cotton mill than you do, I suppose I'm obliged to assist." He turned the slip over and pencilled 2½ percent on the back. Held out his hand and smiled. He wrote T-O-J-P beside the line. What does that mean?'

'To oblige James Pooley. James I think you have arrived!' chuckled Thadeus.

James continued. 'Thank you, one other thing, Inspector Jackson telephoned. He said, "Tell Mr Burke that his second hypothesis is looking good." I told him that you would be at the theatre this evening and he said for you to phone him at home when you return. Is that good news?'

'Unfortunately it is not, James, just Mother Nature playing her games,' replied Thadeus mysteriously.

The play was excellent, except that Ernest wore his hat on the back of his head. Really bad form Thadeus thought. Freddie's leg held up satisfactorily and the extra stick was useful for chasing away a group of youngsters who had decided to play on the Bentley. They set off home determine to experiment with the number of mouthfuls there are in a bottle of Drambuie.

'Good evening, sir. Good evening Miss Freddie,' welcomed Hilton. 'Inspector Jackson telephoned a few minutes ago, sir. He said to telephone him if you return from the theatre within a quarter of an hour. I have the number, sir. Do you wish me to obtain him for you?'

'Yes, thank you Hilton,' said Thadeus. 'And Hilton, can you track down a bottle of Drambuie and a couple of small brandy balloons?'

'Are you sure, sir?' questioned Hilton.

'Yes.'

'Ice, sir?'

'No thank you.'

'Are you sure, sir?' questioned Hilton again.

'Yes,' replied Thadeus again.

Hilton retreated wearing one of his disapproving faces and obtained Inspector Jackson on the telephone.

Jackson demanded a few answers from Thadeus before giving any information. 'Why did you think that it was "odd" that Thurlow had been shot at ten past two?'

'I knew both Thurlow brothers. I have done business with them. I also knew that they enjoy an extravagant lunch most days, accompanied by a substantial amount of wine, followed by a couple of large brandies. For one of them to be in the Room at that time could be considered "odd",' replied Thadeus.

'Edward Thurlow was meeting a couple of Names and was expecting them at two o'clock. They, or, to be precise, one of them, telephoned just before one o'clock. Actually the caller had asked for a meeting with Mr George Thurlow but George told Edward that he could not possibly be there at that time and delegated the job to Edward. George Thurlow did not ask who the names were as he was dashing off to a lunch in the West End,' volunteered Jackson.

'I assumed that something like that had happened. George did tend to treat his brother as an underling.'

'Why did you suspect the young Austin?' questioned Jackson.

'I knew that Mr Algernon Tammis Austin and his two sons were names on the Thurlow syndicate. I also know that the elder brother, also named Algernon, is a close friend of Gussie Downing. They share chambers. Gussie is a self-confessed communist. Young Alfred, the other brother, is a thespian, engaged on the frustrating road to theatrical stardom. This cocktail of information yielded up the young man as my prime suspect for a leading part in the lunchtime drama.' explained Thadeus.

'It is my painful duty to tell you that you were right,' said Jackson without enthusiasm. 'Young Austin shot himself this afternoon.'

'Very sad,' said Thadeus genuinely, without hinting that he was already aware of the tragedy.

Jackson continued with his account. 'Thurlow is posting a "cash loss call" on his names. It will be very bad for the Austin family. Thurlow told me that he had been writing American property business for a couple of years, through an agent in Pennsylvania. The business had gone very well, producing good profits. So he decided to sign up some more agents, in various other states, and carry no reinsurance! It is proving to be a disaster. He has cancelled the binders, but the damage has been done. Young Austin left a note, by the way. "Sorry, I cannot get anything right".'

'Yes. He shot the wrong Thurlow. I imagine the motorcyclist was entirely innocent of the criminal intentions of Alfred?' asked Thadeus.

'Yes, an assistant stage manager from some theatre that I have never heard of. He thought that it was all a student rag-week prank, involving fireworks.'

Thadeus and Jackson chatted for a while, commenting on the tragedy and the unpredictability of human nature. Jackson promised another lunch. Thadeus reminded him that he had paid for that day's meal and therefore was expecting two lunches.

'How do we find out how many mouthfuls there are in a bottle of Drambuie?' asked Thadeus.

'How would a mathematician handle the question?' asked Freddie.

'I would drink a quarter of the bottle, count the mouthfuls and multiply by four,' answered Thadeus. 'What would a doctor do?'

'A doctor would pour the bottleful into a measuring glass and divide the result by about of a fifth of a gill, knowing that that amount represented a mouthful,' was her answer.

'Dull!' exclaimed Thadeus. 'I wonder how Hilton would tackle the problem.'

'He would measure a mouthful of water in one of his kitchen jugs, look at the label on the bottle to find out the total volume of the bottle then get a pencil and paper and work out the figure required,' speculated Freddie.

'Even duller!' responded Thadeus. 'How about a medical student?'

'A medical student would drink the whole bottle carefully counting the number of mouthfuls. Before completing the task he, or she, would fall over in a drunken stupor and reassess the position next morning.'

'Here's to medical students!' cried Thadeus, filling two small Brandy glasses with Drambuie.

Freddie took a glass and raised it to her lips. 'Cheers. Here we go.'

They both slept well that night.

CHAPTER 3

A DOG FIGHT IN ESSEX

Immediately upon completing a modest breakfast of tea, toast and marmalade, Thadeus telephoned Inspector Jackson. He questioned him on the subject of the bottle of Drambuie. Jackson tried to go off at tangents regarding the events of the previous day, and other facts about Sir Percy Dennington, but Thadeus remained disciplined and eventually obtained the following specific facts: Drambuie is manufactured in two sizes of bottle, the full bottle and the half bottle – Sir Percy's bottle had been the half bottle; it appeared to have been full of liquid, except for a couple of glassfuls; there was only one drinking glass at the scene – a Waterford Crystal small brandy balloon – the glass was of the same make and design as the drinking vessels used in the main house; the 'scene', incidentally, had been Sir Percy's office, which was actually a converted horse's loose box. Thadeus had requested full details of this at a later date! Thadeus thanked Jackson for the information and made a note of their next luncheon appointment, which would be subject to confirmation when he consulted the Burke & Co diary at his office.

He next consulted the label on the near empty Drambuie half-bottle that stood, for some strange reason, on the floor of the kitchen. He sat down at the kitchen table, trying to ignore Hilton's extravagant preparation of breakfast for his beloved sister, and engaged in some simple arithmetic.

A half-bottle equals one-half litre – information supplied by the label on the Drambuie bottle. A mouthful could be measured at 25 ml – information supplied by Freddie. The number of mouthfuls per half-bottle equals twenty; information calculated by the Cambridge graduate using a method called 'simple division'.

Freddie's bacon was beginning to smell very appetizing!

Somewhere at the back of Thadeus' memory was the information about fatal dosage of arsenic but the active part of his mind was devoted to assessing the number of bacon rashers required to stabilize his equilibrium.

He instructed Hilton to set aside three or four slices of Norfolk best-back for his second breakfast, at which he would join his sister, as he felt it would be impolite to allow a guest in his house to eat alone. Hilton raised his eyes to the ceiling, speechless.

Freed of any further distraction the answer to the dosage question popped back into his mind: 250 mg, that is a quarter of a gram, multiply that by twenty and the answer is 5g – less than a quarter of an ounce! Not a huge amount in general terms, but enough to frighten a chemist Thadeus thought.

Freddie confirmed this opinion over eggs, bacon and tomatoes a few minutes later.

Within the next four weeks Burke & Company started to flourish. The General Strike was still looming, but more of that later. Thadeus had built up quite a substantial portfolio of general non-marine business, country houses, factories and property investments throughout England and Ireland. Much of this business had come from Thadeus' aristocratic connections, but their efficient service was beginning to attract a wider clientele. He had also established a reasonable book of agents supplying general non-marine risks to Lloyd's.

James was developing a small, but useful book of motor business, both direct and through agents. But what really interested Thadeus was the bloodstock account, horses, particularly racehorses, stallions and mares. An area of business that Thadeus thought could establish the company as a major player within the Lloyd's community.

They had employed three new members of staff. Miss Mills, a lady in her fifties with many years' experience in the city. She had been private secretary to the chairman of a medium sized company of Lloyd's brokers and when he retired she felt that a new position was appropriate. She had worked her way up from an office junior at the end of the last century, and knew 'everything' about Lloyd's brokers. She was, frankly, a bit of a dragon – or should it be dragoness? Everyone, including Thadeus, leapt to their feet when she addressed them. She was appointed office manager. Essentially this title meant that she did everything that the others didn't. James was appointed an assistant director at the same time, to keep him slightly out of her clutches.

Also added was Mr Emery, he was in his sixties and working his way to a well deserved pension that he had already established with one of the large firms of Lloyd's brokers. By a special arrangement with them he had been engaged by Burke & Co to look after the policy documentation. He had substantial knowledge of the Lloyd's Signing Bureau and had been involved within the sub-committee set up to consider the idea of a central policy signing office a few years ago.

The third new member was a twenty-six-year-old young lady, Elizabeth 'Beth' Bateman, previously employed by the Railway Passengers Assurance Company, situated just round the corner in Cornhill, and an occasional lunch companion of Ethel. She was handling claims, as she had done in her previous job. Her telephone manner was excellent and her paperwork meticulous. As Burke & Co did not have many claims at the present time, she was also taking all telephone calls for the office.

During this period Thadeus had had lunch with Johnny Jackson and received a full account of the Armstrong case, involving the use of arsenic, in Wales. A chap poisoned his wife and then proceeded to try his luck on a fellow solicitor. Unfortunately he got the dosage wrong and his competitor was taken violently ill, which lead to Mrs Armstrong's body being exhumed and her husband hanged.

Thadeus had also acquired a description of Sir Percy Dennington's office, the scene of his death. Sir Percy was attempting to establish a small band of thoroughbred broodmares at his farm near Newmarket in Suffolk, the home of English horseracing. To this end he had built two sets of loose boxes, both as a row of six, brick with slate roofs. He had two mares, both in foal, and with recently weaned foals. The two mares were in one unit and the foals in the other. The mare's unit had a foaling box at one end and a box used for storage at the other end. The foal's unit had one of the end boxes converted into an office, equipped with a mahogany roll-top desk, two chairs, a filing cabinet and a bookcase. In one of the bottom drawers of the desk Sir Percy kept a bottle of Drambuie, apparently his favourite tipple, practically addicted to the stuff, very rarely drank anything else. At the time of his death there was a half-bottle in the drawer; it was almost empty. There were no glasses in the drawer. The other, almost full, deadly half-bottle was on the desk with his one glass.

Thadeus made some notes and sketched a drawing of the house and outbuildings, and the loose boxes. He then worked on a detailed ground plan of the area and the office layout. Jackson was most impressed, particularly with the fact that Thadeus had bought these large sheets of paper with him to the restaurant. It was this sketched ground plan that attracted the attention of James Pooley the next day.

'I have been working on a ground plan for Dad's proposed new premises up in Essex,' he explained.

'How is the project getting on?' asked Thadeus.

'Actually it has run into a few problems,' then James, slightly sheepishly added, 'I wondered if I could seek your advice on a couple of matters?'

'And you saw my plans of the Dennington estate and it gave you the ideal excuse to raise the matter?' scoffed Thadeus, softening his observation with the words, 'James, if you have a problem of any sort always talk to me about it.' Thadeus thought, but did not say, that worried and distracted staff were bad for business and therefore bad for the firm, and for him.

It was nearly lunchtime and Thadeus suggested that they should partake of a beer and sandwich at The Lamb, as soon as he had completed a draft slip on which he was working. Thadeus handed his papers to Beth Bateman, who had started work at Burke & Co a couple of days before, and was now manning the secretary's desk while Ethel had taken an early lunch. The two girls were not happy that they alternated at lunchtime as it meant that they were unable to take meals together. Thadeus promised that when Miss Mills and Mr Emery arrived on the Monday of the next week the situation would be reconsidered. What he really meant was that it would become Miss Mills' problem, not his! What the firm really needed was a proper 'office junior' but they could not afford one at this time. The present staff expansion had pushed Thadeus' budget to the limit.

'What's the problem?' asked Thadeus, as they settled on a pair of stools at the bar with their beer, awaiting the ordered sandwiches.

'There are two problems which may possibly be related,' informed James. 'You know some of the facts about the site in Essex, but I will just reiterate the exact position, by way of background. My father was offered a contract by the transport company for work on their buses. Frankly the contact came through a friend of Dad's, with whom he used to work, but Dad gained the contract on merit. He was not the only engineer seeking the job! My uncle, Dad's brother-in-law, works for the War Office and was able to inform Dad about this disused airfield that was being sold, so Dad was able to make an offer, agree a price and pay a deposit within an hour of the information appearing in the newspapers.'

James paused to sup his beer and ask Thadeus if he had any questions. Thadeus said that he might have questions later, but for James to kick-on with the story for the moment. Thadeus had thought of asking James whether his father was an old Etonian, but he held back any criticism of a nepotistic nature saying simply, 'Let us attend to the problems!'

'The first problem is with the bank. Dad has an account with the Co-operative Society Bank. He has banked with them since he left school. He has always been a prudent saver. The business, Pooley Motors Ltd, also have their account with the Co-op; I should mention that Dad is of a socialist persuasion, not involved in politics at all, but definitely "on the left". He feels that the Co-op is the people's bank! The land will cost £3,800. Dad has £500, in cash, in the bank. The company also has assets, machinery and tools. The bank agreed to advance £3,000, leaving Dad to find another three hundred. Now, suddenly, they say that in view of the current economic climate, general strike looming, etc. they have been forced to reconsider the loan and can only advance £1,000 pounds.'

For a moment it looked as though tears might swell in James's eyes.

'What is the second problem?' said Thadeus quickly.

'Dad's friend is under pressure to cancel the work contract because Dad employs non-union workforce.'

At this point tears did swell into James' eyes.

'Pull yourself together James,' instructed Thadeus. 'It is just a "two-pipe-problem" instead of a quick gasper.' With this remark Thadeus lighted the match that he had been holding between his fingers for over five minutes, and applied the flame to the bowl of his silver-topped Calabash.

James smiled and lighted a cigarette.

'Union membership, tell me about that,' ordered Thadeus.

'Dad used to be a union member, but now that he has his own business he is not even eligible for membership. He has an apprentice, aged fifteen, who is also not eligible. The only problem is Philip, the mechanic who has been working with Dad for about six months. He has a strong aversion to unions. When he was demobbed from the army, which is when Dad first met him, he worked as a bus driver. He was newly married and they had a baby child; they now have two. Anyway when the first baby was small Philip was given a local bus route, the number 63 that runs from Forest Hill to Peckham, via Honour Oak and Nunhead. I do not suppose you know much about bus routes?' questioned James.

'It is a vehicle and enterprise that has escaped my studies,' admitted Thadeus.

'Generally bus drivers work shifts; the early shift starts work at about five o'clock in the morning and the late shift does not finish until about midnight. Local busses, like the 63, operate during the daytime only. So it was very convenient for Philip, leaving home at a reasonable hour and always home in time for dinner. After a couple of weeks on this job Philip was moved to a different route, one of the long routes that runs right across London, and needs early and late shifts. The reason was that as he was a new man the job should go to a longer serving employee. The man who got the job replacing Philip was the brother of the trade union steward! Atkins was his name, and Philip thinks that he is behind this problem. Philip does not trust any trade unionist.'

'I can see that it is all a bit of a worry, James,' said Thadeus, 'but let us look at the options. One, Philip must join the union. Which one is it – the Transport and General Workers, or the Engineer's Union?'

'Either, I think,' responded James. 'It was the T&G that he belonged to at the bus garage.'

'Then he must join the Engineers,' instructed Thadeus. 'It is always useless to harbour a grudge; the "grudgor" is the one that suffers, not the "grudgee". He can resign when this problem is out of the way, if he thinks that it is really necessary. Point two, we must find another bank. We will go and see my own manager at Coutts & Co this afternoon. If he cannot help us, he will know somebody who can.'

'I am sorry to be putting all this on to you,' apologized James.

'I love problems! I suppose you thought that the two incidents might be related because the Co-op and the trade unions both sponsor Labour parliamentary candidates. There might be a link. We must investigate!'

The sandwiches and drinks having been consumed the two men returned to their office.

Thadeus made a telephone call to Gerald Parker at Coutts and arranged to meet him, with James Pooley, at 3.30 pm that afternoon. He then gathered up the papers and newly typed slips from Ethel, who had replaced Beth at the secretary's desk, and made his way to the Lloyd's Underwriting Room.

The work proved simple, underwriters just loved office blocks in West London, even if the premium rates were a bit thin! He was back in the office by 3.15, leaving plenty of time for a leisurely stroll through the alleys to Lombard Street.

An elegant young lady, who placed their bowler hats in a cupboard, escorted them into Gerald's private office. James placed his umbrella in a stand himself; the young lady smiled, but appeared to be devastated by the deprival of this duty. Thadeus had the good manners to hand his umbrella directly to the charming female, who gave him an appreciative nod of the head.

Gerald rose from his chair and quickly approached the two men with his hand outstretched. Greetings were exchanged and introductions made.

Gerald was in his mid-thirties, elegantly attired in a full frock coat and high collar, the required habiliment of the bank. Had Thadeus been aware of this meeting while at his matutinal preparations he would have been similarly attired. The lounge suit that he wore that day put him, he felt, at a distinct disadvantage in the forthcoming negotiations.

James outlined the proposed purchase of land in north Essex, describing the old airfield site. The area to be bought by Mr Pooley senior was about two-thirds of the original operational airfield; the other one-third, the eastern side, was to be used by the local council for a new industrial estate, an area where local businesses could be established without interfering with the plans for the nearby towns. Work had already commenced on the site.

The Pooley land included two large aircraft hangers on the northern border, and some huts and small offices at the far western end. The original landing strip had been nearly halved by the division of the land. Mr Pooley intended to retain his half of the landing strip for test-driving buses and other vehicles. He might introduce a skid-pad! All the land transfer documents were ready for signing; only the money was missing!

When questioned more intensely James admitted that there was one small problem concerning a 'right of way'. The previous owners, the War Office, had been able, legally, to ignore this issue, but new owners, including the local council had to recognize the pre-war rights. The pathway crossed the eastern end of the land diagonally, from south-west to north-east. The council proposed to move the right of way so that it left the southern border roadway at the original point, but travelled directly north along the division between the newly divided land. Local rambling and horse-riding groups had been consulted and no problem was anticipated. The council intended to make the redirected pathway into a proper roadway, which would better suite the industrial estate, and Mr Pooley, giving them access to their properties from two sides.

The problem was the other end of the right of way, which obviously also needed to move. This was across the county border in Suffolk and the local council on that side of the divide had proved unhelpful, and nobody seemed to know who owned the adjacent land. Lawyers were working on searches, without much success! The Essex Local Council and, consequently, the War Office, were loath to finalize matters until this problem was resolved.

James left the meeting with two foolscap sheets of notes and questions that needed answers, and a long list of documents that would need to be produced for the bank's perusal, otherwise the meeting went well. Gerald seemed confident that the bank could advance a sum up to four thousand pounds, subject to agreed repayment terms and an interest rate of one and a quarter per cent above the Bank of England lending rate. Following a frown from Thadeus this figure was reduced to a more acceptable three-quarters of a point. As they left the room Thadeus said that he wanted a private word with Gerald and returned behind closed doors for a few minutes. Then Thadeus and James collected their belongings and returned to the office in good humour.

Before leaving the office that evening Thadeus asked Inspector Jackson if he was free for a quick conversation at about 6.00 pm. Jackson suggested a beer at The Lamb, but Thadeus declined, his excuse being: 'I have promised my sister that I will run through some old oral examination papers with her this evening, as she has an important test coming up, and I need all my wits clear and unadulterated for the long Latin words! Can we just meet in the street? Outside my office?'

At 6.00 pm they walked down Gracechurch Street together. Thadeus outlined the shenanigans that were hassling the Pooley family.

Jackson enlightened, 'I am investigating a case of alleged fraud and embezzlement within the T&GWU which may have nothing to do with your problem. The two people involved know nothing about this, and I can say nothing, officially. If the facts concerning the matter were exposed it would ruin my case, not to mention a slight case of slander! Off the record, and putting my life in your hands, I will mention two names.'

Thadeus placed two fingers in front of his mouth indicating his continued silence.

Jackson looked around the street suspiciously, turning casually towards Thadeus' right ear, 'Sid and Len Barber,' he said, and immediately changed the subject of conversation to the weather.

Freddie seemed happy with the questions fired at her that evening, while Thadeus, although armed with the correct answers was still left totally bewildered.

The next morning Thadeus was introduced to Mr Sydney Pooley, father of James, who had appeared especially to thank him for his assistance with the bank. He was slightly taller than his son, wearing a black Homburg and a black overcoat, with a velvet collar. Thadeus thought that this apparel only appeared for funerals, and bank managers. Apart from the black garb he was very much a manual worker, his hands were strong and, although slim, his body was of a sinewy structure. Mr Pooley was armed with two briefcases packed with documentary evidence of the land deal; the bus repair contract, his business accounts and budget figures and details of all his personal wealth. Thadeus advised him that he was confident that the bank manager would be impressed. He did not mention that during his final brief conversation with Mr Gerald Parker he had agreed personally to underwrite the loan against his assets at the bank, secured against the land, of course!

Thadeus invited Mr Pooley to partake of a cup of Beth's excellent and fresh coffee. When served Thadeus asked Beth to close the door of his little office.

'Mr Pooley, have you ever heard of a "Sid and Len Barber"?' he put to the elder man, inwardly crossing himself for the life of Johnny Jackson.

'Two of the worst East End gangsters in London!' exclaimed Pooley Senior. 'Do you think that they have anything to do with my problems?'

Oh God, thought Thadeus, I should not have mentioned the names. Then aloud, 'No, no. I read something about them in the papers and thought that they operated in South London,' he lied.

'They are a couple of brothers, real hooligans; terrified the Isle of Dogs for some years before moving out to one of those new towns in Essex. They live nowhere near the land that I am buying. I came across them when they were involved with the Southwark Trade Council – a devious pair! Sid, the elder one is now quite high up in the

Trade Union Council and I think that his brother is the treasurer of a T&GWU branch somewhere.'

'Oh right!' said Thadeus, casually. 'What time is your appointment at the bank?'

'Not until 2.00 pm,' replied Mr Pooley, 'I was hoping to leave my bags here in the office, if that is all right, while I have a look around St Paul's. Wonderful piece of work, wonderful piece of work,' he enthused.

Thadeus agreed, adding that he thought that it was also 'a beautiful piece of mathematics', then the elder Pooley said farewell to his son and set off along Cornhill.

Before he vacated the office he said, quietly to Thadeus, 'I will not be mentioning our conversation about the Barbers to anybody!'

Thadeus offered a grateful smile.

The rest of the morning everybody was busy on insurance matters; there were plenty of orders and quotations to be completed that week, therefore the staff were surprised when Thadeus announced that he would be leaving the office at 12.30 as he had a lunch date outside of the city. Privately he advised James that his appointment was with his father at the House of Lords, and that he anticipated at least two bottles of decent red wine between them, so it was possible that he would not return to the office that afternoon. He instructed him to telephone him at home if there were any problems, particularly if they concerned his father's meeting at the bank. Thadeus and James then put in a good hour's work in the Underwriting Room; James returning alone to the office laden with files and slips, Thadeus having taken a taxi to Westminster.

Thadeus met his father in the Great Hall and they wound their way through the building for lunch on the terrace. Thadeus had hoped that they would eat in the Lord's refectory surrounded by steaming beef, lamb and pork trolleys, but as things turned out the lighter terrace menu suited him better.

Thadeus' relationship with his father had always been very formal; he always referred to him as 'sir'. His father always called him 'Thadeus' but there was always a slight pause before he used the name, as if he needed to recall the word out of some distant archive of his mind.

They discussed politics, particularly the hopeless position of the Liberal Party and the constant wrangling therein. Shared thoughts on the forthcoming general strike, Lord Ashmoor feared that Churchill would have the nation swarming with armed troops. Thadeus was sure of one thing; the miners were not going to get much help from anybody, a sad reward for the men working at the very surface where nature and civilization meet.

With the cheese, and second bottle of claret, questions were raised about life in the city and Lloyd's in particular. Lord Ashmoor was keen to expand his syndicate portfolio and asked Thadeus to seek out any new and adventurous underwriters that might be of interest.

'How is your venture into the world of bloodstock insurance progressing?' questioned the Earl.

'Slower than I would like, sir,' replied Thadeus.

The Earl removed a sheet of paper from his inside coat pocket and handed it to his son. 'I have told these chaps that you will be contacting them to sort out their affairs.'

Thadeus glanced down the list. 'Good Heavens, sir, half of these accounts will make me the leading bloodstock broker in the world!'

'I thought that was what you had in mind!' puzzled the Earl.

'Yes, sir, I'll get onto this straight away.'

'That chap at the top of the list has a very good horse out at Newmarket next week. Be there!' instructed the Earl. 'And send that sister of yours back up to Edinburgh, she is wasting too much time piddling about at that hospital, and spending money on clothes.'

'She seems to be working very hard, sir,' defended Thadeus. 'I tested her for hours only last evening with past exam papers.'

'Yes, but I see the invoices coming in from London fashion houses, and from Paris! Did you know that she had been over there?'

'Yes, I think she was away for a few days, with some friends,' admitted Thadeus.

'Enough said! There is an interesting debate in the lower house this afternoon. Drop in and see if you can catch some of it, if you have the time,' said Lord Ashmoor rising from his chair and indicating that the interview was concluded.

Taking a seat in the gallery of the Commons, Thadeus was pleased to find a debate concerning methods of taxation taking place in the chamber. Neither the Prime Minister nor the Chancellor were present but there was a good back-bench tussle, every system of raising revenue from income tax, through import duties and purchase taxes, to land value taxation, was being advocated and praised, questioned and ridiculed. The only consensus was the opposition to the reintroduction of window tax!

Thadeus was particularly impressed by the young Labour Member for Burslem, Stoke-on-Trent, with a strong voice, flavoured with a hint of Scottish accent. His preference was land value taxation and he spoke well on the subject. Thadeus could not fault his argument, but what really caught his attention was the member's response to an interruption doubting the ability of the authorities to identify the responsible landlord for tax purposes. 'Very easy!' dismissed the young Scotsman. 'I would walk onto the land with a pickaxe in one hand and a shovel in the other, and I would start digging. It would not be long before somebody tapped me on the shoulder. That would be the landlord!' The House enjoyed that, so did Thadeus; what a good idea!

Thadeus telephoned his office as soon as he returned to his house, told them that he was back, spoke in a manner that amplified his sobriety, and requested that James should ring him as soon as he was back in the office. This duly occurred at a couple of minutes before five o'clock. There were few business problems to worry about; a pair of underwriters had gone 'missing' after lunch, nothing new there! One chap thought that the value of a racehorse could never be as high as £10,000 and that there was probably a typing error on the slip! All routine stuff!

Mr Sydney Pooley had satisfied all the requirements of Coutts & Co and the money was ready to transfer into the newly opened account of Pooley Motors as soon as the outstanding papers were signed. James also informed Thadeus that Philip Mahoney had made an application to join the Camberwell branch of the Engineers Union.

When the final items of the bulletin were despatched, Thadeus advised James that he recommended a visit to the proposed Pooley

Motors North Essex Branch at the weekend; the party to be equipped with pickaxes and shovels.

'Good heavens!' responded James, 'I do not pretend to understand your plan, but Dad already has permission to visit the site at the weekend to look over the aircraft.'

'What aircraft?' Thadeus immediately queried.

'I haven't told you before but in one of the hangers are a couple of Sopwiths,' explained James, 'They were delivered to the airfield just at the end of the war and nobody seems to want them. Most of the ex-war Sopwiths were sold to Australia and other overseas countries but these two got forgotten because there were no personnel on the airfield apart from a caretaker. The War Office says Dad can keep them. It will cost too much to take them away now, especially as the council have cut the runway in half!'

'Good heavens! What sort of condition are they in?' exclaimed Thadeus.

'Excellent, I do not think that they have ever been flown, apart from the delivery flight. The Camel 2F1 has a 150 horse-power Bentley engine, and the Dolphin has a 200 horse-power Hispano-Suiza,' explained James.

'Amazing,' was all an amazed Thadeus could say. 'Can you telephone me this evening at about eight o'clock? By that time I should have been able to work out some sort of itinerary and timetable.'

'Yes, sir,' responded James.

Thadeus replaced the telephone receiver and thought, 'What on earth is "sir" going to come up with?'

That evening a temporary 'war cabinet' consisting of Thadeus and Hilton, assisted by Freddie, demoted to serving coffee, considered the options. Hilton acknowledged that, in a previous life, he had encountered some very hard men, but his advise was more of a cautionary nature rather than protagonistic, if not positively obstreperous or aggressive! However a plan was devised, the magic ingredient being supplied by Freddie. Thus it was that at an early hour on Saturday morning a small convoy entered the main gates of

Boxheath Airport. Philip Mahoney released the padlocks and the strange party drove past the unmanned sentry boxes and deserted guardhouse. They wove their way across to the Suffolk border, the Bentley with its two passengers; Freddie had reluctantly been restrained at home; parked up about fifty yards from the chosen spot. This was an area of light scrubland without trees.

Philip and James put the Morris Oxford next to the Bentley in a suspiciously protected position. Stanley Pooley drove the pick-up truck close to the fairly dilapidated fence. The five men carefully removed about twenty yards of fencing, placing the woodwork in a neat heap on the Essex side. The surveyor's plans showed these to be airport property. Stanley unloaded his cargo, Freddie's magic ingredient, an old Eccles trailer caravan. In the recent past it had been the subject of an accident; that is actually a rather kind description of the vehicle. It was dented all over and the inside resembled a bombsite. It was manoeuvred into position about ten yards inside the Suffolk border. The gang then retreated for a well earned breakfast supplied, and served, by Hilton.

During the two and a half hours that they waited for some reaction to their activities, the party toured the premises. The control tower and its subsidiary equipment had gone, but there were three general-purpose huts, two with old beds and one with tables and chairs. The hangers were the main attractions, particularly the one with the two aircraft. They all spent what seemed like hours gawking at the Sopwith Dolphin and the Sopwith Camel standing majestically at separate corners of the building. James was eager to jump up into the cockpit of the Camel but his father advised him that it was not a toy and that a proper inspection could take place when they had the necessary equipment for handling such a delicate precision machine. Hilton and Philip, who had been partaking of a quiet smoke outside the hanger, alerted the group that they 'had a bite'.

A gentleman in a tweed suit was standing in the newly created gap waving his arms. The team strolled over to meet him. He introduced himself as a local councillor who had been alerted that a possible trespass was being enacted. Was some local by-law being breached – no! Was he in some way representing the local constabulary – no! Was he acting in the interest, or on behalf, of the landlord – sort of!

He knew the owner of the land and knew that the owner would not be pleased by this interruption to the quiet enjoyment of his freehold.

'Excellent,' said Thadeus. 'We are anxious to discuss certain matters related to this landholding with the owner.'

'I regret that that will not be possible, he lives at some considerable distance from here,' was the reply.

Then Thadeus played his wild-card, 'Perhaps we could arrange a meeting with his brother?'

The councillor visibly froze, his mouth opened but nothing came out. He composed himself, saying 'I will see what I can arrange,' and hastily withdrew, walking quickly towards the neighbouring farm.

'We have more than a bite chaps. We will shortly need the nets,' triumphed Thadeus.

'What nets?' enquired James.

'A good question Mister James! I think that we should retreat to the main hanger – with our vehicles!' interposed Hilton.

It was agreed.

Within thirty minutes of their encampment the giant hanger door behind the Camel moved and a gunshot was fired into the air above the heads of the five men standing around the Bentley. As they scuttled to the other side of the large motor car Thadeus just had time to ask James if this sort of thing was covered by his motor insurance. James's vocal system had completely closed down; so had Philip's and Stanley's. Only Hilton was able to express himself in sound, and this he did so by repeating certain well-versed obscenities in short loud bursts!

Before they had time to recover from the shock a new and more terrifying sound split the air. Machine-gun bullets spattered the back wall.

'Good God, it's the Lewis!' exclaimed Philip and Hilton together recognizing the report of the Camel's armament. They had no time to evaluate this new threat, before the firing ceased, and the expletives 'shit, shit!' echoed from the aircraft's cockpit.

'The Lewis has jammed!' cried Hilton.

'Is there not a saying in the east that "one animal's excrement is another animal's nourishment"?' exclaimed Thadeus rhetorically.

Hilton murmured something about 'muck and brass' with reference to east Yorkshire, but Thadeus had stood up, assessed the position, and was running towards the Camel aircraft. He arrived underneath the front of the fuselage and was surprised to find himself facing a very rough-looking fellow at the other end apparently trying to lift up the aircraft's tail plane. Using no words, in an instant, his mind recognized that the villain's idea was to lower the Camel's nose in order to operate the fixed and synchronized Vickers at ground level. He contemplated swinging the propeller as a shield, but there were only two blades, and they were made of wood! As these thoughts flashed through his mind the third, and final, horror started. The Lewis on the Dolphin opened fire. Thadeus experienced one of those moments when time stands still; frozen as Rupert Brooke had ably described in a more favourable situation over a teacup.

The Dolphin's Lewis sent a short burst sweeping across the dusty floor. The scruff at the rear of the Camel fell to the ground clutching his legs and moaning loudly. From his hand fell a handgun. Thadeus rushed down the port side of the Camel and grabbed it. Before he could stand upright the Dolphin was in action again, a well-directed burst hit the occupant of the Camel's cockpit, just as the first rounds left the Vickers on their way towards the far end roof. All was now quiet! Thadeus paused, then ducked under the fuselage and walked with trepidation towards the other craft, gun in hand.

A voice boomed out into the large hanger from a megaphone. 'Thadeus, please do not shoot Detective Sergeant Anderson.' It was the unmistakeable voice of Inspector Johnny Jackson.

An hour later they were all assembled in a private room at the local hostelry. Explanations were being given. The police had arrived as the first shots were fired. The detective sergeant was familiar with the Lewis gun, but it was the first time he had used one to attack a Sopwith Camel. His last victim had been a Hanover C Type over France as a member of the RFC.

What Thadeus could not understand was why even an East End gangster would want to machine-gun five people to settle a dispute over the route of a public right of way?

Jackson explained. 'It might have been the last straw, or more likely the last haystack. My investigation was getting close to his illegal activities, and then he suddenly discovers that Stanley and Philip, two old union adversaries, who knew his name, and knew his signature, were about to unearth his secret land ownership, bought with money stolen from union funds. He also owned the farm, beyond the scrub strip, an area of over 120 acres.'

'How did you know that we were there?' asked Thadeus.

'I telephoned you at home to give you some more information about the Barber brothers. I spoke to your sister, she sounds very nice.'

'She is invaluable,' confessed Thadeus.

Then Jackson enquired, 'How did you wheedle them out?'

'When I was told that we could not meet the landowner, I asked if I could talk to his brother.'

Jackson laughed. 'You chaps will be needed at the enquiry.'

That evening Thadeus felt an overwhelming need to bathe in the beautiful; to rid the body and mind of violence and aggressive impulses. He entertained the clientele of the public bar with parts of Mozart's Piano Concerto No 27.

CHAPTER 4

A DAY AT THE RACES

On the Monday morning Miss Mills and Mr Emery arrived they were introduced to the other staff, James, Ethel and Beth, took their places at the allotted desks, and started work as if they had been there for years. They were both equipped with their own pens, pencils and rulers, which they arranged in accordance with some curious ritual.

Mr Emery possessed a group of geometric measuring devises, the purpose of which was never explained. Miss Mills immediately assumed the role of caring mother figure, and Mr Emery a sort of absent-minded, but kindly, uncle. It took the whole of the first morning to induce them to stop leaping to their feet whenever Thadeus, the esteemed owner, chairman, managing director and boss, emerged from his 'shed'. This act of subservience was frightening the life out of the two young girls!

It was therefore in a holiday spirit that Thadeus set off for Newmarket two days later, confident that the office was now a smoothly running machine.

It was a long trip, over sixty miles from London, but the Bentley enjoyed the open road and purred along proudly. They – Thadeus and the Bentley – stopped at Saffron Walden for a refreshment break before tackling the final leg of the journey, well fuelled.

Within an hour they were passing the July Course, then the Rowley Mile, towards the meeting with Lord Cheddon in the morning room at the Jockey Club premises situated in Newmarket High Street. Just before reaching town Thadeus stopped the motor vehicle beside the road to look across at the newly built Rowley Mile stand. Parking the car in Newmarket High Street, he carefully crossed the horse-walk and entered the Jockey Club rooms. He was a little early for his meeting and took some time studying the excellent collection of paintings displayed around the building, including several fine works by George Stubbs. He viewed some trophies, including the plated hoofs of *St Simon* and *Eclipse*, two of the foundation stallions of the modern thoroughbreds and paused briefly to inspect the silver gilt plaque showing figures of *Godolphin*, perhaps the paternal founder of the whole breed. The plaque had been presented by the King and Queen Mary in the spring of this year.

Realizing that he was due for his appointment he strode purposely through the building eventually finding his way into the morning room, where he noticed Lord Cheddon seated in a leather chair talking to a gentleman with whom he was familiar. Lord Cheddon arose to greet Thadeus and before Thadeus could respond the other guest thrust out his hand and said, 'David Anderson, it is a pleasure to meet you.'

'Good morning, my Lord,' said Thadeus, then turning to the detective sergeant, 'Good morning to you, sir.'

'David is working with our security people, trying to resolve some of the problems between the criminal elements that have been causing trouble on the racecourses,' explained Cheddon.

'At least they seem to be fighting each other rather than the public. Do you have much experience in this field of activity Mr Anderson?' said Thadeus mischievously.

'The Chairman thought I might be able to help,' replied Anderson.

Cheddon went across the room to settle his account with the attendant, and Anderson explained. 'Sorry about the "cloak and dagger" stuff, but not many people here know that I am attached to Scotland Yard. It was because I live in Suffolk that Jackson roped me in for the fun and games at the weekend.'

'Are you joining us for the racing this afternoon?' enquired Thadeus.

'Certainly. All part of the job!' smiled Anderson.

Cheddon had insisted that they partake of Mr Holloway's excellent sausages with mashed potatoes at the Star Inn before departing for the racecourse. He was of the opinion that eating during the afternoon interfered with the sport.

The three of them were driven to the racecourse in Cheddon's Rolls-Royce 40/50 Silver Ghost; a six-cylinder giant in white with red leather interior.

Anderson quickly excused himself as they entered the member's enclosure, explaining that he needed to circulate in the less fashionable sections, where his 'clients' might be found.

The big race of the day was a two-year-old Classic trial with several cracks of the season entered. Cheddon recommended that Thadeus back *Charlie Smirke* in the first race and *Harry Wragg* in the second. Both duly obliged, at short odds, but the two men were in good humour when they met, as arranged, in the paddock before the main race of the afternoon. They selected Lord Astor's *Cross Bow,* a fine looking colt, although Mr Joel's *Napoleon* had *Harry Wragg* on board and could be in the shake-up at the finish. Both were placed but the surprise winner was a colt named *Silent Silver* trained by a Mr Charlie Cook. This horse had opened in the betting at twenty to one but had quickly come in, and started at six to one! Somebody thought that he was a good thing! After the race Thadeus was introduced to the owner, a Mr Sullivan, who had had a modest bet on his runner, but appeared as surprised as the general public at the result. Photographs were taken and interviews given to the press; Thadeus kept out of the way and studied the confirmation of the thoroughbred. He was particularly interested in the shape of the hoofs; they were a good indication of the horse's ability and of mathematical interest in respect of the angles employed in irregular cones. Mr Cook supervised the rugging-up of the winner, watering his mouth personally and fussing around the colt until he was led away. Thadeus was standing beside the gate as the colt was led out of the winner's enclosure, his lad patting his neck and saying 'well done Freddy'. Thadeus thought that if he had known that the horse's stable name was Freddy he might have put a few pounds on him for his sister – Thadeus' sister, not the colt's!

The rest of the afternoon was spent dispersing the modest early winning on losing long-shots and looking around the new stand, which still did not give a very good view of the racing. Fortunately the racing on this course was always of excellent quality and although the view was restricted to horses coming towards you, getting gradually larger, followed by a blur as they dashed past the winning post, the ground was usually in good condition and an excellent test of a horse's ability.

Thadeus did track down Detective Sergeant David Anderson in the Tattersalls Ring and joined him in a glass of refreshing ale, a local brew from Bury St Edmunds. When Anderson heard that Thadeus was staying in Newmarket overnight, he suggested that he may care to join him the following morning and visit a couple of training yards. Thadeus readily agreed, before being told that they should assemble in the foyer of the Rutland Hotel at six o'clock, antemeridian.

After bathing and donning his dinner jacket and black tie, Thadeus strolled along the high street for an evening where he was to be dined and wined at Lord Cheddon's house on The Avenue. After several flutes of champagne the guests, which included several prominent racehorse owners and Jockey Club members, were lavishly feasted with numerous courses, including sumptuous wild salmon and lobsters, local pork and Aberdeen Angus beef. The claret was of vintage years that are normally only read about in imbiber's manuals. Thadeus had difficulty tackling the massive Spotted Dick with lashings of custard, a particular favourite of their host. There were flunkeys everywhere, all of whom were of a pronounced diminutive stature, but efficient enough to grace a royal occasion. Thadeus had not been so regally entertained since he moved out of the Burke family country seat to seek his fortune in London. His father loved entertaining.

There was even time for Thadeus and Cheddon to retreat into the library and finalize insurance arrangements for the earl's bloodstock, an impressive schedule of racehorses, broodmares, yearlings and foals. During several breaks for cigars and cigarettes Thadeus even hijacked two other owners to enlist in his growing bloodstock account.

A tiring evening was followed by a tired morning! Anderson stood on the steps of the Rutland Hotel looking out onto the high street clad in riding boots, cord jodhpurs, a tweed jacket and flat cap. Thadeus feared for the health of his Harris Tweed suit and polished brown shoes from Edward Green's. He must be very careful of his footing on this venture!

Anderson announced that they would 'start at the top' with a visit to Stanley House, assuring Thadeus that this was not part of his police work. 'I am committed to visit all of the training yards at least once each season. There have never been any problems associated with the Honourable George Lambton, but at such a successful yard criminal elements are always trying to infiltrate the lads. Tommy Watson will be there this morning and I think it is always a good thing to make young jockeys aware of the tight supervision applied by the Jockey Club. They are very vulnerable,' he explained.

'Tommy Watson won the Derby last year on Lord Derby's *Sansovino*; you surely do not think that he could be open to bribes?' questioned Thadeus.

'No, certainly not; but what was it your namesake said about vigilance!'

They headed up the Bury Road in the Bentley and turned into the stables. George Lambton was a proper gentleman, immaculately dressed and, despite his sixty-five years, had the appearance of an athlete. He greeted them cordially with a modest smile, asking Anderson discreetly what he particularly wanted to inspect; agreed to introduce the two visitors to Watson; and suggested that Thadeus might like to have a look at last year's Derby winner. Lambton himself escorted Thadeus to the box of *Sansovino*, where the horse was having an early morning wash down. It was explained that the horse was suffering from leg trouble this season and needed constant observation. He was to be walked this morning and might be worked later in the week in preparation for a race over a shorter distance, possibly a mile.

Conquistador, this year's disappointing Derby runner, was outside of his box, tacked up and ready for a canter up Warren Hill. Thadeus was very impressed with the high standards maintained at Stanley House. He did not feel that it was appropriate to raise the question of insurance with the esteemed trainer, but made a point of ensuring that he had a company card before they parted, just in case any insurance problem might arise with which Burke & Co could assist!

Anderson was in the tack room taking tea with some of the lads and lasses when Thadeus tracked him down. Young Watson was at the table with a large steaming mug which he would be unable to finish as he was riding a promising two-year-old that morning. He did not mention the name of the filly.

A while later they mounted the Bentley and set out for a smaller yard, Albert House Stables, not much more than a hundred yards down the same road, back towards the clock tower. This was the home of Charlie Cook, whom Anderson had added to his list of visits yesterday evening, as it was his practice to call on any Newmarket trainer that had a major winner on the previous day. Why? There was always a buzz about the place and plenty of boasting and loose talk but this was not how they found Albert House. All was very quiet. Mr Cook and two lads were smoking cigarettes dangerously close to a pile of baled straw and a young girl was staggering towards the midden beneath a loaded sack of considerably larger dimensions than her own.

Cook appeared startled by the arrival of a Jockey Club official, but stubbed out his gasper and extended a hand towards Anderson then doffed his cap at the Honourable Thadeus Burke. The two lads, both in their forties, disappeared into the tack room. Thadeus was tempted to assist the young, mucking-out lady but proper consideration for his morning attire prevented him. There was not a horse in sight.

Anderson claimed that an inspection of the stable paperwork was overdue and was led off to the office accompanied by a worried looking Cook. Thadeus was entrusted to the capable hands of Jake, the senior lad, summoned back out of the tack room. It was explained that most of the string had already departed for the gallops – they were out on Side Hill and were expected to return in about a quarter of an hour.

A five-year-old mare was brought out of her box for inspection, walked up and back along the short concrete pathway, stood square and then wheeled back to where she was being rested before going off to a stud to be covered next year. Her pedigree and race record was outlined with some authority.

There was suddenly a commotion at the other end of the yard as a young red-headed girl scampered out of the tack room in a state of undress, her shirt and brassiere clutched tightly in her right hand, her ample breasts bouncing delightfully in the morning sunlight. She disappeared quickly into a neighbouring loose box and was heard to scream, 'That bastard in there tried to strip me off!' The words being directed at some unseen colleague. Jake appeared not to have noticed the incident and Thadeus pretended to have been looking the other way. A minute later the alleged 'bastard' emerged and walked slowly over to the office to join his boss.

Jake proceeded to introduce *Alfred The Great*, a bay three-year-old colt that Thadeus remembered had been entered for the seven-furlong handicap on the previous afternoon, but had been scratched. The head lad said that the colt had shown a bit of heat in his off-fore! Thadeus asked if he might inspect the damage and the head lad reluctantly open the stable doors. Ensuring that the horse was brought up close to the doorway in order that a certain amount of light would be cast on the front legs and, incidentally, the legs could be placed onto an area free of straw, Thadeus made an attempt to run his hand along the fetlocks in a knowledgeable manner, murmuring inaudibly.

Anderson's voice could be heard coming out of the office assuring Mr Cook that everything appeared to be in order and enquiring if it would be possible to see *Silent Silver*. Thadeus' attention was redirected towards this good idea, however, *Silent Silver* was out being walked. Mr Cook explained that he did not like to keep the two-year-olds boxed up for too long, even if they had raced the previous day.

They said their farewells and drove the Bentley out of the yard and carefully between various strings of young horses crossing backwards and forwards between stables and the training grounds, parking the car besides All Saints Church.

Anderson partook of a working man's breakfast of eggs alongside the celebrated local sausages at Bob's Café on the corner of Sun Lane. Thadeus restricted his intake to just one poached egg and two tomatoes, being more than complete from his dinner the previous evening. The more robust and active policeman needed the full works. It was during this meal that the sergeant was introduced to Cavalier's Theorem and Euclid Book XII Proposition 15, in particular the volume and measurements of cones, and even more particularly the area and design of frustum, cones with their tops cut off, a shape very similar to an equine hoof. Thadeus advised that the hoofs that he had observed on *Alfred The Great,* a three-year-old by *Lemberg*, were the same hoofs that had been worn by *Silent Silver*, a two-year-old by *Swynford* when winning on the Rowley Mile yesterday. Furthermore, in view of their registered racing names, it was much more likely that the three-year-old should be named 'Freddy' by the stable lads than the two-year-old. Finally Anderson was told that a conversation with a red-headed young lady, equipped with outstanding bosoms, could prove a worthwhile investment – in more ways than one!

Over a huge cup of tea, Thadeus further needed to explain to Anderson that it had become the practice for him to provide the answers in respect of criminal matters, but for the police to seek out the proof.

Thadeus returned to London and work at Burke & Co. In addition to the new bloodstock business, introduced by his father and acquired by himself at Newmarket, Thadeus had received through the post that morning details of paintings to be insured for a prominent collector. They included many works by the French Impressionists, Monet, Renoir and Lautrec; the cubist Braque; Whistler and Turner; and many more exciting names. Thadeus himself owned a Renoir and a Braque and was dazzled by the values applied by this new client. Miss Mills put together the file and slip for the art insurance, as she had previous experience with this class of business, which was new to Thadeus.

The book of business that Thadeus and James took into the Lloyd's market that afternoon was very desirable and the two brokers had no difficulty completing their orders well before 4.30. They had time to stop off for a cup of tea in a café in Leadenhall Market. Sitting at the table, double checking the addition of lines, James advised Thadeus that he had an invitation to attend a horse-racing meeting with Jimmy Payne and a motor vehicle sales agent, who was sponsoring a race at the meeting. This chap had the franchise for the new MG cars in East Anglia and Payne had recommended Burke & Co to handle the insurance deals that would be offered with the new cars. Would it be all right if James had the day away from the office? Thadeus assured his employee that he would be more upset if he did not attend. Would James be happy handling the matter on his own, or did he want Thadeus to travel with him? To Thadeus' chagrin James assured him that, being accompanied by the underwriter, and being aware that the motor man, a Mr Henry Hollington, was of secondary school education from a rather mediocre establishment in East Ham, he was more than confident. The racing was to be next week at Bungay. Mr Hollington had arranged travel up to the top end of Suffolk and back, by a privately hired charabanc.

Thadeus was about to tell James about his adventures at Newmarket, but he realized that time was short and they needed to send out letters and a telegram before Ethel and Beth shot off home.

That weekend tearful farewells were said as Miss Freddie was baggaged off to Edinburgh on the Sunday morning. Although she was travelling first class on a train equipped with an excellent buffet carriage Hilton had provided a huge picnic hamper crammed with her favourite goodies. She was outraged by the telephone calls that Thadeus had made to the university in Scotland and the hospital in Ealing, but most of all by the fact that her younger brother had taken the mantle of their dictatorial, but cowardly, father. She swore that she would never speak to him again! Amending this proclamation to the period only from the time the train departed from Kings Cross until he telephoned her to verify her safe arrival in the northern province later that evening! This Thadeus promised into her hugged ear.

Anderson telephoned during the afternoon with the results of his tryst with the Albert House Stables' red-head, an Irish girl named, of course, Mary. She was well known and well liked in the chosen public house, the Old Plough out at Ashley, the conversation between the girl and the policeman being constantly interrupted by kisses, handshakes and hugs with passing stable-lads – the female being the centre of attention, not the sergeant! Anderson had selected a pub away from the town of Newmarket in the hope of some seclusion but should have known better. Every watering-hole within twenty miles of the town was crowded each evening with stable workers drawn by the demand for light-weighted youth; the only qualification being single figures on the weighing machine. Their diet seemed to consist of no food – just lots of drink!

Thadeus' theory of the 'ringer' was correct. The whole yard was very pleased with the outcome, even Mary had won £100. Mr Cook and his two assistants had pocketed thousands. This information was divulged, not by way of any vengeance against her sexual assailant, but as a matter of pride. Anderson was of the opinion that no case could be brought against Cook; there was no solid evidence and there would certainly be no witness statements. The only gem of information acquired was from overhearing a few words exchanged between Mary and a tall, good-looking youth. The trickery was to be enacted again, in a hurdle race at Bungay next week. He did not know the names of the horses involved and would need to look at the *Sporting Life* tomorrow morning to expand his lead. Thadeus pondered the position and decided to do nothing.

The following Tuesday morning James Pooley and James Payne assembled outside Dulwich Library for their trip to Bungay races. The charabanc already had four passengers, picked up from Penge and as they trundled through Camberwell, up the Walworth Road into Bermondsey, across the river and through the East End of London, they acquired a motley crew of race-goers. Some were equipped with binoculars and cloth caps, others in their best Sunday suits and a few in working togs with a box of sandwiches. The two James's wore tweed jackets, light trousers and brown shoes. As it was a bright and sunny day, J Pooley carried his newly acquired panama hat, purchased from Mr Lock of St James's, where Miss Freddie had sent him to obtain a proper bowler, 'the hairy sort that needed brushing'. He also carried a very expensive pair of German binoculars, loaned for the occasion from Thadeus, who had been his fashion adviser for the outing. The two lads had been racing only once before, when Mr Payne, Jimmy's father, had taken them both to Epsom to watch the first Derby after the war ended; they had backed a horse named *Paper Money*, five shillings each way, using ten-shilling notes. He finished third at seven to one and they made a slight profit.

They were impressed with Bungay Racecourse, the stand and the paddock were quite smart, but very rural; lots of farmers chewing straw and waving sticks. The actual racecourse was over one and a half miles round but you got a good view. They were even more impressed by Mr Hollington. The motor salesman was aged only a couple of years more than the two James's; of medium height, dark black hair brushed back with some sort of pungent smelling hair oil; smartly dressed in a flashy way.

A marquee had been erected beside the saddling enclosure, proudly displaying a notice at the doorway reading 'Hollington Motors'. Inside were tables and chairs as for a banquet, and a buffet meal spread out on two long trestle tables, with a third table piled with bottles of drink. Mr Hollington harangued the party telling them of his early experiences with the motorcar. He boasted that his first vehicle had been stolen, not by driving it away without the owner's permission, but a part at a time. His elder brothers and he had, before the war, when he was only a toddler, nicked, as he called the thefts, wheels, mudguards, a bonnet and even an engine, from which they built up their own motor car – the Hollington Special! He delighted in telling of the time when they watched the gentleman who had lost his engine trying to start the vehicle, spending ages trying to engage the starting handle into an engine cog that was not there! Both the brothers had died within a year of enlisting for the army. Henry had vowed that he would maintain the family name in the motor industry. He had gone to Oxford to enrol as an apprentice with Morris Motors and had met Mr Cecil Kimber, who had taken a liking to him, thought he was a character out of Dickens, called him 'Artful 'Enry' So when MG Cars was founded 'Enry was right there!

He admitted to being better with his head than with his hands, selling was his game, and he was in the right place for the booming motor industry.

Later in the afternoon Mr Hollington, now on first name terms as Henry, enthused about the future of MG Cars, revealing the prototypes than were on the drawing board at Abington. He claimed that Mr Kimber anticipated breaking the world land speed record with an MG!

They discussed insurance arrangements, Jimmy Payne was a bit nervous about some of these cars being engaged in racing, hill climbs and track events, but Henry was not a man that you said 'no' to. Jim Pooley was grateful to observe his broking being handled for him. Jimmy Payne, by way of defence, explained to Jim Pooley, after the business had been concluded, that his uncle Charlie had always impressed upon his nephew that risk was what insurance was all about. No risk, no premium was one of his maxims.

James Pooley crept away between the second and third races to write up some notes regarding the insurance terms for Hollington Motors. The decision to do this work proving to be a wise one as the afternoon, and the food and drink, wore on.

Both of the young men had modest losing bets on the opening race, followed by a recuperation of funds on a short priced favourite in the second.

Before disappearing for his note writing, Pooley had announced to Payne and a handful of other guests, that Mr Burke, his boss in London, had recommended a wager on Mr Cook's runners at that meeting. There were two of them, *Sky Lark* in the third race, a three-mile stayers' hurdle; and *Why Not* in the last, a two-mile-hurdle for novices. One of the Hollington guests, a self-proclaimed purge of the bookmaking profession, suggested a double on both horses, a betting device new to the others. Anyway our two young heroes agreed to have five pounds each in the pool for the double, and to place separately a ten-pound win bet on each horse. These amounts were well above what their pockets could afford, indicating the undoubted presence of alcohol abuse in the system. Perhaps it was this realization that prompted J Pooley to hide away and engage himself in copious note making. He re-emerged from behind the tent just in time to witness *Sky Lark* win his race by a short head at a starting price of twenty-five to one. James had won £250, enough to buy a row of terraced houses in Nunhead. He needed a drink!

Races four and five were run during what had been designated tea-time in the tent, which gave all the guests an opportunity to sober up and scoff various types of sandwich and cakes. During the third large cup of tea J Pooley showed J Payne his insurance notes for Hollington Motors, the underwriter nodded soberly, well fairly soberly, and confirmed that they were an accurate account of the agreement made with Mr Henry Hollington.

They did not have another bet until the last. The prices for *Why Not* were short, and getting shorter all the time. He opened at six to one, but was at five to one within a minute. The insurance men placed their ten pounds each at this price. The bookmakers offered nine to two, then fours, threes, and as the tapes went up *Why Not* was favourite at six to four. He won at a canter!

Another £50 won each. And what about the double – that matter was being resolved at the end of a row of bookmakers near the front of the Tattersalls enclosure.

As suspected some of Mr Hollington's guests from the Walworth Road, Bermondsey and the East End were familiar with a spot physical action and it appeared that it was necessary for the owners of two bookmaker joints to be reminded of their obligations in respect of a double winning bet, and the prices that had been agreed. One of the bookmaking fraternity actually had to be held upside-down for a short period to clear his mind! It was at this point that James felt sure that he caught sight of Detective Sergeant Anderson in the crowd, but nothing was said. The team settled for two hundred to one as a fair compromise from the white-faced bookies. A thousand pounds for a fiver, not a bad afternoon's work. For the bookmakers it was eight times these figures and they were giving not receiving!

As they left the racecourse there was some sort of shemozzle occurring in the pre-parade ring. Two horses, which appeared very similar to each other, were being washed down and attended to by a couple of chaps in white coats who were making careful notes of the horses' markings on a chart. Three or four policeman were also in attendance, and a girl with red hair was kicking the chap who looked exactly like that detective sergeant that James thought that he had seen earlier.

The two James's, having imbibed a substantial quantity of various alcoholic drinks by the end of the day's racing and the correct distribution of vast sums of money, were now sitting on a coping awaiting the arrival of their charabanc.

'Tell me about Cambridge,' ventured Jim.

'You mean, why was I sent down?' questioned a long-faced Jimmy

'Yes,' admitted Jim.

'The short answer is "a woman in my rooms",' explained Jimmy.

'And the long story?' prompted Jim.

'Well,' he paused, 'it started when I met this lady on the stairs.'

'The staircase at the college?' enquired Jim.

'Yes,' he paused. 'She was quite a bit older than me. In fact she was about the same age as my mother.'

'Crickey,' exclaimed Jim.

'My mother did not, and still does not, know that,' said Jimmy emphatically.

'So your parents know all the facts?' said Jim with sympathy.

'Not quite all the facts,' Jimmy emphasized. 'Only Uncle Charles knows the exact details. Dad thought it was a young girlfriend of mine. He thought it was all good manly stuff and the proctor was being a bit stuffy. Mum took the high moral attitude and said I deserved what I got.'

'It does seem a bit hard on you. I bet there are plenty of chaps that have girls in their rooms,' defended Jim.

'There is a bit more to it than that,' admitted Jimmy. 'This lady was a nymphomaniac. I mean, really a nymphomaniac! When we first met she more or less barged her way into my room and raped me.'

'Crickey!' exclaimed Jim.

'Yes. Well she said that she needed a glass for a drink. She actually had a bottle of wine in her hand. I found out later that she was supposed to be engaged on a different enterprise, on a different staircase, in a different college. Well she bounced into my room and demanded a glass, then a corkscrew, and then two glasses, one for me!'

'Good heavens!' exclaimed Jim

'Yes, then she came up right close to me, and… you are not going to believe this… she took hold of my hand and thrust it down the front of her knickers!'

'Crikey, Good heavens,' exclaimed Jim.

'She literally rubbed herself off with my right hand.' Then before Jim had time to exclaim another 'Crickey' or 'Good heavens' Jimmy went into full flow. 'When she had finished, she took her knickers off, stepped out of them, lay back on the bed with her skirt around her waist and said "I suppose you had better have some fun now!" Well, I was a bit aroused I must admit, so I leapt on her. It was bloody marvellous!' Jimmy sank back exhausted.

Jim's eyes were rolling around in his head. Eventually he asked, 'And you were caught in the act, as it were?'

'No, no, the thing carried on for several weeks,' explained Jimmy. 'Oh, there's our coach!'

The two young men were the first on board. They headed for the back seats and, despite a bumpy ride, both fell fast asleep. The tale of J Payne's early sexual adventures were not completed at that time. But they were still in the mind of James Pooley as James Payne was unloaded at his parents' house in Dulwich Village. From the back window J Pooley waved a 'good-bye' to J Payne's rather attractive, forty-something, ruffled haired mother, hoping to God that there were no sexual innuendos being carried by his hand movements.

Eventually deposited in Nunhead, James Pooley was greeted by his fiancée, Eddie, who experienced an evening that she did not forget for very many years.

Thadeus had spent a quiet evening chatting to his sister on the telephone and trying to analyse the chord changes and cadences in a Mozart quartet.

Detective Sergeant Anderson telephoned at about 8.30 and gave details of the events at Bungay Racecourse. The two attending veterinary surgeons had established, by the horse's marking, whorls and white patches, that Mr Cook's two runners had been swapped. Unnecessary evidence as one of the geldings had actually been painted to look like the other one. One had white socks painted on, and the other had them painted out.

'It will probably take a week to get the dye out completely!'

This was a trick used by a felon a few years ago, a certain Mr 'Ringer' Barrie who recently served a three-year prison sentence, then disappeared, probably to Australia. The two head lads had turned King's Evidence and chattered away faster than that man Tommy Handley on the wireless.

'Would you believe that they did not expect both horses to win?'

'Yes, I believe that,' assured Thadeus.

Apparently the winner of the three-mile race had never run that distance before. It was the winner of the last that had been their coup, but they could not get a decent price and had only profited by a small margin. There was a double rolling onto the last race and several bookies were laying off their liability around the betting ring, in addition to the general punters. They had nothing on the first winner at twenty-five to one! Cook was sure to go to prison and the assistants would probably join him for a shorter sentence, or perhaps be lucky and get a large fine. What a disaster!

Mary had escaped; difficult to believe, but she had boarded a train at Norwich station and was on her way to Liverpool. Anderson seemed to have personal knowledge of this flight, perhaps because he did not want her in the vicinity of Newmarket.

The next morning James was a few minutes late for the office. When he went into Thadeus' office to apologize, his employer was studying the *Sporting Life*.

'It looks like it was an exciting day at Bungay yesterday,' said Thadeus looking up casually. 'There were some arrests made after racing – something to do with a betting coup involving a ringer.'

'Crickey!' exclaimed James.

'Yes. Apparently, according to the gossip reported here,' Thadeus continued, 'the whole thing was organized and managed by a south London criminal mastermind. A sort of sporting Moriarty!'

'Crikey, good heavens,' exclaimed James Pooley, and that was all that was said. It did not seem the right moment to reveal his serendipitous accumulation of wealth.

CHAPTER 5

NOUGHTS AND CROSSES

It was the following Monday morning, at the beginning of November, when Jackson called at the offices of Burke & Co suggesting a coffee at The Stray Dog Café. Their coffee, a strange Russian–Turkish concoction, was a particular favourite of Jackson, but Thadeus found it a bit aggressive and had a cup of English tea.

'As you seem to be struggling with the Dennington case, I thought that you might enjoy assisting me with a separate enquiry at a gentleman's club up the West End,' opened Jackson.

'The Dennington case is progressing as well as can be expected,' defended Thadeus. 'I need information about any documents, or paperwork in general, that were found in Sir Percy's office at the time of his death. Do you have any such evidence?'

Jackson was clearly anxious to proceed with the new matter, but could not ignore his friend's request. 'There was a lot of paper in the office, in desk drawers and on the table top; a set of receipted invoices and some unpaid items, feed, veterinary bills, etc. and quite a lot of loose sheets with details of horses' pedigrees. Nothing that you would not expect to find in the office of somebody interested in the breeding of racehorses. I think I told you before that there were several books related to the subject – a set of stud books and results of sales, race results from previous seasons and the like.'

'I would appreciate the opportunity to study those papers', advised Thadeus.

'They were all boxed up and returned to Lady Dennington,' responded Jackson.

Thadeus thought for a moment. 'Well, what is this new problem?'

Jackson explained. 'It concerns a club in the West End, in a mews just off Duke Street; a gentleman's club, drinking, music and some girlie shows, and a bit of illegal gambling. It is named Noughts & Crosses; the music is this new "jazz" from the USA, New Orleans and Chicago.'

'What sort of gentleman do they entertain?' questioned Thadeus.

'I agree it does not sound like a sophisticated venue, but their membership list is impressive. I have obtained a list of members and I think that you will be impressed; there will be several names that you will recognize.'

'Is it the gambling that worries you?'

'No, I can cope with that; keep a watching eye, and make sure that it doesn't get out of hand. There have been a couple of incidents involving a group of Fascists that infiltrated the club, causing a rumpus over the "negro music", again I can cope with this, I think.'

'So what worries you?' prompted Thadeus emphatically.

Jackson finally got to the point. 'There are five owners and I have their names and addresses written down for you, but for the moment let us call them A B C D and E, each owning twenty per cent of the club. A has put in £10,000, cash; the other four have each pledged £10,000 by way of a loan of £40,000 to the club, in particular Noughts & Crosses Limited, from a bank. Each of the four, B C D and E, stand guarantor to the loan, separately, for £10,000 each.'

'You can start a good club for that amount of money,' commented Thadeus. 'Are you going to get to the difficulty?'

'This background is very important,' smoothed Jackson. 'These loans were backed up by Personal Accident insurance, on the life of each of the four, with the beneficiary, in the event of a claim, stipulated as the company, Noughts & Crosses Ltd. So if one of them dies in an accident the company is £10,000 better off, not with additional cash, but by the relief of the loan obligation. In addition to this the dead partner's shares are divided between the remaining partners by a separate agreement within the company articles; anyone dies, whatever the cause, his shares go to the others.'

'And one of the partners is dead!' interposed Thadeus.

'Yes, a motor accident, which I have investigated,' admitted Jackson,

'Why?' questioned Thadeus

'The Lloyd's underwriter involved asked me to look into the matter, a Mr Mannings employer of the late Sir Percy Dennington.'

'You think that there is a link with Sir Percy's death?' queried Thadeus.

'No, but I asked our friend Mr Sydney Pooley to have a look at the smashed vehicle. The accident happened when the motorcar went off the road at a corner, not a sharp bend, just a change in direction of about eight degrees.' Jackson paused in order that Thadeus may appreciate the mathematical accuracy of his evidence. 'The car went straight on, through a hedge and dived down into a ploughed field about eight feet below. The driver was killed instantly.'

'Do you know at what speed the vehicle was travelling?'

'The witnesses estimate a speed of over thirty miles per hour!'

'The witnesses?'

'Two of the club's other partners!' smiled Jackson.

'And what has Mr Pooley uncovered?'

'The front of the vehicle, a Lea-Francis, two-seater sports model, was badly smashed, as you can imagine. Sydney Pooley, who has visited the site of the accident up in Buckinghamshire, is of the opinion that the steering failed. The three partners had been drinking at a public house about half of a mile up the road, and it was a straight run to the fatal corner; this corner was the first time, since leaving the pub, that the steering wheel required any positive movement. The strange thing is that although the casing is bent, the levers of the Ackerman System are in perfect condition. Sydney's hypothesis is that either the drop arm or the coupling rod was disconnected and perhaps tied back in position with tape or string, to stop them falling down immediately the vehicle moved, and they separated from the unit as soon as the steering wheel was turned with some force. But, and this is important, they were reconnected after the accident!' explained a knowledgeable Jackson.

'And signs of tape or string removed at the same time, by the two conspirators?'

'Suspicions but no proof. This is where you enter the drama,' informed Jackson. 'Your friend Gussie Downing is a member of the club and I thought that, with not much effort, you too could join. I am told that they have a very good twelve-bar blues piano player!'

'My brother brought back some gramophone records of this jazz music from his recent trip to America. It is very interesting,' informed Thadeus.

Thus it was that Thadeus and Gussie turned up at the basement premises of the Noughts & Crosses Club that Wednesday evening. Thadeus paid his five pound membership fee and they wandered into a dark and smoky converted cellar, with a stage at one end and a bar at the other. Gussie advised that they had arrived during the interval, the stage was without personnel, but crammed with musical instruments. A gramophone was playing a tune that Thadeus immediately recognized as Dipper Mouth Blues by King Oliver's Creole Jazz Band, one of the recordings that his brother had given him on his return from the USA. Gussie was most impressed with this information and indicated that Thadeus would become a stalwart member of the Noughts & Crosses. They gathered a couple of weak and expensive gin and tonics from the bar, and sat at a table near the edge of the room where they were soon greeted by the welcoming voice of Dulcie Dellar. She was a dazzling young lady, dressed in the very latest fashion, a tightly fitting hat in a sparkling material and a straight dress of similar hue; she carried a lengthy cigarette holder; she was straight out of the movies! Thadeus knew that she was also a shareholder, with what was twenty per cent, and now, following the untimely demise of her husband, Alfred, a twenty-five per cent part-owner of the club. The only lady shareholder did not appear to be adhering to the customary dress code for the status of widows.

The band returned to the stage. There were five of them, all white men and, apart from the string-bass player, all of middle age and of reasonable musical competence. They started their repertoire with a number entitled Tiger Rag, rendered entirely in *presto tempo*. Thadeus did not recognize this piece, but was familiar with the next, again in quick time, possibly *motto allegro*, entitled Clarinet Marmalade. The woodwind exponent was very professional. Thadeus thought that he would have no problem tackling Mozart's Concerto next, if asked.

The club was filling up and an unruly group of young men had gathered at the side of the room near their table. As some of these toughs were sporting coloured armbands indicating their allegiance to the Fascist movement, it was not the appropriate time for a fully-paid-up, but not stupid, member of the British Communist Party to make his presence known; Gussie lead Thadeus down the front, adjacent to the band. There was another break for the musicians to lubricate their throats; pints of beer were delivered under the instructions of the delightful Dulcie

To the surprise of Thadeus the piano player recognized him. Thadeus was unable to return the compliment, but was reminded of a performance in which he had played the cello to this man's keyboard at a church concert over a year ago. Introductions were made with members of the band. The clarinet man had just been engaged for the proposed new BBC orchestra! Discovering that he had some knowledge of jazz, and was a competent pianist, led to Thadeus being encouraged to take the stool and give a rendering from his very limited repertoire. Fitting in between the gramophone and a bout of rowdy behaviour in the bar area, Thadeus gave a passable rendering of Wolverine Blues memorized from his recording by the strangely named master of the ivories, Jelly Roll Morton.

As his fingers held down the final chord, and his hands sprung upwards in his accustomed manner, the lid of the piano was slammed shut with a bang. Thadeus froze, paralyzed by this narrow escape from serious injury, to find himself carrying what felt like a wrestling match on his back. The thugs were leaping onto the stage, throwing chairs out into the audience, and bending the trombone over the drummer's head. With a scream, the double bass artiste, a heretofore quiet young man, rushed into the mêlée carrying his instrument as a battering ram! The spike went straight through the body of an amazed right-wing agitator, and skewered a second deep in the side of his decorated jacket, just below the belt. They went down with an almighty clatter in a cacophony of broken chairs, the remains of the brass section, and blood.

The semi-uniformed brigade fled, pushing their way towards the exit, with the patrons collapsing like earth before the plough. Silence broke out!

Mr Jack Leonard, another shareholder – the one with the cash – emerged from a back office and accompanied by Mrs Dellar, attempted to assure the spectators that all was now back to normal, which it quite clearly was not! There were several injuries in need of attention; what looked like a dead body lying in front of the stage; and blood gushing from a member of the master race, who was now blubbering like a child. Believe it or not, there were three qualified medical men among the gathering, who, very capably, separated the minor from the major casualties; pronounced the passing away of the young white hope and, much to the astonishment of all, discovered that the short, plump cornet player who was at the back of the stage down a gap between the platform and the wall, was similarly deceased: stabbed by a bayonet. His name, as Thadeus knew from the brief handshake meeting no more than five or six minutes previous, was Edward Hardcastle; another late shareholder in Noughts & Crosses Ltd. Now there were three!

When the West End division police arrived it was no surprise to find them accompanied by Inspector Johnny Jackson of Scotland Yard.

The club was sealed and statements taken. Thadeus and Gussie were interviewed personally by the CID inspector. They advised Jackson that they had seen nothing relevant and the rest of the interview consisted of the instruction that they should leave immediately and that they would be contacted tomorrow

First thing next morning Thadeus called Beth Bateman into his office to answer some questions about Personal Accident Insurance. This class of business was a major part of her previous employer's portfolio. Was murder considered as a claim under a PA policy? Yes, advised the young claims expert, in fact her ex-employer, The Railway Passengers Assurance Company, had featured in a landmark legal precedent case in America in 1870, involving a Mr Ripley. It was now generally recognized that provided that the act done against the sufferer was without his, or her, consent it was caused by accident, even if the offending parties' actions were criminal. Manslaughter would come within this category, and murder which would include malice aforethought! When a murderer is executed, that is not a PA claim, as that result must have been foreseen when the act was committed!

Beth quoted from cases in 1918 and 1919 and Thadeus was convinced that she knew what she was talking about. Thadeus made a mental note to ensure that her annual salary was adequate for a person of her experience and ability.

Jackson did not telephone, which was good news as Thadeus had nothing to say, although he had plenty to think about.

The Lloyd's fraternity and the Burke & Co office were getting more and more confused by J Pooley and J Payne both being named James or Jim or Jimmy. By common agreement Pooley was to be called 'James' and Payne was to be known as 'JK'. Pooley had nothing to complain about as his name was unaltered; Payne was happy with the use of the initial of his middle name, Kenneth, as the new moniker gave him, in his opinion, the charisma of a respected executive.

It was in this new mode that they lunched that day at Simpson's, their usual waitress, Cathy asking, 'Kate and Sydney, Gentleman?'

'No, I'll have the sirloin steak,' instructed James.

'Certainly, Mr James, and for you, Mr JK?'

'Same for me,' advised JK, 'and I think that you should just call us "James" and "JK"; or perhaps to be formal, I should be Mr Payne.'

'If you are going to be Mr Payne I should be Mr Pooley,' interposed James.

'You two sort out who you are going to be, while I get on with the main course,' said Cathy, heading for the kitchen.

After much soul searching and further discussion they decided that 'Mr James' for Pooley and just 'JK' for Payne carried the right amount of respect and dignity for use by the underling, who was at least ten years older than them. James expected this reference to an 'older woman' would bring a blush to the face of JK, but no, to James' surprise JK informed him that the whole of the Cambridge episode should be disclosed, brought out into the open, and not become an obstacle between them.

'So, what happened next?' prompted James.

'Well the lady turned up at the college quite regularly, sometimes expected, sometimes not. She usually brought a bottle of white wine with her, if she did not, I had to creep out and buy one! She was sexually quite an athlete. All positions were tried, backwards, forwards, upside down, you name it we tried it!' said JK, in a clear, but hushed, voice.

'Crickey,' was the expected response from James.

'Then one afternoon she turned up unannounced, when I was swotting with a fellow student. I needed to go and get some wine, and when I got back to my room the other fellow said that he would go and get another bottle.'

'Good heavens, I can see what's coming,' exclaimed James.

'Yes. After I had completed the romp to my satisfaction she suggested that I might like to take a walk around the gardens, and that my friend may care for a little drink!'

'Crickey, did you engage in group sex, a threesome?' enquired James, strangely knowledgeable.

'No we never actually got round to that, but it did become the custom for another student to turn up for a session.'

James could say nothing.

'What started the main problem was that some of these other chaps developed the habit of giving me a fiver, by way of reward, as it were.' JK paused and looked blankly at James.

'Good heavens, you were running a brothel at Pembroke College!'

'Yes, that is how the Dean saw the situation, especially after one or two post-graduates on research scholarships had sampled the goods. My study became known as "the white wine room".'

The sirloins steaks arrived accompanied by a mountain of vegetables; they were accepted without comment; implements raised, beer supped and the silent meal commenced. It was not long before both lads burst out laughing.

'Uncle Charlie thought that it was a much better qualification for underwriting at Lloyd's than the first in history that I had been aiming for.'

Thadeus worked through lunchtime, with a sandwich and a cup of coffee, preparing new presentations for both art insurances and bloodstock risks. This type of business was going very well, large values, and therefore large premiums and brokerage, and the Lloyd's market seemed to be eager to participate. He had this week obtained his first order for insuring horses in America, a stud in Kentucky with a band of valuable broodmares. Back in the office, after a successful afternoon in the Underwriting Room, Thadeus found Inspector Jackson waiting to be taken out for a cup of tea. After one letter and three telegrams had been despatched, and four brief telephone conversations concluded, they left for the day and made their way solemnly across Gracechurch Street, into Crown Walk and down the steps into the Crown Coffee Rooms. Without speaking to each other, they ordered tea with toasted buns.

'Nobody saw anything last night,' opened the gloomy Jackson.

'It was all a bit confusing. I could not say who did what, or when. I might be able to recognize some of the thugs, they captured my attention, but the general audience, the bar staff and the club employees, including shareholders, just vanished into a backdrop,' responded an equally gloomy Thadeus.

'We should be able to get something out of the injured Fascist – when he recovers from surgery.'

'I imagine it would not be too difficult to persuade a young brown-shirt to kill a member of a band playing music that originated within the black community of New Orleans.'

'No. The action of the bass player is being treated as self-defence. He is pretty cut up about it!'

'Not as cut up as his victims,' chuckled Thadeus, and they both laughed out loud for the first time that day.

'Tell me about the witnesses at the car accident,' instructed Thadeus.

'Jack Leonard and Oswald Matthews; they were each driving their own cars, not right behind Alfred Dellar, but about fifty yards apart. Dellar went off the road at the bend, the other two cars stopped besides the damaged hedge. They could see the smashed vehicle and the prone body of Dellar draped over the pale grey coloured bonnet, with blood flowing freely across it. Mrs Leonard, who was travelling with her husband and who had worked as a nurse at the end of the war with the Women's Reserve Ambulance, climbed down the bank to see what could be done. The two men were a bit squeamish. She shouted up to them that he was definitely dead and Matthews set off for the nearest telephone call box, or police station or doctor. Actually a bobby arrived on his bicycle at the scene of the accident while he was away and Mr Leonard gave him a statement at that time.'

'Why were they all up in Buckinghamshire?' questioned Thadeus.

'The Leonards live in the area and knew the pub well. It was a working lunch to discuss food and drink, menus, cocktails, etc. for the club.'

'When Mrs Leonard was with the Women's Reserve Ambulance, did she also study motor mechanics? She could have been alone with the car while Matthews was away and her husband was giving a statement to the bobby. And in a pub for lunch all women always disappear for hours, fussing over some feminine inexactitude of dress or make-up.'

'She did not seem to know anything about motors. In her statement she refers to the fact that the, quote, "big glass thing at the front", unquote, was broken.'

'How old is she?'

'Thirty-four, two years older than her husband.'

'Thirty-four, served in the war, and does not know the name of a windscreen – was she ever on the stage? Seems like a well structured performance as a "poor little me" girl – and a bit over acted!' observed Thadeus.

Jackson was silent. 'She's our man! Get on with it Johnny. I must return to the office to finalize a few matters.'

That evening James Pooley told Eddie Whitney, his intended, that he loved her very much, and that with their newfound wealth they would start looking for a detached house with a garage in Nunhead. Also they would buy a cottage in Essex or Suffolk, near Mr Pooley's new works where they could stay, and more importantly where Mrs Pooley, James' mother, could also stay and get to know the area as it seemed certain that there would be difficulty persuading her to ever leave South London. It was not his intention to buy a new motor vehicle yet; he intended to wait for the promised new MG sports car. He thought the bodywork should be red with beige leather interior, Eddie agreed.

Also that evening Mr Oswald Matthews died, within three days of his forty-fifth birthday. Investigations showed that Oswald had been of a homosexual persuasion and that it was not unusual for young men to visit his flat in Curzan Street, Mayfair, most nights. His death was the result of a fall, down a stone staircase, outside of his flat, but within the building. A neighbour, who took a considerable time opening his front door – a tall, bald man wearing a bright green dress and with shaving cream all over his face, living in the flat below Mr Matthews – gave a statement to the local police, informing them that he had heard a clattering noise outside his front door at about 8.30 pm. On opening the door, which involved the use of several keys of different design, he had found Mr Matthews lying spread-eagled on his 'welcome' mat. He was obviously dead; his head was at a most peculiar angle to the rest of his body, it was facing the wrong way! The neighbour thought that Oswald was 'a lovely young man', always very quiet and well behaved, 'a proper gentleman'. He had not witnessed any visitor to Mr Matthews' flat that evening but, from the sounds that he had heard from above, he was of the opinion that Mr Matthews was entertaining that night. He neither explained these noises, nor was he asked too. The young constable left with very brief notes and informed the man that he would be asked to attend the local police station for a full and more detailed statement later. The neighbour said that he eagerly anticipated the pleasure; he just loved uniforms.

This exciting tale was related, over the telephone to Thadeus by Jackson within an hour of the occurrence. The local police had been more than happy to hand the matter over to Scotland Yard. Jackson was ignoring the alleged crime, or crimes, of sexual deviance; the local chaps could follow up this aspect of the matter if they wished to; he was concentrating on a door-to-door enquiry in search of other witnesses to the accident, or murder.

Thadeus had just lighted his second pipe of the evening when Jackson phoned again. A witness had given a description of a young man, very slim, about five foot two inches, at the most, short cropped dark hair, wearing a long cream-coloured riding or motoring coat. He had entered the flats at approximately 7.45 pm and left, in a hurry at approximately 8.30 pm.

It was agreed that none of this was of any help whatsoever, except that the number of suspects and the number of shareholders of Noughts & Crosses Ltd, had been reduced – by one.

Thadeus summed up. 'We have three shareholders dead, Dellar, Hardcastle and Matthews and two alive, Leonard and the female

Dellar, with fifty per cent ownership each. If my theory that Mrs Leonard is the culprit is correct, the next victim should be Mrs Dellar, Dulcie, followed by the remaining hundred per cent owner, Mr Jack Leonard. I am assuming that he will also pass away and that his estate will transfer, in full, to his wife.'

'What can we do except wait and watch?' enquired Jackson.

'We must try and be there at the right time,' elucidated Thadeus. 'A trip to the Noughts & Crosses Club tomorrow evening, if it's open. Are you unengaged?'

'I'll put the Leonards and Mrs Dellar under observation and meet you outside the club at 8.30 pm tomorrow,' finalized Jackson.

The next day was a busy one for Burke & Co. Miss Mills had needed to exert her authority on James Pooley in order that the paperwork for the growing motor account be brought up to date and a new system be devised to ensure that they did not get into such a muddle again. Beth and Ethel were admonished for giggling over last night's radio programme, which Miss Mills suspected of some smutty content. Even Mr Emery had indulged in a telephone argument with an obstructive staff member of the Lloyd's Signing Bureau, ending in a compromising re-presentation of some slips to an underwriter.

Thadeus was pleased be out in the market for most of the day, working hard and entertaining three Cambridge University friends, colleagues of Gussie, with their first visit to the Lloyd's Underwriting Room. The three, all now lawyers, asked some searching questions, unable to comprehend that the whole organization rested on trust, agreements made by word of mouth, and quite often it was months before written records were made of valid contracts. They were taken up to Sweetings for a crowded fish and beer lunch, then they left in a cab for the law courts.

Going straight back to the Underwriting Room from lunch, Thadeus did not reappear in the office until late afternoon, leaving him just enough time to send out conformations of the insurance orders completed that day, before heading home to prepare himself for the evening's venture. Before departing the office it was always his practice to ensure that he had a conversation with all the members of the staff, however brief. All was well. Only James delayed him slightly explaining the copy of *William the Fourth* lying on his desk, not a book concerning the late monarch, but the fourth of a series of children's tales involving the errant schoolboy William Brown written by Richmal Crompton, of whom Eddie was an avid follower. Thadeus muttered something regarding the disapproval of Saint Paul and made his exit. It had not seemed appropriate to mention that the very latest volume, entitled *Still William*, had been observed by him in the front window of a bookshop along Cheapside only two hours earlier!

Jackson was signed in by Thadeus. The two men deposited their coats and hats with the cloakroom attendant, and entered the 'business as usual' club. A new cornet player, younger and more competent than Hardcastle, was blasting away in a solo effort from a work that Thadeus did not recognize.

They sampled the beer from the bar, still exorbitantly priced, but with a full body and more satisfying to the pallet than the previously tested spirits, where the glass appeared to have been no more than waved in the proximity of the bottle. They took a table, again at the side of the room, near the office.

A jazz aficionado seated at the next table kept them informed as the band worked their way through Davenport Blues, That's A Plenty and Canal Street Blues, then a piano solo of King Porter Stomp. Jackson's feet were stomping away with the steady beat.

Thadeus sucked quietly at his pipe. Leaning across the table to tap the dottle into the ashtray, he announced that he would have a look in the office! Jackson nodded, but continued his foot tapping exercises. Pushing open the door after receiving no response to his knock, Thadeus peered and then stepped into the club office. It was well equipped with plush leather armchairs, a large coffee table strewn with magazines and an impressive executive style leather topped desk. The office was unmanned. Thadeus perused the framed prints on the walls; traditional views of London. In the far right-hand corner of the room was another door; Thadeus pushed it open and tentatively put his head around the edge. Facing him, in this very small area, was the face of Dulcie Dellar who was lying over a Pembroke table with the sides hanging down. What he could see of her body was naked and he was pleased to note that her undergarments, scattered on the floor, conformed to the traditional colour for mourning. Behind her, with his eyes closed, stood Jack Leonard engaged in an attempted union of both halves of the club ownership.

'Sorry,' stammered Thadeus. 'I'll call back later.'

'Yes... yes,' cried an ecstatic Leonard.

This affirmative retort did not seem to be the result of Thadeus' statement of apology, as the same word continued in utterance for some time after the door had been closed. Thadeus quickly and quietly made his way back to his seat in the auditorium. In a break between musical renderings Thadeus enlightened Jackson regarding the newly discovered relationship, and they pondered the weight of this contemporary evidence in the continuing murder puzzle.

Twenty minutes passed, then, during the interval an immaculately dressed Mrs Dulcie Dellar, approached the table where the two apprehensive city gentlemen were sitting with their second glass of beer. Before she could speak, however, she doubled over with what appeared to be pain in her stomach. She gasped a couple of times, reached out for support from an adjacent chair-back, then vomited violently into a convenient space between the tables. More uproar in the Noughts & Crosses Club – did not Oscar Wilde say something about one being an accident but two being carelessness?

There were no doctors present this evening and it fell to a quick thinking, and quick moving, Jackson to seek medical assistance from the telephone instrument in the club office, pushing aside a bewildered Jack Leonard who was trying to take the top off of a bottle of stout. An ambulance arrived and the convulsing young lady was unceremoniously hoisted onto a stretcher and carried through a staring crowd of drinkers.

Thadeus took the opportunity of speaking to the doctor that Jackson had specifically requested be in attendance. 'I think it could be arsenic poisoning, try versenate or succimer on her,' counselled Thadeus, using names of concoctions of which he knew nothing, but had been mentioned as possible cures by Freddie. The medical man tried to determine if this advice was coming from an expert source, or the mouth of a beer-swilling drunk. Jackson's police warrant card sharpened up his opinion and the doctor hastened away with a very serious expression on his face.

'We have got work to do,' instructed Jackson, adding, 'I suppose that you got all that impressive information on arsenic antidotes from your sister?'

'Just part of my Dennington case notes!' responded Thadeus ostentatiously.

Jack Leonard again tried, for the second time that week, to persuade the patrons that everything was now back to normal after the unfortunate incident. This time he was successful, the band started playing and the bar started serving. He was then accompanied back to his office by Inspector Jackson of Scotland Yard and the Honourable Thadeus Burke. He acknowledged that he and Mrs Dulcie Dellar were having an affair; they were in love and intended getting married. The affair had been active for over six months. They met at the club and occasionally at a hotel, the Swan at Lavenham in Suffolk. This was the countryside where Dulcie had spent her childhood and they intended to buy a house in the area when he was able to obtain a divorce. His wife was suspicious of the relationship but, as far as he was aware, had no definite knowledge of the affair. Dulcie's husband had certainly known nothing; they had been very careful.

Thadeus cast his eyes towards the ceiling when this information was delivered. Jack Leonard's wife, Mona, had been present at the meeting in Buckinghamshire because she thought that Mrs Dellar would be there also with her husband, Alfred. Leonard had anticipated a scene at the restaurant and warned Dulcie to stay away. 'Might have saved her life,' thought Thadeus.

That evening they had indulged in spontaneous sexual activity. Yes it was a stupid thing to do while the club was open, but... After getting dressed Dulcie had imbibed a glass of champagne; she enjoyed a glass of this French delicacy; she often kept an open bottle in the office, using the trick of placing a tea-spoon in the neck of the bottle to keep it fresh. He never touched the stuff, preferring beer, or better still, a Guinness.

When the club closed for the evening Jackson and Thadeus drove in a police vehicle to the home of Jack Leonard out in Buckinghamshire. The householder arrived, by design, a few minutes ahead of the police car.

The police inspector and Thadeus were introduced to Mona, who, as expected had waited up for her husband's return. She had a pleasant youthful face, short, not more than five foot two inches, and a slim boyish body. The lady of the house was informed of the tragic episode at the Noughts & Crosses club that evening. She was devastated. It was difficult to distinguish if her anxiety was because Mrs Dellar was dangerously ill, or because she was not dead! She had not been near the club this evening, but had been there last night, to help sort things out following the awful happenings the previous evening. She had confined her activities to the office area. There was a bottle of champagne there, she had a glassful herself. She could be of no help whatsoever regarding the alleged poisoning of Mrs Dellar.

As Jackson and Thadeus made their leave from the Leonard's home, Thadeus observed a wooden crate standing besides the front door porch containing six bottles of Guinness. Mona Leonard explained that they were for her husband to take down to London the next day. Thadeus asked if he might be permitted to take one of the bottles in order to quench his thirst on the long road back to town. Jack Leonard thought that this was an excellent idea, took three bottles from the crate and handed out two, and said that he would drink the other before retiring for the night. Mrs Mona Leonard fainted!

At her trial Mona pleaded 'not guilty', despite the evidence that she had actually taught motor mechanics to other volunteers in the Women's Reserve Ambulance, and the rather nasty witness to her agreement with an even nastier fellow Fascist. The arsenic found in the bottles of Guinness was her undoing. Her confession, before execution, including the revelation that she had enticed Oswald Matthews to his appointment with death by promising 'her bum as his birthday present' satisfactorily finalized the matter. The realization that when her husband drank his Guinness that night the only probable outcome of her murderous activities would be a large inheritance for the last surviving shareholder, Dulcie Dellar, or if she died Dulcie Dellar's mother, must have been as big a jolt as the noose around her neck when the trapdoor opened beneath her feet.

CHAPTER 6

WHO WANTS TO BUY A DEAD FOAL?

The next week found Thadeus in Knightsbridge, West London, at the premises of Messrs Tattersalls, the bloodstock auctioneers. He was there to meet some of his bloodstock account clients and maybe pick up a new client or two. His visit to the dispersal of the bloodstock of the newspaper magnate Sir Edward Hulton, conducted by Mr Somerville Tattersall as part of the Newmarket Second July sale earlier in the year, had been a great success and he had captured the insurances of some fine horses, particularly broodmares, and some excellent clients without the assistance of his father's introductions, or the use of his title. This sale at Knightsbridge would not be so grand, but it was necessary for Thadeus to be seen there and satisfy any demands on his professional skills. He did not wish to appear as a dilettante of the high society events only.

To his surprise the first two people he encountered were Jack Leonard and Dulcie Dellar. It was an embarrassing meeting for all three of them; Mrs Dellar particularly found the early conversation difficult, but as Thadeus said practically nothing and Leonard was observing the horses, she eventually confessed that she had anticipated physically throwing him out of the club after he had interrupted the back-room misbehaviour. It was this furious state of mind that had led to her taking only a quick gulp from the champagne glass, an economy which saved her life. Things had worked out extremely well; she and Jack were to get married as soon as the trial of Mona was completed and a respectable period had elapsed and they now owned the Nought & Crosses Club, half each. They did not think that the Fascist threat would disappear in the near future so they might need to change the type of music performed. Thadeus thought that this would be a great pity, not only because the jazz music was extremely enjoyable, but also it was not a good policy to give in to 'thuggee', as he thought the practitioners of thuggery should be called, after the

Hindi. Jack, who had returned to the group, agreed that they should 'fight the bastards'.

Thadeus took the opportunity to ask Jack why he had a crate of Guinness at his home when there was plenty of the precious liquid at his club. He was enlightened by the information that this crate, and several more of the same, came over from Dublin in the horsebox of a friend. It tasted just the same as the London brew but was psychologically better!

Thadeus' second surprise was to meet Gussie Downing and his mother Lady Frances Downing, she who never visited London. Horses apparently were an exception to this rule and anyway, according to her, Knightsbridge was not really in London. They were accompanied by a lady who was introduced as Lady Daphne Dennington, widow of the deceased Sir Percy Dennington, the late Lloyd's underwriter.

The two ladies were school chums, known and indecently disclosed by Lady Frances as 'Fanny' and 'Daffy'. Lady Frances laughed like a horse, and Lady Daphne giggled like a schoolgirl with shamefaced embarrassment.

Gussie was in attendance to ensure that his mother behaved herself. He even more indiscreetly informed Thadeus that one of the reasons that his mother never came to London was that on some past occasion she had fallen into bad company. Thadeus frowned, but asked no questions. The other reason for Gussie's presence was to make sure that 'she did not buy any more bloody horses'.

The distinguished figure of Mr 'Sommy' Tattersall mounted the rostrum in the corner of the grey-bricked enclosure and the day's business was begun.

The catalogue consisted of broodmares, maidens or barren and in foal, with a second session for weaned foals.

There was no surprise in the meeting of Robert Byrne, a bloodstock breeder and owner of a stud farm in County Kildare, Ireland and a long-time client of Thadeus before, and now with Burke & Co. What was a surprise to Thadeus was the subject of conversation. Robert immediately pointed out a large man, aged about fifty, with a mop of grey hair.

'His name is William Hitchen. He's a veterinary surgeon; known, behind his back, as 'Wild Bill' Hitchen.'

Thadeus anticipated that this chap had a reputation for raucous behaviour, probably involving long drinking sessions in illegal public houses often set up in a disused cow-shed behind a small Irish farm. But no, Robert explained that the moniker derived from his habit of being fast with a gun; particularly in euthanizing horses before the insurance company or Lloyd's underwriter were given the opportunity to inspect the alleged injury.

Foals were his speciality. On several occasions, according to Robert, a foal had been submitted to a bloodstock sale and the price run up to a figure far exceeding the true value. Outrageous amounts were not involved, too suspicious to both the auctioneer and insurers. They usually bid between nine hundred and eleven hundred guineas, not enough to attract attention, but a good result for a foal worth no more than one or two hundred. The foal then, within a few weeks, has an accident, usually late on a Friday night or Sunday morning and along comes Wild Bill to diagnose immediate destruction for humane reasons, and the carcase has gone off to the local hunt before the ink on the claims papers is dry. The vendor – who is the bidder as well in a different guise – and the vet split the profit!

'Why are you telling me all this?' asked Thadeus.

'Because these bastards bought a foal from me. It was a very poor specimen, born in late May and never going to make a racehorse, so I put it in, with no reserve, at a weekly sale in Ballsbridge and he made twenty-five guineas. Blow me if the same colt does not turn up here, in Knightsbridge, and make eight hundred. Then I find out a month later that the foal is dead and the subject of an insurance claim. Nothing off my farm deserves that!'

'Being in the insurance industry you think that I can balance the books?'

'Yes, we can track all these incidents down.'

'Might take a long time?'

'You would be surprised. There is the saying in Ireland: "always remember that your friend has a friend". People will talk.'

Robert Byrne went away to inspect a broodmare, carrying a foal by Blandford, for whom he intended to bid.

Thadeus thought about all the blarney with which he would be inundated if this matter was to be pursued. It would be much more fun to set up Wild Bill for a fall! But how?

While Thadeus was pondering this problem he was approached by Lady Daphne Dennington. She had followed his movements from the position that the two ladies had occupied on the arcaded balcony to ensure a decent view of the proceedings.

'Mr Burke, may I seek some assistance from you?' she enquired with a delightful smile.

Thadeus implored her to use his Christian name and confirmed that he would be pleased to help her in any way he could, if it was within his powers.

'Thadeus,' she recommenced, 'since my husband died I have not entered his office. He had a separate room built into one of the stables for all his office work, especially concerning horses, and including some personal financial matters. The police were in and out of the office for several days and they very kindly sorted out some of the important personal papers for me. They gave me the bank statements and up-to-date copies of the utilities invoices and papers relating to the current running of the house but his business papers remain in the office room. My solicitor has been in there and recommends that somebody with more experience in the horse business investigates. He knows, and has recommended, some people in the Newmarket area who could help, but I do not really like the idea of our neighbours rummaging in our affairs.'

She paused. Thadeus nodded but said nothing so she continued.

'One thing that definitely needs attention is the insurance arrangements; for the horses, the mares and foals and in respect of the buildings, which is divided between business premises and private accommodation. I am sure that you could resolve this problem easily and, perhaps, at the same time give me an opinion regarding any other matters that might need action.'

'I would be pleased to assist. I am confident that any insurance worries can be dealt with quickly,' he assured the lady. 'I should be able to be in Newmarket at the weekend, or within a week at the latest.

I will telephone you tomorrow, after I have had the opportunity to study my diary engagements.'

She thanked him profoundly, and Thadeus pocketed one of her visiting cards, checking that it included the telephone number. He was surprised to find two separate numbers, business and private.

Robert Byrne came bounding over and Lady Daphne took her leave with Lady Frances discussing some accountancy or book-keeping matter.

'I have just bought Lot 25,' said Robert. 'Please arrange the usual insurance for her, purchase price four thousand guineas. The details are in the catalogue.' Then he shot off again, leaving Thadeus with his thoughts.

Thadeus had found from carefully observed experiments that in crowded surroundings it was always a good plan to stand still. Find your spot and stay there. This way anybody who was looking for you would eventually find you, and after a while they would get to know your established position. Also, as most people had developed the habit of moving around, always seeking a new vantage point, it was probable, if not mathematically certain, that anybody that you were yourself looking for would eventually pass by your chosen location. His chosen location was besides 'The Fox'; a statue of the furry beast that was the symbol of the auction company.

Out of this peace arose his plan to undo William Hitchen. It would require several players, carefully co-ordinated, and a lot of luck – also a bit of bad luck, but this will be explained later!

As the laws of probability had predicted, Mr Hitchen passed by the stationary Thadeus within an hour. Thadeus accosted the veterinary surgeon.

'Mr Hitchen, may I introduce myself? I am Thadeus Burke a specialist in the insurance of thoroughbred horses.' Thadeus bowed his head and handed the man one of his business cards. 'If I can be of any help to you, or your clients, I am here and at your service.'

'A Lloyd's broker!' acknowledged Hitchen, studying the card.

'The finest insurers in the world,' pattered Thadeus smoothly.

'I suppose you know that I am a vet. If I arrange insurances for one of my clients, do I get a commission?'

'An arrangement with which I am extremely familiar,' assured Thadeus.

'I might have a foal to insure this afternoon,' stated Hitchen.

'I will be here,' smiled Thadeus.

The second stage of the plan was in place!

Before accosting Hitchen, Thadeus had engaged in another conversation with a veterinary surgeon that had needed no introductions. Mr Peter Freeman, with a practice in Newmarket, was an old friend and had assisted Thadeus many times with difficult veterinary questions related to insurance, both for acceptance of cover and with regards to claims. The first stage of Thadeus' plan was to obtain the services of a reliable and trusted vet for the examination of any foal that, perchance, Thadeus might be asked to insure that day. The foal would undoubtedly be fit and healthy, otherwise it would not be in the sale, but Thadeus' brief specified a particularly attentive examination, and recorded notation, of the animal's markings. He wanted every white patch and whirl, blemish and scar, set down with exactitude.

Mr Freeman was suspicious of Thadeus' intentions, but did not complain and agreed to be on hand when called.

Mr Freeman's services would be called upon at a later date, and perhaps not in such an obliging manner, however, there seemed no reason to disclose unnecessary complications at this early stage.

Lunch with Gussie and a decent bottle of claret were the next items on the programme. They escaped from the ladies, who were seeking tea and sandwiches, and settled themselves in an often frequented establishment in Beauchamp Place, where they discussed politics and the merits of a good rabbit stew. Seated in the corner of the restaurant was Mr William Hitchen together with a tweedy country gentleman, short and stocky, with a stubby black moustache. Both parties ignored each other.

The *l'addition* was settled and they made their way back to Tattersalls in good time for the opening of the second session, involving weaned foals.

The youngsters were a poor lot, mostly by unfashionable stallions, and not very well prepared. Robert Byrne had bought the only two attractive lots in the day's catalogue in the morning session; nice mares, in foal to Blandford and Lemberg.

Sommy Tattersall treated all beasts equal and gave each of the afternoon's entries into the ring an introduction fit for a potential Derby winner, but there were no records set.

The auctioneer worked hard for a handful of four-figure bids, one of which was knocked down to the tweedy country gentleman, with a stubby black moustache, and the lunch companion of Mr William Hitchen. This same veterinary surgeon who, within ten minutes of the purchase, arranged insurance on the foal in the sum of one thousand two hundred guineas, with Lloyd's Underwriters through the obliging offices of Burke & Co.

Hitchen was far from pleased when Thadeus announced that it was his practice to have all purchases at sales examined for insurance purposes by a veterinary surgeon appointed on behalf of the insuring underwriters. Hitchen protested that as he was himself a vet, this unnecessary intrusion, was an outrageous and an unethical device. Thadeus assured him that, with a certificate of soundness completed by the underwriter's own veterinary surgeon, the insurance policy enacted was of a much more secure nature; there could be no repercussions, in the event of a claim under the policy, arising from allegations regarding the health of the insured animal.

Hitchen was aware of the sort of problems that often arose over disputed claims, and, to the relief of Thadeus, accepted the situation, only insisting that the results of the new examination should be made known to him as early as possible, in case he needed to make alternative arrangements. Within thirty minutes Mr Freeman was able to dissolve this cloud of doubt with the simple words, 'The foal is fine.'

Mr Hitchen was content and advised Thadeus, and Mr Freeman, that the young colt would be leaving for Gloucestershire by trailer that evening.

Before leaving the sales complex Thadeus was handed a three-page report consisting mostly of diagrams of the outlines of a horse marked, in red ink, to show every nook and cranny of the newly insured foal's physiognomy.

The third stage of the plan was in place!

Back in the City of London next day it was Thadeus' immediate duty to inform Charlie Norman of the insurance arrangements for a bay colt, born on 18th March 1925, by *Henry Bee* out of *My Sunshine*, on behalf of a Mr Gerald Letting with an address in Gloucestershire. Charlie, the leading underwriter on the Burke & Co bloodstock binding authority, was not happy. Even after Thadeus had assured the underwriter that in the event of any financial loss as a result of the broker's actions the deficit would be reimbursed by the broker, from Thadeus' own pocket, Charlie continued to bleat on about the legal implications and the 'Good name of Lloyd's', 'the reputation of the City of London' etcetera. Having satisfactorily got all of this off of his chest, out in the open, and amplified his own innocence in the forthcoming drama, particularly with regard to any unforeseen repercussions, Mr Norman wished Thadeus good luck with the enterprise and duly initialled the paperwork presented by Thadeus in all the right spots as Thadeus jabbed his finger on the appropriate places.

Charlie Norman then proceeded to tell Thadeus about a most unusual insurance that he had underwritten the previous day. It appears that an American lady engaged in the art of clairvoyance had, at one of her sessions, foreseen that the German ex-Kaiser Wilhelm would be returning to the throne in November of this year. Investors in the German Republic were in a panic and vast sums were being spent on insurance against this eventuality. They were paying a premium rate of fifteen guineas per cent!

'It is Christmas come early,' enthused young Mr Norman. Actually the underwriter was aged thirty, five years older than Thadeus, but mentally a little less mature. On this occasion Thadeus thought that Charlie was quite correct in his analysis of the situation. Should Thadeus make a telephone call to America and solicit some of this business from agents of his acquaintance? No, he was too busy on other matters, and yet it may be important to show that he was concurrent with the market movements. No, it was not for Burke & Co.

James Pooley's desk was still piled high with brochures of motor cars, obtained at the Motor Show at Olympia last month. Thadeus doubted if all these papers were of great assistance to the Burke & Co motor account, but the study of the documents seemed to occupy much of James' time. It was extraordinary how many separate motor car manufacturers there were in England! James was busy and could not be involved in the Gloucestershire foal enterprise.

Hilton could be involved and would be tackled later that evening.

Thadeus spoke on the telephone to the Thoroughbred Breeders Association at their offices in Newmarket, asking them many questions and making copious notes of telephone numbers and addresses. Another telephone call, to Peter Freeman, gave him the details of a veterinary practice in Gloucestershire. Then he spoke to Inspector Johnny Jackson, who advised him that his plan would 'simply not work'. Also Jackson could, and would not, help in any way. Jackson did, however, give Thadeus the name and private telephone number of a police inspector in the Gloucestershire Constabulary with whom the London CID man had, in the past, co-operated on a nationwide search. According to Jackson this man was mad enough to be attracted to the project. More telephone calls were made. Thadeus was getting decidedly nervous about the enterprise!

As promised, Thadeus also telephoned Lady Daphne Dennington, on the private number, and made arrangements for a visit to Newmarket on Saturday. He would avail himself of the kind offer of accommodation at the Dennington's stud that night, and work in the office of her late husband the next day, returning to London that evening. Unless he was in Gloucestershire!

The next day a dubious Hilton started to put together an unusual combination of picnic baskets, to be loaded with sandwiches and drinks at the allotted time, and a small arsenal of weapons, borrowed from friends of his undisclosed distant past.

That very evening an Inspector Hobson telephoned from his home in Cheltenham with the message that the game was afoot! Hilton drove the Bentley out to a hotel in the village of Broadway; Thadeus was too anxious to trust himself to drive.

Inside the house of a smallholding two miles from Cheltenham Racecourse, Mr Gerald Letting and Mr William Hitchen were partaking of a glass of whisky each, waiting for the peace of night to envelope the farm. Outside a youth named Jack was lugging machinery about the yard. Jack was not very bright, but he was very ugly; opportunities for his advancement had been few. Outside the farm, in a gateway on a narrow country road, a police Black Maria was parked, inside of which sat Thadeus, Hilton, Hobby, as Inspector Hobson was known, and a local veterinary surgeon. On the floor of the vehicle lay a large package, wrapped in cloth.

William Hitchen downed the last gulp of Scotch and instructed Jack to get on with the matter in hand. Jack stalled, complaining that he had not got the tractor in position yet. Letting cuffed the lad's ear and sent him out into the yard to finalize the arrangements. It was nearly ten minutes before the youth returned. He was then instructed by Hitchen to get the foal out of the barn, take it over to the tractor and break its leg. Jack left the room, but was back within a minute stuttering about a problem, something to do with the foal being asleep on the ground.

'Just break its leg with an iron bar and drag it over to the tractor,' said an impatient veterinary surgeon.

'But…' started Jack

'No buts, just get on with it,' interrupted Letting.

Jack left the room once more, returning five minutes later with the announcement that the job was done. He was then told to go to bed.

The two men refreshed their glasses and Hitchen wrote out a certificate confirming that he had attended the premises of Mr Gerald Letting that night at approximately eleven o'clock and found the newly purchased colt foal in considerable pain with a fractured cannon bone. He had performed euthanasia immediately to relieve incurable suffering.

Standing up Hitchen said, 'I had better go out there and make sure that idiot broke the right bone otherwise I will need to write all this out again. And I must put a bullet in its head. I do not want to forget that!'

The door flew open and the vet returned. 'The bloody thing is dead already!'

'What, before you shot it?' asked Letting.

'Yes. I lifted the head, fired a bullet into it, and then realized that it was stone cold!'

'Does this change anything?' asked a worried Letting.

110

'No. Just make sure that the hunt takes the carcase away first thing in the morning,' assured Hitchen.

Outside in the Black Maria the team of four were starting on Hilton's picnic. The wrapped package had disappeared and been replaced by a lively young colt foal by *Henry Bee* out of *My Sunshine*. At the same time a young police constable, in uniform, but accompanied by his girlfriend, knocked at the door of the Letting farmhouse. The young man was enquiring if all was well, as he thought that they had heard a gunshot.

'We had to put a foal down,' advised a sad farmer.

'Nature can be very hard,' commented the local bobby.

Then his girlfriend interrupted. 'Do you want us to take him down to the kennels? I live there, and we are on our way home now. We are in the farm truck.'

Letting thought it was extremely helpful and directed the couple round to the back yard. Wrapped in canvas the dead foal was in the back of the truck and away before Hitchen came out of the toilet.

'This is all too bloody convenient for me,' exclaimed a suspicious Hitchen. 'First the animal is already dead before I shoot it; then the bloody hunt are out collecting carcases in the middle of the night!'

'The copper heard the shot and I know the girl, she lives down at the kennels.'

'Well it is you who will need to make the insurance claim. Wait a couple of days. I will be up in Scotland.'

The occupants of the farm went to bed. Jack was not yet asleep, kept awake by the crisp sound of the new £5 note under his pillow.

The police van set off for the local veterinary surgery and unloaded the healthy colt foal, stolen that night from Mr Letting. The dead foal that had been first deposited on the farm of Mr Letting and then collected and driven away, also arrived at the same surgery, where it was placed in the mortuary awaiting despatch to Bristol University for a post mortem.

That weekend, on Saturday morning, Thadeus again drove to Newmarket. This time his destination was a sixty-five acre stud farm near Dullingham, the home of Lady Daphne Dennington. The journey was uneventful and as he had set out late he did not turn into the gate of the stud until nearly three o'clock. This was his plan; he had advised Lady Daphne that he would arrive during the afternoon, and he did not wish to get involved in lunch. The main dwelling house was a long thin building with a utility room at one end, then a well equipped kitchen; next to this was an ample dinning room, then a very large drawing room. The next and final room on the ground floor was a library. Upstairs were two bathrooms, equipped with walk-in showers, and three bedrooms. The furniture was mostly Victorian with a smattering of antiques. The facilities of the utility room, the kitchen and the bathrooms were all modern, in the very latest designs. The Denningtons had clearly spent a considerable sum restoring what was probably an eighteenth-century construction. A morbid cloud hung over the mistress of the house as she conducted Thadeus on a tour of what had been a very proud home for the titled couple.

Outside Thadeus recognized his map, but allowed his guide to direct his attention to the various outbuildings and their usage. He briefly inspected the office but did not dwell, preferring to wait until the next morning for a thorough investigation of the contents. They strolled between two paddocks separated by a pathway wide enough for a vehicle and fenced with well preserved wooden rails. Two mares grazed comfortably on the far side, but wandered casually across to greet the visitors. The bay was introduced as *Happy Days*, a twelve-year-old, whose pedigree Lady Daphne could not remember; and the grey, a younger model, was *Fire Lightning*, she was by *Lemberg* and had won four races. The paddock on the right was empty and it was necessary to return and cross between the loose boxes to the third paddock containing the two weaned foals, still kept discreetly out of the sight of their mothers. Lady Daphne did not know the sires of these two colts, all the paperwork was in her late husband's office. She apologised for her 'daffyness' assuring Thadeus that she was very interested in the horses, and, of course, at some time she and her husband had discussed the breeding of the mares and made decisions together about the use of stallions, but she had not written it all down, or learned it all by heart, as she had not expected him to suddenly depart this world.

Decisions needed to be made regarding the future of the foals. Should they be sold? It was already too late for them to be entered into any decent bloodstock weanling sale. Could they be prepared for next year's yearling sales, and by whom? Here at the farm, or sent away to someone with more experience? Lady Daphne's questions were intelligent ones; Thadeus would be busy the next day.

The farm's staff lived in three cottages situated on the far side of the property. An estate manager, with his wife who supervised the management of the house, and their son, in his late teens, who assisted around the farm and, with Lady Daphne's help, was seeking a place at an agricultural college. Next door were the cook and her odd-job man husband; the third dwelling being occupied by the cook's daughter and her newly-wed husband who worked as a laboratory assistant in Cambridge. Daily cleaners came in from the village. The Denningtons had been comfortable, indeed Thadeus found out the next day from papers in the office, that Lady Daphne Dennington was a very wealthy lady and certainly not in reduced circumstances. On this occasion Thadeus encountered only the cook and her daughter, who prepared and served a simple dinner of soup, followed by locally cured ham with a white sauce, and a choice of ice-cream, all the way from Norfolk, and/or cheese from an excellent little shop in Stetchworth.

Lady Daphne excused herself for an early night and Thadeus retired for a full pipe of tobacco and a browse around the library before bed.

The next day the household was alive early. At Thadeus' request the cook's daughter prepared a breakfast of eggs and tomatoes and he collected the keys for the office and went to work. He soon had several heaps of papers laid out on the floor in different categories: personal, to be retained by a solicitor, and personal, to be handed over to an accountant. Business papers to be disposed of to the same professionals. Nothing appeared to be in urgent need of action, but the ledgers would need updating. He unearthed the passports of the two mares, and the covering certificates for the foals. They were indeed well bred, but had not yet been registered with Weatherbys.

The insurance policies on the mares, affected, not surprisingly with the Manning's Syndicate at an extremely attractive premium rate due for renewal in February next year. There was no insurance document related to the foals.

The insurance policy documents for the house and outbuildings, and for the cottages, were all due to expire on the 31st December, as was the motor policy for Lady Daphne's Rolls Royce, although the name of the assured required amendment. Thadeus made a note to have a look at this vehicle which must be in a garage or barn somewhere. All these insurance documents were put in a pile that Thadeus intended to remove to his own office in London. A cardboard folder contained several loose sheets of paper on which were handwritten details of horses; colour, name, age, sire and dam, some with more expanded pedigree references. Most of these foolscap sheets were white paper, but a few were from those yellow legal foolscap pads that are popular in the city, not only with lawyers. Thadeus was sure that the Mannings' box at Lloyd's used them; they might be connected to Sir Percy's work, so they could also go down to London.

It was noon before Thadeus emerged ready for a report to Lady Daphne. There were a handful of documents that her solicitor should keep in his strong-room. If she wanted her accountant to continue the book-keeping records established by her late husband a meeting would need to be arranged. She decided that she would seek his assistance but continue the work herself. She was happy for Thadeus to remove all the insurance papers and make any arrangements that he thought necessary. He informed her that, after closer study of these documents in London, he may require instructions from her, particularly regarding changes in value of some property. Did she want the pedigree research books placed in the library? No, they were to stay in the office and, one of these days, she would go in there! The various pens, pencils and rulers could also stay, but Sir Percy's silver pen and pencil set would now live in the house, where she would use them daily.

It was a sad parting, full of melancholy; Thadeus did not adjudge it appropriate to ask if he could play with her Rolls Royce before he left.

It was Monday morning when Thadeus received a completed claim form from Mr Letting. The farmer had telephoned the office on the previous Thursday and spoken to Beth Bateman regarding the sad and unexpected demise of his colt foal. Thadeus wrote a reply that it is apposite to quote in full:

Dear Mr Letting,
Colt (1925) Henry Bee/My Sunshine
I am in receipt of your completed claim form in respect of the above mentioned colt foal. Unfortunately, at the present time, I am unable to proceed with settlement of this claim until certain unexplained matters are clarified.

You are probably not aware that after your foal was taken to the hunt kennels as you disclose in the form as part of their own routine arrangements, the carcass was examined by their consultant veterinary surgeon. Regrettably he found that the cause of death was not euthanasia as anticipated, but as a result of illness or disease. He therefore took the precaution of sending the carcase up to Bristol University for a full post mortem report.

This examination revealed even more startling information. The foal had in fact died some twenty-four hours previous to the time of your alleged accident, and not following a fractured bone, but of pneumonia. Although it is true that the animal had suffered a broken cannon bone, and also been inflicted by a bullet wound to the head, both of these injuries were dated post mortem and were imposed upon an already dead horse! More puzzling is the fact that this foal showed signs of being painted; some of the natural markings had been changed.

When this information was communicated to my office last week I immediately compared the detailed report from the university with the examination certificate prepared by Mr Freeman on the day of sale. Imagine my astonishment when I discovered that the dead foal which is the subject of your claim is different in many important aspects from the foal that you bought at the Tattersalls Sale.

This dilemma can only be resolved by an explanation from your own attending veterinary surgeon Mr William Hitchen. I have endeavoured to contact him but, at the time of writing, without success.

I will write to you further as soon as I am able.

Kindest regards.

*Yours sincerely
Thadeus Burke
Managing Director*

Gerald Letting spoke to William Hitchen at the latter's Scottish retreat.

'We will deny all knowledge of this other foal; it is the result of a mix-up at the kennels, or at the university.'

'Then what happened to the foal that you shot at my farm?'

Silence, then, 'It has probably been eaten by the hounds.'

'Two dead foals, both with broken cannon bones and bullets in the head?'

'Why not?'

'And both delivered to the same kennels on the same night?'

'Damn, damn, damn, it is that bloody insurance broker, he has stitched us up!'

'Well I'm not taking the rap for this. It was your idea.'

'Thank you Mr Letting, I knew I could rely on you,' was Hitchen's final comment before slamming down the telephone instrument.

Thadeus was never able to write another letter to Mr Letting, much of what he might have said would have been slanderous, so he decided to make a personal visit to the gentleman out in Gloucestershire. He took with him a decent bottle of Scotch, and apologized profusely to the bewildered farmer. He was genuinely shocked to find that he was not the first, allegedly, to be caught up in Mr Hitchen's dead-foal ploy. The foal that the vet had gone out and shot in the head that night had been the property of a stud farm owner some twenty miles away who had been unlucky enough to loose his charge the previous day, and had reported the fact to a friend at the Thoroughbred Breeders

Association, as had at least one other unlucky owner in the area over the last week. Mr Letting's own foal by *Henry Bee* was safe, sound and thriving at a veterinary surgery a few miles away, and would be returned to him as soon as he had signed a prepared statement that was placed before him. Why should he absolve from guilt some person, or persons, unknown, who had stolen his foal? The answer was in order to prevent a prosecution as an accessory to an insurance fraud. He was more reticence about naming Mr Hitchen as the protagonist in the charade but was persuaded, maybe by the return of his premium paid for the now null and void insurance policy.

This matter being concluded it remained only for a reluctant Mr Freeman to make a formal request to the Royal Society of Veterinary Surgeons for the resignation of the membership of a Mr William Hitchen. Surprisingly Mr Hitchen's letter of resignation arrived in the same post as Mr Freeman's letter, apparently 'Wild Bill' had decided to retire and become a trainer of racehorses, in Ireland. Thadeus' friend, Robert Byrne was not amused by this final twist, commenting only that he would inform a friend.

CHAPTER 7

A PARADOX FOR LUNCH

Thadeus arrived at the Lombard restaurant a few minutes before one o'clock for lunch with Mr Edward Mannings. The restaurant was obviously near Lombard Street but situated up a narrow alleyway that ran from Gracechurch Street through to St Clement's Lane, past the Red Lion public house. Lunch invitations from Mr Mannings were rare events, this honour being bestowed on Thadeus as a result of the £10,000 that he had saved the Mannings Syndicate, together with the life of Dulcie Dellar. Mr Mannings, a distinguished figure, wearing a wing collar with a college tie that Thadeus did not recognize, was already seated at the table, sipping a glass of tap water and studying the menu through a pair of gold pince-nez. The intention of the meeting was that they discuss personal accident business with particular regard to the Burke & Co account, which was minimal. Thadeus had not relished the idea as the underwriter was well known as being short on conversation with no sense of humour whatsoever and lacking in the manners department. But he was a senior underwriter, a member of the Committee of Lloyd's and a moving light within the non-marine market.

Thadeus greeted the seated man enthusiastically and received a grunted acknowledgment.

'The steak tartar here is very good, that is what I have ordered.'

Obviously the idea of hors d'oeuvres or appetizers was out of the question and Thadeus instructed the waiter that he would join his host with the same choice of dish. The guest did manage to solicit a half bottle of fairly ordinary red wine, and the business conversation started with Mr Mannings listing endless options of benefits available under his policies, ranging from death during a railway journey which would pay double, through to the loss of a small finger on the left hand of a violinist, apparently worth only 2½ per cent of the sum insured. This restaurant had the habit of presenting the ingredients of their steak tartar set out on a platter in virgin state for inspection by the gourmet before returning them to the kitchen in order for the chef to apply his mystical influence to the concoction. Thadeus contemplated questioning the yellow of the egg by way of a relief from the haranguing, but resisted. He resolved to give his full attention to the experienced underwriter; there were things to be learned here, although the lecture was poorly presented.

The two men at the next table, which was at least six feet away, were speaking German in loud voices which annoyed Mr Mannings intensely, such that he started to speak English in ever increasing tones. Thadeus was tempted to scream *diminuendo, diminuendo!* as if to an assembled orchestra. Fortunately one of the Teutonic language broadcasters left the table for a few minutes, giving Thadeus the opportunity to ask some appropriate, and hopefully intelligent, questions. Coffee was ordered, the underwriter announcing that he despised the underwriters who took two-hour lunches, returned drunk as skunks – such people had no respect for their names. The small German battalion had reassembled but were now speaking in hushed voices, Mr Mannings also dropped into *sotto voce* fearing that the old enemy was attempting to acquire his trade secrets.

The taller of the two luncheon neighbours, the one that had left the room earlier, left the room again. Weak bladders these Huns, thought Thadeus. Mr Mannings settled the bill, after carefully checking each item, and they left the restaurant leaving the little fat German speaker alone with his thoughts, and a cold cup of coffee. As the two insurance men made their way through the alleys towards Lloyd's, Thadeus mentioned that he had visited Lady Daphne Dennington in order to assist her with some of her husband's bloodstock paperwork.

'Good,' complimented Mannings. 'She's a fine woman; she used to work for me, typing and that sort of thing; that is where she met Percy – very disturbing about poor Percy.'

'You have no idea of anything that might have worried him?' questioned Thadeus.

'No, no money worries. His family has bags of cash; shipping, I think, or is it cotton? Anyway something to do with boats. And her family has just as much; made their pile out of the slave trade, then property,' enlightened Mr Mannings.

'Did he ever make any possibly revealing remarks?' probed Thadeus. 'In hindsight, I mean.'

'No, although on a couple of occasions in the last week of his life, I thought that he wanted to say something to me. But as you know I'm not one for nattering.'

True thought Thadeus; he liked Edward Mannings, plain but honest.

They shook hands at the entrance to the Royal Exchange building.

'Go out and get me some decent business young Burke,' was the underwriter's goodbye, as he strode across towards his box.

The room was still fairly lunch-time quiet. Thadeus strolled down the centre isle, met no one whom he needed to contact, nodded politely at a handful of idle but expectant faces, then headed away towards his office. From their days together at Crawford & Amos, Thadeus remembered that Ethel was a reasonably accomplished pianist. If his memory was correct her repertoire was limited to popular musical numbers, but her studies had included a rigorous indoctrination of musical theory and literacy, which would have encompassed knowledge of the standard instruments of the orchestra. With a modicum of training the young lady might be capable of handling a personal accident account aimed at instrumentalists, under the guidance of Mr Emery. Some of these virtuosi would possess valuable digits and other desirable property for an insurance broking firm. He could design a special scale of benefits for various artistes. Woodwind players could cope without legs but the loss of an arm would put them out of business. His recollections led him to believe that, in addition to a truck-load of scaffolding with which they invariably appeared, a bass-trombonist needed only one arm and a pair of lips; gruesome stuff but it could be fun.

Ethel was delighted with her anticipated promotion but Mr Emery carried a dubious *déjà vu* expression. Miss Mills demanded an unnecessary chaperone role and it was agreed that the idea had possibilities, but the two older members of the staff would reserve judgement until the proposed documentation had been given an exacting perusal.

The afternoon was interrupted by a visit from the police. Inspector Johnny Jackson, accompanied by a smartly dressed lady stenographer with her hair severely tied back, required an interview. Routine enquiries had revealed that the Honourable Thadeus Burke enjoyed lunch today at the Lombard restaurant. Seated in the close vicinity had been two gentlemen from the banking profession, a German from Hamburg and a Swiss from Zurich.

At the end of their meal the Prussian gentleman had finished his coffee alone and the Swiss gentleman had left the restaurant and disappeared completely from the face of the earth! Thadeus questioned this assumption as the vanishing act had taken place only three hours previous it was more probable that the Swiss banker was just shopping in Fenchurch Street. He was informed that the missing person should have appeared at a further important meeting at Martin's Bank in Lombard Street with an international group of bankers from various European countries at 2.45 pm.

More relevantly, he was advised that Herr Haushofer from Hamburg had disclosed to the police that his friend and lunch partner, a Herr Blum, was involved with large money transfers arranged by the NSDAP, the extreme anti-Semitic political party in Germany. The Swiss banker, being Jewish, was in fear of assassination or kidnapping by the Frontbann, an organization from storm troop remnants structured as a private army by a Captain Röhm. This last named man had apparently taken it as a personal insult that the relevant funds were being distributed within the Swiss Union Bank by a member of the hated Israelites.

Jackson assured Thadeus that this matter had no connection with the East End of London groups, who were mere boy's clubs compared with the activities of the Führer Hitler's first-class honours graduates in violence and mayhem. The incident needed to be taken seriously. Scotland Yard was very concerned by the rise of anti Jewish elements in the capital, and other parts of the country.

Thadeus gave a full statement concerning all that he could recall from the neighbouring lunch table. His education had included only one year of German language, limited to *Deutsche Leben Erste Parte*, so he understood none of the adjacent conversation during the first *forte* movement, then the Swiss had left, presumably for a visit to the lavatory, but strangely enough, during the *pianissimo* second section, Thadeus had picked out reference to several numbers; *funf und drei, sieben und acht* cropping up and being delivered with careful pronunciation.

Had Mr Mannings been interviewed, asked Thadeus, and to the surprise and disapproval of the stenographer, Jackson informed him that he had, by a brief telephone conversation only, but had been of no help, finding the pair of money-men an annoying interference with his important business engagement.

The stenographer was even more confused when Thadeus rose from his desk and informed the inspector that he was going over to Lloyd's with the intention of visiting the Mannings box where he needed to pick up some papers. If there was any news Jackson would be telephoned before the end of business hours. Jackson added the information that the Swiss had not visited the lavatories but had stood outside the restaurant for a few minutes smoking a cigarette; one of the cooks engaged on a similar relaxing break had observed him. Then Jackson left, followed by the puzzled lady.

Thadeus engaged in some brief conversations with the office employees, primarily of a caring, enquiring nature, making a note of an outstanding invoice that was of concern to Miss Mills. James Pooley was out, in the market engaged in the placing of insurance on a large factory complex in Birmingham, and a schedule of valuable yearlings in Ireland; Thadeus might call him from the rostrum when he arrived in the underwriting room. Lightly equipped with his rolled umbrella, gloves and bowler hat, Thadeus made his way down Cornhill, arriving at the Mannings box five minutes later. Charlie Norman, the youngest member of the Mannings entourage, was expecting the visit, having been instructed by the syndicate boss to prepare a comprehensive collection of policy wordings and rating schedules for personal accident insurance, sufficient to occupy a separate filing cabinet at Burke & Co. Thadeus disclosed his uncrystallized thoughts regarding a scheme for musicians and was directed by Charlie to a schedule of benefits that the syndicate had specifically drawn up for a violinist only a few months previous. Thadeus was warned by Charlie that the boss was not an enthusiast for jazz music and had serious doubts concerning the morals of the practitioners of that art form. Thadeus thought that the temptation to trade-in a small finger for an adequate nose-full of cocaine might indeed prove the undoing of careful actuarial work, in some areas of the United States, and some venues in London!

The evolving idea in the head of Thadeus turned to the inclusion of insurance in respect of musical instruments within a comprehensive policy aimed at musicians. Certainly the box wrote all risks business and there was no reason why an attractive package could not be arranged. What about a third party section, enquired an enthusiastic Charlie, another speciality of the Mannings empire? Think of the damage that could be done with a trombone, or the bow of a double-bass!

'What about the spike on the bottom,' thought Thadeus!

The boss loved innovative ideas and spent a lot of time unravelling puzzles and codes. Did Thadeus know that Mr Mannings had worked in the Directorate of Military Intelligence during the war? His excuse had been that he was too old to fight and die, but Charlie was of the opinion that his employer was a sort of Isaac Newton of the insurance world, and he spoke five languages!

The great man himself appeared behind young Charlie and peered over at the notes, with the experienced eye of a Lloyd's man, capable of reading up-side-down at twenty yards.

'What are you going to call this project, insurance *con tutti*?' An interjection that startled Charlie and surprised Thadeus with its shade of humour.

'I have a cousin who is a conductor and thought that there might be an opening for a spot of enterprise for a small broker,' explained Thadeus.

'Orchestras, not omnibuses, I assume!' quipped the leading underwriter.

Good heavens, thought Thadeus, Mannings is in good form!

Continuing his surprises, the underwriter then said, 'You can expound your theory over a cup of tea, Burke. Your treat, I bought lunch!' And he strolled off towards the Captain's Room with Thadeus gathering an armful of papers and raising a farewell hand at Charlie Norman. No time for a call from the rostrum for James.

'You can pour: I always get tea all over the table,' instructed Mr Mannings as they took their seats besides the window.

'Everyone does. I think the committee gets its teapots second-hand from Lyons Corner House,' commented Thadeus.

The serious business started, 'Did you have a call from the police about a missing Swiss banker?'

'Yes. I expect you know more about the matter than I, being fluent in German,' prompted Thadeus.

Mannings gave an acknowledging smile. 'I like to keep my own affairs to myself, and think that others should enjoy the same privilege,'

'But we both share a fascination for a mystery,' suggested Thadeus.

'I have heard rumours of your involvement with the world of crime, but for myself I adhere strictly to the maxim "do nothing unnecessary".' warned Mr Mannings.

'So what did you hear?' questioned Thadeus, with direct eye contact at Edward Mannings.

'They seemed to have been business correspondents, possibly never met before. Spent some time talking about tramping about the mountains wearing leather trousers, not a habit that they enjoyed; their conversation ridiculed the pastime. Can you imagine those two in Lederhosen; they would have made a music-hall act!'

Mannings really was sparkling today. Thadeus kept quiet and listened.

'I do assure you that I did not spend our lunchtime together listening to next door's conversation.'

'They were so loud it was difficult to avoid,' excused Thadeus.

'Quite so. I got the impression that they were up to some sort of shenanigans, something to do with money arriving in Zurich then being transferred to Munich, then Hamburg, and then back to Zurich. I might have got it all wrong, but the little one was definitely trying to persuade the tall one to do something about which he was showing reluctance.'

'That would fit,' said Thadeus. 'Apparently when he tall one, the Swiss chap, left the room; it was not for a pee, but outside of the building for a cigarette. Probably pondering a difficult decision. Then, when he returned they started speaking in low voices!'

'Yes, I did not take a lot of notice of that session,' said Mannings, attempting to pour a second cup of tea. 'These bloody pots are useless, I shall bring it up at Committee.'

'I thought that the quieter conversation was about money, lots of large numbers being used,' suggested Thadeus.

'No, those numbers were bank account identification numbers,' revealed Mannings.

'Good heavens!' exclaimed Thadeus, immediately reminding himself that he must stop using that phrase, he was beginning to sound exactly like James Pooley. 'Did you tell the police all this?'

'No, I thought that you would do that. Leave it to the experts, not one of my maxims, but I thought that you might keep me out of it,'

'I'll certainly try, but I am sure that they will need some form of statement eventually,' confessed Thadeus. 'It's a pity that we did not write those numbers down.'

'5353007788,' advanced Mr Mannings casually.

'Goodness gracious, how did you remember that?'

'You do not become a third generation Lloyd's underwriter without being able to memorize a simple number like that. Now *pi* or the *golden ratio* would be a lot more difficult.'

'They certainly would – they have no ending!'

'I also heard a rumour that you were a bit of a mathematician. Check that bill carefully before you pay it,' chuckled Edward Mannings.

They shook hands, parted company and Thadeus returned to his office just in time to catch James Pooley before he left for the evening. All was well, James had been successful with his broking and despatched confirming telegrams. Thadeus congratulated his colleague then he too headed home for a quiet period of meditation to allow the events of the day to settle into an ordered pattern.

In the middle of that night Herr Blum was found murdered in the docks area around Wapping. This was the information communicated to Thadeus by Jackson early the next morning when he arrived at the insurance broker's mews house for breakfast. Hilton prepared the 'full

English' which the police inspector consumed with enthusiasm along with several large cups of tea. Thadeus was restricting himself to toast and marmalade and made gentle crunching noises as the story of the night's escapade unfolded between mouthfuls of sausage, bacon, mushrooms, tomatoes and eggs.

Blum had been discovered by three Danish sailors returning to their lodgings after a night of hard drinking in the Chinese Quarter of Limehouse. They were from Copenhagen and could all speak German. Thadeus interrupted the tale to express his misgivings regarding the coincidences of a German-speaking Swiss being discovered by three German-speaking Danes, after having had lunch with a genuine German-speaking German, next to a German-speaking Englishman; not to mention that his life was being threatened by an organization run by a German-speaking Austrian – and all of this in London!

'If the Danes had not spoken German we would not have known what Blum's last words were,' explained Jackson.

'I thought there must be some reasonable explanation for them taking language lessons,' said Thadeus sarcastically.

'Denmark is very adjacent to Germany. Do you want to hear this story or not?' threatened Jackson.

Thadeus was silent and Jackson continued to tell how the three sailors found Blum stretched out in the roadway of one of those narrow streets down by the river, a labyrinth of warehouses. His back was broken and his limbs lay at odd angles. They think that he fell, or was pushed, out of a loading bay, some of which are three or four stories up. They tried to assist the injured man but, in the sailor's lingo 'he was a goner' – Danes being familiar with colloquial English!

'The dying man mumbled something in Latin, a sort of last rites and then said, quite clearly 'Herr Haff, Haff' several times.'

'So you are seeking a Herr Haff?' prompted Thadeus.

Jackson looked somewhat embarrassed as he was not actually looking for anybody.

Thadeus continued. 'First of all a dying Jew is not going to mumble a last rites in Latin! Secondly, when dying in a London street you would expect your audience to be English! I suggest that these drunken sailors are interviewed again, sober and separately and try to reconstruct exactly what they heard into a recording machine. Only then can we see if we have any clues or not!'

Jackson confessed that, having been up all night, his mind was a bit foggy, but breakfast had revitalized his mental state. Anyway, he had already instigated further questioning of the witnesses, with recording machines, and in the presence of a German interpreter. He asked Thadeus if he needed a lift into the city.

'No thanks,' said Thadeus, slowly. 'I feel a hypothesis coming on!' An hour later Thadeus telephoned Jackson to advise him that the whole crime had been worked out and that, in consideration of a lunch at "The G & V", say 12.45, he would reveal the solution. Thadeus made a couple more telephone calls and then drove the Bentley up to the city, where he found Charlie Norman already chatting to Ethel and Miss Mills over cups of coffee.

'Thanks for coming over to the office so promptly Charlie,' said Thadeus. 'I thought it would be a good idea for you to meet Ethel, and we can throw some ideas around about how we might operate a scheme for musicians. Are they behaving themselves Miss Mills?'

'As well as can be expected,' was her diplomatic reply, as Ethel leaned across and tucked Charlie's puckered collar back inside his jacket.

Thadeus pushed on, 'I have spoken this morning with a violinist who is about to purchase a Stradivarius for four thousand guineas and will certainly require insurance on the instrument. He was less enthusiastic about accident insurance but as he is going to be spending a lot of money on cover for the valuable fiddle I thought we could produce a PA policy that would be attractive, and throw in the TP section also.'

'We need to walk before we can run,' said Charlie sternly.

'We are not in the business of standing still, are we Miss Mills?' said Thadeus turning to the elder lady.

'I think we can safely say that we do not stand still for long,' responded the senior mistress of the office.

'We have all the tools here, at hand. Let's see if we can get something out to this chap today; then we might try and get a piece written in *The Gramophone* next month,' enthused Thadeus.

Thadeus excused himself in order to take a telephone call, winked at Mr Emery and disappeared into his office. Well, disappeared as much as he could within a glass box.

The call was from sister Freddie, checking on the arrangements for Christmas, to which Thadeus had given very little thought. She appeared to be bored with life up in Scotland and was looking forward to some sparkling parties in London. Thadeus thought that the festive period should be held in the bosom of the family, with an appearance at the family seat in Rutland; but followed by a rollicking good time at Hogmanay in the north, perhaps one of those wild hotels in the border country.

Dull, dull, dull, thought Freddie, it was her intention to descend upon him in the capital city within days; certainly in good time for invitations to be answered. Hilton should be instructed to make arrangements and obtain adequate provisions and she would send details of train timetables and suggested venues for collection of both her person and her luggage. Why do women ask for a chap's opinion on a subject about which they have already made up their minds? Made up or not Thadeus felt certain that his sister's Christmas appointments would be the subject of strong parental control, regrettably administered by her younger brother who seemed to have been handed the baton of responsibility in this respect.

Back to work. Miss Mills had beat a retreat from the musical battleground and sent in her cavalry in the shape of Mr Emery, who was at that very moment correcting Mr Norman's erroneous attitude towards comprehensive policy wordings, with particular reference to the agreed value aspect of a Stradivarius violin. The idea of sorting claims out before they happened seemed to be a new one on young Charlie. Ethel also seemed to be learning fast.

At 11.15 the junior underwriter was due back at the box. Thadeus accompanied him to the Underwriting Room, apologizing for lumbering him with his office work and thanking him for putting himself out to assist. Thadeus was of the opinion that it was important for office and underwriter to have a good rapport. Mr Mannings was a strict believer in business being conducted at the box and Charlie had been surprised that he had been allowed out.

Arriving at the Mannings box Thadeus was reminded of the yellow legal foolscap pads that they used and took the opportunity to question Charlie on the subject. The boss liked the idea of instantly recognizing his papers from other people's papers. Brokers did not walk off with something they shouldn't, and they did not leave their own rubbish lying around on his box. It worked well, except that some brokers had taken to using these fancy pads also.

Thadeus mentioned that he had observed some of these yellow sheets at the office of Sir Percy Dennington and wondered if they might be important for the syndicate records and should be returned.

Charlie Norman thought not; it was Sir Percy's practice to make a note of interesting horses at any time that the information happened to pass through the box. Sometimes he was underwriting a bloodstock risk himself as leading underwriter, or perhaps adding a line to a large placing, or maybe just perusing a claim file. He was particularly interested in seeing the breeding of horses owned by prominent owners such as the Aga Khan or Lord Derby. Sometimes the horses had never even reached the racecourse but Percy investigated the pedigrees to find out what stallions they were using and which female families were successful. Percy had explained it all to him one day over lunch. It was all a bit beyond Charlie but Sir Percy loved playing with his pedigrees. He took his notes home and did research from stud books that he kept, and worked out pedigrees going back for six generations. Sir Percy's ambition was to breed a Derby winner one day!

Lunch time was approaching and Thadeus was becoming increasingly nervous of his commitment to Inspector Jackson. Frankly his hypothesis hung on a very dubious thread. Fortunately Jackson was in boastful mood amplifying the benefits of routine police work. Herr Blum had not 'disappeared', he had gone from the restaurant directly to a branch office of the Union Bank in Bishopsgate, arriving in an agitated condition, dealt with some post that had been couriered over from Switzerland, and despatched several telegrams. He had been observed a little later walking along Leadenhall Street towards the Aldgate Pump.

Then he immediately disclosed the results of the more thorough examination of the three Danes, in particular their interpretations of guttural utterances. It was admitted that German was probably not the dying man's chosen language, although this was not yet entirely ruled out. The experts at the Yard, having studied the disc recordings all morning were of the opinion that the following words were involved, definitely 'say no'; then a difficult word, which could have been 'parrot' or 'a pair' or 'a dose'. Thadeus was tempted to ask if the alleged parrot was German speaking, but resisted this frivolity. Finally the words used repeatedly could have been a German surname but were more probably the English word 'half'.

Thadeus smiled broadly, he could not believe how closely the dying man's utterances were related to his own wild speculation.

He revealed it to an astonished Jackson, 'Zeno's Paradox, half, half, half, half.'

'What the hell does that mean?'

Thadeus amplified the explanation, 'Zeno was a Greek mathematician, about 450 BC, famous for his paradoxes, the most important, or at least the most well remembered, was the story of Achilles chasing a tortoise. Achilles was an accomplished athlete and with each leap he was able to halve the tortoise's lead, but of course the tortoise was still moving and therefore even though he kept halving the lead he never actually caught up with the tortoise; there was no last leap.'

'That is ridiculous,' commented Jackson. 'Obviously the faster will catch up with the slower; I think Zeno needed some lessons from our traffic division.'

'The paradox concerns divisions of space in relation to motion.'

A still mystified Johnny Jackson responded with, 'But what has it got to do with a murdered Swiss Banker in the middle of London?'

'Imagine that you have a bank account in Zurich into which small and large sums of money appear; probably contributions being made from the USA or Ireland, Spain, or Italy or even England, and from within Germany, by sympathisers with the National Socialists in Germany. You do not know what the balance of the account will show at any particular time. But if you set up a standing order at, say the first day of each month, arranging for half of the balance to be transferred to a separate account, you would not need to know the figures involved, or make any changes to the instructions, and be confident that the donor account would not run out of funds, and that your recipient account would get richer and richer.'

'You concocted all of this out a few garbled words from a dying German speaker, translated through a trio of drunken Danish sailors? Ridiculous!' said Jackson, and tucked into his steak and kidney pie.

At that very same moment James Pooley was carrying his midday meal of the Blue Plate Special purchased at the Aerated Bread Company's self-service restaurant in Cannon Street across to a quiet corner where he intended to study the copy of the workshop manual for the new open-top Morris Cowley motor vehicle that he intended to buy from Mr Hollington later in the week; with the agreement of Eddie: The book having been sent through the post in advance by the obliging client. Settling to his task he was annoyed to find that the pair of ill-attired and dirty building site operatives, that he had taken great care to avoid in the queue for food, had taken seats right next to his selected table. More disturbing was the appearance of a small fat German gentlemen who with a Teutonic 'here, here' handed the dishevelled duo envelopes which they proceeded to tear open, check the contents, and then started throwing bread rolls about the restaurant with riotous abandonment to the embarrassment of the quickly departing fat chap, and the great consternation of the ABC's management.

A full account of this episode was related by James to an astonished and shocked Miss Mills later in the afternoon: the office manager having first admonished the assistant director for frequenting such an outrageously American-style establishment; a venue that no respectable city gentlemen should honour with his presence, at least no respectable city gentlemen who anticipated a progressive career at Lloyd's. This conversation was conducted within earshot of the chairman of Burke & Co, the Honourable Thadeus Burke.

The tale led to Thadeus making an urgent telephone call to Inspector Jackson of Scotland Yard. This action led to a Herr Haushofer, the representative of a bank in Hamburg, being arrested within an hour.

Jackson later, over a glass of ale in the Red Lion, related that he had never seen a suspect crumble so fast under exposure to a brief and amateur lecture in ancient Greek mathematical history. Apparently Herr Blum had developed the habit of fraudulently diverting funds accumulating in his bank at Zurich for the benefit of the NSDAP, the political party led by Herr Hitler, into a separate account operated for the benefit of a fledgling Jewish political opposition group. Herr Haushofer, who was himself a member of the NSDAP, had discovered this movement of money as a result of discrepancies between records kept both at his bank and within secret party documents to which he had access. The result was that during a banker's convention held in London, he had persuaded Herr Blum that his project was useless and that the German Jews were pocketing the money themselves, which was, incidentally, not true, and that Herr Blum had a simple choice to make! Either he could be exposed to the Swiss Union Bank, lose his job and spend a considerable time in a Swiss jail, or face the Frontbann who would delight in disposing of him in a most unpleasant manner; or, and by far the best option, change the beneficiaries of his clever scheme into a more personal arrangement involving just Herr Blum and Herr Haushofer. With the assistance of an intake of tobacco smoke, Herr Blum had made the obvious decision.

New account details, already set up in Hamburg before leaving, copies of which were found on the person of the little fat German while in police custody, were communicated to the reluctant Jewish banker who enacted the change of bank account number by telegram that very afternoon. Blum's clever scheme used an ancient Greek devise known as Zeno's Paradox! Amazing!

That evening another, even more disturbing telephone call was received by Thadeus from his sister, Freddie. She advised that she had this week inserted an entry within *The Times*, Court Circular on page 17, it read: *The Honourable Lady Frederica Burke has left Claridge's and taken residence at 11-15 Sloane Mews, SW.*

This notice appeared between the announcement that Lady Kathleen Curzon-Herrick has left Claridge's for the country and the information that the Master of the Rolls and Lady Pollock will return to 2 Lygon Place from Scotland at the end of next week

'Freddie, you have not been residing at Claridge's and you do not now reside at Sloane Mews – *I* do!' admonished Thadeus.

'I need a London address,' she stated emphatically. 'If you feel that my embroidered announcement warrants further proceedings you must report me to your friend Inspector Watson.'

'Sister dear, have you been drinking, or sniffing anaesthetic?'

'Both,' was her giggled reply.

'We will speak of this matter at a later date, when you are of a saner attitude. How are your studies progressing?'

'All finished. I've passed my final exams with grades that have astounded my professors and all I need to do now is sit on my bum, waiting to be proclaimed a Doctor of Medicine in May. How is your study of toxic materials proceeding?' asked the sibling, ignoring her brother's serious pose.

'As it happens I saved a young lady from arsenic poisoning recently,' boasted Thadeus.

'Did you give her a shot of Aunty Dot?'

'No,' admitted Thadeus, guessing at the medical slang for antidote, 'I happened upon her engaged in a spot of illicit sex, and she was so infuriated that she took a mere sip of the intended poison, before rushing at me with a mouthful of vomit.'

Freddie roared with laughter, 'You should report this incident to that Mr Freud in Vienna. A short paper, I think, entitled "The fortuitous advantages of voyeurism"; it will wow them over there. Must rush; Love you.'

'Love you too,' replied Thadeus into a buzzing disconnected telephone connection.

Why was crime so much easier than family matters?

Herr Haushofer was delighted to find that he was to be hanged in England rather than face his native ex-colleagues; his repatriation to Germany had loomed as an option at one time; notwithstanding this he made a point of saluting his Führer as he stood on the gallows. He was a nasty little man who infuriatingly refused to explain exactly how he had managed to get the sad and disillusioned Herr Blum from Leadenhall Street into the hands of the hired building workers for disposal out of the top floor hatch of a warehouse in the Wapping area. Thadeus and Jackson wasted hours of precious time with speculations involving fast cars, doctored drinks and an unconscious body wrapped in a carpet, but neither the inventive insurance broker nor the combined routine efforts of the Metropolitan Police could exactly reconstruct the *modus operandi* for the assassination of the Swiss banker.

Several months later a prostitute, serving a sentence for grievous bodily harm in Holloway Prison, boasted to a fellow inmate how she had accosted a tall, dignified foreign gentleman, in broad daylight, in the City of London, lured him down an alleyway in order that two of her protectors could bundle him into the boot of a small Austin motor vehicle. She had been rewarded with a brand new £5 note! She was particularly pleased to broadcast that as a result of her enterprise the 'bloody four-by-two' had been thrown off the top of a huge building.

Sometimes the reality of human behaviour is beyond the reach of the reasonable mind.

CHAPTER 8

CHRISTMAS WITH THE FAMILY

Christmas Day 1925 fell on a Friday, the following Monday was also declared a Bank Holiday. Burke & Co had democratically decided that the office would be manned on Christmas Eve by a skeleton staff consisting of Mr Emery and Ethel Henson, with a voluntary James Pooley also in attendance for a few hours, particularly at the time when the Lloyd's Underwriting Room was in business. Tuesday 29th December would be handled by Miss Mills and Beth Bateman, with James again attending if necessary. It was anticipated that this would be sufficient, the insurance renewals of Lady Daphne Dennington having all been arranged and debited to the client earlier in the month, as had other renewals due at the year end. The Honourable Thadeus Burke would be leaving for Derbyshire on the Wednesday before Christmas and not returning to the city until the following Wednesday.

All the staff had been given a crisp new five-pound note each as a present and thanked for their diligence and loyalty during the year. Changes of salaries, if any, would be disclosed on New Year's Eve.

Lady Frederica Burke had been unceremoniously bundled, quietly screaming and shouting, into the back seats of the Bentley, together with a mass of leather suitcases and coat-hangered dresses, and Hilton had driven the siblings up to the family seat. Lady Frederica was sober and repentant and had promised both her male companions her best behaviour for the whole weekend. A promise that held firm, until she announced sedately that 'if they did not stop for a break soon she would pee in her pants'; the gentleman immediately obliged, drawing into a wayside inn, more in fear of damage to the rear seat upholstery than the young lady's comfort. The hostelry provided a beer for Hilton and two small gin and tonics for the other two travellers, the female medical expert having assured the company concerning the capabilities of bladder capacity for the remainder of the journey.

Headley Hall stood at the centre of two hundred and fifty acres of parkland and woods overlooking a man-made lake, equipped with its own small island. The Bentley entered through the open iron gates and crunched its way along the chestnut tree-lined avenue, arriving outside the Ionic columned portico in good time for tea, or in the case of Miss Freddie, a very large Gin and It.

As baggage and parcels were unloaded and carted off towards their allocated rooms by Hilton, assisted by a bevy of servants, Lady Ashmoor and her daughter-in-law, Lady Geraldine Burke came out to greet the visitors. The two newcomers responded impeccably exchanging hugs and kisses with the relatives. They were informed that the men were in the billiard room and that tea would be served shortly in the drawing room, no doubt the new arrivals would appreciate the opportunity to visit their rooms and dust themselves down before joining the company. Thadeus led Freddie straight through to the music room where he poured them both a very large gin and tonic each. 'Bottoms up!' They cried, sealing the foundations of a conspiratorial weekend.

After bathing and dressing in a lightweight tweed suit Thadeus made his way to the billiard room, greeted his father Lord Ashmoor and brother Lord Edward Burke, helped himself to another, more modest, gin and tonic, and stared aimlessly at the coloured snooker balls bouncing around the table.

Miss Freddie appeared in a dazzling French dress, with a close-fitting hat, and carrying a long cigarette holder, the end of which held a black cigarette. Both her father and elder brother looked at her disapprovingly; her younger brother, Thadeus, raised his eyes to the ceiling and puffed his pipe casually. Freddie challenged brother Edward to a frame, received a twenty-one point advantage, and won by thirty, finishing with the last four colours. Conversation had been trivial up to that point and Freddie's final black ball put an end to all vocal exchange. Lord Ashmoor left the room without a word, and Edward excused himself as he needed to dress for dinner early because he was expecting two guests this evening. Questioned on this subject by Freddie, she was informed that a Mr and Mrs Matthews, art dealer chums of Edward were joining the table this evening on their way up to Lancashire.

Left alone Freddie and Thadeus knocked a few balls about to the repeated female chant of dull, dull, dull. Freddie decided to go downstairs and cause a bit of chaos in the kitchen. She was actually seriously interested in the art of the cuisine and intended taking notes from the cook Gladys in preparation for her entertainment table back in London.

Thadeus decided to interrupt his brother's preparations, under the guise that he might acquaint himself with the proper habiliment for eating with the nobility, although he was confident that Hilton would already have spied out any modern and recently introduced deviations; none were expected in this house, more likely the reverse and he might find himself exposed as the only guest not wearing cross-garter hose! No, Thadeus' reason for the intrusion was to find out about the Matthews, who appeared to be the only opportunity for sport this evening, apart that is from the very real possibility of sister Freddie popping up, half naked, from the middle of a large blancmange! Father was right; something had to be done about that girl. She had completed her studies but could not yet start the work with which she was eager to be engaged. It would be a frightful mistake to send her abroad; what a pity women were not allowed in Lloyd's, she would make an excellent broker. He would arrange accommodation for her at Sloane Mews. Thadeus actually owned the whole mews, a total of twenty-two houses, a property that had been bequeathed to him in the will of his late brother Jonathan. Thadeus had acquired title to the dwellings on attaining his twenty-first birthday, an arrangement that came to fruition posthumously after his brother had won the small development in a game of backgammon.

Edward's rooms were crowded with both male and female servants busying themselves with brushes and cupboard doors, assembling garments for a small safari. Art, paintings in particular, had always been Edward's passion; they were the subject of his university studies, and now his principle occupation. For three years he had operated the Athena Gallery in Cork Street, run on a daily basis by an efficient and knowledgeable manageress, with whom Thadeus and Freddie suspected he was having an affair, although they had no evidence of this whatsoever. The suspicion had arisen at the opening night of an exhibition, last summer, glances and mannerism indicating a close liaison. Observation prompted the outspoken Freddie to whisper into Thadeus' ear: 'He is swiving her!' On reflection this was the first occasion on which Thadeus became aware of his sister's diversion from her usually impeccable Oxford English into what was becoming a more habitual use of the vernacular. With the imminent appearance of the letters MD after her name, this was a digression requiring urgent correction. Thadeus made a note in his little black book to give this matter his early attention when they both returned to London.

Retreating into the withdrawing room section of the suite Thadeus stood with arms folded, studying three small oil paintings propped against the far wall. Art had not been his subject – his own collection of paintings having been recommended by his brother – but he thought he recognized the assembled trio as the work of Cézanne, a sloppy, amateurish sort of Frenchman whose efforts were commanding enormous prices in the London and New York art markets. The landscapes were very similar. Thadeus often wondered if all these Frenchmen were afflicted with some disease of the lower limbs, in addition to Monsieur Toulouse Lautrec, a painter whom Thadeus admired greatly, as they did not seem to travel around much. One of them had painted the same cathedral in different lights hundreds of times and this man Cézanne spent all his time in the same mountains with only a minimal collection of paint tubes.

'What do you think of those Thady?' came the voice of Edward.

'Cézanne,' ventured Thadeus.

'Very good, I'll make an art expert out of you yet. But are they genuine or fakes?' an unexpected question from his brother.

'Is there any difference? I think this chap faked his own pictures.'

'If they are his own hand they are worth a fortune, if not, they might as well be painted over by you.'

'I will have some spare time over the weekend for a bit of brushwork if needed,' offered Thadeus. 'What do Mr and Mrs Matthews think of them?'

'Astute as ever, Thady! Mr Matthews, who is arranging a sale of the paintings, is sure that they are genuine. He has a full provenance going back to when the paint was still wet. His wife, however, thinks that all three are fakes.'

'Not a loyal and devoted spouse,' suggested Thadeus.

'Professional pride. She is a couple of years older than him, started in the business a little before him and is very keen to keep her senior status.'

'They sound like an absolutely awful pair. Are you the umpire in this match?'

'No, I think the works are genuine and I have a client for two of the paintings. If I can get the right price from Matthews my profit will be the third piece for myself. I've always told you that art galleries do not make money by the paintings that they sell, but by the ones that they don't! They will be here any minute now, you'd better push off and get dressed.'

'Oh, right,' acknowledged Thadeus. 'White tie?'

'Of course!'

'I hope you're going to change the frames, they look as if they were made yesterday,' added Thadeus, as he made for the door.

'That is in hand. Off you go,' instructed his brother.

Thadeus made his way up to his own rooms on the next floor, pausing to knock on Freddie's door to check on her progress. He was dragged in to pronounce his opinion on the two or three dozen garments displayed around the two rooms. 'The blue one,' he adjudged.

'Which blue one?'

'This one,' he pronounced, touching the cloth gently. 'It has various shades of blue.'

'I will think about it. Thanks!' and he was ushered out.

At dinner Lady Freddie shone like the sun to Mrs Dorothy K Matthews's moon, as W B Yeats might have said. Her many shades of blue silk whirling about Mrs M's little black dress like a squadron of Sopwiths around entrenched infantry. She behaved impeccably in both her use of the English language and table manners. Her only slight deviation came when Mrs Matthews revealed that her friends called her 'Dot' and Freddie responded with the assurance that it was not her intention to refer to any other human being with the diminutive title related to a small mark on a piece of paper and that as a result she would have to remain no more than an acquaintance of Mrs Matthews. Dorothy Matthews saw the funny side of this remark, although Freddie assured Thadeus later in the evening that there wasn't one!

Thadeus, his brother Edward and Mr George Matthews discussed art values. Starting at the Renaissance, they moved quickly through the Baroque and Dutch Masters and dallied at Turner and Constable before having a heated debate on the Impressionists. Thadeus confined his contribution to questions, except for the latter school, which he had briefly swotted in his rooms from a book entitled *The History of Painting*. His knowledge of Renoir and Degas astonishing the table companions; his assessment of Henri de Toulouse-Lautrec rendered with the confidence of a director of the Louvre. Mr Matthews countered with more stories about James McNeill Whistler than the artist himself could have conjured up. Lady Ashmoor lodged an injunction against the intention of the trio to discuss Fauvism and Cubism and they accepted the directive to rejoin the company in more festive conversation.

The following day George Matthews missed breakfast, his wife advising the assembled family group that he was suffering from a stomach complaint. Freddie administered a powder of some sort to settle the art dealer's agitated organ. This seemed to restore the guest to normal activity, but it was decided that he was not in a fit state to travel on the long journey to Lancashire. He and his wife accepted the invitation to stay on for a further night, proposing that they should need to be away first thing on Christmas Day in order to meet their family commitments in Bolton.

Lord Ashmoor was out all day shooting. His wife, daughter-in-law and Freddie spent the whole day discussing and arranging Christmas lunch with the staff. A rapidly recuperating George Matthews and Lord Edward Burke haggled over the price of the three Cézannes, which had now been taken out of their plain wooden frames in readiness for reframing at Matthews' workshop in Bolton during the holiday break. Dorothy Matthews gave Thadeus an art lesson. Mrs Matthews was quite an academic and matured visibly when assuming the teacher's role. Her knowledge of dates and names was astonishing and she was capable of projecting her own understanding to the mind of a student. She delighted in explanations of techniques, from fresco and mosaic to the development of modern European painting. When they reached the subject of the Impressionists and Cézanne in particular her objective attitude stepped up a gear; she was able to convey the nuances of colour and patterns in a manner that left the disagreement with her husband over the authenticity of the three paintings that were in the house as purely transient opinion. She did, however, decline to use the three pictures as examples in her lecture. Good for you, thought Thadeus, the lady did possess dignity.

This did not stop Thadeus later in the afternoon creeping into the library where the three canvases lay on a table to continue his studies, aided by a magnifying glass. Only Freddie disturbed him, seeking her first drink of the day. They sat by the fire supping a couple of large gin and tonics, and discussing the Matthews.

Dinner was light in preparation for the more substantial traditional meal anticipated for the next day. Wine had been imbibed in moderation in preparation for the attendance at midnight mass at Saint Mary's, the village church. Freddie carried her white leather prayer book, a gift from Thadeus during their teenage years and Thadeus carried his black leather reciprocal present. It was a chilly night and the small party wore hats and long coats. Led by Lord Ashmoor, the local aristocracy graced this occasion each year, except that this time Lord Burke and his guest George Matthews had pleaded indisposition, much to the annoyance of Lady Ashmoor; so his Lordship was accompanied by his wife, his youngest son, his only daughter, his daughter-in-law and a rather overawed Mrs Matthews. This did not stop her participating raucously in the traditional Christmas hymns, as did both Thadeus and Freddie. Lady Geraldine Burke was quiet and kept close to her mother-in-law. They both came into prominence at the ceremonial handshaking which Lord Ashmoor hated, Mrs Matthews did not understand, and Thadeus and Freddie suffered embarrassing remarks about their present adulthood compared with their locally remembered childhood. It was 1.30 am before the party was home and in bed.

At 6.30 the next morning the Matthews drove away towards Bolton, George at the wheel, three carefully wrapped Cézanne canvasses secured to the seats immediately behind him, and Dorothy asleep on the second set of back seats of their Austin 20 Open Road Tourer

Christmas Day. It had long been the Burke family habit to exchange only modest presents between them, Lord and Lady

Ashmoor having established the principle that if any member of the family discovered something that another member of the family needed, or might be pleased by, then it should be acquired and presented without unnecessary ceremony. Only Thadeus and Freddie ignored this ruling, T Burke creeping into F Burke's bedroom before breakfast with a leather handbag of French manufacture that he had acquired in Old Bond Street and a matching long dark brown mink coat. Thadeus was asked to close his eyes while his naked sister slipped into her new coat and cavorted about the room, announcing that it would probably be the only garment that she would wear all day. Part of her dance involved the whirling away of a chenille cloth to reveal a stack of books; a complete leather-bound set of the *General Stud Book*, all twenty-five volumes, together with a card inscribed: 'To the bestest brother and most famous bloodstock insurance broker in the world.' Thadeus was delighted.

Both were late down for breakfast, but were forced to play their full part in the consumption of grilled kidneys, scrambled eggs, finnan haddock and cold ham, accompanied by hot toast or freshly baked wholemeal bread, jams and marmalade, toasted teacakes and scones, tea or coffee. The four youngest members of the Burke household then set off for a much needed walk through the local countryside. It was sunny but very cold, which delighted the fur-clad Freddie, better equipped than her tweed and leather attired companions.

The two girls discussed modern trends in make-up, Geraldine being mystified by some of the terms and phrases used by her sister-in-law, although she asked intelligent questions and gave her full attention to the particulars of colourings for the eyes. Magazines mentioned by Freddie were noted down at the back of a small diary carried by the slightly elder woman.

Thadeus and Edward exchanged opinions on budgeting and cash flow, the latter being a particular problem for an art gallery.

'Never buy, until you have already sold!' warned Thadeus

'You must speculate to accumulate,' responded Edward.

Both the men benefited from their outspoken opinions of bankers and accountants, each making notes of important names that may be of use at a later date.

Christmas lunch was started at four o'clock in the afternoon and was conducted with the precision of a Masonic lodge meeting, opening with grace rendered in a graceful voice by Lord Ashmoor. Dishes and drinks were presented and removed by a disciplined staff with diligently practised and correct movements from exact and accurate positions. The ceremony was closed with the loyal toast – 'the King' they all cried in unison, followed by the family – 'the Family Burke', again in unison. Then the mysterious silent toasts, Lord Ashmoor to his wife, Edward to his wife, Thadeus to his sister and finally by two boys to their father. Then, seated, the unofficial toasts, Freddie to her mother, Geraldine to her mother-in-law, Lady Ashmoor to her children. The conclusion being a series of raised glasses across the table in every direction. It was a very satisfactory method of emptying several bottles of good claret.

In these small gatherings Lady Ashmoor had never allowed the females of the species to be dismissed from the table in order that the men could enjoy their cigars and port in splendid isolation. Only on occasions of entertainments devised for business purposes was she prepared to condone the introduction of what she correctly surmised to be smutty conversation unsuitable for the ears of a lady and therefore led the female withdrawal. She regarded 'business' as an activity rated no higher than 'gathering and hunting'. Her four sisters had strongly supported the suffragette movement, but Lady Ashmoor had abstained, being of the opinion that the position of women was already far above that of a male.

After a polite period of drinks and conversation in the drawing room Freddie excused herself in order to retire to her rooms to write some letters, and Thadeus took the opportunity to slip away towards the library. He was anxious to try out his new stud books and had the ideal material for a full test in the collection of papers from Sir Percy Dennington's desk that he had brought with him, knowing that there would be many unfilled breaks during the weekend. He started his research with a mare named *Lisma*, the property of one of his own clients and probably noted down by Sir Percy from one of his own slips during his days at Crawford & Amos. There she was on page 499 of the latest volume, a chestnut foaled in 1907 and still working, carrying a foal this year to *Sky-rocket*. Working backwards through volumes XXIV and XXXIII, etcetera, he followed *Lisma* and her dam, *Luscious*, then the grand-dam *Alveole* and onward until he reached *Maid of Masham* in the sixth generation of the pedigree. All this information matched exactly with the carefully written presentation by Sir Percy, except that he had also set out the full pedigree of *Lisma's* sire *Persimmon* so he had both the male and female lines. Thadeus did not have available details of sires' pedigrees and therefore would need to limit his further research to the distaff lines only. He could start checking some more of Sir Percy's workings but that seemed rather boring. He turned instead to the simple lists on the yellow box-paper; five sheets listing sixteen horses in total. There were also two white sheets of paper listing the same sixteen horses, five on one sheet and eleven on the other. Closer study of the pile of documents revealed that several of these eleven horses had had their pedigrees analysed and set out in perfect triangular fashion by Sir Percy, but none of the separately listed five horses. On closer inspection there was only one of the eleven missing so Thadeus set about reconstructing this forgotten or mislaid item. He had pursued the female line of this one back to the fourth dam when his sister arrived with the specific objective of disturbing his peaceful enjoyment of his chosen situation on the planet Earth, an offence that Thadeus had many times spoken against at political meetings. He had also spoken on occasions on the duty of the strong to protect the weak, and here was his weak little sister in need of a large drink and a companion at a game of cards, or backgammon, or billiards, or something stimulating.

Thadeus bowed to his duty and started by pouring from a jug of Pimm's that he had ordered, but not touched, half an hour previous.

Freddie browsed through the papers and stud books that Thadeus had spread over the library table. 'What are you up to here?' she questioned.

Thadeus explained that these were papers left on the desk of a man who committed suicide but left no note. Lady Freddie insisted upon a full reconstruction of the evidence and her brother obliged with a detailed account of documents. 'These sheets are full, six generation projections of various horses, some well known to me, some unnamed foals or yearlings of good breeding,' he commenced, pointing out two Derby winners and a Two Thousand Guineas winner. 'These sheets are of particular interest; a set on yellow paper, almost certainly completed at the gentleman's Lloyd's box. You will observe that different coloured inks have been used, indicating that some of the information was added later.' He pointed at a name in the list. 'Here we see the name of the horse, the sire and the dam, but the sex, colour and age have been added after some research. These entries on the five yellow sheets of paper have been later transcribed onto the two white sheets. Some of these named horses have then been analysed to show their full pedigrees.

'I was in the process of completing the task by reference to my new Christmas present.'

'Well, let's get on with it!' said the girl, and took a seat at the table.

'Not too dull for you?' jibed her brother.

'Certainly not – in any profession diligent use of records and the preparation of a valid analysis, supported by material evidence, is essential,' admonished the young medical student.

It was not long before the pair of siblings were wandering around the table leafing through the large books and making notes of horses' names seeking to fill gaps in the triangular tables. Freddie, who was working on the white paper list of five horses transcribed from the several yellow sheets, was having trouble establishing the pedigrees.

'Here we have an un-named foal, or yearling, born in 1923, by a stallion called *Phalaris* and out of a mare called *Mary Mona*, but she did not have a foal by that stallion in that year; she did have foals by him in the previous year and the year after, but not in 1923.'

'Probably just an error with the year of birth,' advised Thadeus.

'I do not think so,' responded Freddie. 'Here is a horse named *Icarus*, born in 1922, by *Polymelus* out of *Miss Matty*. This mare appears in volumes XXIV and XXV but she has never been to *Polymelus*. I have checked two others and although the stallions and mares are real, the horse on the list does not exist! They are deliberate and fictitious inventions.'

A puzzled Thadeus checked through Freddie's workings and together they checked the fifth and last name on the list. Again all the names shown were actual horses except that the combination giving rise to the listed animal was non-existent.

'Well done Doctor Burke,' said a thoughtful Thadeus. 'I think a reward in the shape of a large glass of Pimm's is in order.'

'Too late, my appetite for study is fully awake. I will retire to my rooms and continue the investigation in which I am engaged on the subject of allergies.' She kissed the top of her brother's head and left the room.

Thadeus continued his study of bloodstock pedigrees, involving reference within the library to other racing records. His suspicions were confirmed, *Miss Matty* was the dam of *Papyrus*, winner of the 1923 Derby, the horse *Icarus* would have been a full younger brother, very valuable! Other named mares were either classic winners with fictitious offspring, or fictitious females closely related to top race-fillies, half, or full sisters. Too good to be true! Thadeus cleaned, prepared and lighted a pipe-full of tobacco and sat down in front of the blazing fire.

Christmas evening was a period set aside for games, involving both the family and staff. As in previous years the staff included a couple of new young maids, aged fourteen or fifteen and earning not more than twenty pounds per annum, and every effort was needed to prevent embarrassment for these new charges, much cheating and waving of arms and mouthing of answers was permitted for their assistance. Not so on the occasions when Hilton was at the centre of some playful inquisition, he was allowed no mercy, having on many previous appearances taken the top prize. By some simple shenanigans his name was drawn first in the list of 'volunteers' for the serving of supper, he was in no need of a crisp new five-pound note distributed by Lady Ashmoor; his three previous trophies being kept, framed and dated in his rooms at Sloane Mews.

Fatigue, and near suffocation from cigar smoke, forced the party to retire just post-midnight. Mary, Freddie's personal maid, took the fiver, having shown an outstanding knowledge of anatomy.

Saturday was the hunt and Sunday the church: passion and desire, repentance and forgiveness – all four emotive activities being displayed at both ceremonies. Saturday afternoon Thadeus made a telephone call to a friend and client who was an art dealer and collector in Manchester, and asked some questions. Sunday morning he received a return call and answered some questions; then early evening, just before the second visit of the day to the church, he received another call and made some notes. Thadeus had also taken the opportunity over the weekend to quiz his brother on the prices of the pictures. It was disclosed that George was asking a total of £12,000 for the three, Edward had hedged, suggesting that he may only be interested in two of them, the larger pair, for which he had in mind a figure of £7,500. It had been agreed that a further appraisal would be made after reframing, which George thought would vastly improve Edward's opinion.

On Monday a late rising and a lengthy and casual breakfast was followed by the reappearance of the travelling Matthews. The Matthews unloaded their precious cargo straight into the library, having parked their vehicle at the eastern side of the house and entered through the casement windows, under the direction of Hilton. They joined the extended breakfast, now playing well into extra time, Edward munching toast and reading the *Illustrated London News*. Dorothy Matthews tucked enthusiastically into newly prepared eggs, bacon and tomatoes, Thadeus having made short work of the first batch of his favourite matutinal repast. George supped coffee, reluctantly tapping a single boiled egg. Lord and Lady Ashmoor were long gone from the room, Freddie and Geraldine soon left on some mission involving a mountain of magazines. Thadeus excused himself intent upon his first pipe of the day.

The three remaining, quietly nibbling breakfasters chatted amiably, George Matthews confirming that he would accept a figure of £10,000 for the three pictures and Edward said that he would just have a final look over the paintings but was sure that a deal could be struck. The paintings in the library were wrapped in plain brown paper, but George insisted that they should be protected with cardboard and he had some corrugated material in the car, used during travelling, which he would leave for Edward.

Suddenly they were flabbergasted by a loud cry of, 'Oh damn and blast!' in a male voice coming from the direction of the library, accompanied by female cries of, 'Oh, no'. The art-expertise trio set off towards the library full of fear and trepidation to find Thadeus, Freddie and Geraldine moving Cézanne paintings and at the same time mopping up a rapidly spreading red liquid.

'What the hell have you done?' exclaimed a goggle-eyed George Matthews.

Edward Lord Burke and Mrs Dorothy Matthews had mouths open but no sound was emerging.

'I am sorry. I was decanting a bottle of port and the tongs slipped,' admitted Thadeus.

'I was trying to help,' was the useless admission from Freddie.

'I did not see the accident,' added Geraldine.

'Where did all this cloth come from?' asked Matthews, surprisingly.

'It is, or was, my petticoat,' admitted Geraldine. 'We've cleaned up everything. There's no damage to the table or the pictures – it is just that the back of the frames are a bit red!'

Edward, George and Dorothy inspected the works of art, handling them very carefully to ensure there were no dripping edges or hidden pools of liquid on the canvases. The three were all shaking with anger.

'Get out!' Edward ordered Thadeus.

He left and the two ladies followed him without a word.

The work of Cézanne was as the painter intended, untouched by the accident. The new gilt frames were fine, only the back white wood faces showing the influence of vintage port.

Lord Ashmoor stopped Freddie in her flight and questioned her on the disturbance before summoning Thadeus into his study. 'That was not a bottle of my 1904 that you splashed around the library I hope,' was his simple statement.

'No, sir,' responded Thadeus. 'It was a bottle of LBV.'

'You are telling me that you decanted a bottle of Late Bottled Vintage'

'Yes, sir.'

'In the library?'

'Yes, sir.'

'And you expect me to believe this balderdash?'

'No, sir, but it does seem to have deceived Edward and his associates.'

'I am getting accustomed to your devious plots and ploys Thadeus. I expect you pick up this sort of nonsense in the city, but be careful of involving your sister and Geraldine.'

'Yes, sir.'

'I am buying your sister a new motor vehicle ready for when she is qualified. I want you to make sure that it is suitable for a doctor, not a girl about town. Send her in to see me, please.' With this final directive His Lordship closed the interview and waved his son away.

Thadeus dashed through the ground floor of the house and out through the east door, past an Austin 20 Open Road Tourer with the hood up and into the walled garden where he consulted with Hilton, Henry the footman and Alfie the odd man. After a considerable amount of nodding by all four, he strolled back into the house. The Matthewses had gone upstairs for a wash-up before they left for London. Freddie was hovering in a passageway and, after a few words, Thadeus directed her towards her father's den. Edward was alone in the library with his cheque book spread in front of him and a pen poised for writing.

'What do you want?' he asked gruffly, but politely.

'Are you absolutely certain that those three paintings are genuine?' asked his brother.

'Yes.'

'Show me,' instructed Thadeus.

More by way of superiority than co-operation Edward rose and went to the separate reading table on which the three painting were now displayed.

'People tend to think that these Impressionists were quick dabbers of paint, rushing off two or three canvases a day. It is not so, Cézanne would spend a month or maybe two months completing a work. When the average artist paints a tree he will mix an appropriate green and use that colour for most of that subject, adding shading later to bring out the perspective and lighting. See here.' Edward pointed at a tree in one of the compositions. 'Cézanne would create a subtle change with almost every brush stroke, because of this each square inch of his work has a special vitality.'

'Thanks, fascinating. You are happy with them then?'

'Yes, except that Matthews insisted that the 10,000 was guineas not pounds. Probably as a result of your incompetence.'

'I am sure that it was,' said Thadeus. 'We will talk later.'

He left the room and went up the back stairs to join his sister at the window of her bedroom. Hilton had brought the Austin round to the front of the house, just below where they stood. Edward, Lady Ashmoor and Geraldine were saying their farewells, the younger lady moving her hands about in an apologetic manner, the Matthews raising theirs in a 'no harm done' acknowledgement. George patted his wallet pocket as a gesture of satisfaction at the sale, and Edward shook his hand warmly and kissed Dorothy on the cheek. Hilton and Henry held open the car doors and the two art dealers drove down the drive at the end of which they would turn left towards London. Thadeus suggested to Freddie that they would be stopping at the first pub they came to, for a post mortem on the morning's events. Before vacating her chambers he asked her what sort of car she intended to purchase with her father's money.

'A Bugatti Type 37 Grand Prix two-seater,' she smiled. 'It will not be on the market until next year. Your colleague James Pooley obtained a brochure for me.'

'Did you mention this to father?' asked Thadeus

'Yes.'

'And he was happy with this purchase?'

'Yes. We discussed a suitable vehicle for a newly qualified doctor and it was agreed that a small Austin might be appropriate. However, I pointed out to him that it might not be appropriate for a young titled female doctor from the aristocracy, the only daughter of Lord Ashmoor.'

'What an excellent broker Freddie would have made,' thought Thadeus.

A light buffet lunch was announced. Edward filled his plate and beckoned Thadeus to follow him into the unoccupied drawing room. 'The full story please,' said Edward simply.

'I was suspicious of the Matthews pair, particularly by the attitude of Mrs Matthews; a lady of outstanding knowledge on the subject of art and paintings in particular. It seemed to me to be very odd that she had voiced an opinion regarding the authenticity of the Cézannes; I thought that this might be a hedging manoeuvre.'

Edward said nothing, and Thadeus continued.

'I spoke to a friend in the art business in Manchester over the weekend, not the best time to obtain an opinion, especially Christmas weekend. He made some brief enquires. The Matthewses are not well liked in Lancashire, but in particular he advised me that there had been an occasion a couple of years ago when they were involved in a case of some forged paintings. Their main defence in this case had been that Mrs Matthews had warned that she was doubtful regarding the origin of the pictures and had disclosed this opinion to the buyer.'

'These pictures are perfectly satisfactory. What was all that nonsense with the port?' said Edward in a milder tone.

'That was devious, I admit. I had arranged for Hilton and a couple of the staff to rummage in the Matthews's motorcar during breakfast. In the back they found three identical paintings in identical frames wrapped around with corrugated cardboard. Copies of the three Cézannes! I think it was their intention to exchange the paintings that you had inspected and bought, for the fake copies before they left.'

'You are sure about this?'

'Yes. Your wife was also a witness. So I arranged for an accident in order that the frames were marked.'

'It is true that they had suggested over breakfast that they might wrap the paintings in corrugated cardboard for me. They are small works; a bit of confusion, some coming and going, they might have got away with it. They certainly would not have had time to effect reframing,' mused Edward.

'If you look at the smallest of the paintings, you will notice that on the back the framer's label is upside-down, in relation to the picture. The frame on the smallest picture in the car had the same error!'

'When a framer works on a group of frames he will make identical ones together, in order to save the necessity to adjust the measurements on his machines. And he would glue his labels at the same time.'

'True,' admitted Thadeus

'And you have overlooked the most obvious explanation; the vendor of the paintings might have requested copies to be made to replace the ones that he was selling. Not unusual at all!'

'True. No harm done then, except that the back of your frames are red,' admitted Thadeus, again.

'Of course I know who the vendor is. I could check with him,' Edward was musing to himself again. 'The Matthews could say that they thought it would be a good idea to make copies for the vendor anyway, even if he did not request them!'

Thadeus crept out of the room leaving his brother lighting a large cigar.

Neither the three Cézannes nor the two Matthews were ever mentioned again.

CHAPTER 9

A NEW YEAR

New Year's Eve was a Thursday and it was agreed that Burke & Co would cease business at a 4.30 in the afternoon and be closed all the next day.

A bottle of champagne was shared within the office and Thadeus had a chat with all the members of the staff, outlining his plans for the new year ahead and the role of the individuals within those proposals. A new shorthand typist would be taken on in order that Ethel Henson could move smoothly across to a more active participation with the personal accident account, and Beth Bateman could be relieved of all general typing duties. A junior general helper would be sought – a youngster straight from school – who could run messages, make tea and deal with menial tasks; everybody looked forward to his, or her, arrival. Salary changes were revealed; a nominal increase for Miss Mills and Mr Emery, who had not been with the company long, a good smile-raising improvement for Ethel and Beth, and a substantial advance for a very grateful and much deserving James Pooley.

Banter was exchanged regarding the anticipated celebrations for that evening, involving much giggling from the two young girls and sober pronouncements from the two elder member of the group. James was set for a family party and Thadeus was to attend something organized by his sister.

That evening Ethel Henson was at the house of an old school chum who was blessed with hundreds of brothers, sisters and cousins, most of whom played ukuleles or the piano. It was better than a trip to the music hall.

Elizabeth Bateman was at her mum's with a new boyfriend who spent most of the night trying to drag the girl into an unoccupied bedroom. At midnight her new year's resolution was to get rid of him. Miss Mills was joined by a spinster neighbour and they listened to the wireless with a bottle of sherry.

Mr Emery ate at a local restaurant, strolled home, stopping at a pub for a packet of twenty Players White Label for eleven pence and two bottles of beer for a shilling. At home he sat in his large armchair and quietly consumed his new purchases, rising at intervals to change the gramophone records as they proceeded through the whole of Sibelius's Second Symphony. He did not notice the time when he went to bed.

James Pooley's evening was also mostly musical provided by a series of Mrs 'Poolies', his grandmother, his mother, the wives of his father's brother and his cousin, the monopoly broken only by his unmarried not-quite-Pooley fiancée.

An uproarious knees-up welcomed the first of January.

In a house at Gordon Square, Bloomsbury, two ladies were seated for dinner, Mrs Alexandra Canham and Lady Gwendolyn Kirkling, waited upon by a maid, Miss Roselyn Matcham.

'I thought that we were to have finger buffet?' queried Lady Gwendolyn.

'Later darling,' smiled her companion and they both laughed coarsely.

'Rosie would you mind taking off all your clothes; just leave on your cap and stockings,' Lady G instructed the maid.

'Certainly madam.' The young girl slowly disrobed in front of the fire, retaining only the two requested items.

'Alex looks a little flushed Rosie, why don't you remove her knickers?' suggest an excited Lady G.

'Certainly madam, a very good idea,' said the girl, and Mrs C stood up and moved to the hearth rug. Rosie knelt and disappeared under the full skirt of Alex's dress, one hand reappearing and delicately dropping a pair of frilly panties onto the floor. The girl remained beneath the garment for several minutes, during which time Mrs Canham's breathing rate increased and a glow spread across her face. Lady Gwendolyn lay back in her chair and pleasured herself with her fingers, thinking what a wonderful evening it was to be.

'The Honourable Thadeus Burke and Lady Frederica Burke,' was announced as the pair entered the ballroom at Clifford House.

'We sound like a married couple,' commented Thadeus

'That is the idea. It was my instructions. This place is full of lesbians, I do not want female hands all over me tonight!' smiled Freddie taking a glass of Champagne from the proffered tray. This ploy was very effective, for Lady Burke found herself surrounded by older gossiping women and the Honourable Thadeus was spurned by every attractive lady he approached. At midnight they partook of the traditional sensual kissing – together. Between times Thadeus had engaged in heated debates on the subjects of the future of Europe, the Jewish problem and the delights of New York. Freddie had imbibed several bottles of champagne, had her bottom fondled by an ugly, artificially blonde-haired woman and diagnosed diabetes in four fat friends of the hostess. One young lady had decided that midnight was an ideal time to take off all her clothes, only to find herself at the centre of a pitched battle between the separate genders of her audience. Thadeus had been obliged to step in and rescue the poor creature. She thanked him enthusiastically and intended to hand him one of her visiting cards, but could not find one about her person! Freddie was not amused by the incident and indicated that in her opinion it was time for them to leave the party.

The Burke siblings were very pleased to find the faithful Hilton outside the house in the Bentley at 12.30 precisely, which was the exact time that the London fire brigade received a telephone call to attend a conflagration at a house in Gordon Square, Bloomsbury.

Friday 1 January 1926 having been declared a private holiday by Burke & Co, all the revellers indulged in a much-needed recuperation period. Freddie spent most of the day passing water through her body in an attempt to flush out a self-diagnosed case of champagne poisoning. Hilton was occupied with recovering her various possessions and garments from the car, the kitchen, up the stairs, in the bathroom and the bedroom floor. Thadeus attempted to play 'the blues' on his cello, without much success. Numerous telephone calls inviting the pair to attend horserace meetings were rebuffed.

Over the weekend, in more sober mood, it was decided that the pair of young nurses living at No. 9 Sloane Mews would move along the row into No. 3 Sloane Mews. The women were not lesbians, several young men having been observed entering and leaving the dwelling at various times during the late evening, and during the night. No. 3 suited the female colleagues admirably as it had been recently renovated, including a new kitchen and bathroom, both equipped with the very latest gadgets; an unchanged rent was an added bonus. This left No. 9 unoccupied ready for a similar renovation in preparation for the tenancy of Miss Freddie, except that she had decided to forgo the pleasures of a new kitchen, preferring instead an ample garage space for her anticipated new Bugatti. A doorway was to be installed into the upper hallway wall gaining her access to her brother's residence next door, and use of his kitchen facilities – which included Hilton! It was agreed that the presence of a resident doctor on the premises was more than adequate to compensate the loss of rental income. Thadeus absorbed all these indulgences with good grace.

It was late on Monday morning that Inspector Jackson informed Thadeus that Mrs Alexandra Canham, aged thirty-six, was a divorcee, the daughter of a wealthy mine-owner in Yorkshire who had settled a substantial sum of money on her at the time of her marriage to a Mr Arthur Canham. He had left the matrimonial home within six months and gone to live in Italy, the couple had been divorced two years later. In view of the lady's sexual preferences it was probable that the marriage was a device to obtain her inheritance.

Lady Gwendolyn Kirkling, aged thirty-three, was from an old aristocratic family in Suffolk; her elder brother had sold the family estates and gambled away the proceeds before being killed in the first year of the War. Lady Gwendolyn had already succeeded in marrying a rich American, from Chicago; he had died in a boating accident in Devon within twelve months. The boat capsized, she swam ashore, he did not! Suspicious of course, but no evidence of foul play.

Miss Roselyn Matcham, aged twenty-two, lived in rented accommodation in Pimlico and worked as a private maid and companion to a Lady Margaret Kemp of No. 49 Chelsea Gardens, who was killed in a motor accident about a month ago. Lady Kemp had provided a glowing reference for the girl's landlady, who stated that she had never seen much of the girl, spent most of her time away;

paid her rent promptly in advance, always dressed well and drove a small motor car.

All this information was delivered from three sheets of typed notes; there were several more sheets, the contents of which were not revealed. As there were two proper titled ladies involved Jackson was consulting Thadeus, whom he now regarded as his undercover agent in the aristocratic world, a sort of plain-clothed Black Rod.

Without Lady Kirkling's family name his man could be of no help but Lady Kemp rang a bell somewhere in the back of his memory. Thadeus thought that she was the one that drove racing cars, outrageously flamboyant, dressed like a man and wore a monocle. 'I can check that,' suggested Jackson, blowing his nose for the third time that morning, 'if she died in a motor race not too long ago.' They would both check the facts; James Pooley would know something about her, though perhaps only the cubic capacity of her car.

'Are you going to tell me the rest of the story?' pushed Thadeus

'Beer and shepherd's pie in the Lamb,' suggested Jackson.

Before departing the office James had given them a thumbnail sketch of Lady Kemp, better known to James and the motor racing fraternity as 'Mad Maggie', including the information that she was killed outright when her accelerating Fiat was impeded by the bridge at Tours, in France, during an overtaking attempt, in November. He was of the opinion that a police enquiry would have been difficult as Maggie and her Fiat were spread about two hundred yards down the track, a revelation that brought gasps of horror and disgust from the eavesdropping office employees. Jackson made notes of the incident, and the relevant magazine references, in an efficient manner. James was puzzled by a question on the lady's sexual life, seeing no relevance to the enquiry at all; neither did he have any suggestions on a source for any such facts.

Perched on stools facing the Leadenhall market the remarkable tale of the Bloomsbury New Year's Eve fire was recounted by a sweating Jackson, constantly moping his brow and complaining about the heat. At 12.30 that night the police received an anonymous telephone call 'those lesbian bitches are frying in hell' was all it said. An hour later police efficiency linked the note of the call with the circumstances of the fire. The cause of the fire could be suspicious and was currently being investigated by specialist officers, but it was the scene at the not-badly damaged building that had sent ripples of gossip and innuendo around the police stations. The ground floor of the house was an artist's studio with a high ceiling and a balcony. The room, which had suffered only smoke damage, contained a refractory table spread with the refuge of a meal, and the floor was spread with various lady's clothes and undergarments. At the back was a kitchen, badly burned, and above this was a small bedroom containing a large bed with three dead female occupants laying side by side, all naked, with the middle one, who was later identified as Roselyn Matcham, facing the 'wrong' way. Jackson paused at this point in the story for effect; Thadeus did not respond, so he continued. The bed also contained what has been described as 'sex toys' and the wardrobe, which filled most of the rest of the room, was full of theatrical gear, predominately for schoolgirls. Thadeus again did not respond to Jackson's glance. The three unfortunate women had died of, according to the diagnosis/guesswork of the attending police surgeon, carbon monoxide poisoning resulting from ruptured gas pipes below, and/or smoke. This was still a grey area; full post mortem reports were not yet available.

House-to-house enquiries had revealed a woman who lived in the road behind Gordon Square was responsible for the telephone call; a police officer who took the opportunity to walk up to the top floor of her house found a telescope set up to view the back bedroom opposite, apparently used by her husband, a man with a keen interest in lesbian activities. The emergency call had been duplicated, not in the same words, by the residents next door who were holding a New Year's Eve party and just after midnight were cavorting in a processional dance routine that required entrance to the garden from the back kitchen door and re-entrance to the house through the French windows, and vice versa. During one of these manoeuvres a red glow was observed in their neighbour's ground floor, resulting in speedy fire-fighting efforts by the younger male members of the gathering, thence the minimal damage incurred and the preservation of the bedroom evidence.

'And numerous witness statements,' suggested Thadeus.

'Indeed!' confirmed Jackson. 'I have copies of several with me in this folder. I thought that you may be interested in glancing through them?'

The inspector knew that his friend would be enthusiastic to study the papers and assist with the investigation, a habit that was beginning to annoy his colleagues back at Scotland Yard.

'I will need to peruse these during the evening, as I must work in the Room this afternoon. Is that all right?' said Thadeus reaching out for the folder eagerly, assuming his question as rhetorical, adding, 'Do you know if the ladies left any wills or bequests, and do you know who were the beneficiaries?'

'There are notes within the papers,' said Jackson smugly.

Thadeus received the same reply to his questions about fire brigade activity, names and addresses and next of kin. They vacated the public house and returned to their allotted places of employment, where Thadeus prepared for a trip to Lloyds, and Jackson informed his sergeant that he did not feel well and intended to go home to bed.

One of Thadeus' first visits of the afternoon was to the Mannings box for a conversation with Charlie Norman, whom he found sitting quietly staring into space.

'Mr Burke, how nice to see you again; how is your personal accident account proceeding?' said Charlie springing to life.

'Slowly, but with promise,' was Thadeus' cautious reply, then changing the subject completely, 'I was interest in finding out some more information about the list of horses that Percy Dennington had recorded, particularly the ones written down at the box.'

'I cannot add anything to what I have already told you,' confessed Charlie.

'I know that you underwrite a Quota Share Treaty for bloodstock from the Thurlow syndicate, and I was wondering exactly what other business you underwrote,' quizzed Thadeus.

'What makes you think that we write a Quota Share of Thurlow? Or perhaps I should say how did you know that we write that?' retorted a suspicious Charlie Norman.

'It is not a secret,' emphasized Thadeus. 'When a bloodstock risk was shown at this box, Percy always asked the broker if Thurlow was writing an additional line as he needed to be careful that he was not over-lined.'

'True but I cannot give you specific information about risks that do not concern you – not without the approval of Mr Mannings.'

'I would not dream of compromising you,' assured Thadeus to a dubious Charlie. 'I would appreciate just a broad outline of the account, in the widest terms, then if I require more specific details I will certainly approach Mr Mannings.'

Mr Norman co-operated. 'Well, we write business to you, both from when you were with Crawford & Amos and now at Burke & Co; you will have full details of those risks.'

'True,' thought Thadeus 'but completely unhelpful!'

Fortunately Charlie Norman continued his assistance. 'Then there was, and still is, the occasional risk that we write 100 percent, or lead with a decent line: these are usually small risks, low values, a hunter for example; often they are for friends of the boss. Then there are the big market placings, Derby or St Leger winners, which require the support of several underwriters, where we write a modest line. Percy would always make a note of these.'

'Do you get separate advises of the Thurlow underwriting? A bordereau of premium and claims for example?' pressed Thadeus.

'Yes, a monthly bordereau, but I cannot show you that file,' emphasized Charlie.

Thadeus continued. 'That's the lot? You do not underwrite any other reinsurance?'

'No,' said Charlie, showing signs of annoyance at this interrogation.

'Right. I am very grateful for your assistance,' said Thadeus. 'Ethel sends her regards,' he added, bringing a smile back to Charlie's face.

Thadeus excused himself to respond to a call from the rostrum and went off to meet James Pooley and discuss their planned broking for the afternoon, noting intended visits to underwriters, and swapping slips accordingly. A serious conversation with Mr Edward Mannings would have to wait until another day.

In the evening, after a modest dinner without any alcoholic drinks, Thadeus retired to his study to peruse Jackson's papers. Re-reading the portrayals of the victims and making notes; reading the witness statements, setting aside those considered relevant, then re-reading that group and making notes. Finally he studied the autopsy report and the fire officer's report; then he listed a series of questions that needed answers. The 'victims' notes showed the names and addresses of the three ladies and the beneficiaries following their deaths. Mrs Alexandra Canham had left a will bequeathing insignificant amounts to friends, including her partners on the fatal night, and the residue of her estate, estimated to be a considerable sum, to her younger sister, a Miss Delores Chapman, who was engaged on a cinematograph career in California.

Lady Gwendolyn Kirkling had left no will but, according to her solicitor, had been content for her possessions to pass to her natural next of kin, her twenty-five-year-old sister Lady Victoria Cardwell, currently residing in Suffolk.

Miss Roselyn Matcham was the most interesting. Documents found at her flat indicated that she was also now the owner of 49 Chelsea Gardens, home of the deceased Lady Kemp; a visit to these premises revealed that Miss Matcham was a very wealthy woman, sole beneficiary to the estate of her late mistress. There were indications that she was in the process of drawing up a will, the draft papers showing percentages divided among her female friends. In the absence of any signed document the whole of her estate passed to an elder brother, a Mr Joseph Matcham with an address in Streatham, South London.

At this juncture Thadeus had taken coffee and allowed his sister to look over the scribblings; she announced in an aloof tone that Thadeus knew Lady Victoria Cardwell, having cavorted naked with her very early on the previous Friday morning.

'So your intervention saved me from a bout of illicit sex, and access to a large fortune?' suggested Thadeus.

'No brother dear, she is engaged to a captain in the army. I saved you from embarrassing yourself, both in bed and later in hospital.' She swallowed the last mouthful of coffee, and wriggled her little finger at him in contempt. 'I do think that it would have been better mannered of you to ask the name of the lady before stripping her naked, dragging her down on the ground and rolling around on the floor with her!'

Thadeus' protest was drowned by his sister's laughter. Thadeus next tried to draft a synopsis of the events in the neighbour's garden derived from the witness statements. The host and hostess had been a retired colonel and his good wife; most of the guests were adorned with title, rank and decorations: Thadeus unceremoniously reduced the lot to letters of the alphabet, marking the top of the statements with A B C, etcetera and using these abbreviations for his synopsis, which read thus: 'A' noticed that the kitchen next door was on fire. These simple words précised numerous descriptions of 'red glows', 'flames', 'sparks' and a thesaurus full of other similar nouns. 'B' immediately leapt over the wall and entered through the unlocked kitchen door. 'C' 'D' and 'E' joined him via a garden ladder. 'F' and 'G' joined them later. The fire was only against one wall, consisting of cupboards. The team had thrown water over the conflagration from buckets and saucepans, until 'C' found a length of hosepipe, which he attached to a water-tap and succeeded in dowsing the flames. The fire brigade arrived, having already turned off the domestic gas supply at the mains for the whole street as soon as the fire was reported, unnecessarily broke down the front door, dragged huge hosepipes through the house damaging several valuable antique pieces of furniture, and saturated all the ground floor and most of the upper floors with water; ensuing a massive insurance claim for some poor Lloyd's underwriter. 'B' 'C' 'E' and 'F' went off to hospital for treatment of minor burns and smoke inhalation. 'D' and 'G' went straight home to clean up. Only 'B' came back to the house later that night. The post mortem had exposed the cause of death as carbon monoxide poisoning, assisted by the fact that the bodies of all three victims revealed substantial quantities of alcohol and barbiturates; Mrs Canham had a prescription for these drugs. The fire officer's report included the discovery of a fractured gas supply pipe near the stove, behind a cupboard.

Having re-read these notes several times Thadeus sought the assistance of Freddie on the symptoms of carbon monoxide poisoning. Her answer was precise: headache, fatigue, shortness of breath, nausea and dizziness. She added that these were also the exact same symptoms as a night of lesbian orgiastic cavorting. When questioned on her source of this extra enlightenment, she just poked her tongue out at him.

'So following a heavy dose of carbon monoxide these ladies would just have fallen asleep?' he asked.

'Yes, followed by coma and death!' was the medical opinion.

'So, why a fire? And what sort of arsonist would ignite a room containing a broken gas pipe, and beneath a room full of gas – it would explode like a bomb!'

Hilton, who had joined the confab, spoke. 'If I might suggest, sir, if we call the poisoner 'X' and the arsonist 'Y', then either X and Y are two different persons, or X performed the poisoning earlier in the evening and returned later for the fire.'

'What about the fractured gas pipe?' queried Thadeus.

'That must have been carried out after the fire brigade had disconnected the supply,' stated Hilton.

'Exactly, and probably after the fire had been extinguished: X and Y are two people; and X must have attended the party and been involved in the fire-fighting escapade. Y is an unknown.'

'Y could be one of the fire-fighting latecomers, and one of those that left to clean up, and escape. G is your arsonist!' pronounced Freddie.

'And B is the poisoner; he acted fastest, knowing that there was a good chance of the place exploding; went to hospital as was expected of him, and returned later to check any repercussions.'

'Another problem solved. Shall we arrange for a hanging tonight, or wait until the morning?' said Freddie, 'Can you reveal the actual names of B and G, or should they now be reclassified as XB and YG?'

The group laughed and Thadeus fumbled through the papers, which were now spread in different parts of the room.

'XB can be exposed as Captain Gerald Carstairs, aged thirty, with an address at Peasenhall, in Suffolk. YG is listed as a Mr John Marks, also aged thirty, with an abode in East Dulwich.'

The room was tidied, papers return to order and cocoa served in large mugs, after which they all retired to bed.

Next morning Thadeus telephoned Johnny Jackson at his office, to be told that the inspector was away, sick with influenza, a sudden affliction. Thadeus telephoned his home and spoke to the ailing policeman, who coughed and grunted that he would prefer to be left alone to die in peace; anyway it was not his case, the matter was being handled by an Inspector George Harding, of the Metropolitan Police, West End Branch. Thadeus telephoned Inspector Harding and reccived a very cool reception.

The incident was being regarded as 'accidental death by gas poisoning', Thadeus was informed by Harding, who also enquired as to what the hell it had to do with him.

Thadeus, using his best broking ability managed to solicit answers to two questions from the unhelpful man. There was no reason whatsoever to suspect Captain Gerald Carstairs, who was a friend of the family, being in the same regiment as the colonel's son, as were several other guests at the party and yes, there was a problem with Mr John Marks as he could not be traced to the given address in East Dulwich but if he was involved in the fire it had nothing to do with the death of the three women. It was a separate matter being pursued by the South London Constabulary.

Thadeus suggested, in the mildest possible manner, that it may be rewarding to interview a Mr Joseph Matcham at an address in Streatham, South London; and possibly arrange for the police officer who had taken the name and address of Mr Marks on the pavement outside the house in Bloomsbury, to be present at the same time. This advice was acknowledged without enthusiasm.

Thadeus and the Burke & Company team spent a busy day catching up on incoming post, delayed by the Christmas and New Year breaks. A row of tenanted thatched cottages in Devon, and cash in transit between shops and banks in Liverpool, deprived Thadeus and James Pooley of their lunch-time meals; pleading their case in the Lloyd's Underwriting Room until it closed at 4.30 pm. Over tea and toasted teacakes they counted up the lines, 96 per cent on the fire and perils risk in Devon, and only 85 per cent on the cash in Liverpool; they decided to trudge around the fringe company market first thing next morning. Returning to the office Thadeus found that, following telephone instructions from his sister, a pound and a half of scallops, with shells, had been purchased on his behalf in Leadenhall Market, by Miss Mills and placed outside on the window-sill of his office to keep cold; they were to be part of his evening meal.

Back at Sloane Mews an exhausted insurance broker was greeted by a large gin and tonic and the news that his sister, assisted by Hilton, had prepared a dinner from a French recipe using garlic, olive oil, onions and tomatoes, and a pound and a half of scallops, with shells. Indications from empty bottles in the kitchen showed that white wine and vermouth were also involved. Four bottles of Pouilly-Fuissé sat in the wine cooler awaiting the corkscrew. Retiring for a shower he found his full black tie regalia laid out ready for his correct appearance at the dinner table.

'It's your man Watson on the telephone.' It was Freddie calling up the stairs.

'Prescribe something for his influenza; I'll be down in a minute.'

Thadeus finished towelling, donned a dressing gown and descended to take the telephone instrument out of the hand of his sister as she was about to launch an exposition of dietary needs for the modern policeman.

'You are back on your feet?' assumed Thadeus

'No, I have just been woken up by that bloody Harding; he does not speak to anybody below the rank of sergeant and only then if they are in uniform.'

'Your sense of humour has returned at least,' mused Thadeus.

'I'm dosed up with pills and powders, most of which your sister tells me are useless. Stay in bed and sweat it out is her advice; you don't think that she...?'

'No I do not,' interrupted Thadeus to Jackson's obvious lewd interpretation of Freddie's recommendations. 'I suggest you tell me whatever it is you phoned about before you run out of breath.'

'That man Matcham from Streatham was the man pretending to be Marks from East Dulwich. His tale is that he went to Gordon Square, Bloomsbury to see his sister, wanted to borrow some money, realized that she was upstairs being naughty with her friends, went into the kitchen, the door of which was unlocked, hung around and smoked half a packet of cigarettes, suddenly found that a kitchen cupboard was sprouting flames and that the neighbours were pouring in, hid in the downstairs toilet, then crept out under the cover of smoke, joined the fire fighting and then made his escape; sorry about the false name, etcetera – panicked.'

'And Harding believes this story?'

'It more or less tallies with the facts, except that he left out reference to his intention to burn down the house with his sister in it!'

'Yes, a very lucky man; innocent and rich! Did he have any observations that might assist with the poisoning enquiry?'

'Harding is a man of few words, as you know. When I get back I will speak to the team that interviewed him.'

'Thanks, Johnny. Times are also important, when did he get there, did he wait in the garden, did he see anybody else go into the kitchen? Ring me when you are up and about.'

They said goodbye and Thadeus scooted upstairs to change as Hilton hit the gong. A dinner gong was not really necessary in a mews house but Hilton regarded it as an essential accoutrement to his trade. Melon with ground ginger, coquilles St Jacques à la Provençale, cheese and Port, and one bottle of Pouilly-Fuissé left over; Thadeus could not think of a better way to end a very satisfactory day.

Wednesday morning James Pooley completed the previous day's unfinished broking with a collection of small, but sound and respectable companies.

Thadeus considered his plans for a trip to Peasenhall then telephoned Sergeant Anderson, attached to Suffolk police and of great assistance in a Sopwith, and at Newmarket and Bungay, and about to become an accomplice in Peasenhall.

David Anderson asked several questions and received several unsatisfactory answers, resulting in his full agreement to co-operate. He could rustle up a posse of police constables, including WPCs if necessary, but he was adamant that a period of surveillance was required before any action could be anticipated. He would arrange for a plain-clothes team to get down there this afternoon, two men and one woman, with substitutes waiting to be brought on for variety; it would be good practice for them – all night if need be! He would telephone Thadeus, at the office or at his home, when there was some news. Thadeus felt frustrated by this intelligent strategy, a mental impairment that coloured the rest of his day. He had intended to visit Mr Mannings to seek out information about the Thurlow bloodstock treaty, but he was not in the appropriate state for such a delicate conversation; instead he made a nuisance of himself in the office, questioning Mr Emery and Miss Mills on matters of procedure, reading Beth Bateman's claims register and reorganizing her filing system. They were all pleased to see him take James out for lunch, hoping it would be a long one. The two men strolled along Cornhill, up Cheapside, down Bow Lane and into Sweetings for a plate of fish, haddock for James and skate for Thadeus, they both declined white wine and drank Guinness. James was interrogated on home life and his wedding plans. He and Eddie were in the process of buying a detached house in Nunhead, with a garage and a garden. He still had his motorcycle but the new car would arrive next month. His father's business was flourishing; he now had another engineer working for him. Thadeus' enforced participation in the verbal exchange consisted exclusively of questions about his sister's new Bugatti, which had not been built yet, it was an entirely new model and would probably not be on the road for two months at the earliest; Mr Hollington had it all in hand.

They talked a bit of Burke & Co insurance business, then Thadeus announced that he would take a taxi home, he had not brought the Bentley in that day; perhaps he was suffering from influenza, infected by Jackson.

James headed for the office and Thadeus, equipped with an early edition of the *Evening News* boarded a cab for Chelsea. Upon his arrival home he was put to bed, accompanied by three hot-water bottles, and buried beneath a mountainous layer of blankets. Freddie went to the kitchen to prepare a reviving concoction, involving Irish whisky, hot water, lemon, sugar and cloves, a mixture that she had not learnt in Edinburgh, but on Naas racecourse in Ireland during a visit in the days when Thadeus was at Trinity College Dublin.

The patient was fast asleep when Anderson rang and spoke to his sister.

At 2.00 am Thadeus awoke to find himself laying in cold, damp bedclothes and in need of another shot of the Irish remedy, so he arose and cloaked his body in a heavy cashmere dressing gown and crept downstairs to the kitchen. As he waited for the kettle to boil he heard the front door open and several different footsteps ascend the staircase and enter the drawing room. He switched off the electric light, turned off the kettle, stealthily followed the intruders to the upper floor and swung open the door.

'What are you doing out of bed,' demanded his personal medical consultant in an admonishing tone.

Through bleary eyes he could make out four images; his sister, Hilton, David Anderson and a young brunette WPC in uniform, but for her hat. 'What's going on?' he croaked pathetically.

'We have been over to Peasenhall, clearing up your unfinished mystery,' said Freddie casually.

Had Thadeus been fitter he would have exploded, 'Why has my sister been allowed to partake of a police raid!', 'Why did Hilton not stop such an ill-advised venture!', 'What was this maniac Anderson doing involving civilians in his police work?' and 'The appearance of a WPC shows that there was danger to a female of the species!' the thoughts returned to the 'Why was my sister…?' question, and the cycling and recycling thoughts made his head ache; he sat down and was silent.

Hilton appeared with a refreshed Irish remedy which Thadeus sipped while Freddie dramatized the evening's events.

'This is Lily, a good friend of David's, who packs a punch that could finish 'Bombardier' Billy Wells,' she introduced the WPC and Thadeus' eyes were screwed up at the revelation of her talents that compared favourably with the British and Empire heavyweight boxing champion.

'David phoned at about seven o'clock for you, but I told him that you could not be disturbed under any conditions, strict doctor's orders! The surveillance team had reported the arrival at Captain Gerald Carstairs' house of another army man, a major in the Guards, full uniform, red jacket and sword, the lot. He drove up in a small Austin and unloaded several baskets of provisions, bread, vegetables and fruit, etcetera, and a case of wine. The team reported that he was a known "ginger beer".'

Freddie paused at this point to explain to Thadeus that the term 'ginger beer' is apparently a cockney rhyming slang expression denoting 'homosexual'. She assumed that the cockneys must have used James Joyce for their compilation.

'The "ginger" major left but returned an hour later in a Bentley, together with another army officer, a captain this time, and a very smartly dressed lady.'

She interjected, 'This was the point when David phoned me.'

Thadeus was about to say something but she continued unabatable.

'Hilton and I leaped into the Bentley, our Bentley in the garage below, and headed at breakneck speed for the Suffolk Road and Peasenhall, I navigated. By 9.30 we were parked outside a grocers, in the high street, actually there is only one street in the village, opposite the "Target House"' – she emphasized this new technical idiom – 'which was on the other side of the river. David and Lily were in an Austin just in front of us, that is why we parked there.' She paused to take a sip from the Hilton-prepared large mug of cocoa and made a face at the bland tasting liquid, inappropriate to the startling adventure tale that she was telling. Champagne or one of those exotic American cocktails, would have been more apposite.

'Lady Victoria Cardwell, that was the identity of the lady, came out of the house at 10.15 precisely; Lily put it in her notebook. I sprang from the car, ignoring all protests from Hilton and the police, was across the bridge and facing Lady Vic in a matter of seconds.'

She paused and requested something stronger than cocoa from Hilton, who was now looking slightly shamefaced and eager to leave the room. She grabbed Thadeus' warmish whisky and took a large swig.

'"Hello", I said, "I almost did not recognize you with your clothes on!" A quotation from a music hall turn, but effective, she almost fainted on the spot, dropped the pair of shoes that she was carrying from her car and screamed in panic. All hell broke loose, the army poured out of the front door of the house and police officers, plain clothed and uniformed, local and special, male and female metamorphosed from every direction of the Peasenhall landscape.' Another pause for a substantial swig from the newly served hot toddy.

'It was all over within fifteen minutes,' she concluded and resumed her seat in silence.

'All over? What about Billy Wells and the resolution of the poisoning mystery?' Thadeus was feeling a lot better.

'Lily followed me across the bridge and when one of these captain fellows grabbed me, she hit him, first on the nose with her left and then with the other fist in the solar plexus. He folded up and rolled into the roadway.'

There was much chortling at this description, everybody became animated as the scene was re-enacted, as a mime for Thadeus' benefit.

'And then?' prompted the ailing one-man audience.

David Anderson took up the story. 'Lily took Freddie out of range…'

'Not far, I could still hear what was going on, and could have been back in the battle at a moment's notice,' protested Freddie.

'The major came out with his hands above his head in surrender mode, waving a white handkerchief, protesting his innocence and demanding that he be allowed to tell all. The Suffolk police have got his statement, but briefly Captain Angus Cain, that was the chap who attacked your sister and was floored by Lily, persuaded his old friend and billet mate, Captain Gerald Carstairs, to poison his fiancée's sister for a fee of £2,000. Angus and Victoria knew the layout of the place in Gordon Square and when they found out that Gerald was attending a party in the next house, a plot was hatched and they gave him a good briefing. Gerald kept an eye on the next door bedroom lights; when he assumed that the ladies were otherwise occupied he popped into the kitchen, crossing the wall at the bottom of the garden, used a piece of hose-pipe to link the gas stove tap to a knot-hole in the upstairs flooring, and slipped back to the party. Imagine his surprise to find a fire in the kitchen before he had time to dismantle his device, he shot over the wall, turned off the tap and removed the pipe, then stoked up the fire with a cane chair and waited for the cavalry.'

'The whole place, and the house next door, could have exploded like a bomb?' questioned Thadeus.

'Yes, apparently Gerald Carstairs is not over-bright, according to the Major, but he does drive a long, straight golf ball.'

Lily had kindly agreed to accommodate David Anderson for the night, or what was left of it, at her flat in Camberwell.

A long way from Suffolk thought Thadeus, but repercussions arising from the evening events were beyond his ability at that time; he would reappraise the situation in the morning.

CHAPTER 10

A FAREWELL CONCERT

It was not until Monday 18th January 1926 that Thadeus returned to his office in the city, having spent a whole week in bed sweltering under blankets, the heat suspended for short periods when Hilton propped him up in a chair while he changed the bedclothes. Freddie had raided the local pharmacist down the King's Road and scheduled a diet of pills and potions for various times of the day. Despite all these efforts the influenza took its course and the body recovered, improved by the rest and revitalized from the victory over the parasite invaders. The weekend prior to his reappearance at Burke & Co had been highlighted by vigorous performances, both at the piano and with the cello. Freddie's flute embouchure and Hilton's singing throat were severely tested.

It was therefore in sprightly mood that his first act after arrival at his desk was to telephone Mr Edward Mannings to seek a private audience with the great man: a dubious secretary was no match for a refreshed and invigorated Honourable Thadeus Burke and 11.15 am that very day was entered into the diaries.

While laying abed the batch of five fictitious horses had circulated around Thadeus' head, his attention flitted from one memorized pedigree to another, until his head ached and he either fell asleep or deliberately directed his attention outwards to clear his mind. In these quieter moments the quandary settled into clear patterns; all the horses were well-related, brother or sisters, or half-brothers or half-sisters, to valuable horses, so also, theoretically, valuable; carefully constructed; it was easy to make up a pedigree of a horse, but using actual sires and dams, it was necessary to ensure that the invented horse did not actually exist already; research needed. The only possible reason for arranging insurance for a fabricated horse was to make a false claim, no point in paying premium for something that did not exist unless there would be a profitable result! He needed to look at the Mannings syndicate claims records.

At his desk he studied personal incoming mail. Miss Mills had, following his instructions, opened the envelopes and taken out non-personal items for action in the office, leaving only three, apart from get-well messages, remaining for his attention. There was a reminder that a service was due on the Bentley, papers to be signed relating to the new Lloyd's underwriting year, and an invitation to a concert to be held at the Guildhall that Friday. He dealt with the last first; Haydn would be an ideal send-off for Freddie who was returning to Edinburgh at the weekend, two quick telephone calls and a cheque in the post resolved that. Next he signed all the Lloyd's documents, wondering what they were all about, but confident that Mr Wren, his Lloyd's agent, would have contacted him if anything were amiss. Then he booked a table for late Friday evening at a French restaurant near Covent Garden for an après-concert dinner with his sister. The Bentley could wait until his diary for the week had been finalized.

A business session with James Pooley followed by similar with Beth Bateman and it was 11.00 am and time to walk round to Mr Mannings' office, straight across Gracechurch Street, through Leadenhall Market into Lime Street, a very handy location for access to the new Lloyd's building. The recent fall of snow had melted in the city, warmed by the many basements.

Thadeus was early, which was opportune as Mr Mannings' 11.00 am appointment had cancelled, and he was able to walk straight into his office.

Thadeus closed the door and took the proffered chair and they exchanged pleasantries about the weather, which was still extremely bad, heavy rain and floods, racing at Hurst Park had been cancelled, newspapers reported that the Thames had risen six inches; and health was discussed, the bout of influenza cases that were inflicting the City of London in particular.

'Why have you come to see me?' questioned Mr Mannings suddenly and bluntly.

'I would appreciate being permitted to look through your claims records for the past twelve months or so, bloodstock in particular,' was Thadeus' equally blunt reply.

'I assume that as you have approached me, it is not me that you intend to have arrested?' The underwriter was already moving forward quickly.

'It concerns some papers left by Sir Percy Dennington.'

'So you do not want anybody else on the syndicate to know of this investigation?'

'Preferably not!'

Mannings placed his hands in a prayer position, resting his chin on the extended thumbs; paused in thought for a full minute and then spoke in deliberate, precise sentences. 'I want to know of any action that you intend to take that may affect this syndicate, or me, before it happens. I have just completed my reinsurance arrangements for the new underwriting year and am frankly, not very happy with them. I shall appoint you as a new reinsurance consultant to review the 1926 programme, and analyse our results, premium and claims. That should give you a clear run; I will write to you, you can come into the office next Monday.' He stood up.

There was nothing more to say except, 'Thank you Mr Mannings', returned by a handshake, accompanied by a simple 'Thadeus.' The interview was concluded.

The next day the promised letter arrived, marked 'Strictly Private and Confidential', two sheets, one a formal appointment as reinsurance consultant, the period and remuneration being yet to be finalized; the second a personal, hand-written note reiterating the need to be kept fully informed at every stage and assuring the recipient of the writer's allegiance to the memory of Sir Percy and his commitment to a satisfactory conclusion to his friend's untimely death. A postscript invited Thadeus to visit Mr and Mrs Mannings at their home in Buckinghamshire at some time in the near future. Thadeus hand-wrote a brief acknowledgement.

The week passed peacefully, as it should during January in a Lloyd's insurance broker's office, there were no dramas of missing documents, mis-filed papers, or forgotten telephone messages, spilt coffee cups or any of the usual accidents that arise when two paths of fate cross in the middle of a flourishing workplace.

The Friday evening concert had been selected for Freddie's final London occasion as the programme included the aptly named

'Farewell Symphony' No. 45 in F# Minor by Franz Joseph Haydn. Devised by the composer to awaken his employer, the Prince Nikolaus Esterhazy, to the plight of his musicians separated from their families for long intervals at Eisenstadt, a summer retreat of the prince. The final movement of the work allowed each instrumentalist to leave the platform upon completion of their written participation in the score and steal away from the concert hall. The performance by the City Orchestra that evening was to be a re-enactment of the first performance in which the composer led on first violin, including the use of candles to light each music stand, the flame to be extinguished as the post was vacated. Thadeus and Freddie knew the piece but had never seen it performed in such authenticity.

Thadeus left the office early in order to properly prepare for the event, frock coat and white tie with his best silver topped stick; his hat would accompany him but be left in the car, from which it might appear for dinner. Freddie wore an evening gown in daffodil yellow with flared skirt and embroidered with silver beads, lined throughout with Jap silk, accompanied by a matching close-fitting brimless cloche hat and gloves, and a pair of opera glasses; she looked stunning.

They took their seats and Freddie slipped her reading glasses from her bag and studied the programme sheet, where she found that the bassoon player, Kathleen Dandle, was known to her for they had shared the same music tutor some ten years previous. Pursuing different instruments, they had participated together in the study of music theory and accompanied each other to the Royal College of Music literacy examinations, until Freddie had quit at grade five; Kathleen continuing to the final grades in order to ensure her qualifications for a teaching profession, required by most musicians since the demise of Prince Nikolaus and his ilk. Freddie remembered that Kathleen was renowned for her numerous boyfriends, she was a particularly attractive girl, and other students chided her about her name being very suitable for the art of childrearing.

The first piece was a cello concerto, also by Haydn, in C major, a robust rendering including an ambitious cadenza. Thadeus applauded the soloist with enthusiasm, more for his courage than his technical ability. The stage was cleared and the piano brought forward for two of Mozart's violin sonatas, K305 and K377, so beautifully conceived that it was impossible to criticize anything but the acoustics, and the inability of one's own mind to attend silently to the sound.

Wine was served in an ante-room during the interval and Freddie sought out Kathleen Dandle from the group of musicians gathering at the far end of the chamber. Her friend was delighted to meet her old chum again after so many years and the two girls chatted excitedly about the direction that their lives had taken and the plans and ambitions of teenage years that had been abandoned.

His sister safely ensconced in happy memories, Thadeus chatted to various Lloyd's characters, underwriters and brokers of his acquaintance, noticed the Chairman of Lloyd's in light conversation with the Commissioner of the City of London Police, then decided to sneak out on to the steps to puff his pipe for a few minutes. The initial preparation of his lighting-up procedure resembled a bonfire! Passing through the concert hall he stopped to observe the stage being set up for the final piece of the evening. In order to create the dramatic effects required, the position of the instrumentalist was unusual; the orchestra was not large in number but the chairs and music stands had been set widely apart, using the full width and depth of the performance area and long candleholders placed beside most members.

The double bass was lying on the floor next to a very high music stand extended to its full height, using the very limits of its rods and ratchets, and a candle was clipped to the top; it all looked dangerously precarious. Thadeus thought that when the player appeared they would have the appearance of those two movie stars, Laurel and Hardy, with the lighted candle playing the part of the thin one's quiff of hair: they had a long solo passage tonight, deserving of a filming. The first and second violins, instead of sharing a stand side by side, were placed opposite each other, awaiting the final moments when their muted *pianissimo* would be the only remnants of sound in the crowded hall.

A group of early enthusiasts began shuffling along the rows and Thadeus turned back towards the ante-room, against the flow of people, to track down Freddie, who was now engaged in conversation with Charles Payne, the motor insurance underwriter, Kathleen having taken up her post on stage early in order to assemble her assortment of reeds. Thadeus interrupted a discussion on the merits of cheap insurance premium rates exclusively for the Bugatti motor vehicles. Rescuing a grateful Mr Payne he guided his sister into the concert hall.

They took their seats. The house lights, already dimmed, were turned off, leaving the assembled orchestra glowing in candle light. No conductor, the principle violinist drew prominently the first note of the *allegro assai* and the band roared into powerful rhythmic form. The second *adagio* movement in the dominant key of A major beautifully rendered with muted strings was followed by a charming minuet and trio in the key of F# major. Then the final *pièce de résistance* beginning with a lively *presto* back in the home key and a sudden drop in pace to the *adagio* in A major with an F# minor finale.

Kathleen's bassoon solo was rendered delightfully, an instrument accustomed to a supporting role stepping into the limelight with dominating confidence, Freddie could not restrain a loudly whispered 'bravo' as her friend departed the company. The last petals of the *adagio* fell away as the sound diminished through lack of instruments and adherence to the written dynamics. The final pair, the two principle violinists stood, bowed and blew out their candles. The audience exploded and rendered a standing, rapturous applause. The auditorium's electric lights went up. The stage was left in shadow as it was empty but for a clutter of musical paraphernalia. Only the first horn still sat there, very still, *senza* sound, *senza* candle-light, *senza* life; he was dead, stabbed through the neck with a long knitting needle.

The players trooped across the front of the stage under spotlights stepping forward to receive their individual acclaim, then a final bowing line, and the march off left.

Thadeus and Freddie hastened through their row, hoping to catch Kathleen before departing for their dinner date. They ignored the kerfuffle taking place at the back of the stage and went into the bar where the instrumentalists were either having a drink or saying their goodbyes. Kathleen was dressed in her outdoors coat and ready to go, having had plenty of time to disassemble, clean and pack her bassoon, reeds and various accoutrements in the period following her departure from the orchestra.

It was agreed that she should be invited to dinner with the Burke siblings and she accepted readily, begging that she be allowed to attend the mandatory orchestra debriefing with the leader. At that time she was engaged in a round of drinks with the two oboe playing gentlemen; Freddie scribbled a note of the restaurant address on a piece of paper and she and Thadeus left her to make her way by taxi.

'Do not be surprised if she turns up with a man – or maybe two,' warned Freddie as Thadeus opened the door for her to enter the waiting cab.

Kathleen was alone when she arrived at *chez Paul* forty-five minutes later and bubbling with news. Freddie sat quietly sipping her third gin and tonic, and Thadeus completed the bottle of *Chablis* that he was only tasting for acceptability half an hour ago. The newcomer ordered vodka with soda water and salted cucumber, a habit that she had picked up touring in France.

'France or Russia?' queried Thadeus.

'No definitely France, somewhere in the middle bit,' he was assured.

Kathleen took a long, lingering guzzle at her drink and exclaimed to an expectant audience of two, 'Sorry I'm a bit late, I was arrested for murder and needed to talk my way out of it with a very aggressive policeman.' She smiled and took another long swig. 'He was about to insist that I be handcuffed and dragged away to Bow Street for further more detailed examination, when I mentioned that I was late for dinner with the Honourable Thadeus Burke and his sister the Lady Frederica Burke. His attitude changed immediately, and I was escorted to a police car and driven at speed, with bells ringing, straight up to the front door here.'

'Inspector John Jackson, I presume?' interjected Thadeus.

'Yes. Do you know him? I might have exaggerated that bit just now about his aggressive nature.' She finished her drink and looked around for an attentive waiter.

'For God's sake Kathleen, read the menu, order up some food, a starter at least, before we all die of starvation. I will keep the glasses coming!' Freddie snapped her fingers and two waiters appeared instantly at her side, she handed over Kathleen's empty glass with a directive thrust: 'Smoked oysters, for my friend,' she demanded, 'and we will have our hors d'oeuvres now,' she demanded of both attendants. 'Start the story from the beginning,' she demanded from the bassoonist.

'Yes, "head girl".' Kathleen saluted and commenced her tale. 'As you know the woodwind section, all three of us, were having a drink waiting for Graham, that's the leader, and his wife Gwen, the orchestra secretary, to come off stage, pat us on the back, say "we'll see you on Wednesday", that's our rehearsal day; but instead a high-ranking police officer, a commissioner or something like that, ushered us into a separate room, a grand place like a library or a club room, with panelled walls. We were asked to wait there until the rest of the players came in, the strings drifted in, and Rupert the second brass man; Graham and Gwen last. Graham tapped on a table for silence and announced in a grave voice that Ralph, the first horn, was dead – stabbed!'

A new bottle of Chablis had arrived and Kathleen raised a salute and drank half of the glass that had been poured for her.

'Obviously we were all shocked and there was a general hubbub and suddenly your man Jackson stormed into the room, banged on the table and announced that we would all have to be interviewed by the police, immediately, and separately. He was ruthless; constables filled the room and we were led away to disconnected rooms, some upstairs, some along a corridor, I was down the corridor guarded by a woman police officer until Jackson came in. He held a piece of paper listing the instruments in the order that they had left the stage as indicated in the last movement.'

She paused to swallow the other half of her wine and Thadeus asked her to repeat this list as he wrote it down in his little black notebook.

'First oboe, second horn, bassoon, that's me, second oboe, first horn, double bass, cello, third and fourth violins, together, viola, and finally the leader, first violin, that's Graham, and the second fiddle, Sarah, together.'

This was delivered slowly, and Kathleen waited until Thadeus had stopped writing, then, looking over at his notes, added, 'The oboes and horns come off together, then me on my own, the bass, on his own, the next three strings, together, and the other three strings stay on until the end; the viola should leave but he prefers to sit in the dark for a few minutes rather than risk an accident as he might walk into a stand or something.'

Thadeus added some brackets to his list and held it up for Kathleen's approval.

She nodded and diverted her attention to the oysters that had been placed before her. 'Yum, yum! Can we take a dinner break?'

The three of them settled into gentle social banter and worked their way through fish entrées, sweet soufflés and crêpes for the girls, and cheese for their masculine attendant. The brie was in excellent condition, practically dripping off the plate, and the large glass of 1904 Warre delicious.

While Freddie and Kathleen went off to powder their noses, Thadeus sketched a plan of the concert stage showing the position of all the players as he remembered them and when Kathleen returned he asked her to indicate which side of the stage each person had departed the performance. Everybody went off stage left, except the first oboe and one of the subordinate violins. Stage right was not so easy, exit there entailed going down some steps and walking round the back of the stage behind curtains; Gwen, a 'bit of a fuss-pot' stood guard at that side to prevent accidents. Kathleen's evidence to the police had been that she was the third member to leave, as far as she could remember there was one candle burning in front of one oboe and another beside the horn, they were over to her right; she left her stand, with the sheet-music in position and just carried her bassoon out with her, round the back of the double bass. She went straight to the bar, where her instrument case was, cleaned the bassoon with her 'pull-through', packed her reeds and ordered a drink. The first oboe was already in the bar when she arrived, and the double bass player came in next, he had left his instruments lying down on the stage; one of the horns came in from his car later, and the cello and two fiddles near the end.

One disclosure that attracted the attention of both Freddie and Thadeus was that at rehearsal, the previous Wednesday, Ralph, the deceased horn player and Gwen had had an argument. Kathleen was standing outside the rehearsal rooms waiting to be picked up by a young man with his car and she heard Ralph accuse Gwen of diverting a portion of the orchestra funds for personal use. The orchestra survived on donations from city institutions, Lloyd's was one, and the horn player accused the wife of the leader, who was also the treasurer, of including her personal wardrobe within the allocation towards miscellaneous expenditure, that sometimes included special costumes for the orchestra. Gwen went mad at the outrageous suggestion and threatened an action for slander if this opinion was ever voiced again. The other members of the musical group were all nice, quiet people, except the bass player, who was a tall, over-weight chap who, after a few drinks, had the habit of starting an argument, or better still, a fight. Kathleen tended to avoid him.

The bill for the evening settled, Kathleen thanked Freddie and Thadeus for their hospitality and took a taxi home, leaving her telephone number with Freddie in anticipation of another meeting when she was back in town.

It had been a long day and Freddie and Thadeus decided to partake of their nightcap at home. In the taxi back Thadeus promised not to allow any more detective work to pervade the weekend. Freddie was 'travelling light' and therefore it took no more than four hours at the most to pack her trunks and cases ready for the next day's railway journey. Saturday evening Hilton joined the table for a friendly, in house, farewell dinner and Sunday morning Freddie was shipped north.

When Thadeus arrived at his office Monday morning there were already two telephone messages written out and placed upon his desk by the early rising James Pooley. The first was from Mr Mannings' secretary asking if his appointment at their offices could be changed until the next day as the office that they had set aside for his work would not be ready today. He telephone her straight away confirming that this was perfectly acceptable and that he looked forward to seeing her at about 11.00 am tomorrow morning; there was no sound other than, 'that will be fine Mr Burke' but Thadeus was sure that he could hear the secretary's thoughts classifying him as a late-rising idler who was going to bring shame and ruin to the whole company. He smiled – she may be right. The second message was from Inspector Johnny

Jackson asking if it would be possible to meet for coffee in the Captain's Room at 10.45 am. Thadeus asked Ethel to ring and say that he would be there.

James and Thadeus discussed the accounts position and it was agreed that they must employ a bookkeeper at least, if not a fully fledged accountant. James, Miss Mills and Mr Emery between them could not keep the figures up to date, together with their other ever increasing duties. It was important that premiums were paid promptly and this needed overall supervision, in addition to the work of the account handler. Thadeus also required statistical analysis of the different branches of business that they handled and this was impossible at the present time. A bookkeeper, an office junior and it would not be long before they needed an extra pair of legs in the Underwriting Room; three new staff. Thadeus would speak to an employment agency and see what they could come up with, in the mean time both James and he would ask around in the Room to see if any applicants might emerge. Fortunately business was still very good with the new firm.

James had a coffee appointment with Jimmy Payne to sort out a couple of difficult claims, so they left together for Lloyd's.

Inspector Jackson was already ensconced on a sofa in the corner of the Captain's Room reading *The Times*. Thadeus sat down opposite him and James hovered briefly shaking hands and exchanging pleasantries until 'JK' Payne walked in and he headed off for the other corner of the room.

'Good morning, inspector, quiet weekend?' opened Thadeus.

'No! You and your sister are the only material witnesses that I have not interviewed over the murder of the horn player on Friday evening.'

'My sister has departed for Scotland,' informed Thadeus. 'What have you got so far?'

'I saw the bassoon player, Kathleen Dandle, at her flat in Hampstead yesterday afternoon – she is a very nice young lady – she told me that you had had a conversation about the matter at dinner, and that neither of you seem to have seen anything relevant.'

'Nothing important,' responded Thadeus, distracted by an image of Miss Dandle that had come into his mind, cradling a baby Police Constable on one knee and a WPC on the other.

Coffee was served and Jackson divulged the evidence uncovered so far. Saturday morning he had inspected the bank account details of the murdered man and papers kept at his house, and discovered large sums, £700 in all, being paid into the account by the bass player. The big man had been questioned on this matter the same morning and confessed that he was being blackmailed by Ralph, but was adamant that he had nothing to do with his murder. The bass chap had been arrested and charged for manslaughter in 1913 in Manchester; he was involved in a pub fight, hit a man who fell, hit his head on a table and died. The charges were later dropped and a verdict of accidental death declared at the inquest, but it was not a story that he wanted broadcast. In the trenches the bass player had established a reputation for killing the Hun with his bare hands, one of his specialities was the bayonet through the neck; silent and the enemy died, asphyxiated by his own blood, just like poor Ralph. Thadeus interrupted at this point to remind Jackson that the bass part continued after the first horn departed the stage, or would have departed had he not been dead, and included a long and very fine solo passage. He could not have crept right across to the other side of the performance area to stab the brass man in the middle of his own performance. Jackson acknowledged this but was keeping his options open, the bass player was still in the frame.

The other highlight of the weekend had been the perusal of the orchestra accounts ledgers by an accountant in the service of the fraud section at Scotland Yard, following Kathleen's evidence about the row with Gwen. The numbers man found that a purchase of dark blue dresses from Harrods for the lady members of the orchestra had included an extra garment for Gwen, hardly the crime of the century, and it could be argued that the treasurer was one of the lady members, but a slanderous rumour could be very damaging and Gwen had every opportunity to commit the crime from her post at the right-hand stage exit, and a knitting needle was a woman's weapon. Gwen was Jackson's number one suspect.

None of the artistes had seen anything amiss during the performance as, during the dress rehearsal it had been noticed that if you glanced around the glare from the candles created a blind spot on the pupil and when you returned your eyes to the sheet-music you could not see the notes, so they all kept their eyes firmly on their separate musical scores.

It was possible to get onto the stage from the back-centre, up behind the curtains; this entrance had been tried by a constable and a WPC and it was not very difficult. From this position anybody could have murdered the man, not just a member of the orchestra.

Having received assurances that neither himself nor his sister were under any sort of suspicion, Thadeus packed and lighted his pipe and mused for awhile as Jackson continued his scouring of the daily news and new coffee was ordered.

Eventually, as Jackson grew impatient, Thadeus tapped out the dottle into an ashtray and announced, 'The second horn, Rupert, did it!'

'Gwen confirms that Rupert left the stage by the steps at her side of the stage just after the first oboe,' defended Jackson.

'And he was not seen again until appearing in the bar, returning from his car, much later?' queried Thadeus, drawing on the conversation at c*hez Paul* with Kathleen.

Jackson checked his notes. 'He has no collaboration for this but his instrument and other paraphernalia were in his car when searched that evening.'

The surprising next question from Thadeus was, 'Did Ralph earn a good living from his horn playing?'

Jackson again looked at his notes. 'Yes, after the blackmail exposure I arranged for the accountant to inspect his papers at the house and our man was quite impressed, sometimes he was engaged twice on the same date.'

Thadeus smiled.

'Find the reason behind Ralph's blackmailing of Rupert,' he instructed a puzzled police inspector. Then he settled the bill and the two men parted.

At lunchtime Miss Mills told Thadeus of a man whom she knew from her previous employment who was now out of work having become surplus to requirements at the company which had suffered the disastrous loss of a large account at the end of the year. The man was a bookkeeper, and a very competent person in Miss Mills' opinion, aged thirty-seven, married but without children. She felt that she should also disclose that he had only one arm, having lost his left upper limb in 1917 in France.

A brief telephone call and minutes later Thadeus and James were partaking of a beer with Clement Simpkins; they liked him and he was asked to join Burke & Co on the first of next month, a week away. As they rushed back to the office James pointed out that if the new man filched any cash they would know which pocket to look into. South London humour was still beyond Thadeus' understanding.

As a penalty for his poor taste James was enlisted to move furniture around the office in preparation for the new arrival, and work out where the new lad, or lass, would sit when recruited. This task proved impossible as the room, originally designed for three people, already housed five. There was another vacant office available to let, on the same floor at the end of the short corridor that ran in front of the lift well and staircase, the present Burke & Co office being right opposite the lift doors. Thadeus had already made enquiries at Hargreaves & Simpkin as this detached office space would be ideal for his own office and he could bequeath the 'shed' to James. Thadeus disclosed his plan and James resumed the reorganization with renewed vigour.

The afternoon at Burke & Co was busy but boring; no excitement either in the office or at the Lloyd's Underwriting Room, successful but routine!

Many letters and telegrams needed to be dispatched before the end of the working day and Thadeus was relieved by the welcome bustle of departing staff and the sombre stroll to his parked car. All was quiet upon his arrival at Sloane Mews; Hilton was cooking some sort of bean stew from ingredients purchased from the street market; the sortie among the stallholders a welcome relief from the machinations of the architect and builders advising on the conversion of Freddie's new dwelling, next door. Thadeus was updated on the progress as he sipped a modest glass of *Pastis*, awaiting the experimental dinner. Following a very adequate repast he considered some activity for the rest of the evening; the absence of his sister left a gap to be filled with quiet contemplation and study. He retired to the drawing room with a newly acquired copy of Plato's *Timaeus* to revise his calculations of the philosopher's ratios for the act of creation; he had worked through the application of the two fractions, 9/8 and 256/243 to construct a musical octave and found that by using the larger fraction for the full tone intervals and the smaller one for the semi-tones, it appeared to work for all keys, and was puzzled as to why Plato had not been followed instead of Pythagoras, thus avoiding the latter's notorious *comma*. Then the early musicologists could have avoided the inharmonious equal temperament. He was working out the vibrations for B major, with five sharps, when Inspector Jackson rang.

'Perhaps you would be good enough to explain to me how he could have done it?' were the policeman's first words.

'You have unearthed the motive then?' queried Thadeus.

'Yes!' replied a submissive Jackson. 'Rupert Percival was married in France to a French girl in 1916, a copy of the marriage certificate was found taped to the underside of a desk draw in Ralph's house. Rupert was also married to a young lady organist in Essex in 1921, according to his current curriculum vitae.'

'I think that you will find that he has been paying for this misdemeanour by performances on the horn in Ralph's name, Ralph getting the fees.'

'Routine enquiries, armed with photographs of the two men should expose that deception if it is true, but how could he have done the deed?'

'My reconstruction would be that he left the platform, following the first oboe, and was seen by Gwen; he must have left his candle burning and his instrument on the floor; he then walked round behind the curtain, climbed back onto the stage, waited in the dark for a passage of sixteen bars' rest, that he knew was coming, then, as Ralph set down his instrument Rupert stepped across, stabbed him through the neck and blew out his candle. He then crossed to his own chair and stand, picked up his horn and from then on played the part of the first horn; left the stage, in the role of first horn, passed behind the double bass and went straight out to his car.'

'If challenged he would simply deny it; we would have no proof.'

'The second oboe might have seen something suspicious.'

'He wears glasses; when he is playing he uses reading glasses. He told us that if he looked up he would see nothing clearly, even if the lights were up.'

'When are you going to interview Rupert?'

'He is on his way to the Wood Street station in a police car, as we speak.'

Thadeus thought for a moment and then asked, 'What happened to all the sheet-music for the performance that was left on the players' stands?'

'It was all handed over to Graham, the leader, this afternoon.'

'Get it all back immediately.' instructed Thadeus. 'I will meet you at the station within half an hour.'

When Thadeus arrived at Wood Street he was told that the sheet-music had not been picked up by Graham, although he had been informed that they would be released to him if he called at the station that afternoon. He had decided to call round tomorrow.

'Good news,' said Thadeus and immediately started to sort through the sheets placing them across a table separated into their different playing parts.

In the next room the interview with Rupert Percival had begun; Jackson was interrogating the man very professionally, going over the statements several times and asking repeated questions. The horn player was getting frustrated and annoyed, as was his solicitor who had been brought in with him. Jackson put to him the scenario suggested by Thadeus, with the words 'I suggest…' pre-empting each stage of the verbal re-enactment, Mr Percival replied at each stage with the words, 'No' or 'Rubbish'. As Jackson came to the end of his alternative attacks on the suspect, Thadeus entered the room carrying a set of music-sheets. He sat down behind the attendant police sergeant and listened to Rupert's continual denials. Jackson paused, shuffled his papers and considered his next move. In that brief suspension of hostilities Thadeus leaned forward and said to Rupert Percival, 'When the individual players vacated the stage they left their music-sheets on their music-stands to be collected up by Gwen or Graham?'

'Yes, of course,' responded Rupert abruptly.

'Then how can you explain that on the stand at your position on the platform at the end of the performance was the score for the first horn, not the second horn?' asked Thadeus seeking clarification, and holding up a set of musical sheets headed 'First Horn'.

Rupert Percival's mouth opened and his lips went up and down for a few seconds. 'It must be some sort of mistake!' he blurted out.

'A mistake of yours I would suggest,' said Jackson, leaning forward, with renewed vigour.

The solicitor seemed less confident and requested a short break in order that he may consult with his client. They appear to have spent the time considering what Rupert's mitigating circumstances would be at his trial, as when the two men were recalled to the room they were advised that Mr Percival wished to make a new statement.

CHAPTER 11

A VISIT TO THE WHIRLING DERVISHES

At 11.00 am Tuesday morning Thadeus appeared at the offices of the Mannings syndicate ready to take up his role as new reinsurance consultant to review the 1926 programme and analyse their results, premium and claims.

A small office had been set aside for his work and a pile of papers, folders and entry-books were stacked onto the only desk in the room by a thoughtful secretary. He shuffled the documents into some sort of order; the 1926 reinsurance programme details, letters and cover notes; the syndicate statistics, premium figures, split into classes, and claims, similarly divided; a specific file related to bloodstock claims for the years 1924 and 1925 and a separate file for the Thurlow Reinsurance Treaty for the same years. Thadeus reached for this last document first and took from his briefcase a file of his own containing five sheets of paper, each headed by the name of one of the false horses recorded by Sir Percy Dennington. He turned the sheets of the Thurlow Monthly Claims Bordereaux 1925, backwards, starting at December, and slowly ran his eye up the column headed 'animal' showing the name or breeding of the horse that had been the subject of the claim; he found two of the horses on his list. Turning to the 1924 bordereaux he found the other three. Each time he located a sought item he noted down on his personal file; the original policy number; the name of the insured, the address was not shown for any of the entries; the period of insurance, always annual policies, the first running from February 1924 until the last commencing in March 1925; the sum insured, all even thousands, a two, two fours, a five and a six, totalling £21,000; the date of the loss and the cause of the claim, two cases of colic, two fractured bones, and one colitis X, brief categories but no details. He had acquired a lot more information but his investigation had not progressed much further, except that the direction had moved from the Mannings syndicate to the Thurlow syndicate. The next step would seem to be an inspection of the original claims files and, preferably, also the original placing files; documents that would be in the Thurlow offices in Finch Lane.

Thadeus turned his attention to the 1926 reinsurance documents, reading through the letters and studying the official cover-notes. At a point in the negotiations the reinsurance broker had stipulated that the contract must have a ninety days cancellation clause, and Mr Mannings had cleverly accepted this but stipulated that it must be both ways, either he or the reinsurer could get out of the deal within three months, so, if Burke & Co could do a better job than the present reinsurance man, there could be a nice piece of business for the firm fairly quickly. Thadeus started to take the task seriously; Mannings would have known this – a shrewd man!

By 1.00 pm Thadeus had decided two things. The first was this programme would prove expensive to the Mannings Syndicate because although the minimum and deposit premiums were low, and the adjustment rate reasonable, in the event of claims the reinstatement premiums and upward rate requirements were outrageous; his study of the figures showed that the lower levels would most certainly be hit by claims. It would take some time to project an accurately estimated result for 1926 based on the 1924/5 underwriting, but Thadeus felt sure that the reinsuring underwriters could find themselves in a much better position than the original underwriter. The second decision was that, although he was capable of handling the figure work, given sufficient time, he may not be able to arrange the placing of such a reinsurance programme, and that his search for an additional broker should be upgraded to include reinsurance experience.

He advised Mr Mannings' secretary that he had completed his preliminary examination and taken note of various statistics that would need time to analyse. He would telephone her before the end of the week concerning the next step; he had separated the documents into two piles, those that he would require again, and those that he would not. She appeared impressed with his diligence, and he left to pick up a sandwich in Leadenhall Market before returning to his own office.

Munching his chosen luncheon accompanied by a mug of tea Thadeus browsed through the morning paper; the report of the fire at

Hampstead tube station and the continuing progress of the Lawn Tennis Champion, Mademoiselle Suzanne Lenglen in California: no fear of snow out there! Ethel interrupted his perusal of the news with the announcement of a telephone call from Gussie Downing.

There were several surprises from Gussie, including the fact that he was telephoning from the offices of the Thurlow syndicate in Finch Lane where he was supervising the inspection of documents concerned in the discovery examination that was part of a High Court action. The plaintiff concerned was a cloth manufacturing company suing Thurlow & Others over a claim that they had denied; one of their machines had broken and a piece of flying metal had severely injured a local councillor who was visiting the plant. Investigation of the claim had revealed a lack of servicing for the machine in breach of the policy warranties. The engineers responsible for the service contract had been joined as co-defendants, which suited Thurlow as if they were found liable for the claim they would be seeking recovery under their subrogation rights against the engineering company, and this action could be considered at the same time. Gussie's leader, a KC, had suggested that he attend all the meetings to gather as much first-hand information as possible.

All this was related as a preamble to the main item of the telephone call, which was that at the Thurlow offices he had met a Turkish gentleman, Azimi by name, Gussie was not sure whether this was his surname or his Christian name, if he had been a Christian, which he was not, being a follower of the Sufi tradition; and this Turkish chap had invited him, and a guest, if he wished, to a performance of the Mevlevis in an exhibition of their famous whirling dance. The show was to take place at a hall in Barron's Court on Thursday evening and Gussie thought that Thadeus might be interested in attending. Gussie's invitation included the background information on Azimi who worked for a Turkish insurance company, had just returned from a trip to the USA and was currently working with Lloyd's underwriters and brokers studying their methods of claims' settlement. Gussie's activities had attracted the Turkish man's attention.

Gussie went on to denounce the alleged new truce between the Labour Party and the Communist Party as complete rubbish and, while in political mode, amplify the alleged wholesale defection of the Liberal Party to the Conservatives.

Thadeus' response to all this chatter was a simple 'yes' to the invitation to the Mevlevis performance, even this miniscule role in the conversation provoked Gussie into a further diatribe on the travel arrangements, whereby he would take Thadeus along to the hall in Baron's Court but he, Thadeus, would have to make his own way back home as he, Gussie, was committed to driving Azimi to his lodgings in Wimbledon.

The telephone call had exhausted Thadeus and he ordered a new cup of tea from Ethel and lighted his pipe, stared into space for a while, then doodled some diagrams of his new office arrangements, having finalized the lease terms first thing that morning.

James appeared in the office and Thadeus divulged his idea of a new broker experienced in reinsurance. James confirmed Thadeus' opinion that reinsurance brokers were a bumptious lot, and expensive! They would both make discreet enquires, avoiding anyone working for Mr Mannings' present reinsurance broker.

That afternoon and the following morning the whole personnel at Burke & Co worked very hard, which left the Wednesday afternoon free for Thadeus to measure up his new office and arrange the purchase and delivery of furniture, traditional, in mahogany and leather, with a bent-wood hat-stand for his accoutrements. He contemplated phoning Freddie for advice but resisted in fear that she would recommend a modern art deco ambience.

He would move in next Monday, the first day of February, provided the decorators had completed their tasks over the weekend.

On Thursday morning the details of several applicants supplied by employment agencies were perused; bookkeepers were rejected, they already had one; a mountain of school-leavers seeking their first job was handed over to Miss Mills for scrutiny and judgement; the four brokers seeking a new post were studied by Thadeus and James. Two of the applicants were well known to them and both rejected, bumptious and expensive; the third was a sad case of an under-paid older man with a reputation as a good workhorse, but no imagination; and the fourth was a man in his mid-twenties who had worked as a reinsurance placing broker, until he had been sacked for drunkenness.

Thadeus was prepared to take his chances with the lush, but he was sure that James would go for number three; no competition from that fellow. Surprisingly James knew the alcoholic miscreant, a south London lad who travelled to work via London Bridge Station and walked across London Bridge with thousands of others, including James. The man, William Penrose, had lost both brothers in the war and his wife had died in childbirth; James thought him a quiet and efficient chap, articulate and well groomed, but he did have the unfortunate habit of taking to the bottle in a serious way; James had put the inebriated Lloyd's man on the right train home several times. It was agreed that William Penrose would be interviewed by Miss Mills and Mr Emery; if he passed that test they would give him a trial run.

Thadeus had left the Bentley at Sloane Mews that day as he was being chauffeured down to Baron's Court in Gussie's new 6-cylinder Chrysler two-seater purchased from Eustace Watkins Ltd in Piccadilly for £525, another gem imparted during the prolonged telephone conversation. Gussie duly pulled up outside 3 Gracechurch Street at exactly 6.00 pm and they headed west in the splendid new machine, parking in a back street and walking round to the hall where the Mevlevis were to perform. The venue was crowded with a mixture of European and Oriental men and women harmonized by a tranquillity that an anticipated profound philosophical experience always seems to provoke. Gussie disappeared at exactly 7.00 pm to collect Azimi at the local underground station. Thadeus mingled with the crowd, browsing through some Sufi literature displayed on a stall, until they returned and introductions were completed; then they took their seats in the hall, in the second row back from the central performance area, which was not a raised stage, but a large polished wooden floor at the same level as the seating.

With no introduction the musicians started to play, a slow, soft drum beat with a plucked *tabla* and a hovering *ney*, a reeded flute, then the Whirling Dervishes entered, taking the floor in groups of three, with their long flowing cloaks and *sikke*, tall honey coloured hats, turning slowly, the revolutions increasing as more participants joined the assembly. A male and a female voice added a lingering chant, moving over three octaves; the effect was stunning, although the room was filled with sound and movement, the result on the mind was a pervading peace and stillness, much as Thadeus had often found at performances of compositions by Mozart or Vivaldi, when the vigorously vibrating strings serve to remind you of that which does not move or change.

Thadeus could have sat there for hours, but eventually the troupe slowed, stopped and was led off, after a concise bow; there was an appreciative *mezzo* applause. It was announced that there would be a twenty-minute break for coffee in an adjoining room; to be followed by readings from the works of Rumi and some Sufi stories.

Thadeus avoided the Turkish coffee of which past experiences had provoked insomnia, and watched Gussie gulp down a small cup, after which his eyes inflated and Thadeus thought that at any minute springs and cogs would burgeon from his ears; Azimi smiled and sipped contentedly. Gussie entered into conversation with two young ladies of his acquaintance, and Thadeus questioned the Turkish insurance man vigorously on the subject of the Thurlow claims department, but nothing of importance was revealed. He had read some bloodstock claims files but found them rather succinct; one piece of paper said the horse was fit, and another piece of paper said that the same horse was dead; QED – a claim! Thadeus agreed that Azimi had acquired a good understanding of bloodstock claims. Thadeus was recruited to Gussie's growing female entourage, and Azimi moved around the room chatting to various men and women with whom he was obviously acquainted. Politely declining to take one young lady back to his home so that she could try out his Bentley, he was providentially distracted by a view of Azimi across the room engaged in a heated argument with a short plump man of Turkish appearance. The small chap was poking Azimi in the chest with his index finger and delivering a sneering reprisal but as the little man stormed off and his opponent turned and walked towards him, he realized that it was not Azimi. His puzzled expression must have alerted the stranger who came straight up to him and introduced himself as Ahmad Babrak Durrani and acknowledged that he did bear a striking resemblance to Azimi, whom he had met earlier. 'He is my doppelgänger – or maybe I am his!' he smiled and moved into the hall.

In the second half Thadeus found the poems of Rumi difficult to grasp at one sitting. He made a mental note to track down a good translation for future study. The Sufi stories or myths were delightful. Thadeus particularly liked the tale of the wise man, a seeker of truth, who was summoned before the king, who demanded that the sage divulge three truths to him, otherwise he would be incarcerated within the palace. The wise man pronounced his name and asked the king if it was true that this was indeed his name – the king replied 'yes'. Then the wise man asked if it was true that the king demanded three truths from him – the king replied 'yes'. Then the wise man asked if it was true that the king would imprison him within the palace if he did not reveal three truths from him – the king replied 'yes', and the wise man was allowed to leave. Thadeus felt that this simple tale had several meanings at different levels of understanding; he resolved to hold the memory in his mind awaiting some enlightened moment.

Out on the streets of west London, Gussie and Azimi said their farewells and the pair headed off for the Chrysler, and Wimbledon; Thadeus walked to a nearby main road corner giving him two chances of hailing a taxi. Engaged on the same mission was Ahmad Babrak Durrani on his way to a hotel in Kensington; they agreed to share the solitary cab that appeared.

Ahmad was in the diplomatic service, employed by the Turkish government, a servant of Mustafa Kemal Ataturk, who in his wisdom had in the previous year banned membership of Sufi orders and closed their *tekkes* as part of his desire to direct the country towards a proper Western mentality; a great pity because what the west really needed was an influx of eastern wisdom. Ahmad agreed, he felt that the European nations were mentally akin to the Sufi story's blind men each describing an elephant that they had examined by touch alone; unable to communicate intelligently. Unfortunately most of the Middle Eastern countries were now inflicted by the desire for personal wealth and following the European path to self-destruction.

Ahmad closed his eyes and appeared to take a moment of prayer, then said, 'Thadeus one must be weary of criticism, it divides and separates, we are all one.' He elaborated on the purpose of the whirling dancing explaining how the participants seek that inner peace and stillness, beyond sound, before the Word. A silence that is always the same, unmoving, can be glimpsed, the more often it is attained the stronger the attraction and the easier the next effort. He emphasized that they had not witnessed the full Mevlevis ceremony, just a demonstration, and recommended that his new acquaintance seek out a member of the Sufi order in London, where he might be able to know more. Thadeus directed Ahmad's attention to the poems of Rupert Brooke whose beautiful observations of this state are worthy of study, especially 'When beauty and beauty meet'. They shook hands and exchanged visiting cards as the cab arrived at the Kensington hotel.

It was not late when he arrived home and he telephoned his sister to relate the experiences of the evening. She was well and he went to bed with a clear and tranquil mind.

The next morning his heightened awareness was disturbed by a telephone call from Inspector Jackson.

'If I ever take up a musical instrument, Thadeus, please promise me that you will not attend any performances of my playing,' was his opening remark.

'I think I can safely make that commitment. What has happened?'

'Your name appears in a statement made to the police last night by your friend Gussie Downing. A Turkish chap that he was giving a lift to was killed by a hit and run driver in the Baron's Court area.'

'Azimi – how awful!'

'That's the chap. He and Gussie were at Gussie's car, parked in a back street. The driver's side nearest to the pavement, which is a traffic offence as a parked vehicle should be facing the correct way to ensure that the tail lights reflect towards oncoming traffic, and Azimi went round, on to the road, to get in the passenger side and a motor vehicle ran him down. He was dead on arrival at the hospital. Gussie's new car was damaged on the near-side wing and the back bumper torn off.'

'I arranged the insurance on that car only yesterday,' informed Thadeus, continuing Jackson's casual display of material facts.

'Gussie thinks that it was not an accident. He heard a vehicle start its engine moments before he opened his car door and is sure that it was the same vehicle that accelerated straight at his friend and mowed him down.'

'We had better meet, I may have some additional information for you,' said Thadeus

'Two minutes, in the Crown Tea Rooms,' said Jackson

'I'll be there!'

Over cups of coffee Thadeus concisely disclosed his present progress with the Dennington case, opining that Sir Percy's death had been a murder and that his knowledge of the fraudulent bloodstock claims had been the motive for the killing. Furthermore Azimi was, this week, working at the Thurlow offices perusing claims files and to Thadeus's knowledge, these included bloodstock papers.

'Do you think I should have a word with Mr Sturge, go in there and turn the place over?'

'If a man has just been murdered because of those files they would have been destroyed this morning,' opined Thadeus adding, 'I might have a more subtle way of penetrating that office.'

'Keep me in touch,' ordered Jackson. 'Routine enquiries will continue on the hit and run incident – that should reveal something. I must get back to the job I am working on at Billingsgate.' He held his nose by way of further explanation.

Thadeus had not been back in his office more than a half hour when another call came through from the Scotland Yard man.

'Despite your assurances I have decided to forego, forever, any sort of musical career: Mayhem at jazz clubs; death at classical recitals and now two deaths following oriental chanting. Your name has appeared as chief suspect in another murder last night.'

Thadeus could say nothing prompting Jackson to question that he was still on the line?

After a weak 'yes' Jackson disclosed that prompt and efficient police enquiries had led to an interview with a taxi driver whose fare, a man of Arab appearance, at about 9.30 last night, was dropped at a hotel in Kensington, the other passenger, a young English man was taken on to Sloane Mews.

'The man of Arab appearance was Ahmad Babrak Durrani, a Turkish diplomat, who was found dead in his hotel room at 7.30 this morning, shot through the head; and I think that young English man taken to Sloane Mews was you!'

'I have a lot to tell you about this one too,' confessed a shocked Thadeus.

'Shall I have you taken away to a cell somewhere, or buy you a spot of lunch in the George & Vulture?'

'Twelve thirty, early in and early out,' agreed Thadeus.

How awful, two lovely, lovely people dead – why? he thought as he replaced the receiver.

Thadeus had no appetite for city stodge that day, sipping a glass of white wine with a plate of smoked salmon and brown bread and butter. He related the story of his evening at the Sufi demonstration and his meeting with Ahmad, most importantly the striking resemblance between the two men murdered that night. He thought it probable that Azimi had been mistaken for Ahmad, or just possibly the other way round. Of course the obnoxious looking little fat Arab who had accosted Ahmad during the evening coffee break was the prime suspect. He must be found! A little voice at the back of his mind whispered 'be wary of criticism'. Thadeus smiled, drank his cup of coffee, paid the bill, to Jackson's surprise, and decided to start the weekend early.

Saturday morning Thadeus and James supervised the new office decoration, which was not easy as the one-man room had two ladders, bridged by a plank of wood supporting a workman painting the ceiling; a second workman painting the window surround and a third chap, on his knees working around the skirting board. Thadeus checked that the parquet flooring had been covered adequately and that the Venetian blinds were delivered and ready to be hung some time over the weekend. Mr Emery had volunteered to oversee the furniture arrival on Sunday morning; he had been equipped with a set of keys and a handful of Bank of England one pound notes.

At 12.00 midday Burke & Co dispersed leaving the decorators at their toil. Beth, who was engaged on a shopping spree in the West End that afternoon would return to Gracechurch Street later and lock up. Thadeus also needed to visit shops in the Knightsbridge area and had left the Bentley at home, intending to take taxis to the various places on his list. He was, therefore, surprised and pleased to find Gussie

Downing sitting in his car outside the office offering his services as chauffeur.

'An excellent claim's service at Burke & Co – insured it Wednesday; smashed it up Thursday; repaired it Friday, and here I am on Saturday morning taking the man responsible for a slap-up lunch,' he chortled.

'Most opportune; you are going to come in very handy. Where are we going?'

'Upstairs at Simpson's in the Strand, proper grub!'

Gussie had telephoned Hilton and discovering that Thadeus was without transport that morning had booked a table by the window at Simpson's, and was now entirely at his friend's command. The only price for this exemplary behaviour was a lecture and cram-swot on the subjects of 'subrogation' and 'contribution', and the difference between them, if there was one!

Thadeus readily agreed, withholding for the present the main reason for his enthusiastic welcome of the assistance. He had experienced shopping ventures with Gussie on previous occasions and had marvelled at the young barrister's ability to engage with shop assistants at the ladies' underwear departments. Tucked inside his jacket for a week was a shopping list given to him by his sister Freddie before she set out for Scotland. It was not scribbled illegibly as a doctor was supposed to write, but typed out in the manner of a legal document in numbered paragraphs, listing shop names, name and description of garments, sizes and colours and estimated prices. She had omitted the verbal instructions, such as 'make sure it doesn't make my tits look too big' so was fortunately in a state that could be unveiled to Gussie the female undergarment expert. What Thadeus found embarrassing, Gussie revelled in; their previous raids on Harrods had seen Gussie equipped with a two-page list, which he explained to the girl sales assistant as being 'items that were needed by his mother'. If the young lady was surprised by this she was even more astounded when he proceeded to hold up pairs of nylon stocking to eliminate any latent blemishes, and ping the fittings on suspender belts to ensure reliability. On one occasion his behaviour with a pair of brassieres had warranted the intervention of a more senior, and older, woman supervisor.

Over lunch Thadeus ensured that the instruction on insurance terminology, with particular reference to underwriters recouping their losses by way of policy conditions, was delivered in his most verbose mode, thus leaving no guilt complex concerning the modest request for assistance at the ladies underwear sections of the Knightsbridge department stores an hour later. However, as they entered the first shop Thadeus reflected on the reaction of his sister when she became aware that data concerning her panties might become the subject of debate on the staircase of Brick Court, and took on the task himself. In an aloof and efficient style that he thought might have been used by the original James Lock, some centuries back, when inspecting material for his hats, he conducted the purchases with aplomb, even managing to stipulate that the brassieres should not 'give the lady's bosom the appearance of over development'. His only moment of anguish was that he nearly choked when he overheard one of the sales assistants whisper to a colleague: 'She don't want her tits to look too big.'

The additional use of the Chrysler to carry an Afghan rug, required for the new office, back to Sloane Mews, together with numerous boxes of Freddie's unmentionable undergarments, did not seem to call for added consideration, but Thadeus supplied it nevertheless by way of a supper invitation.

Having let Gussie off the underwear venture, he had another plan in mind.

Hilton prepared a light meal, the two gallants having over indulged at lunch time. The menu consisted of a type of fishcake made from potato and anchovies, with lemon and capers, accompanied by steamed shredded cabbage. It was delicious; Gussie had two helpings. The guest also consumed most of the cheese reserves of the house and a considerable amount of Claret such that he did not return home that night, but dossed down on a couch in the drawing room.

The libretto for the evening's performance had taken the form of a revelation by Thadeus that he was working on a proposed reinsurance programme for a Lloyd's underwriter – the first truth; and that this work made necessary the study of specific claims information – the second truth; and that certain claims essential to this scrutiny were in the offices of the Thurlow syndicate – the third truth. And that, for reasons of discretion and confidentiality, and to save embarrassment between two separate groups of underwriters, Thadeus did not want it known that he had looked at these files. If the king himself did not insist upon four truths, why should Gussie!

Lawyers are very quick on the uptake. 'You want me to nick some file from the office for you?' said Gussie.

'In a word – yes,' admitted Thadeus.

'Fine. I am sure that it is in a good cause. Give me the details tomorrow, or better still Monday. Will it get my client, Mr Thurlow into trouble?'

'Not if he has been a good boy, but if he has been a naughty boy it might be his undoing.'

'Fine, I'm all for justice!'

'The only problem was, when Gussie sobered up, would he remember any of this?' thought a tired Thadeus.

At breakfast at midday on Sunday, Gussie was as bright as a 100-watt bulb, armed with pen and paper he took note of the five claims files required by Thadeus, and disclosed that a part of his present work schedule was the perusal of industrial injury insurance payments over the past five years, and that this entailed removing files for study at his home; it should not be a problem slipping a few 'wrong' ones into his satchel. The proviso being: 'I do not want to find myself in the nasty brown stuff – old college chum!'

They chatted about the merits, and more merits, of the Chrysler motor vehicle for a while then Gussie announced that he was going home to bed.

Monday morning – a new week; February – a new month, a new office and a new employee. The first person to grace Thadeus' new rug was Clement Simpkins, although everybody else had poked their nose around the door on some invented pretext to view the new inner sanctum. Clem came equipped with a huge leather Gladstone bag, which he explained was for carrying books and ledgers around the city on the 'ticking up' ventures, when the broker's accounts were verified with the underwriter's records. He assured Thadeus that when he arrived at the door of an underwriter's office he, and his bag, brought fear and trepidation to the hearts of the syndicate's entry boys. If there was a discrepancy they knew it was their error.

'Good,' said Thadeus. 'Just make sure that it is! Welcome aboard.'

Thadeus thought that, loaded with ledgers that bag must weigh several hundredweight; one arm or not, that man must be as strong as an ox!

The internal telephone rang for the first time, it was Ethel announcing with a girlish giggle that there was a policeman waiting for an audience to discuss an alleged case of office trespass. Jackson bringing a touch of police harassment to Burke & Co!

Thadeus tried to ignore the outline of a grinning face pressed to the opaque glass door-window, just above the engraved words 'Private'.

'Come in,' he shouted out, trying not to laugh.

'I am going to get the word "investigator" chiselled on to your door after the word "private" was the inspector's opening remark, 'just like Sherlock Holmes.'

'I think you will find that Mr Holmes described himself as "a consulting detective"' corrected Thadeus. 'You appear to be in fine fettle this morning police inspector.'

'Yes. I have solved all the little crime problems that you set for me last week and am here to promote the good name of the Metropolitan Police Force.'

'You have got that bastard who murdered Azimi and Ahmad? Well done you!'

'Not quite, I know how and who, but the bird has flown back home.'

'Just give me his name and I'll bring him in for you,' boasted Thadeus seriously.

'Shall I tell you the story?' asked Jackson

'I do not think I can stop you,' admitted Thadeus.

Jackson told how routine slog had found the hit-and-run vehicle, abandoned in Fulham, an Austin hired from a garage in Putney. The garage owners had been questioned and given the name and address of the hirer; a false name, Ali Bin Mohammed, which is the Arabic equivalent of John Smith; a street that did not exist; and an area in London that did not match the postal district number. Challenged on the accuracy of their records the female half of the garage ownership said, 'How was she to know that Southwark might not be NW8 – in a foreign language?'

The hirer was a short fat man of Arab appearance! And he left his fingerprints in the vehicle! More routine slog discovered that a short fat man of Arab appearance had stayed at a hotel in Kensington – not the same one as Ahmad – and the man had left his fingerprints in the room! He had registered as Sadar Shah Hasham with an address in Turkey. Examination of the scene of crime at Ahmad's hotel revealed the same fingerprints! An open and shut case!

At this point Ethel appeared with tea and biscuits for both men on a newly purchased tray, having gently knocked at the door and received permission to enter. She could not resist remarking, 'I think you need some pictures on the wall, sir.'

'Quite right Ethel. I have the matter in hand!' Thadeus assured the girl. 'So how did the bugger get away?' he put to Jackson.

'We have witnesses of a man matching the description boarding a train at Victoria Station and more witnesses of a man boarding a boat at Dover.'

He went on to describe the procedure followed over the weekend in liaison with the French police and elucidated on telephone conversations with the Turkish authorities who had no record of such a person. However, his personal contacts at the Foreign Office knew Sadar Shah Hasham well; a thug in the employ of Mustafa Kemal Ataturk, a prominent member of his private security force. Of course they could do nothing officially.

'Any idea of the reason for the assassination?' asked Thadeus

'My man at the FO thinks that a member of Hasham's family is next in line for Ahmad's job.'

'Two upright and honest human beings slaughtered as a nepotistic favour? Tragic and disgusting,' said a sad Thadeus.

Jackson left to be replaced by Miss Mills who had just completed an interview with William Penrose. Thadeus did not feel up to this discussion but he took a deep breath and heard the senior lady's report. She liked Bill and thought that he was a capable and honest recruit, but he did have a drink problem. Life had not been kind to him and Miss Mills knew more about this infliction than Thadeus anticipated; her sister, who had lost her only two sons in the war and was then deserted by her husband who took off with a 'floozy' in 1921 had taken to drink. This divulgence was difficult for the office manager and she pleaded that it would stay as a close secret between them. Her experience showed that alcoholism was not just a bad habit, but an illness and it could be cured. Her sister had enrolled at a clinic under proper medical supervision where they used methods like hypnosis and acupuncture, not a group of temperance activists, and she had recovered within a month and had not touched a drop since! Her opinion was that this young man should be given a chance, but subject to a commitment from him to undergo treatment.

'Is he still here in the office?' asked Thadeus.

'Yes,' she replied.

'Send him in,' he instructed.

A few minutes later William Penrose, the company's potential new reinsurance broker entered the room. They shook hands and the new man sat down in one of the new leather visitor seats.

Thadeus studied the chap's curriculum vitae, looked up and said, 'What do you think of this R/I programme?' and handed him the précis of the Mannings arrangements.

'He would be better to run a higher deductible, pay more money and get one free reinstatement. If he had a good result he and his reinsurers would do well, if not they would both suffer equally. I have not seen his past results but my guess is that this programme will cost him dear,' said William in a competent, but not ostentatious manner.

'I will employ you for one month, during which time I have a particular job – that one! You have asked for a salary of £200 per annum, I will pay you £15 for the one month. After that period I am stipulating that you obtain treatment for your drink problem, I will pay for your medical care, and when you are cured and able to return to work we will discuss your future remuneration, which will not be less than £200 a year.'

'Thank you, sir,' he said.

'And for God's sake try and stay away from the booze until we get this Mannings treaty put to bed. Can you start tomorrow?'

'Yes, sir. Thank you, sir.'

They shook hands once more and the new reinsurance broker left, hopefully going home, not to the nearest pub!

Had he done the right thing? Should he have consulted Freddie? What would Ahmad have done? Act as the moment dictates – wasn't that a Sufi instruction!

CHAPTER 12

THE CHELTENHAM GOLD CUP

February 1926 was a busy month for the coal miner's president Herbert Smith – 'our Herbert' to his followers – seeking but failing to obtain unpretentious increases in earnings for his members at the same time as it was revealed that the Marques of Bute's royalties from coal excavation on his land amounted to £115,000 per annum!

It was a busy month at Burke & Co. as well, though not quite as rewarding and certainly not with such little effort.

William Penrose, the new reinsurance broker worked on the Mannings Treaty with very good results. Mr Mannings was pleased with the new arrangements, gave notice to cancel his existing programme at 31st March and gave Burke & Co an order to replace his reinsurances at the 1st April. William placed the whole programme with a Lloyd's lead, followed by several large London insurance companies, then completed his slips with a strong collection of Lloyd's underwriters. The brokerage was sufficient to pay the new man's salary and his trip to the health clinic for three weeks. Thadeus read the enticing brochure and felt quite envious of Mr Penrose, who although restricted to a rigorous diet enjoyed daily massage and the use of a well equipped gymnasium; the boss might try this himself some time. William's well-being was substantially assisted by a romantic liaison with Beth Bateman, love at first sight for both of them; her threats regarding the consumption of alcohol proving stronger than the clinic discipline. He was a new, new man by the end of the month.

Bartholomew Coen, the office boy aged fourteen, arrived in the second week of the month. He was straight out of *Oliver Twist,* except he was Jewish and his boss a Christian. Hailing from Whitechapel, he had more brothers and sisters than Old Mother Hubbard could cope with and a similar number of uncles and aunts. His dark grey, or blue, suits were immaculate, his father being a tailor; his white shirts were fresh every day, from his aunt's shop; his shoes were a problem, rarely fitted and were sometimes odd, usually the same colour but different designs, there was clearly a deficiency in the cobbler department of the Coen clan, or more likely the little lad fared badly in the mêlée underneath the stairs at the matutinal uprising. Ties were another dilemma, he did not have one; William and James donated two each and taught him how to tie them. He could not be described as well educated, even his writing and reading were not strong, but his memory for numbers, names and faces was such that Ethel felt that he could have become a successful stage turn.

Gussie's undercover espionage work at the Thurlow offices had unfortunately proved unsuccessful; there was no trace of the requested claims files, either by number or names. Thadeus was assured that they were just not where they should be! However, two days later Gussie telephoned to depart the useful information that, working from the given policy numbers and a policy register coding system, he was able to ascertain the name of the producing agent for this particular bloodstock business; a firm of solicitors in Newmarket called Woodford & Kinloch. Gussie knew of this partnership as his mother used them for some of her horse charity ventures. Although he had never visited them, he regarded them as a respectable outfit.

Thadeus tracked them down and arranged a visit to their offices in the Newmarket High Street. He advised Mr Woodford that he was representing certain Lloyd's underwriters, and needed to inspect some files related to bloodstock business placed at Lloyd's by the partnership; both statements being truthful, but not necessarily when put together!

When Thadeus arrived at the lawyer's building he was cordially greeted by Mr Woodford who did not seem in the least bit surprised that their bloodstock account should be investigated: it had proved a disaster for the underwriters involved! He related how insurance was not really something that they knew much about, usually preferring to divert any enquiries from their clients to a professional insurance broker in the town, for which they received a small commission payment.

The bloodstock business that the firm had handled for a short period arose from the interest of a young articled clerk, who knew the insured owners personally and handled all the work himself: the commission to the partners had been surprisingly generous. The young man, Archibald Wickham, had been killed in a motor accident about four months ago; he was run down one evening, as he travelled to his home in Diss on his motor cycle, by a 'hit and run' driver. Thadeus acknowledged that there had been a spate of these crimes recently.

Declining lunch at a pub out at Dullingham, Thadeus sat down with the only bloodstock insurance file that the firm possessed, a ring-binder containing all their papers. There were very few sheets of scribbled telephone messages and copies of each of the insurance certificates, the latter showing the addresses of the insured owners. Thadeus wrote down the addresses, which were new to him and at first glance appeared to be false, but he would get Jackson to check these. The hand-written notes were mostly draft instructions for what later became the insurance policies; there were no details of the claims occurrences, except for one startling telephone message, taken in a separate hand that might have been the firm's telephone operator.

It read: 'Yearling by *Phalaris* out of *Mary Mona* died of colic. Please phone Mr Hitchen.' There was a telephone number and the note was dated 15 May 1924.

'Well, well, well,' said Thadeus aloud. 'Wild Bill strikes again!' He copied the words verbatim into his notebook. At 2.30 he took his leave of Messrs Woodford & Kinloch and called in briefly to see Daphne Dennington. She was very busy waiting for a mare to foal down, and her Rolls Royce was being serviced at the garage, but they had a cup of tea and chatted about the new breeding season and the stallions to be used this year before he drove back to London.

The next day he telephoned Inspector Jackson of the Yard and gave him the addresses to verify, and asked him to seek details of a fatal accident involving Archibald Wickham. The telephone number used by William Hitchen nearly two years age was no longer available. The same day Jackson confirmed that the addresses were all fictitious; the roads did not even match with the towns and counties. The next morning a typed memorandum concerning the death of Archibald Wickham arrived at Sloane Mews.

The twenty-two-year-old Archie was found dead in a ditch beside a main road in Norfolk at dawn on a Monday morning; his damaged motor cycle lay close by showing evidence of a collision but no lead as to the perpetrator of the crime. In addition to the details of the multiple injuries sustained, the post-mortem report exposed signs of recent sexual activity – the deceased lad had a good weekend!

There were no further developments regarding the Dennington case that month, which was fortunate as the insurance work at Burke & Co was mushrooming in all directions. Thadeus and James were confined to their offices from dawn till dusk, emerging only to transport bundles of slips forwards and backwards, to and from the Lloyd's Underwriting Room.

The month started on a happy note when Thadeus was invited by a crowd of ex-Trinity College Dublin men to attend the Cheltenham Gold Cup to be run at Prestbury Park on Tuesday 9th March 1926 – a very welcome break for an exhausted insurance broker. The Bentley was polished and packed with suitcases and a small suite at The Lygon Arms in Broadway booked for Sunday night through until Thursday morning; this was a fixture that needed preparation and recovery intervals.

Both Oliver Cromwell and King Charles the First had made their battle plans in the hotel building which was a good recommendation for Thadeus' anticipated savage attack on the bookmaking fraternity.

Sunday evening he unpacked, strolled around the village, sampled the local ale and the hotel cuisine, spoke to Freddie on the telephone who informed him that her graduation ceremony had now been brought further forward and would take place on Tuesday 13 March, just before the Easter break. This was a whole term earlier than the rest of the diploma presentations in order to give more time for the rebuilding programme planned for the medical department during the summer. Thadeus would of course be there for his sister's big day and she volunteered to seek accommodation either at a hotel or with some friends of the family that she had already raided several times during her five years up in Scotland. Thadeus was looking forward to this event and retired to bed contemplating additional activities to enhance the occasion.

Monday morning he was up with the lark, give or take a couple of hours, bathed in grand style and just caught the last serving of breakfast. Clothed in bucolic habiliments he lounged in the drawing room with a copy of the *Sporting Life* and studied the runners for the next day. The big race was of course the Gold Cup introduced by Mr Cathcart only two years ago, a weight for age contest over three and a quarter miles and a race that could establish the National Hunt Champion for the season; the Grand National at Aintree being a handicap. Next year the course was to introduce a similar race for hurdlers over two miles.

Thadeus browsed through the field. Mr Filmer-Sankey's *Ruddyglow* was the favourite at evens, or slightly odds-on in some places; Mrs Dixon's *Old Tay Bridge* was second favourite at three to one, this gelding had run in the inaugural race two years previous, so he knew the course and trip. Thadeus fancied *Koko*, carrying the same weight and at tens with the bookies. He decided that an each-way bet at that price, or better in the ring, would be good value. The other races on the card were also quite competitive, modest pin-selected gambles might be in order. Suddenly his eyes were drawn to a runner in the fourth race, trained by a Mr W Hitchen from Ireland. Well, well, well, thought Thadeus once again.

Thadeus had lunch with Lord Harry Cheddon who was staying nearby at a friend's house in Winchcombe. The earl had a runner in the first on the next day, a failed flat-racer being given the opportunity of a new career over fences; the owner did not recommend a flutter. There were also several bookmakers resident at the hotel for the meeting, at least three of whom came across and shook hands with Thadeus' ennobled companion, a bad sign thought Thadeus who had every intention of continuing to enjoy the angry glances from the gentlemen of the turf accountancy profession whenever possible.

The evening dinner appointment with the Trinity old boys is better left undescribed in print; suffice it to say that a new venue will need to be sought for next year! Thadeus found himself with a large taxi fare to pay as he disembarked, as the last passenger on the route from the town of Cheltenham, via various villages and farms, to the safe haven of the Lygon Arms. A serious cash-recovery plan was required for the next day.

Gold Cup day 1926 and Thadeus was greeted at the entrance to the Prestbury Park racecourse by the imposing figure of Mr Wild Bill

Hitchen; too astonished to utter even 'Well, well,' his arms were clasped at his side by the ex-vet who boomed, 'Welcome Mr Burke.'

Thadeus managed a weak 'Mr Hitchen!' and the new racehorse trainer acclaimed, 'All is forgiven dear boy; I am released from the drudgery of swindling Lloyd's underwriters and firmly established in the honourable profession of trainer to the gentry – and all thanks to your assiduousness. Let me buy you a drink.'

At these words Thadeus could almost hear the body cells of his kidneys offering a plea to their Maker for a recycled role in any reincarnation strategy that might be included within His creation, perhaps a minor situation at the back of the eyeball or a cushy little number as part of the ear lobe could be considered.

The Trinity mob had ensured that any body-part not poisoned with alcohol had been drowned in the stuff; nevertheless five minutes later Thadeus was at a bar in front of a pint of Guinness trying to make polite conversation with a man whom he had previously numbered among his enemies. The black stuff seemed to revitalize him, presumably finding a welcome from the remnants of last night's intake.

Hitchen strongly advocated a bet on his runner later in the afternoon. Wild Bill had backed the gelding at fifties, then at twenty-fives, twenties, and finally at sixteen to one. The winnings were going to repay his mortgage arrangements.

Could Wild Bill be trusted, or was this a perverted form of revenge? Thadeus decided to test the man's new-found amiability with a few questions about non-existent horses that pretended to die for the amusement of insurance claims officers.

Hitchen laughed riotously and ordered another round of coloured Liffey water. 'I am a new man!' he pleaded. 'All my previous sins have been confessed and eradicated by more Hail Mary's than you can wave a stick at.'

Thadeus made to flip the froth from his new pint at his drinking companion in priest-like manner. 'Well be good enough to re-confess this little episode to me.'

'I was given the details of the horses involved, name, colour, sex, age and breeding; then asked to invent a cause of death and prepare a certificate to that effect. I think I gave a couple a colic demise and another two broken legs, then, after reading an article in an American veterinary magazine I tried my hand at Colitis X – never had a case of that myself but I gave a good report.' he chuckled

'Your memory is very good,' said Thadeus

'You need a good memory if you are dishonest,' instructed the Irishman.

'Who gave you the details and instructions?' was the number one question, eager to emerge from Thadeus' lips.

'I am not a sneak dear boy. Back my horse today and you can get all the money back for your underwriters.'

Thadeus pushed this question further but Hitchen's lips were sealed. He acknowledged that he knew Archie Wickham and confirmed that he had spoken to him on several occasions; the news of the lad's death was genuinely a surprise announcement.

They shook hands and departed towards their different appointments.

Up in Harry Cheddon's box all the talk was for the favourite in the first race, a decisive winner of several races during the season, but at eleven to ten Thadeus considered it poor value. However, the price looked generous within fifteen minutes as the gelding trotted up, crossing the winning line as the second horse jumped the last fence. Lord Cheddon's five-year-old, who started at one hundred to one, was pipped on the line for a place, much to the relief of the owner, having broadcast widely that the gelding had no chance. The host had engaged the services of a retired tic-tack man for the amusement and enlightenment of his guests and this elderly gentleman had given a running commentary on the laying-off activity in the betting ring involving the short priced favourite which was more exciting than the race itself.

For the next race Thadeus selected an each-way chance at ten to one, good value over two miles of hurdles. His choice crossed the line in second place but was awarded the race after a steward's enquiry.

As Thadeus queued to collect his winnings he noticed a familiar face similarly engaged at an adjacent bookmaker, Sadar Shah Hasham, clearly not a strong adherent to the Islamic faith. Thadeus ducked out of his line in fear of being recognized, but followed the alleged assassin through the crowd until he entered a private box on the ground level opposite the grass viewing area.

Tracking down a police constable on crowd duty Thadeus enlightened the astonished young PC of his observation, and instructed him to contact the local station, preferably Inspector 'Hobby' Hobson, and also to make the information known to Inspector Jackson at Scotland Yard.

Within fifteen minutes Inspector Hobson and a posse of uniformed officers arrived at the course, meeting with Thadeus at the appointed place, and proceeding to the private viewing box presently entertaining Hasham. Hobby outlined his plan to march straight into the box and arrest the villain. Thadeus recommended caution and suggested that a couple of constables be despatched on that duty, and that he and the inspector stand on the pathway in front of the target box. This they did, and within a short time a disturbance was heard inside and a sweating and dishevelled Sadar Shah Hasham vaulted, or rather rolled over, the sill of the balcony at the front of the box and stumbled onto the path. Gratefully he accepted the helping hand from a large ex-Trinity man, lifting him to his feet, his demeanour changing as a pair of handcuffs were placed around his wrists by an agile police inspector.

The Turkish diplomat being safely carted away in a waiting Black Maria, Thadeus carefully briefed Hobby on the matter of press reportage, insisting that the whole of Fleet Street be made conversant with the arrest, and the crime involved, and particular emphasis be given to the fact that the wanted man had been spotted collecting his winnings from a bookmaker on Cheltenham Racecourse and that the detainment had been carried out in the middle of a heavy drinking race-day party. He felt that these disclosures should ensure that no question of diplomatic immunity or extradition would arise for the professed follower of the Islamic tradition.

The horses were already down at the start for the Gold Cup so Thadeus rushed over to the rails and reinvested his £500 win on the previous race as an each-way bet on *Koko* at tens. He was back in the box as the flag went down and *Koko* went to the front and stayed there with quick and accurate jumping; treating the first and second favourites with contempt the eight-year-old crossed the line a comfortable four lengths clear. Thadeus' fund was now well into four figures and he needed to carefully consider his wager on Mr Hitchen's hope; he collected £3,000 in cash from his bookmaker, leaving the balance as a credit on his account, and wandered into the Tattersalls ring. It took nearly twenty minutes to dispose of the total sum among the bookies; the majority of the cash being placed at sixteen to one; then five hundred on at fourteens, and the last few hundred taking the generally now available twelve to one. Back in the viewing box he was standing next to a chuckling ex-tic-tack man again watching the betting shenanigans from his high point: the bookies might be agitated but it was an equally nervous Thadeus who trained his binoculars on Hitchen's brown and bright yellow colours, worn by a tall but skinny Irish jockey: He had nothing to fear, the magnificent looking gelding sat at the back of the field until the final bend, then shaken up by a couple of cracks from the whip he stormed through the rest of the field and galloped up the hill to take the race on the bridle. An even more nervous Thadeus entered the betting ring to collect a total of £45,000, in cash, from a collection of straight-faced settlers, some of whom he had observed at breakfast that morning, and would again confront over dinner this evening. This reaping was assisted by a couple of new friends from the box, and a small leather suitcase purchased hurriedly from a vendor's stall near the paddock.

It seemed appropriate for the last two competitions to be watched in anonymity, so after depositing his loaded suitcase in a locked cupboard in Lord Cheddon's box, Thadeus walked across to the inside of the racetrack to view the action from a grassy mound opposite the last fence. Purchasing a cup of coffee from a stall situated beside an inner roadway, used by official observers and both human and equine medical attendants, he strolled around to find a vantage point for the fifth race. To his surprise there, sitting on a spread rug together were three people that he knew, but did not know that they knew each other; they engaged in an impromptu picnic consisting of only champagne: Mr William Hitchen, who Thadeus thought would have been deep within a congratulatory celebration among an Irish contingent; Lady Frances Downing, not unexpected at any horse event of any kind, and Mr Algernon Tammis Austin, the father of Alfred who was the young chap that had shot and killed Edward Thurlow.

Thadeus placed himself in front of this small audience and toasted them with his paper cup of coffee, the surprise on their faces reminiscent of the final scene in an American movie. No introductions were necessary but explanations of the gathering naturally arose; Lady Frances had met Mr Hitchen at Tattersalls in Knightsbridge, possibly on the initiative of Thadeus, she thought, changing her recollection to the introducer being Daffy Dennington, who had sought the vet's assistance by placing his right arm up a mare's backside for a possible pre-purchase examination; Hitchen confirmed that this was indeed their first meeting. Lady Frances was at Cheltenham attending the inaugural meeting of a charity being established for the welfare of retired National Hunt horses and their separate wanderings into the inner section of the racecourse had netted Mr Austin, who had a country residence nearby and was known to Lady Frances from her involvement with an embryonic action group investigating the underwriting losses of the Thurlow syndicate at Lloyd's.

Thadeus refused an offer of Champagne and was suspicious of the curious trail that had gathered together this particular trio but the volunteered elucidations were reasonable. Lady Frances asked Thadeus if he had encountered her son Gussie recently in the city, and Thadeus was glad to report that the junior barrister was well and actively engaged in representing Mr Thurlow in the defence of a disputed insurance claim; she was pleased to hear this and suggested that both he and her son should join her at the Norfolk home, at some not too distant time, for a weekend vacation. Thadeus thanked her and said that he would arrange something with Gussie when they next met.

After the quartet watched the next race together Thadeus returned to thank his host Lord Cheddon, and then after receiving in return a whispered 'thanks for that one in the fourth!' made his departure after the last race.

Embarrassingly large wads of encased notes were concealed in the locked boot of the Bentley and the car and driver clambered out of the muddy parking zone and on to the road towards the village of Broadway.

Thankful for Hilton's foresight in arranging a lock-up garage behind the hotel for the Bentley, Thadeus went round to the front of the building just in time to witness the return of the bookmakers in their collectively hired coach. They were clambering out of the charabanc door, the governors, clerks, board boys and tic-tack men; while two girls were unloading the hods, those big leather bags or satchels used by bookies for their cash, and some ledgers, from the rear of the vehicle and placing them on the pavement for collection by the owners or their staff. Thadeus watched for a while as the luggage was distributed then entered the hotel main entrance, retaining the memory of 'Long John', a bookmaker with a Gladstone bag of the same size and description as that of the new bookkeeper at Burke & Co, except that Long John's had his name and profession painted on the sides; the tall man had set off for the public house on the other side of the road where he apparently lodged; he was assisted with the large bag by the two girls. Thadeus' mind speculated on the outcome of this event.

Pushing open the double doors Thadeus was greeted by applause from two lines of hotel staff, and a contingent of the bookmaking fraternity; the corridor between the assembly led straight towards the bar, at which a smiling bartender stood in eager anticipation of a substantial drinks order. Mr Herbert Hope, a gentleman whose name also appeared on one of the unloaded hods suggested, to the background of further animated applause, that it might be in order for the day's lucky punter to purchase a round of drinks for the poor and distressed bookmakers. Thadeus gladly conceded to the proposal and announced in a loud voice that he was 'in the chair' and that the congregation were at liberty to consume the tipple of their choice at his expense, begging only that he be allowed to visit his room to clean up before joining them.

Thadeus needed another long drinking session like a hole in the head, and intended to dally at his ablutions to the maximum acceptable polite limit.

He ordered an urgent, large pot of tea from room service and stood in front of the open casement windows filling his pipe. From this advantage point he observed that across the road Long John and the two girls were loading their bags and things into an old Austin, into which they all climbed and drove off up the main street towards Oxford. As they passed beneath a lighted street lamp Thadeus, equipped with his racing binoculars, noted the car registration number. He then telephoned Inspector Hobson at his home number, informing him that he knew that a crime had been committed; knew the modus operandi and the perpetrators, but did not yet know who the victim was. Hobby said he would act and thanked Thadeus for the tip on Mr Hitchen's runner at Cheltenham that day; the whole station had benefited through the use of an illegal bookie's runner, granted special immunity for the occasion.

Thadeus showered, drank his tea and changed into lighter clothing more suited for a place beside the huge fire downstairs, then descended to mingle unobtrusively with the intoxicated crowd clutching a glass of ice-cold water. It was not long before an agitated youth, Mr Herbert Hope's board boy, entered the bar area and whispered a few words to his governor, who set down his glass of whiskey and dashed from the room.

'So, Mr Hope, you are the midwife to my woe,' Thadeus quietly quoted Richard the Second's queen to himself. He ascertained Mr Hope's room number from reception and ascended the stairs in that direction, knocking at the door and entering without permission, he asked if he could be of any help.

'Some bastard has absconded with my cash and left me with a pile of newspapers,' was the exact and succinct response. He went on to pace up and down the room illuminating the small group of listeners with details of his successful strategic ploys during the afternoon that had proved so beneficial, up to this point. He had posted odds-on for the favourite in the first race, added a point to the prices for the fancied horses in the Cup and laid off most of the gamble on that Irish runner in the fourth.

'Now some thieving bastard has pocketed my reward. What happened to those two tarts?'

'I think you will find that the game that they were on paid better standing up,' suggested Thadeus.

'You think it was them?' asked the youth

'Agents for Long John, who by the way is now Long Gone!' enlightened Thadeus, explaining that he was aware of the crime but needed to await the emergence of the victim. He returned triumphantly to his rooms and partook of his fourth pipe of the day while speaking on the telephone to James Pooley checking on office endeavours, the only matter of importance to arise being the decision to purchase, at company expense, a decent pair of black shoes for the exclusive use of Bartholomew Coen within the City of London limits; the lad having appeared the previous day wearing one brown and one black. Thadeus concurred with the modest acquisition the cost of which in his opinion could not have procured a decent pair of socks!

Inspector Hobson telephoned two hours later with the news that unfortunately Thadeus' hypothesis of unlawful goings-on had been wrong!

Acting on information received, the policeman had arranged for a traffic patrol vehicle to stop Long John's car, with suspicions of driving without due care and attention, which was not difficult following a boozy meal enjoyed by the three occupants at an Italian restaurant in Chipping Norton. The decidedly drunken group were very helpful and obliging towards the police officers, allowing a full search of the entire vehicle including opening up cases and bags. One leather bag contained nearly £3,000 in cash which the owner went to great lengths to explain to a bemused sergeant had been acquired at the races that day, and he went on to support every penny of the money from his ledgers, that were also in the car boot.

Asked for the destination, they replied that they were returning to a pub where they were lodging in Broadway; asked why they had carried their entire luggage out to dinner with them, they replied that they did not trust the security in public house dwellings.

Thadeus, now facing possible actions for slander, needed to make a rapid reappraisal of the situation. Where was the duplicate leather bag that he was so sure the alleged villains had switched during the coach disembarkment? Had they stashed it somewhere in Chipping Norton, or left it hidden at the pub across the road? He watched the Long John band return to the pub and reinstate their belongings into their rooms from his vantage point at the casement window in his room at the Lygon where he had sought sanctuary since the disturbing phone call.

It was past midnight and during his third pipe of the evening when plan B unfolded in his mind.

Out of bed early and with a room service breakfast the low-profile Thadeus carefully perused the view opposite the hotel, sweeping his binoculars across from the confectionary shop on the left, through the pub's car park, over the entire front of the hostelry and on to the gentleman's outfitters at the right.

Eventually his vigilance was rewarded and he observed Mr Herbert Hope's board boy cross into the public house car park and drive out in a highly polished Rolls Royce, which he parked outside the hotel, just below Thadeus's window. The Hope team, together with the tools of their joint, as a bookmaker's site at the racecourse is called, including only one leather hod, drove off eastwards. Thadeus, having written down the vehicle registration number, again telephoned Inspector Hobson and suggested the employment of the same traffic surveillance ploy as was used the previous evening; this time Thadeus' accusations were more speculative and reserved.

Within an hour Hobson telephoned the hotel. Thadeus was wrong again! Hope's Roller had stopped on a pedestrian crossing while the lad popped out to buy some cigarettes, giving the following police car the opportunity to once again interrogate another vehicle's occupants. Thadeus was right about one thing; there were two identical leather hods in the car boot, one empty and the other containing exactly £1,000 in bank notes. This was explained by Mr Hope personally as a reserve bag, manufactured some three months ago following an incident at Hurst Park when the stitching on the usual hod had broken, and he had decided to purchase and employ a duplicate in the future, retained in his motor vehicle and containing a small cash emergence fund – just a grand!

No harm done and Thadeus already had plan C waiting in the wings for just such an emergency. In hindsight plan C was the most obvious solution as plans A and B had been too easily detected; all the plans started from the large hod carried by Long John; Thadeus was certain that within that bag when it was first loaded onto the coach at the racecourse was a small duplicate of Mr Hope's bag filled with old newspapers. This was lifted straight out of Long John's bag and placed on the pavement outside of the hotel, then within the cover of the coach's rear boot-hood Mr Hope's racecourse bag had been placed into the tall bookie's bag, which was then shut and placed alongside the other unloaded hods and later transported across the road to the lodgings in the pub. As a result of the police searches it was evident that the Hope racecourse bag must have been left in the pub rooms and picked up by one of Hope's employees during the evening and put in the boot of his Rolls Royce, stationed in the pub car park. Thadeus suspected why these manoeuvres were enacted but needed some telephone conversations to verify his new hypothesis. First a call to Lord Cheddon to find out the name and telephone number of the extic-tack man who had entertained the group in the earl's box the previous day: Next a call to that man, who was at home in his flat in London, having returned to town by railway late last night.

This call confirmed all Thadeus' suspicions and included a brief précis of the Race Gang Wars when a gang from Birmingham had tried to break the monopoly of the London producers of the 'lists', the sheets that displayed the runners for each race for use on the bookmaker's boards. Thadeus thanked the tic-tack man for his exact and numerate observations of the Tattersalls Ring and Rails betting movements before the fourth race yesterday. Hope had laid the Irish horse very heavily, taking most of the ceded bets at ten to one; he must have lost a fortune on Mr Hitchen's winner.

Could it be proved that he then devised a plot, with the assistance of Long John, to recoup his losses at the expense of his cash in transit insurers, aided by a respected Lloyd's insurance broker as witness? Thadeus surmised that the 'stolen' bag contained more than £1,000 and that Long John's team had taken the surplus as their reward for the operation. The proof would entail long and arduous analysis of the books and ledgers used at the Gold Cup day meeting. Routine police work thought Thadeus! Having fired blanks on two previous efforts Inspector Hobson was sceptical about supporting a third raid upon possibly innocent members of the public, even if they were bookmakers. However, over the next ten days he and other police officers around the country, slowly and methodically interviewed and scrutinized the betting participants and their records. Some, particularly those from the northern tracks, were pleased to assist in every way, delighting in the knowledge that their evidence might bring down the cocky cockney. Thadeus' enquiries in Lloyd's revealed that the underwriter involved on the insurance was 100 per cent Thurlow & Others. George was very appreciative and employed one of his most aggressive claim's adjustors for the task of unmasking Mr Hope.

It was only one day before Thadeus set off for Scotland that the bookmaker was confronted by an overwhelming mountain of statistical and statement evidence, sufficient for his loyal clerk and board boy to turn King's evidence immediately.

Mr Hope's tic-tack man refused to comment, except with a prominent and communicative use of two of his fingers of one hand, preferring to serve a gaol sentence with his master.

CHAPTER 13

THE DOCTOR'S GRADUATION

Freddie's graduation was finally set for Wednesday 31st March 1926 and extensive secret activities were undertaken by Thadeus, James Pooley and Mr Henry Hollington the motor vehicle entrepreneur, to ensure that her new Bugatti Type 37 Grand Prix two-seater was not only manufactured in France, but also delivered to England and then driven up to Scotland. Following numerous strongly worded bilingual international telegram despatches, the important surprise was due to be landed at Folkestone two days earlier from where Thadeus would drive the car straight up to Edinburgh, stopping somewhere overnight and arriving in the Scottish capital a day ahead of the planned presentation to the newly appointed and sworn-in Doctor F. Burke. The human endeavours proved satisfactory, but Mother Nature, not linked into the international communication network, delivered a fierce storm across the English Channel right through the weekend and Monday, preventing vessels crossing from France; the vehicle would disembark Tuesday morning God willing!

The Bugatti was fast, easily capable of travelling over four hundred miles in twenty-four hours but Thadeus did not wish to risk the possibility of missing his sister's ceremony; a new car needed running in at a reasonable pace, and there might be engine problems or a puncture. James Pooley had the solution. Thadeus would travel to Edinburgh by train, a very enjoyable journey in first class relaxing with good food and drink, meanwhile James, accompanied by J K Payne, would drive through the night taking turns at the wheel, like in the Grand Prix du Mans, a race for which this car was designed.

Thadeus wondered if, with the co-operation of some pluvious insurance underwriter, the pair of them had arranged the inclement weather in order to engage in this exciting venture; if they drove up and Freddie drove back, as she undoubtedly would, Thadeus was to be deprived of all opportunity behind the wheel of this racing legend. A disappointed Thadeus phoned his sister to advise that he would be arriving on the night train leaving Kings Cross late Monday and arriving in Edinburgh Tuesday morning; he also telephoned their favourite restaurant, from previous visits, to book a good table for dinner Tuesday evening; of course he was unable to cry down the phone to his sister concerning the outrageous twist of fate that had deprived him of his motor-racing ambitions, as she was to know nothing of the planned four-wheel surprise. His sister was cheerful and pleased to hear his news, as were the two Lloyd's colleagues chattering excitedly over road-maps of the British Isles in the Burke & Co office as Thadeus left the city by taxi for the mainline LMS station, he having worked late finalizing outstanding matters, and they using the firm's typewriter and paper to note down their itinerary.

Hilton met Thadeus on the platform where he had loaded his master's suitcases into the allotted sleeping compartment and together they distributed the luggage around the little mobile room; Thadeus' suits and shaving paraphernalia placed in their appropriate places, a selection of newspapers, magazines and books set down near the bed; the manservant returned to Chelsea in the Bentley. Thadeus lighted a pipe of tobacco and browsed at the news awaiting the anticipated call for dinner, which was to be served soon after departure. The big steam engine puffed its high-temperature water vapour high into the arches of the station and the wheels turned to follow their allocated lines to the north. Thadeus stared out at the night lights of London and its suburbs. The carriage attendant knocked on the compartment door to announce that dinner would be served shortly and requesting that he take his seat in the dining carriage at the rear of the train. Thadeus needed no second reminder, it was well past his normal dining hour and he was hungry, so he set out down the corridors clutching a copy of the *Horse & Hound* and took his allocated seat by the window; within a minute he was joined opposite by a very beautiful lady, elegantly dressed, in her late twenties or early thirties, Thadeus guessed. He rose from his seat and greeted her, introducing himself and receiving a bright smile and the name Alice Kurtner, from South Africa, visiting friends in Perth. They ordered their meal, smoked salmon for two, Dover sole for him and sirloin steak for her; Thadeus ordered a Chablis and a Claret. They chatted amiably about the weather and travel generally and the fact that one should never order soup on a train, neither looked at their magazines, hers being *Vogue*.

They both showed disappointment when the outside seats at the table were taken by two men in plain suits and ties indicating that members of the third class were now joining the dining carriage to take up the spare seats; they were introduced as John and Fred, no surname was supplied or requested; they both ordered soup and fillet steaks with chipped potatoes. Conversation between the foursome was sparse right through until the cheese and remnants of the red wine, then Fred lifted from beneath his seat a folding chessboard and a box of chess men.

'Do you mind if we play a game or two?' he asked.

There was nodded consent. The table was cleared by the waiter and four coffees and two ashtrays delivered; the board unfolded between John and Fred and chess pieces were carefully placed in their positions.

Thadeus picked up a rook of Staunton design. 'Nicely weighted,' he commented. 'Just right for the railway.' He replaced the piece on its appropriate square.

The two chess players lighted cigarettes handing a packet of Players White Label to Alice, at her request; she lit a gasper; Thadeus insisting that he preferred to wait until later for an opportunity to smoke a full pipe of tobacco. Play proceeded with king-pawn openings and movement of the knights then, within the next play white made a bad queen move. Black went on to win after about twenty moves, it being lucky for white that there was no clock ticking. They turned the board around and changed colours but Fred still won the second contest. The two men invited their table companions to engage in a match; Alice and Thadeus accepted and played one game, the lady confessing to beginner status, confirmed by Thadeus needing to allow reinstatement of her queen on three occasions, before she gracefully resigned.

The train chugged on blowing its whistle in regular proud intervals, then started slowing down, the waiter advising that they would stop at Peterborough for water and coal; legs could be stretched if desired. The idea of strolling up and down the platform at Peterborough station did not appeal to either Thadeus or Alice, the latter declaring that she would retire to her compartment to freshen up and probably visit the first-class lounge in about a half of an hour for a night-cap, a clear invitation to Thadeus to join her, John and Fred not being in possession of the correct tickets.

Thadeus also left the two men with a similar excuse and made his way back to his compartment where he set up his own chess set, kindly provided for the journey by Hilton, on his wooden board, in the positions of the first game witnessed that evening, after the players had played three moves each and considered whites reply to Kt-B3; he considered a copy-cat Kt-B3 was the best option, then as he thought about white's next move he was aware of some commotion on the platform outside his window; there were several uniformed policemen engaged in an arrest, the prisoners being led from the train in handcuffs were no less than John and Fred his erstwhile dinner companions.

Holding his hands against the window pane to shade the inner glare he was even more amazed to see the face of Detective Sergeant David Anderson of Scotland Yard staring back at him indicating with a waving index finger that he should proceed to the carriage exit to his right, where no doubt the mysterious events would be elucidated upon. Thadeus followed the hand signals and shortly found himself shaking hands with the signaller, his ally on three previous adventures, and it was explained to him that the two arrests were on the instructions of Inspector Jackson in London and that the detainees were wanted for questioning in connexion with a robbery at a jewellers in Old Bond Street, a particularly vicious attack that had left two men dead and two more in a serious condition. John and Fred were brothers, although they did not look alike, sharing the surname of Lampard, part of a gang resident in Fulham, very possibly they were the ringleaders. John's fingerprints had been found on the get-away car, he was the muscles of the partnership, his brother the brains. Thadeus informed the sergeant that he had just finished a passable dinner with the alleged assailants; Anderson laughed and said that he was looking forward to telling Jackson. Thadeus, acting on a whim, requested that an Alice Kurtner might be worth checking out by the CID duo. Whistles were blowing and green flags waving so Thadeus said goodbye and rejoined the train.

He returned to his compartment and washed, brushed his hair, changed his shirt and tie and put on a light tweed lounge suit, then set out for the first class piano bar to join Alice. She was seated with her back to the window in conversation with a stocky gentleman, both smoking cigarettes and nursing small glasses of liqueurs. Thadeus went over to their table and offered to refresh their drinks, they accepted and Thadeus signalled the attendant for replenishment and brandy with ice for himself. The stranger was introduced as Alex Wengler from Amsterdam travelling to Edinburgh on business, the nature of which was not disclosed.

Alice ordered a new packet of cigarettes as the brand that she was smoking, Players White Label, were not to her liking; it was the packet that had been handed to her by Fred at dinner and she had left the table with them in her bag by mistake; Alex said that he enjoyed those and exchanged the Players for a new packet of 'Autograph' Corked Tipped, opened and presented by the bar attendant. Thadeus watched this play-acting with some amusement, especially when the Dutchman opened the Players upside-down and all the cigarettes fell onto the carriage floor. Alice laughed as both the men stood and collected up the scattered gaspers, the farce being amplified by Thadeus treading on the empty cigarette packet and crushing it flat beneath his foot; everybody was in hysterics by the time Alex had reconstructed the mutilated tobacco container back into a reasonably acceptable and useable packet of cigarettes.

Thadeus declined a further round of drinks ordered by Alex advising the company that, as he was aware that the train arrived at its destination at 7.00 am, and that breakfast was served forty-five minutes before that, he was of the opinion that an early night was necessary. He left the couple of foreigners toasting some alien deity with new, full glasses.

Thadeus slept well despite the rocking of the rolling-stock, to be woken only by a consistent soft knocking at the compartment door. He arose, naked, and opened the door a fraction, anticipating the smiling face of an inebriated South African lady, but instead found himself facing a small hand pistol held before the grim visage of Alex Wengler.

'I apologize for the intrusion Mr Burke, but the train is just entering York Station, where I am afraid I must disembark – with these,' he announced, pushing his way into the sleeper and scooping up Thadeus' chessmen from the board that he had left in position since his encounter with Sergeant Anderson hours earlier. All thirty-two of the game's pieces were slid into a small open mouthed sack; the playing board was left *in situ*. Thadeus said nothing, his unclothed state not prompting lengthy verbal exchanges. He just nodded sleepily as the Dutchman and his booty departed with a brief 'Thank you, *et bon voyage.*'

The rest of the night was undisturbed, except by several involuntary chuckles prompted by the semi-conscious sleeping mind of the traveller rehearsing the tale that he would tell his sister the next day.

Alice Kurtner was not at breakfast, served just after dawn as the train trundled gently through the suburbs of the Scottish capital. Thadeus sat alone and availed himself of a poached egg with tomatoes and bacon, accompanied by tea, toast and the day's edition of *The Times*.

At about the same time James Pooley was parking his car at a garage owned by a business friend of his father's behind Victoria Railway Station. He and J K Payne unloaded their suitcases, one each, and trudged sleepily round to the platform where the train for Folkestone was shortly due. They too anticipated a proper cooked breakfast before taking their reserved first-class seats, in which they hoped to replace the missed nightly slumber.

Thadeus also could have used more rest but as the meal was cleared by the dining carriage attendants, the steam engine entered Edinburgh Station, Platform 1. He stood up, stretched and made to leave the carriage, taking a couple of bank notes from his wallet as reward for the excellent service he had received from the LMS staff. He received grateful acknowledgements for the two quickly pocketed five-pound notes, and a surprise apology from the table waiter for having no carrier bag available for the chess set that had been left on the dining table the previous evening. As Thadeus paused the waiter explained that he understood from Mrs Kurtner that the pieces and board were his property; the attendant had enquired while serving the lady coffee and toast in her cabin earlier. Thadeus made no complaint, but requested that the man be good enough to arrange for the delivery of the chess pieces to his hotel, either by hand or through the postal service and, most peculiarly, that the items be placed within a round cake tin, packed to prevent rattling, and presented as a parcel at the hotel reception desk. Any murmur of discontent was quickly dissolved by another five-pound note, to cover postage costs; another of the same denomination for the acquisition of a cake tin; and a third as compensation for the time and effort required to fulfil these strange instructions. Having just been handed more than a month's wages, in cash, the chap was delighted to oblige the eccentric Englishman.

At the platform barrier stood sister Freddie, the early hour failing neither to rumple her natural bright and elegant demeanour nor restrain her fashionable clothing selections; she waved enthusiastically as he stepped from the train. He saw her and increased his pace, leaving the porter trundling behind. They hugged and directed the luggage to be strapped on the back of her tiny Morris Cowley, tipped the attendant, over-generously again, and Freddie steered the vehicle cautiously out of the station precinct and along Princes Street towards the Great Northern Hotel, which was only a few hundred yards away, parking the car at the back and registering for the two suites that Freddie had booked for a couple of days.

Thadeus notified the receptionist regarding his expected delivery of a cake, much to the bemusement of his sister. He then wrote a brief telegram to Inspector Jackson in London – 'Check out an Alex Wengler from Amsterdam'. Freddie was further baffled by his insistence that they leave the hotel immediately and purchase a chess set; this did not take long as there was an appropriate store within walking distance of the hotel lobby. Freddie watched silently as Thadeus resisted all attempts to sell him ivory or stone examples, some of which were carved as the leading protagonists in the Battle of Waterloo, or the American Civil War, and insisted on a plain wooden set in the Staunton design, in black and white and nicely weighted, with green baize bases; he did not require a playing board.

'They were the cheapest chess set in the shop,' admonished Freddie, a fanatical believer in extravagance.

'Yes, but I expect them to be stolen within twenty-four hours,' defended Thadeus.

They retreated to Thadeus' suite and over hot freshly ground coffee, a newly packed pipe of tobacco for him and a cigarette for her; he narrated the tale of the train ride from London to Edinburgh.

'I think that you should seriously consider taking lodging at a police station,' suggested Freddie, 'then criminals of all types, from murderers to jewel thieves, could simply walk in and surrender to the authorities without the unnecessary disturbance to your relatives and friends. You could share a bed-sit with your friend Watson.'

'Nothing is going to upset your great day,' assured Thadeus, 'Tell me about tomorrow.'

'There are sixteen new graduates, two of whom are women, and we will all parade in front of the Chancellor and receive a short identical congratulatory speech each and a diploma to hang on the wall; then we will all troop off to have photographs taken wearing borrowed gowns and mortar-boards; then we head for the car-park and go out trying to run over people that we can legally repair.'

'What about the Hippocratic Oath?' asked Thadeus.

'That does impose a duty to refrain from harm, so we had better leave out the motoring proposals.'

'I mean when do you swear the oath? At the graduation ceremony, or separately?' said Thadeus, trying to return the girl to sanity.

'After we have been done by the Chancellor and are all clutching our diplomas, the head of the medical department reads out the full oath in English. Quite interesting actually; it will be a literal translation from the Greek, all ten verses, the witnesses being Apollo, Asclepius, Hygeia and Panaceia. The English schools use an adaptation to Christianity, no bad thing, but I prefer to enter the profession in the traditional manner; some English schools do not even allow female graduates to receive their diplomas at the public ceremony; just stick it in an envelope and hand it to them as they go out through the gate.'

Thadeus kept quiet as his sister let off steam.

'Then, on a prompt from the cheer-leader, that's me, we all shout loudly and clearly "I so swear!"'

'It's going to be a great day,' said Thadeus putting his arms around her.

It was agreed that they both needed a rest; Freddie went to her rooms and one of them would telephone the other some time before lunch.

Thadeus had undressed and got into bed, and it was noon when he awoke. At this time James Pooley and J K Payne had obtained possession of the Bugatti with paperwork supplied by Thadeus and Mr Hollington, donned their leather and fur flying jackets, leather helmets and goggles, garments supplied by ex-members of the RFC who were working on Sydney Pooley's Sopwiths with a view to getting them back in the air, and felt like proper racing drivers as they set out across Kent towards London; James at the wheel, with J K to take over on the other side of the capital. Water, oil and petrol checked and all was well.

Freddie, who only needed a brief rest, was back in her outer clothing by 10.30 and wandering about the hotel lobby when Thadeus' parcel arrived. The motherly lady in charge of the front desk enquired of Lady Burke regarding her brother's cake! Freddie said that she would deal with the matter, signed the chitty, and disappeared with the cake-tin out to her car and drove off towards the university buildings. She returned at the same time as a newly spruced-up Thadeus was seeking her whereabouts. She led him straight off for a light lunch of smoked fish with salad and a glass of Chablis.

The meal set out before them she asked, 'What does a jewel robbery, a lady from South Africa and a man from Amsterdam have in common?'

'Diamonds,' answered Thadeus correctly.

'And where would these diamonds be hidden?'

'In the base of a chess set – having eliminated the cigarette packet ploy,' answered Thadeus, correctly again.

'And how do we confirm that this hypothesis is correct?' was Freddie's final question.

'We remove the baize covering and break open the base of the pieces, and look inside,' suggested Thadeus.

'Philistine!' exclaimed the girl. 'We seek the assistance of the medical profession. We find somebody who has access to a radiography facility and arrange for the x-ray of the chess pieces and print out the results, which is what I have already done this morning.'

'And what did we find, oh super intelligent sister of mine?'

'Massive, uncut stones in each of the main pieces, nothing for the pawns, sixteen in all, of huge value, probably six figures.'

'And where are they?'

'The cake tin and its contents are secured in my locker at the medical centre. We will phone Watson after lunch. Eat your fish; it's good for the brain.'

Thadeus commenced his meal but continued the analysis of the crime. 'John and Fred, the two arrested villains, obviously left their chess set on the train deliberately, not for me, so clearly for Alice Kurtner. They probably put a message inside the cigarette packet; she read it and removed it when she returned to her cabin. She is probably the person who is buying the stolen goods, and she decided that it would be safer for me to leave the train with the booty and recover them later, so at any moment she is going to steal back the set from my room.'

'Good analysis, I hope she gets on with it soon, then we can have a quiet dinner with no disturbances. We will make a loud exit from the hotel this afternoon and go shopping – do you have lots of money with you?'

'I had a very good Cheltenham; masses of notes in my pocket and a very healthy bank balance.'

'Excellent. We will get rid of that!' enthused his sister.

The Morris Cowley set of for Perthshire to look at property; Freddie having found out the size of Thadeus' race winnings decided that a Scottish retreat up on the eastern coast would be in order, especially as she needed somewhere to garage the 'heifer' – her pet name for the small car – that she wanted to neither sell nor take back to London. It was a great afternoon. Estate agents bobbing and grovelling, as the dazzling young lady surveyed castles, mansions and shooting lodges, demanding instant responses to her every question. They returned to Edinburgh at 5.30, Thadeus driving as Freddie continued her study of brochures and notes, eliminating choices and scheduling the desirable freeholds in order of preference.

Such was their euphoria that they forgot to telephone Inspector Jackson, and, even more disastrously, Freddie forgot to purchase some new dresses. Entering Thadeus' room they found that the chess set, left prominently on a small table in front of the fireplace had disappeared; stolen!

'Excellent!' stated Freddie. 'Now for a very good dinner.'

At about this time the two-man intrepid Bugatti team was sitting down to a late tea or early dinner at the White Lion in Baldock. J K studied his watch and found them to be ten minutes ahead of schedule. It was his turn to drive so James sampled two pints of the local brew, downing the final drop in front of a finger tapping colleague eager to start out for Yorkshire and the Scottish border.

The Burke siblings' repast was far more relaxed. Cocktails involving ingredients previously unknown to the restaurant staff, brought in from a nearby public house on Freddie's instructions; Beluga caviar with sour cream and blini, served with iced vodka and salted cucumber, another eye-opener for the barmen; Scottish beef and the best Claret on the wine list; Crêpe Suzette flambé at the table, preceded 1904 Cockburn's port and an inebriated stagger back to the hotel. It was, in the words of the almost-doctor 'Bloody good!'

They made a flamboyant entrance into the hotel lobby at exactly midnight, just as the Bugatti team were unwrapping their earlier purchased cheese and tomato sandwiches outside the town of Thirsk, over halfway to their destination; the enthusiasm for motor racing waning. James pointed the bonnet north and the splendid vehicle purred through the night air on the next stage towards the border crossing at Coldstream, at which time the Burkes would be fast asleep.

Freddie appeared at breakfast in sombre attire, black shoes, a dark blue dress, no hat or gloves, a single gold chain and a gold wristwatch; her hair fiercely brushed and a modest application of make-up. Thadeus was also subdued in black shoes, a dark grey suit, white shirt and a floppy blue bow tie with white spots; Freddie considered this last item carefully before giving her approval. They set out for the university by taxi and sat quietly, each clutching dark blue overcoats;

the day was sunny but cold; they were both nervous. Thadeus had received a telephone call from James, the lads were in Scotland and expected to be in the university car park on time; the news prompting a 'well done you'.

The ceremony went according to plan, no hitches whatsoever. After the handshaking and kissing between the sixteen new doctors, Thadeus and Freddie found themselves alone in the rose garden where they put their arms around each other and both sobbed like babies; they needed to sit at a bench and clean up their faces before Thadeus unobtrusively steered his sister into the allotted 'second ceremony' area.

There was the pale blue Bugatti, sponged and newly wax-polished, attended by what appeared to be two wartime fighter pilots just returned from a long dog-fight over enemy territory. Freddie was speechless and tears flowed again; more handshaking and kissing before she climbed behind the steering-wheel and pressed the self-starter and the engine roared to life amid cheers and laughter. Thadeus took the passenger seat and the pair cautiously manoeuvred the way back to Princes Street; the two lads electing to enjoy a walk to the hotel for drinks on the veranda, where they were all to meet an uninvited and unexpected guest, Inspector Johnny Jackson of Scotland Yard.

The policeman advised that he had flown from Croydon Airport to Edinburgh at dawn that day in less than four hours!

While Champagne cocktails were being distributed, and after a rousing toast to 'Doctor Burke', Thadeus drew Jackson aside. 'You did not fly up here at taxpayers' expense just to congratulate my sister on her doctorate!'

'No, we have a lot of talking to do,' said Jackson seriously.

Freddie was now surrounded by Scottish friends, both social and medical giving the two men the opportunity to slide out of the gathering un-noticed and occupy an empty antechamber, where Thadeus related the whole diamond-business story, including the identification of the diamonds that was new to Jackson.

'I wish I had heard all of this yesterday, back in London,' he admonished. 'One thing I can tell you is that no uncut diamonds were reported stolen in the Bond Street robbery; are you sure your sister was right about that?'

'She spent a summer vacation working with a firm of diamond dealers in Hatton Garden, which included a fortnight in Amsterdam. And she has a small collection of samples, in addition to her jewellery,' said Thadeus by way of justification.

'One positive thing is that this news matches up with what I know about Alex Wengler. He is an independent insurance adjuster working for a Dutch insurance company on a claim of theirs in respect of – wait for it – stolen uncut diamonds valued at nearly a quarter of a million pounds,' informed Jackson.

'I think that you might find that he is now working for himself,' said Thadeus. 'My worry is that both Alex Wengler and Alice Kurtner must now know that they have been duped by me, and that I must have the stones; they will be back. By the way who is Alice Kurtner?'

'She is a South African diamond dealer, quite legitimate, but suspected of handling stolen goods in Johannesburg, Amsterdam, London and New York; a very well connected lady. But your main worry should be the reason why I have come up here; there are two hoodlums, part of the Fulham gang, on the London train due in Edinburgh this evening, and I think that you will be on their calling list.'

With that disclosure Jackson and Thadeus returned to Freddie's party, joining the general banter and sampling the buffet lunch nibbles. Pooley and Payne had availed themselves of the offer to stay at the hotel that evening and return to London the next day, so although they showed signs of weariness they had showered and changed their clothes and were now reasonable representatives of the Sassenach clan.

The champagne was beginning to dominate Freddie's bloodstream and she announced that she would go up to her room for a rest; she was assisted to the lift by James and J K, who also needed some sleep. The remnants of the crowd said their goodbyes leaving Thadeus and Jackson to smoke their pipes and mull over the growing economic unease until these two early-risers also decided to rest and regroup at 5.00 pm; the train from London was due in Edinburgh at six.

By 5.30 everyone was revitalized and assembled in the resident's lounge, refusing proffered drinks and unenthusiastically studying the dinner menus, glancing occasionally at the small posse of plain-clothed Scottish policemen placed strategically around the room and foyer.

'Good heavens' exclaimed James Pooley, leafing through Thadeus' copy of the *Horse & Hound*, then holding up a page in the direction of J K Payne who turned a bright shade of red.

'Something exciting in the magazine?' questioned Thadeus.

'No, just a coincidental reference to something that J K and I were discussing on our journey,' said James hastily folding the paper over and throwing it casually on the coffee table in front of him.

Payne lit a cigarette and strolled from the room, Pooley following muttering 'sorry' they returned within fifteen minutes apparently reconciled, just as one of the expected visitors strode purposefully into the room, stopped and promptly about turned.

'Hello Alex,' said J K Payne. 'Remember me? Lloyd's underwriter – you did some work for my uncle, Charles Payne, when one of our insured motor cars was involved in an accident at a railway crossing in Holland. I came over there and we had dinner together.'

'Yes of course; nice to see you,' said Alex Wengler.

'This is a broker friend of mine,' said J K, introducing James Pooley, 'and over there is his boss, Thadeus Burke the head of the most up-and-coming Lloyd's brokers in the City.'

Thus it was that the Dutchman found himself facing the Englishman once more; Thadeus being fully clothed in a lightweight tweed suit, and Alex Wengler without a gun in his hand.

'This is Inspector John Jackson from Scotland Yard, a good friend of mine,' introduced Thadeus. This was no opening move, they were in the end-game now.

'I suppose I owe you some sort of explanation,' said Wengler

Thadeus and Jackson smiled and nodded; the two Jameses looked puzzled.

'You have the diamonds I assume?' started Wengler, and received more smiles and nods. 'I followed them from the original theft in Rotterdam, through various hands, to a respectable but vulnerable gentleman in Old Bond Street, London, who was to arrange a private sale. Unbeknown to me one of the shop staff had discovered the deception and informed a gang of jewel thieves; he was paid £500 for his help; poor compensation for his widow – he, and the first gentleman, were shot dead by the gang on the night of the robbery. Strangely it is not difficult in any large city to find people as bad as that; I, and the police, quickly had them under surveillance.'

'Are you still carrying a gun?' interrupted Jackson.

Wengler removed the weapon from an inside holster and was instructed to hand it over to the police constable who was standing behind him. The two lads had discreetly moved away.

'Was your aim to get the stones for yourself?' asked Thadeus

'Certainly not,' snapped an outraged Wengler. 'I am surprised that you, a Lloyd's man, should think this. I am being paid to do a professional job. I have a good reputation all over Europe, possibly a little unorthodox in my methods. Also there is a substantial reward to be claimed.'

This latest disclosure attracted the instant attention of a listening Freddie. 'How much?' she demanded.

'Part of my work will be to assess the position in that respect,' said Wengler.

The matter concluded the three men shook hands, Jackson reminding the Dutchman that he should not leave town, and the Dutchman reminding Jackson that he had no intention of leaving until his work was completed.

'What do you think?' Jackson asked Thadeus when Wengler had left.

'Part of an adjuster's ability is that he is impossible to read, it's a cultivated art. I think that he is all right, but I do not think that he should be put in the team just yet.'

Thadeus and Jackson pondered the things that Wengler had omitted from his scenario, but they were able to fill in the gaps satisfactorily. Freddie went to her room attended by a police constable; James and J K Payne decided to take a stroll around the town, which was new to them. Word came through that the villains from London had 'landed' and were in a taxi heading towards Princes Street. A plan was put into action. Jackson went into the lobby leaving Thadeus alone except for a surrounding of undercover agents.

What the team in the hotel did not know was that although the two villains knew that they needed to find a man named Burke, their surreptitious telephone calls had given them the impression that there were two people registered under that name, a Mr T Burke and a Dr F Burke, so they had decided to take both of them for a little ride, as soon as they were able to steal a convenient vehicle from the hotel car-park, which did not take long, the Bugatti was too small for four people so they took a large Austin. Entering the hotel they separated immediately which puzzled the observers, the elder one putting some questions to the porter, and the younger one making enquiries at the desk. The elder one took a seat in the nearly empty lounge next to Thadeus, his left hand around a pistol held in his pocket; the youngster stood by the ground floor lift doors waiting for the appearance of Doctor Burke.

After a few minutes the lift doors opened and out stepped a strawberry haired young lady who strode purposely towards the lounge; the youngster waited on. The young lady walked up to the elder villain and leaned down face to face, 'Doctor Burke at your service.' The man attempted to rise, his mouth falling open, into which Freddie placed a small revolver. 'Say aah,' she smiled.

Thadeus reached across and removed the pistol from the man's pocket. 'Do not ever do something like that again,' said a genuinely angry Thadeus to his sister, as several police officers grabbed the man and manhandled him away.

The junior villain had been equally surprised when he accosted the next arrival at the ground floor lift doors. 'Doctor Burke?' he enquired. 'No. Inspector John Jackson of Scotland Yard,' replied the gentleman, who was holding a revolver, aimed between the eyes of a startled young man.

'Whose damned fool idea was it to use Freddie in this enterprise, armed with a gun?' Thadeus demanded of Jackson as soon as the excitement was over and the two criminals carted off to more suitable accommodation.

'She insisted,' stammered the police inspector.

Thadeus stamped up and down for a few minutes then sat upright on a straight-backed chair with his eyes closed.

'He's meditating,' whispered Freddie to Jackson. 'He'll be fine.'

Sure enough fifteen minutes later Thadeus opened his eyes, stretched, smiled and enquired of the gawping bunch, 'What about some drinks?'

'Good idea Mr Burke. I'll have a gin and tonic,' came the voice of Alice Kurtner, entering the room from behind our hero.

'Alice! I thought that you were in Perth,' exclaimed Thadeus kissing the lady on the cheek.

'Change of plan. I'm needed on business in New York; staying here tonight then sailing from Liverpool tomorrow,' she rattled out.

Thadeus thought that she had met with Alex Wengler and was fully briefed with the current state of play. As Alice engaged in social chit-chat with him and Jackson, Freddie made a telephone call to the university and gave instructions to a uniformed police sergeant, resulting in his appearance at the ladies' locker room in the medical department some fifteen minutes later and the removal of a cake tin and its contents to a strong-room at the police station. Freddie did not like the look of Alice Kurtner!

CHAPTER 14

THE MINING DISASTER

Thadeus had an early night and slept well, as did James Pooley who skipped dinner and opted for bed at 8.00 pm; young Payne and Freddie danced on into the night and were not expected to arise before noon. Jackson had been up early and was already at the local police station canteen when Thadeus and James ordered their breakfast. As the inspector contemplated the interrogation of his new captives and worked on a draft statement that could be signed by Alex Wengler, and while Freddie and Mr Payne slumbered, the two breakfasters scoffed egg and bacon with tomatoes and toast.

'What was all that kerfuffle about the article in the *Horse & Hound* last night?' ventured Thadeus.

After a respectful amount of procrastination James told his employer the tale of J K Payne's dismissal from Pembroke College Cambridge, leaving out the more explicit imagery, but giving a clear account of the comings and goings on the staircase. What was new yesterday was that during their journey up to Scotland, James had asked JK if he had ever met the lady in question since the undergraduate's extracurricular studies. His response was that he had not, but he had seen photographs of the lady on occasions in the *Tattler* and in the *Horse & Hound*; then came the much regretted disclosure that he had read an article penned by her in last week's *Horse & Hound* concerning charitable collections for retired racehorses.

Chris Byrnes' adage 'remember that your friend has a friend' came into Thadeus' mind, but with the young man's uncle Charlie having numerous friends who would adore such a tale Thadeus thought that the story now must be common currency around the Lloyd's fraternity. There was no need for the lady's name to be voiced between the two breakfasting colleagues.

Freddie was up and about by 10.30 and busily arranging the final details of the shipping of her worldly goods from both the hotel and her Edinburgh digs by road, rail and air to the tiny mews house in Chelsea. Numerous other items were scattered around the Scottish kingdom in houses of friends and relatives but they were to be the subject of a separate exercise. She had found a policeman who was taking well deserved leave to visit his brother and his family in London and who had volunteered to drive the Morris Cowley down south in a week's time. She had decided that her Scottish interlude had ended and that a property in Perthshire was not needed, and with the anticipated huge reward from the Dutch insurance company for the diligent recovery of their diamonds she would buy a house in the city where it was her intention to work. The place and appointment would be unveiled to Thadeus from the passenger seat of the Bugatti during one of his spells at the wheel so that he did not get too animated.

J K Payne had to be dug out of his room at noon like a fox at ground, which was appropriate as the next waiting incumbent was the daughter of an English Master of Hounds and his wife occupying Thadeus' vacated suite.

Eventually they all departed; Alice Kurtner towards New York; Jackson and Alex Wengler down to London in a large black police Wolseley; James and JK in first-class cabins on the train to Kings Cross and Thadeus, clad in the leather jacket borrowed from James, and Doctor Freddie in her mink coat and a helmet borrowed from JK, pointed the bonnet of the Bugatti vaguely in the direction of the South – Freddie at the wheel receiving instructions in the art of double de-clutching.

They decided to head for Durham where a friend of both was teaching mathematics at the university, stay in that city overnight and then go across to Rutland to visit their parents for another 'doctorate' celebration. Burke & Co was progressing satisfactorily; Thadeus and James had telephoned the office regularly to check on any problems.

On the road Thadeus disclosed his suspicions about Lady Frances Downing, who had now become his prime suspect in the Sir Percy Dennington murder. He set out the salient points to Freddie. Lady Frances was a school friend of Percy's wife and knew Percy well; she also knew and used the firm of Newmarket solicitors, Woodford & Kinloch, who had handled the false insurance claims. She had a ravishing appetite for sex with young men, and there was a young man involved at the lawyers processing the fraudulent claims, Archie Wickham, who had also died in suspicious circumstances, the body showing signs of recent sexual activity. She was familiar with the *General Stud Book* and surely capable of inventing bogus pedigrees and, the most damning evidence, she knew the vet, William Hitchen who admitted to being involved, although both of them had pretended that Thadeus had introduced them when caught together at Cheltenham, but Thadeus knew that this was untrue.

'What are you going to do?' asked Freddie

'She has invited me up to Norfolk, with Gussie, for a weekend – I will go and confront her!'

'You will need a doctor on hand armed with antidotes for your nightcap drink of Drambuie – I will come with you,' declared the caring sister.

It was agreed.

With Thadeus at the wheel Freddie announced her intention to take up an offered appointment at Addenbrooke Hospital working in paediatrics; and to buy a house or flat in Cambridge with the money that she hoped to obtain from the Dutch insurance company for the safe return of their diamonds. She also announced that she had abandoned the idea of a place in Perthshire, having served her time in Scotland, and cautiously suggested that Thadeus might like to purchase, with his ill-gotten Cheltenham cash, a stud in, or near, Newmarket where he could pursue his ambitions to breed racehorses and provide a proper home for his hardworking, much loved only sister!

'*Ad idem*,' exclaimed Thadeus, assuring Freddie that he held the exact same plan in his own head.

These matters resolved they enjoyed an alcohol-free lunch and motored into Northumberland.

It was a bright and breezy day. Progress was good and they soon came upon the little mining village of Pitside. As they approached they were harangued by hooters and claxons and baulked by a throng of people, men, women and children, running along the road.

'What's up?' Thadeus asked an anxious looking woman running with her small child in her arms.

'There's a fall at the mine,' she choked out, continuing her trot.

'Climb in here and show us how to get to the pithead,' ordered Freddie.

Thadeus sat up on the luggage and the newcomers took up the passenger seat. Freddie put on her headlights and blasted away at the horn, while the new lady screamed at the crowd to make way for a doctor.

Within fifteen minutes Dr Burke stood in a bright yellow dress behind the iron grating of a mine shaft lift, waving *au revoir* to her sceptical brother, bound by the dictates of her Hippocratic Oath, descending hundreds of feet into the bowels of the earth. Squeezed in with her and several very large miners and officials was a small man with a doctor's bag introduced by himself as Vernon Topping; it was also divulged, again by him, that he had imbibed a few drinks and that Freddie should keep a close eye on him. Her response was that she only qualified yesterday and that a reciprocal arrangement might be necessary – it was not appropriate to laugh out loud!

The light blue Bugatti with the dark brown mink coat bundled across the front seats attracted some hostile attention until the attending police constable announced that this was 'the doctor's car', after which the vehicle and its contents took on a 'holy grail' status and the machine was guarded by a burly crew of mining stewards.

Thadeus sat quietly on a stone wall and smoked two whole full pipes of tobacco, his leather flying jacket giving him an undeserved Great War reverence, which he used to assist the two arriving ambulances onto the site.

After an hour Freddie and Vernon reappeared at the gates, now both clad in dungarees several sizes too large for them; the arms and legs rolled up so that they both walked with a peculiar childlike gait. Laid on the floor of the cage were four stretchers carrying four men, two of which had sheets covering the faces, ominously indicating death. The other two showed bewildered blackened faces peering anxiously around the gathered crowd. The two injured men were set down on a grassy bank and the corpses placed into one of the ambulances.

Vernon went to the deceased miners and Freddie attended the wounded; starting with a giant of a man who, when questioned, gave his name as Taffy Jones.

'Welsh I assume,' said Freddie as she cut up the front of the man's trouser leg with a pair of surgical scissors revealing the naked and dirty skin.

'He is the captain of the rugby team,' announced one of the attendants, as if this in some way excused his nationality.

'Well Taffy,' said Freddie after examining the man's left leg, 'is this arrangement whereby your feet face in different directions a cunning ploy that you use in the scrum? Or would you prefer that they both faced the front?'

This remark took a while to be digested by the small group, then one began to laugh raucously, to be followed by other howls of amusement as the quip was explained Chinese whisper fashion around the grassy bank, one side interpreting the story with convulsions and the other with puzzled expressions.

Taffy managed a weak grin which quickly turned into a grimace. Freddie did not await the full applause that the observation deserved instructing a pair of the largest attending orderlies to sit on each of the rugger-player's shoulders, with an additional volunteer squatted on his right foot, by which time the doctor had acquired a firm grip on the patient's left ankle which she held tight in both hands and threw her full weight, all seven stone six ounces of it, backwards. Taffy let out a yell that could have been heard in Cardiff.

Ignoring the concerns of the patient and attendants Freddie carefully ran her hands up and down the leg, back and front, then pronounced that there was no permanent damage to bone, muscle or ligament, but that the leg had suffered serious trauma; all that was needed was rest, several months; he might be back on the rugby field in time for the end of next season.

Freddie's next patient was not so lucky; he would loose a foot; he accepted the diagnosis with composure, but the young doctor could see the private tears waiting to be shed in solitude by the lad, not yet out of his teens.

'I suppose I'll get a stump, like my uncle Bert,' he said.

'Nonsense,' assured Freddie. 'A good looking young man like you will need a proper artificial foot; they make them very well nowadays; inside a year you will not know the difference.'

'I can't afford them luxuries,' said the teenager.

'Well I have contact with a charity organization that deals with just this sort of help,' said Freddie, making a note in her little black book of a name and telephone number that the young man should contact when the time came. It was a Mr T Burke with a number in London.

'Any problems?' said Vernon, coming over by Freddie.

'I don't think so,' she said. 'You might just have another look at the youngster, I think that he will need an amputation.'

He came back. 'No doubt whatsoever, I'm afraid, the foot is completely smashed.' Then, pulling her aside said, 'Come and have a look at these two dead chaps.'

'Do I have to?' questioned Freddie

'I'd like you to check the body temperature of both men,' said the senior man seriously.

The face and thorax of the men were badly damaged; the hospital orderlies turned the cadavers over revealing naked bottoms into which Freddie inserted clinical thermometers, after having read from the instruments the atmospheric temperature; waiting five minutes she then noted down the body heat measurements. She thanked the orderlies for their assistance and returned to Vernon who was taking a cigarette break, having supervised the hospitalization of the two injured men.

She took a proffered gasper and said to the senior man, 'There is just over four degrees difference between those two bodies!'

'What does that indicate to you doctor?' he asked.

'Their deaths occurred two or three hours apart,' answered Freddie.

Vernon looked at his watch. 'The accident occurred nearly two hours ago; that would seem to match with the body temperature of Eric Halliday, the warmer one, but the other one, a Mr Gerald Moore Bowden, must have died much earlier – a puzzle!'

'There is a senior-looking policeman over there, I think that we should ensure that a full post mortem is carried out on both men,' suggest Freddie.

Vernon agreed and they both put the matter to Assistant Chief Constable Willerby Bewicke-Copley, who showed no enthusiasm for the suggestion, but agreed to arrange for a senior police pathologist to be at the mortuary when the bodies arrived before disappearing into an adjacent building to give the necessary telephone instructions.

Two more medical men had turned up and Vernon directed them towards a few cut hands and bruised toes that were hovering in the vicinity, suggesting to Freddie that they might retire to a nearby hostelry for a stimulating glass of whisky.

'A bit early for me,' she advised. 'But I could handle a sandwich. My brother is over there – I'll get him to drive us to the pub.'

They said their farewells to the mine officials, the weeping teenager's mother and what appeared to be another rugby player, but was in fact Taffy Jones' missis, extracted themselves from the dungarees, Freddie emerging as a butterfly and Vernon returning to the status of a caterpillar. With Thadeus perched back on top of the luggage the owner drove her car the mile to the Spread Eagle.

While Vernon was at the bar ordering drinks from a clearly well known landlord, open outside hours because of the emergency, Freddie enlightened Thadeus on the new mystery.

Vernon made short work of his double Scotch before the two new guests had started to sip their small beers and Freddie was still assessing the problem of getting the enormous cheese and pickle sandwich up into her mouth without the use of a crane.

Thadeus ordered another round for the thirsty medical man and asked him if he knew the two dead men personally?

'Eric Halliday has been around the pit for a couple of years, came over from Nottinghamshire; he has a sister who lives in the village, a widow whose man was killed in the War. Gerald Bowden only came up from London three months ago,' he informed his listeners.

'You do not find many coal miners in London,' noted Thadeus.

'He is a communist agitator,' retorted Vernon. 'Registered with me as soon as he turned up from a posh address in Eaton Square.' He gave a 'knowing' look and took another gulp at his drink, setting the empty glass down on the table with a bang. 'He would not know one end of a shovel from the other!'

'You did not like him?' suggested Thadeus.

'The miners do not want a revolution and the unions do not like the communists, they are all Labour Party men – and he had too much money for the folk around here.'

'You would not be surprised to find that he had been murdered then?' pushed Thadeus.

'No,' said Vernon, toying with the idea of another drink but resisting and informing the Burkes that he would return to his house and have a bath.

He kissed Freddie on the cheek and said 'Thank you my dear', shook hands with Thadeus and left.

'I need a shower and some new clothes,' announced Freddie. 'Where are we going to stay?'

'I have already booked rooms in Durham, we can be there within an hour,' replied Thadeus, adding 'You might be required here tomorrow so we had better phone the governor and tell him we will be a day late at Headley Hall.'

'And you do not want to leave a mystery unsolved!' added his sister.

Thadeus smiled.

The hotel in Durham was small but well equipped, though they had to take turns in the only shower, situated between the connecting rooms. While Freddie caused havoc with the domestic staff, reduced during the off-season period, sponging and ironing her minute travelling wardrobe of only four dresses and a half-dozen pairs of shoes, supported by a separate suitcase full of undies, Thadeus made several telephone calls to London. First, Inspector Jackson; what did he know about Assistant Chief Constable Willerby?

'More interested in promotion than crime,' was the reply. The inspector knew nothing about Gerald Bowden from an address in Eaton Square, but would investigate and report back.

More luck with Gussie Downing. Gerald Bowden was not a member of any communist organization that he knew, but he did know the man, having met him, or a man with the same name, at a house party in Eaton Square; 'a pompous little bastard' only one interest in life – making money.

Freddie was now organizing for the Bugatti to be valeted so Thadeus wandered into the hotel bar for an aperitif and the opportunity to study the dinner menu.

'I saw you up at Pitside,' declared a voice at his right elbow.

Thadeus nodded and the newcomer introduced himself as Howard Carter, a journalist with the *Durham Record*.

'I was just passing through,' admitted Thadeus.

'You were in the Bugatti with the lady doctor,' said Howard, a practitioner in the art of leaking information, as from a pipette.

'Yes,' said Thadeus, a practitioner in the art of leaking information as from a dry sponge.

'Two men dead,' was the next instalment from the journalist.

'Yes,' was the acknowledgement.

'Nobody will miss that little shit from London, pretending to be a communist,' was the next observation fed in by the hack.

'I have no knowledge of him – enlighten me,' said Thadeus inviting Howard to partake of a glass of something.

Howard ordered a large gin and tonic, thanked Thadeus and divulged his full collection of Mr Gerald Moore Bowden stories. It did not take long. Howard's treasure chest of facts on Karl Marx, the Soviet Union and the communist canon had all been gleaned from newspapers, primarily from the headlines alone, but even these had been sufficient to fox and outwit the London pretender.

'So what was he up to?' asked Thadeus, gaining the upper hand in this question and answer session.

'I thought that you might know that,' parried the journalist.

'The victim kept the company of well dressed gentlemen, lady doctors and Bugatti owners did he?' The newspaperman was stunned by this latest thrust and just tapped his nose in an 'I know but will not tell' manner.

'He was a mineowner's stooge wasn't he?' a killing blow from Thadeus that had the hack choking on his G and T.

'You did know him,' admonished Howard.

'I know nothing about the man other than what you have told me,' a response from Thadeus that really upset the journalist.

'This is not the time or place to talk about it and I have an appointment that I must not miss with a lady who has just given birth to triplets.' Howard Carter handed Thadeus his card, thanked him again for the drink and left the bar, just as Freddie was entering.

'I've been speaking to Eric Halliday's sister-in-law,' she announced. 'She works in the ladies' lavatory on the ground floor, sister of the dead husband of Eric's sister Cherry. Lives in Pitside!'

'So you know all about the late Eric?' enthused Thadeus. He wanted this information before revealing his newly acquired data about Gerald Moore Bowden.

'A gambler,' was the response that summed up Freddie's analysis. She paused, and receiving no reaction from her brother continued. 'Came up from Nottingham to stay with his sister as the only alternative to the workhouse: owed tons of money to bookmakers; fled, absconded, moonlightflitted!'

'Is there such a word?' asked her brother, ordering a large gin and tonic for his sister.

'There is now!' she announced. 'He's in big trouble with the bookies again in Durham and Newcastle.' She stopped speaking, pleased with her contribution to the investigation.

'He *was*,' corrected Thadeus. 'It is not possible to sue the estate of a deceased person for gambling debts?'

'Do you think that the bookmakers could be involved in his death?' queried Freddie.

'No,' said Thadeus. 'I think it more likely that somebody paid off, or promised to pay off, his gambling debts if he disposed of Gerald Bowden in a mining accident.'

He enlightened his sister on the interview with Howard Carter. They both pondered the possibilities over a poor dinner accompanied by an appropriately poor bottle of wine. They had had a long day and retired to bed early.

Thadeus was awoken next morning by the shouting of his sister, clad in only the top half of her pyjamas, screaming at him, 'Look at this. Look at this', and throwing a copy of the day's *Durham Record* onto the bed covers as she turned and stormed back to her room, with the words, 'Who do we know that had an interview with a journalist from the *Durham Record* – yesterday?'

Thadeus calmly read the front page headlines: 'Murder allegations by incompetent doctors at Pitside tragedy.'

The article, by a woman news editor, set out the story of how a novice doctor, qualified only the previous day, and a local GP, well known for his frequent drinking bouts, had made unfounded accusations of foul play at the regrettable Pitside mining disaster. Assistant Chief Constable Willerby Bewicke-Copley confirmed that pathological examinations by the police, involving a senior consultant from Newcastle University had found nothing incongruous with the understanding by mining officials that the two men had died together at the scene of the accident at the same time, crushed by an unexpected fall of rock.

Thadeus picked up his bedside telephone and called Howard Carter at his home number. Before he could say anything, Howard had opened with. 'I'm ahead of you. I have an appointment with the official police pathologist at her home in a half of an hour. She is not going to work today! Do you want to come along? You can be my sub-editor – nobody ever knows what they do.'

The address was dictated to Thadeus. He told Freddie what he was up to and immediately took a taxi to the house just outside the City of Durham. In the cab he read a more realistic account of the mining accident in the *Daily Chronicle*. The accident occurred in an abandoned coal seam, away from the current workings, miners were alerted by the noise and clouds of dust emerging from the area. The two dead men were below several tons of debris and two serious injuries were sustained to rescuers by a slide of rocks as the digging commenced. Official mining safety officers took charge quickly and further catastrophe was averted.

Dr Haddon was in her fifties, requalified to pathology from nursing five years ago, a pleasant lady and a good friend of Howard Carter.

'Hello Howard,' she greeted them. 'Come and have some tea.'

Behind enormous cups the two intruders heard her tale. 'Outrageous! Outrageous!' she declared. 'The ACC is an idiot, and that buffoon from Newcastle Varsity that he insisted on calling in, even worse. The man went on and on about temperatures at different depths of the earth's surface and the effect of coal dust on putrefaction – complete tosh! They did not want to hear what I had to say; the ACC declares the deaths as "accidental" and signs for the bodies to be released to the next of kin: Then he phones that tame news editor of his at the newspaper office!'

Howard was loving this, scribbling away at his notebook, a large grin on his face. He asked the lady a few pertinent questions, exact names and exact times and then the most pertinent question: did she think that the examining doctors at the pit were right in their diagnosis?

'I examined the bodies an hour after them and "time of death" is notoriously difficult to fix, but they examined the bodies only an hour or so after the accident was reported. I cannot see that they could both make a mistake at that time. I observed that the one marked "Bowden" was showing definite full-face rigor, whereas the other one had no more than a slight touch on the eyelids. If you went back now a couple of hours would make no significant difference. I shall write to the Chief Constable – then I shall resign,' she concluded solemnly.

'Better if the Assistant Chief Constable resigned!' said Thadeus.

'Do you think that that is possible?' she asked.

'That is our plan,' stated Howard.

They thanked Doctor Haddon for her time and headed for the nearest cafe.

'What now?' they both asked.

It was decided the Howard should pursue the background of Gerald Bowden and Thadeus would visit Cherry, the sister of Eric Halliday; they would make contact later in the day. Thadeus returned to the hotel where Freddie was taking breakfast in her room. Her temper had cooled down and she was able to absorb the summary of the morning's work with equanimity.

'I'll dress and go down to the lavatories and find out Cherry's address,' she said, practical as ever.

Within an hour they were knocking at the lady's front door. She did not answer but Freddie noticed the upstairs curtains move and called out through the letter-box that she was the doctor who had attended her dead brother the day before and shortly afterwards the door was cautiously opened and the pair admitted.

'I thought that you were those bloody bookies,' she explained.

'They were after the money that he owes?' ventured Thadeus.

'Yes. I told them that there was nothing here and that they could "piss off" but it was not true; there was fifty pounds in brand new one-pound notes in Eric's room. I don't know where he got it from.'

Freddie consoled the woman and Thadeus inspected the cache of money, which was still bound with paper bands showing the name of the issuing bank – Martin's Bank, a branch in Newcastle. He made a note of the numbers in his little black book. He would contact his father who was a director of that bank and instigate a search for the drawer of this cash.

Back at the hotel he telephoned Jackson but was informed that the CID man had no jurisdiction in Northumbria or Yorkshire, although of course he had contacts in the area and would try and promote an internal investigation into the allegations against the Assistant Chief Constable, but it would have to be a low-key affair.

The news about Gerald Bowden was more promising; he was certainly not a member of the Communist Party, in fact he was a signed up member of the Conservative Party, although not particularly active. His father was a greengrocer in Balham but young Gerald had fancier ideas. He had started several investment advisory agencies, all of which had failed and been put into liquidation; kept high-flying company; was well known with some titled ladies about town and had been paid off by their fathers on at least three occasions. It really is amazing what the police can find out, thought Thadeus, wondering if Jackson's office kept a file on him.

Thadeus relayed this data to Howard Carter, who already had the names and address of the ladies involved with Gerald's romantic entanglements, one of whom had been at school with Freddie! He did not divulge the exact findings at Cherry's house in Pitside, referring only to 'some cash' being discovered, which was enough to get the journalist excited and start pounding away at his typewriter.

Freddie was still keeping out of the limelight so they drove out to a seaside village, south of Sunderland, and indulged in a lobster with a bottle of Chablis, huddled on a chilly beach.

'So you think that this Chief Constable is a crook?' proffered Freddie

'Unlikely that he is involved in a murder,' said Thadeus. 'But I think he is involved in a cover up operation, possibly innocently, maybe not!'

'Mornin', miss,' said the chirpy voice of a small lad in large boots. 'I saw your car at Pitside yesterday.'

Thadeus stood but was unable to shake the hand of the minor and/or miner as it was swathed in bandages, an attribute that he proudly declared resulted from his scrambling through a gap between the roof and the fall at the accident yesterday; and, more importantly, gave rise to a one-day holiday, with pay, and two pounds in compensation, which was why he was down at his mum's eating fish and chips.

'The owner's have agreed compensation for the accident?' queried Thadeus

'Oh yes, sir!' he answered. 'It was all done with the union men first thing this morning. There's money for Eric's sister, and Taffy Jones, and a new foot for the lad from Hartlepool, and between two pounds and five pounds each for all the damaged men; including me.'

'What about the other dead man, Gerald Bowden?'

The lad chuckled. 'I don't think that anybody is bothered about 'im; the bosses and the union men are going to sort something out in London.'

'He came up here looking for bother, and bother he got, eh?' said Thadeus.

'That's about it, sir!'

'That explains the cover up,' said Thadeus as they got back in the car, having finished their *al fresco* meal and said farewell to the little lad. 'Nobody wanted a further investigation; they are all happy with the result; life is cheap up here.'

'But my reputation is in tatters and a man has been murdered for cash!' stated Freddie emphatically.

'Justice must be done, seen to be done, and published on the front page of the *Durham Record*?'

'If I might quote from one of your Negro jazz pals – right on brother,' said Thadeus' sister.

Freddie drove the Bugatti back to Durham and Thadeus lay back in the passenger seat thinking how the happy youth's euphoria would change as the report of the Samuel Commission filtered down to the illiterate workers, and the mine owners' new terms of employment, including longer hours plus reduced wages, were translated into hard fact; and the killer punch that if the miners did not accept the stipulations they would be locked out from the first day of May. At this moment the coming storm was still being contained within Eccleston Square the headquarters of both the Trade Union Council and the Labour Party, but the strike bulletins and propaganda leaflets would soon be flooding the universities and workplaces. Right on brother, indeed, black from birth or coal-dust, harmony in the communities was about to be tested to the limit.

Eric's cash had been collected from the bank in Newcastle on a signature from the Honourable Bertie Snowling, youngest son of Lord Carstairs, the owner of the Pitside mine, information that had no source and could not be used under any circumstances; Thadeus understood the rules.

A war cabinet was formed and convened under the chairmanship of Dr Freddie and held in her room: the members being her brother Thadeus, and Howard Carter, newly self-acclaimed freelance journalist. Madam Chairman made notes and before long it was clear the Gerald Bowden's greed knew no bounds, there was already the nucleus of a best-selling biography piled on the table. Thadeus and Howard concurred that Bowden was employed by Carstairs or his family to discredit the miners' proposed strike activities, but that he probably turned the tables on the owners and demanded more money from them to keep the ploy away from the press. Howard confirmed that Bowden had hinted at a good story that might be for sale shortly. Bertie Snowling was a ferocious gambler on the horses and would have had contacts in the bookmaking fraternity with information about Eric Halliday and his financial management shortcomings.

The theory was that Eric killed Bowden during a lunchtime break and put the body in a disused tunnel, returning later to bury it, but fumbled the job and died along with his victim under a fall of the disturbed rock-face. All three of the assembled retribution team were agreed on what was necessary to flush out Snowling, a man, from London, purporting to be a friend of Bowden and who was in possession of valuable information for sale to the highest bidder – the blackmailer's reinsurance programme. Did anyone know a person who could fill this role?

Thus it was that Thadeus telephoned Bertie Snowling from a telephone box at Durham railway station that evening with the good news that the young nobleman had been the first choice to purchase the draft press release in respect of the Halliday/Bowden murder mystery. A rendezvous was agreed, a cricket ground outside town, in the middle of nowhere. The parties did not set out for the assignation alone; Snowling had recruited three hefty rugby-playing mates with no love for lily-livered southerners; Thadeus was accompanied by six strong policemen, two press photographers and a fast get-away car. Some blood was shed by Thadeus' nose, expertly handled by his personal medical attendant, but the police officers specially selected by Inspector Jackson from a Newcastle precinct, prevailed and the Snowling contingent were manhandled away in a Black Maria. The police sergeant, an ex-London colleague of Johnny Jackson, was given very specific directions about what evidence needed to be sought, starting with a bundle of pound notes held by a woman named Cherry at a house in Pitside.

The story did not make the front page of the *Durham Record,* as Howard had sold the tale to the nationals, all of whom were eager to publish, each with their own slant on the news, but united in their acclamation of dotors Topping and Burke and condemnation of Assistant Chief Constable Willerby Bewicke-Copley, whose early retirement was the subject of four column inches by a lady news editor on page five of the local paper the next week.

Bertie Snowling's appointed lawyer was brilliant and succeeded in preventing the trial from even reaching court; there were no actions for slander or liable instigated; Bertie wisely decided on a career move, to Rhodesia

Following supper with Dr Vernon Topping and Howard Carter, who was promised an even better story for the national newspapers shortly concerning the murder of a prominent Lloyd's underwriter, the Burke siblings celebrated another successful enterprise with their parents over the Easter weekend, with much churchgoing and pink eggs boiled in cochineal flavoured water. They returned to London to receive a letter from Alex Wengler, the intrepid insurance adjuster, advising that he had successfully negotiated an *ex gratia* payment to Dr Frederica Burke of £12,500 from a Dutch insurance company, receipt of which needed only her signature on the enclosed release form. They also heard from Gussie Downing that his mother was dead; crushed beneath her hunter after he ducked away from a hedge and they both smashed their way through a five-bar gate.

Her only son took the news with solemnity, grateful that his mater's undergarments were of the finest quality, avoiding the lady's feared embarrassment in front of the hospital staff at the time of her long anticipated death in the saddle of an equine companion.

Gussie's surprise being only that she had left an envelope marked 'private and confidential' addressed to the Honourable Thadeus Burke.

The funeral was arranged for the following Friday and both Thadeus and Freddie would attend the ceremony and subsequent wake, to be followed the next day by a visit to the races at Fakenham.

CHAPTER 15

THE END AND A NEW BEGINNING

Freddie spent the early part of the next week organizing her new home at Sloane Mews and telephoning estate agents in Cambridge about her intended residence in that city.

Thadeus returned to his neglected office and hung his painting of Newmarket Heath by Alfred Munnings on the wall of his new office, which was now equipped with an internal buzzer system, installed by the lad Bart Coen, and purchased by him, with company money, from his uncle who operated a stall on Petticoat Lane specializing in strange electrical appliances. The lad had also devised a detailed code pattern, one short buzz for James Pooley, one long buzz for Bart Coen, etc., right through the whole office staff, finishing with four short, and one long buzzes for 'help I am being attacked by a madman'. All this was carefully typed up and a copy distributed to all personnel. Thadeus played with the system all morning.

The letter from Lady Frances Downing had been sent down to London by Gussie. It read:

My Dear Thadeus,

If you are reading this letter then I must be dead; I expect that I broke my neck in a fall from a horse. Please ensure that no blame is attached to the animal and that he is well cared for in my absence.

I have heard rumours that you are investigating some fraudulent bloodstock insurance claims, which is the purpose of this unexpected letter.

Yes, I did it! For reasons that I will not expose I needed some serious cash so I invented well-bred horses from my pedigree books and arranged their insurance with that lovely young man at Woodford & Kinloch who tragically died in a motor accident, so the wheeze stopped.

You know that Bill Hitchen helped me; I helped him when he was stuck with a foal and no owner at Tatts a few years ago, and although he is a terrible crook, he is a very nice man.

The money is long gone. Little Archie sent it abroad for me and I shuffled it away for a very good charitable purpose. Anyway those buggers at Lloyd's do not really need it!

I regret that we never got to know each other better; I expect that you are bedding that lovely sister of yours, I do hope so.

That's about it. Case closed, look no further.

Love,

Fanny Downing

This needed to be discussed with Inspector Jackson but after the extravagance in Edinburgh, the penury of the mines and the solemnity of Headley Hall, consideration of any sort of social activity, such as lunch with Johnny Jackson, left Thadeus cold so he summoned the policeman to his office for a sandwich.

Thadeus ran over the case against Lady Frances, as outlined to Freddie the previous week and confessed to Jackson that he had expected to be able to name the lady as the murderer of Sir Percy Dennington; the motive being his discovery of her fraudulent claims. But the lady made no mention whatsoever of Sir Percy in her letter, and her reference to Archie Wickham, anticipated as another of her victims, was very consolatory

The only new factor was that this letter gave them the opportunity to approach the Lloyd's Committee, in particular Mr A L Sturge, and obtain his approval for an official inspection of the claims files held at the offices of the processing Brokers for the Woodford & Kinloch business, Messrs Pearson & Salter. They would not take kindly to an inspection of their files by another competitor broker, but the presence of a Scotland Yard detective and the backing of Mr Sturge should prevail. All the various other more devious methods that Thadeus had employed to gain access to full information had yielded very little; he was not hopeful of finding anything startling and it may be that these claims were not connected to Percy's murder, or maybe suicide.

After a long telephone conversation with his sister about the merits of purchasing a bicycle shop in Trinity Street, Cambridge, with a two-bedroom flat above for nearly £2,000 – it being decided that the freehold with a rental income from a tenant in an industry flourishing in Cambridge, and within walking distance of Addenbrooke Hospital, was an excellent opportunity – Thadeus met Jackson at the offices of Messrs Pearson & Salter.

Mr Pearson introduced his claims manager, a Mr Wright, and the four of them sat around the boardroom table in front of five beige folders. Thadeus read carefully through each file, turning the pages slowly, sometimes going back and re-reading; the three others just watched. Mr Wright explained that they handled very little bloodstock insurances and there was no particular separate system for this class of business, any member of the claim's department might have dealt with any of these claims and any of a group of claim's brokers may have presented the papers to the underwriters. Thadeus opened each of the five files at the page on which the underwriter had actually agreed settlement of the claim, and took a clean sheet of paper from a foolscap pad provided by Pearson; he then made observations aloud to the small audience.

'The settlement of this claim…' he placed a finger on one file, 'was agreed by Edward Thurlow. This one… ,' moving his finger to the next file, 'by his brother George; this one by Mr Edward Mannings and this one by Sir Percy Dennington; and the final one by George Thurlow again. I know that because of the quota share arrangement it was, and still is, possible for a broker to use either box for bloodstock claims depending on who is available, but this diversity is either by design or very fortuitous for the fraudulent claimant.'

Both Mr Pearson and Mr Wright leapt to their feet with shouts of protest.

Thadeus paused. 'I think that Lady Frances was very lucky, because if these five files had been brought before the same man he would have noticed the similarities and raised the alarm. Same agent, same veterinary surgeon; it could not be missed.'

'The claims range over a period of fourteen months,' defended Mr Wright, who had obviously read the files before the visit, as would be expected of a diligent claims manager under scrutiny.

'I cannot see Messrs Pearson & Salter risking their reputation over such a paltry sum as £21,000,' smiled Thadeus.

The group laughed, without enthusiasm.

'I can see no problem with the broking here, can you inspector?' asked Thadeus of Jackson.

'No,' said the embarrassed detective, thinking that Thadeus was getting his own back for the employment of Freddie with a gun in Edinburgh.

'However, there is one thing on this file agreed by Mr Mannings that I would like to look at closer,' said Thadeus seriously. 'On this page with his agreement to settle the claim there appears to be some writing that has been erased – the surface of the paper is disturbed and there is the faint outline of some writing.'

He held up the relevant sheet for inspection by the assembly, all three showing signs of confusion. They each took turns at a closer inspection of the offending area, bending right on top of the spot and holding it at different angles and under different lights.

'Do we have a soft lead pencil?' questioned Thadeus.

Pearson was on his feet immediately bawling at a girl in the outer office corridor, 'Soft lead pencil. Quickly, quickly.'

A harassed, senior looking lady, rushed in with the requested utensil.

Thadeus took the implement and started to shade across the suspect image, looking up he said, 'I think that this has been done before,'

'Sir Percy Dennington had all these files last year,' said Mr Wright. 'I thought that you knew that?'

'We certainly did not,' said Jackson roughly.

Thadeus finished his work. 'Ring 901,' he announced.

'Means nothing to me,' said Pearson, and Wright agreed with him.

'Just an *aide memoir*,' suggested Jackson. 'Someone made a note of a phone number, and then rubbed it out.'

'Yes,' said Thadeus, and the whole case opened up before him.

Thadeus and Jackson took their leave of Messrs Pearson and Wright, Thadeus assuring the pair that there would be no further imposition on their time. Jackson, in less generous mood, gave one of his 'do not leave town' speeches.

'You seem excited,' said Jackson to Thadeus when they were back in Leadenhall Street.

'There is work to be done,' was the mysterious response.

One of the pieces of work to be done was to telephone Lady Daphne Dennington, at her home, which Thadeus did the next day. After an exchange of pleasantries including condolences on the sad loss of her schooldays' friend, Thadeus, apologizing for his impertinence, asked if she would be good enough to glance at the bookshelf in the office to see if Sir Percy had a copy of *Horse Breeding in Theory and Practice* by Burchard Von Oettingen, which he would be obliged if he could borrow for some pedigree research on which he was working.

She said that she would certainly look, but at the present time she was in the house and, as he knew, Percy's books were still out in the stables, however, if it was there she would bring it with her to Lady Frances's funeral service tomorrow!

Friday morning Thadeus and Freddie were up at dawn and, after a gulp of tea and a bite of toast, leaving London in the Bentley and on their way to Cambridge for an appointment with a gentleman who would show them around the flat in Trinity Street. They arrived at 9.00 am precisely and spent exactly thirty minutes on the inspection, including a conversation with the bicycle man, who promised a free bicycle and complimentary servicing for the vehicle to the new owner of the freehold in consideration of advantage at his next rent review the following year. The Burke siblings were delighted with the premises and gave the estate agent details of the family solicitor and told him to proceed with all haste before one of the colleges snapped it up.

Back in the car they set out for Norfolk and the funeral of Lady Frances Downing, arriving at noon, in good time for the ceremony. It was an affair of great dignity, the vicar speaking in a clear articulate manner and the speech by the master of the local hunt delivered with sincerity and charm. Gussie, assisted by a bevy of legally trained volunteers, gave the occasion the appearance of a courtroom drama, lots of nodding and pointing, witnesses being summoned forward and backwards, before the coffin was finally sentenced to its earthly resting place.

Lady Frances's only son informed the congregation that his mother had left explicit instructions that all those in attendance at her final appearance should be granted the opportunity of sufficient alcoholic beverages as to ensure that their bodies and minds would not forget the occasion, to be served back at The Hall.

Thereafter, almost as part of the interment, following the sprinkling of dust, ashes and clods of Norfolk clay, the gathering trooped ceremonially onward, the one hundred yards or so, into the ancestral home of the Downings. Mr Edward Mannings holding the arm of a tearful Lady Daphne Dennington; Mr George Thurlow, solitary and distinguished; the Honourable Thadeus Burke and his sister Doctor Lady Frederica Burke, the latter clad in black from head to toe, an appearance that had already alarmed horses, cabbies and cyclist in the City of Cambridge, especially as she had somewhat overdone the pale make-up in her early morning alacrity; members of the Downing clan, from aged brother-in-law to newly born second cousin; and a goodly band of local farmers accompanied by a surprisingly large turnout of their sturdy offspring.

Gussie gave a short speech of welcome, including the unnecessary divulgence that his late mater's last will and testimony had read simply, 'I leave everything to my son Gussie, a nice boy but as daft as a brush'. Possibly Gussie's astute legal mind opined this to be a wise announcement in the present company, that included kith and kin from all parts of the country.

Drinks begun to flow and the tone of conversation loosened into less formal banter, chuckles and good-natured cries of astonishment were heard around the huge room. Mannings and Thurlow discussed serious-looking Lloyd's matters and Lady Daphne floated from group to group unable to settle.

Gussie, now in relaxed mood, joined Thadeus and Freddie with an enormous glass of gin and tonic and they chatted about days gone past and retold well-worn tales of mutual embarrassments or successes, then Gussie announced that he needed to grab Daphne Dennington before she disappeared to discuss his mother's charity accounts and make arrangements for a meeting to formalize transfers and dissolutions of funds and closure of banking arrangements, and so on.

'Lady Daphne handled your mother's charity finances did she?' asked Thadeus.

'Oh yes. She is an absolute wizard at figures: if she had not married so young she could have qualified as an accountant, or graduated and become a mathematician or an economist.'

Thadeus and Freddie did the circuit of polite farewells, were handed a copy of *Horse Breeding* by B. Von Oettingen from the hands of Lady Daphne's chauffeur, and headed back to London, stopping for dinner at a Chinese restaurant in Limehouse.

Racing at Fakenham for the next day had been cancelled due to hard ground.

Saturday morning Thadeus announced that he was going to pay a surprise visit to Lady Daphne Dennington, also there were two stud properties in the Newmarket vicinity that could possibly be for sale, at the right price. Freddie insisted on a role in this latter venture, so the Bugatti was put back into action.

A leisurely drive of two hours found them rejecting the first of the equine establishments. With so much mud around the paddock gates they feared that animals would submerge from sight, giving problems with any insurance policy that stipulated a post mortem to substantiate a claim, although Thadeus thought that possibly one of the marine transit clauses might allow loss by sinking. The academic considerations being halted by Freddie's exclaimed: 'I'm not going in there with any shoes of mine!'

The next appointment was more promising, on the Cambridge side of the town, which pleased Freddie who disliked the proliferation of stables and pubs in the municipality that gave the area, in her words 'a veneer of horse-dung and vomit'.

The elderly widow who had struggled with the property for several years took to Freddie like a long lost daughter; they inspected the main house together. Thadeus patrolled the four large paddocks and wandered in and out of stables and barns, returning to find the new female friends engaged in scone making in an enormous kitchen; they hardly noticed him take his leave and drive away towards Dullingham and Lady Daphne's small empire.

'You have not read that large book already?' welcomed Daffy Dennington.

'I only consulted one chapter,' excused Thadeus. 'Actually I wanted to speak to you about Lady Frances' charity accounts and the work that you have been engaged on for Mr Mannings.'

This statement clearly distressed Lady Daphne for she sat down on a nearby wooden chair, head sunk into her lap and wept like a small child. 'Fanny has gone. Percy has gone. My whole world is destroyed,' she choked.

'You appropriated some money from Lady Frances's funds?' suggested Thadeus.

'Yes, but not much! I told Fanny and she said not to worry; she had a scheme to put it all back.'

'Twenty-one thousand pounds,' said Thadeus

'No, only half of that amount,' defended Daphne. 'Mr Mannings and I needed it, temporarily.'

'Did Fanny have other financial problems?' questioned Thadeus

'Yes, she was experiencing difficulty with the cash call for her Lloyd's losses on the Thurlow syndicate.'

Thadeus thought it was ironic that Lady Frances had devised a fraud to reimburse her cash paid to the Thurlow syndicate, and the money taken by her friend Daphne to fill some hole that had arisen in the hidden Mannings syndicate scheme; and her fraud was financed by the two Lloyd's syndicates themselves.

'You did not know how Fanny obtained the extra money?' asked Thadeus

'No, I think that it was something to do with her horses,' explained Daphne

Extraordinary, thought Thadeus

'Your husband did not talk to you about an insurance fraud that he was investigating involving false pedigrees?'

'No. He was upset because he had discovered somehow that I was handling accounts work for Mr Mannings. We had a terrible row; he demanded an explanation and I told him all about the work I had been doing. Then that weekend he committed suicide.' Again the poor lady burst into tears. 'I killed him,' she croaked.

Thadeus handed Daphne a handkerchief, but remained seated, objective and alert. 'Credit insurance?' he said.

'Yes. How did you know?' her tearful face looked up.

'Tell me all about it,' he directed.

Daphne leaned back in the uncomfortable chair with a look of thankful relief on her face. 'I used to work for Mr Mannings handling underwriting accounts, meeting brokers and the auditors, this was before the War. Then I married Percy and that was the end of my city involvement. Percy went into the army and I carried on here, and on occasions assisted Mr Mannings when there was a big panic on because of the lack of staff; all away fighting. When the war ended we bought this place, Percy returned to Lloyd's and I ran the home. Then in 1923 that man Harrison got into lots of difficulty with his syndicate suffering huge losses writing credit insurance and the whole market had to bail him out; it cost them over £300,000.'

Thadeus nodded, he was familiar with the fracas, and remembered the Committee coming and goings being the subject of all the conversation during his first year at Lloyd's.

Daphne continued. 'From 1st January 1924 Mr Sturge banned all direct credit insurance or any sort of financial guarantee business being conducted in the Room, other than as reinsurance. Cuthbert Heath opposed him and the embargo was quite illegal; the Lloyd's Act of 1911 stated specifically that it was the duty of Lloyd's to provide guarantee business,' a questionable statement from Daphne. 'Anyway Mr Sturge won the day and Heath had set up his Trade Indemnity Company and handled his credit business as reinsurance and everybody was reasonably happy; except Mr Mannings! He had spent a lot of time and money setting up his own credit insurance scheme. It was kept secret; he did not want Cuthbert Heath to find out about it. I did most of the work up here in my home. He issued a blanket policy commencing on the 31st December 1923 so avoiding the necessity to use the Lloyd's Policy Signing Office, and I operated the scheme from here with agents and monthly bordereaux; and a separate bank account in Norwich, the same bank as used by Fanny Downing.'

Thadeus went across to the drinks cabinet and poured them both a large whisky and water each, and Daphne continued.

'Unfortunately the business started badly and we had very high losses; one of the agents was selling motor cars on hire purchase agreements to itinerant farm workers in Norfolk and some of these chaps only earned thirty shillings a week; they were selling the cars for twenty-five pounds and disappearing. We sorted it all out eventually, hiring a private detective to find the vehicles, repossess them and resell them, but it took a long time and was an expensive operation.'

'Who was that motor agent?' interrupted Thadeus.

'A man named Hollington,' said Daphne. 'We had a serious word with him and he has been a good boy since, one of our best customers.'

'Are you still operating this scheme?' asked a worried Thadeus.

'No, we ceased business at the end of last year; we could not think of a way of continuing the illegal policy. The 1925 policy was renewed by a letter, which would not stand up in court.'

'So the early losses were funded by Fanny's charity fund?'

'Yes, we could not get legal access to the Mannings syndicate funds.'

'Because you kept separate books, not seen by the audit committee?'

'Yes,' came the sheepish reply from the lady. 'The final net result of the two years underwriting was a profit of nearly £18,000,' a proud but pathetic conclusion to her narrative.

The telephone rang. 'It's your sister,' announced Lady Daphne.

'Do you think that I will go to prison?' asked the lady as Thadeus took his leave, under instructions to return to Newmarket and rescue Freddie from a demonstration of marmalade making.

Thadeus assured Lady Daphne Dennington that he would do everything he could to resolve the dilemma without the involvement of the courts. He drove off thinking that already Lady Daphne was talking on the telephone to Mr Edward Mannings.

Freddie was delighted with the stud and they agreed that it should be purchased, the present owner being willing to deal exclusively with them regarding the future of the property, although Thadeus emphasized that a thorough budget and business plan would need to be considered before a final decision on their venture into bloodstock breeding could be reached. Freddie needed some convincing that it was not just a question of going out one afternoon and buying a few mares, sending them to be covered by stallions and then entering the progeny into the Tattersalls sales; staff would need to be interviewed and employed. The whole thing might take years to come to fruition, like a home the expanse of land required hefty maintenance costs.

Although thrilled to bits with the idea, Thadeus was pleased to change the conversation on to his discoveries of the afternoon and deliver some explanations to his sister about credit insurance, bills of exchange and Lloyd's underwriting liabilities; she could not understand why the activities of Daphne Dennington and Edward Mannings needed such underhand and secret consideration.

'What is credit insurance, and why is it so dangerous?' was her enquiry.

'When money is borrowed the borrower signs some document to confirm his intention to repay the loan.'

'Obviously,' said Freddie

'This document may take many forms and in most cases be accompanied by a guarantee from a bank or private individual of known wealth; traditionally a bill of exchange was used, a financial instrument recognized in the money market and a transferable document that the lender could sell to obtain his money at any time he desired.'

'I do not see the point of that; if he needed the money, why lend it to someone else?'

It seemed a sensible question. 'The interest earned by him on the loan would exceed the discount he incurred selling the bill.'

'And if the borrower dishonoured the deal someone else would pick up to loss!'

'Yes, and some years ago Mr Cuthbert Heath devised an insurance policy that would handle the guarantee simpler and cheaper, called a credit insurance policy.'

'Seems like a good idea. Why did Lloyd's not like it?'

Another good question. 'Well, in 1923 an underwriter named Harrison wrote a lot of this business and got into terrible trouble with dishonest clients and then made matters worse by trying to deceive the Committee of Lloyd's about his audit figures. He ran up a total liability of nearly £400,000 and the rest of the underwriters had to bail him out to protect the good name of Lloyd's.'

'One bad apple does not make – something,' said Freddie, forgetting the full proverb.

'That was Mr Heath's opinion, but the Committee took the view that this class of business was beyond supervision in a market that traded on individual unlimited liability and underwriting names, and the Lloyd's market generally, could not be exposed to such risks. A guarantor who cannot go broke is just too much of a good thing to be ignored by fraudsters!'

'But you tell me that Mr Mannings did not lose any money, in fact he made a profit, as I expect did Mr Heath. What is wrong with that?'

'Mr Heath abided by the rules using a reinsurance vehicle, Mr Mannings did not!'

'You are losing me slightly. But in a nutshell, if his secret business was discovered Mr Mannings would be drummed out of Lloyd's?'

'Yes,' said Thadeus, thinking that a return to the subject of bloodstock breeding would have been the preferable option.

'Poor Daphne Dennington, no wonder that she thinks her husband committed suicide when he discovered these shenanigans. She must have been in hell this last year, poor lady! If her husband was murdered she will probably find it a relief. What about that clerk at the Newmarket solicitors, Archie Wickham; who murdered him?'

'It must have been a genuine accident, or perhaps a jealous rival for the favours of Lady Frances. Some of those farmer's lads at the funeral looked capable of the simple task of running down a motor cycle ridden by a clerk; did you notice that one of them was carrying a gun over his arm – as he stood at the graveside?'

'It is a job for the police; Jackson cannot expect you to do all his work for him,' said Freddie, closing the subject.

Nobody slept well that night. Sunday was a day of relaxation and contemplation.

Freddie was reading notes on paediatrics and general child care, then she casually mentioned that last year at Edinburgh she had partaken in some voluntary fertility testing, using experimental equipment and drugs and had come up negative. 'Barren!' she said. 'Not a good marriage prospect!'

Thadeus and Hilton were dumbfounded but Freddie seemed totally undisturbed, happy with the thought of all the kids she would have around her in the new job.

The two men found themselves completely inadequate for the situation.

James Pooley and his fiancée Eddie Whitney came over for tea in their new car; Freddie and Eddie discussed home decoration colours and kitchen equipment; Freddie for her new flat in Cambridge and Eddie for her new house in Nunhead; then they moved on to the latest fashions in clothes and dancing. Thadeus and James, after some conversation about the prospects of the Newmarket property and the possibilities of using the house for company entertaining during the sales and racing weeks, and an update on the continuing progress of James' father's motor business on the Essex/Suffolk border, hammered out the questions of credit insurance and the Harrison affair, a debate that could have run all night; it was stopped by screams of, 'Dull, dull, dull' from the two girls.

Monday morning Thadeus sat at his desk opposite Clement Simpkins. They were discussing the month's figures, when the door opened and Edward Mannings entered. Thadeus stood to greet the underwriter.

'Sit down and give me the letter that Lady Frances wrote to you,' he demanded, taking a revolver from his inside pocket and pointing it at Thadeus's head.

Thadeus did as he was told, but at the same time pressed the button under his desk five times, four short and one long. He stooped down to his bottom left-hand drawer and fumbled through the papers therein, taking out one sheet, looking at it then replacing it and taking out another.

'Don't prevaricate,' snapped Mannings menacingly.

Thadeus appeared flustered and pulled out the whole drawer; Clement sat motionless. Then the door burst open and William Penrose staggered into the room holding a bottle of red wine. ''Scuse me boss,' he slurred. 'I've finished that slip you gave me and thought that I might pop off home.'

'Get out Penrose,' commanded Mannings turning towards the new arrival.

Realizing that this was a stupid thing to say, he was about to say a few more words when pain seared across his face. Clement Simpkins had reached across and grabbed the wrist holding the gun in a vice like grip; the poised fingers were frozen in time and space, and beginning to turn white.

'Give me a hand, William,' said Clement politely.

'Certainly, Clement,' replied Penrose, removing the weapon from the hand of Mr Mannings. 'I trust that you seeing me with this bottle in my hand does not breach my contract of employment,' he said to Thadeus.

Simpkins continued to hold tight to his victim until James Pooley arrived with a ball of string, and proceeded to tie Mr Mannings, unceremoniously to the second visitor's chair. James punctuated the activity with several 'Sorry Mr Mannings' to which the gentleman smiled wintrishly and stared bleakly out of the window.

Then Jackson arrived, summoned by Miss Mills, with a pair of handcuffs and two burly constables.

'Why don't you sit down and tell us all about it,' suggested Jackson

'I am sitting down,' responded a gloomy Mannings.

Thadeus thought it was about time he said something. 'Lady Frances did not mention you in her letter at all,' he disclosed to the prisoner.

Mannings chuckled. 'I knew Fanny when she was in her teens; in those days she had an appetite for older men, as she got older she switched her allegiance to younger models. What a girl!'

'Poor chap. He's had a complete breakdown,' said Jackson later that afternoon. 'Lucky that you spoke to me on Sunday and we were prepared for him – well, sort of prepared for him.'

'A two-man posse, one with an arm missing and the other drunk is not what I call preparation,' admonished Thadeus.

'We were on hand – no harm could have come to you. Anyway Simpkins is as strong as an ox and Penrose was not drunk.'

'You were not facing a loaded revolver,' emphasized Thadeus.

'Neither were you! My man unloaded the weapon in the lift – he is an ex-pickpocket, turned poacher,' laughed Jackson.

'You bastard,' said Thadeus. 'Did Mannings poison Sir Percy?'

'Yes; told us all about it – very sad. Took a small bottle of Drambuie up to the stud, together with a bottle of whisky for himself; tried to persuade Sir Percy not to grass on him, failed and suggest a drink for old times sake. Percy dropped dead and Mannings continued right through the whole of his bottle, fell asleep and drove home the next morning before anybody was about. For a long while he convinced himself that it had all been a bad dream.'

There was a pause for reflection, then Jackson asked, 'Why was he after the letter from Lady Frances?'

'I expect that Lady Daphne heard about the letter at the funeral on Friday, perhaps Gussie told her, it was no secret that she had written to me. When I confronted her about the Mannings credit insurance arrangements on the Saturday, she must have assumed that Lady Frances knew of the matter, maybe a slip of the tongue between the two friends. Anyway she thought that Lady F's letter had put me on to her; she told Mannings this, and it became his passion to redeem it with all haste.'

'It is extraordinary that a man of his standing should resort to criminal action like we witnessed today,' said James Pooley.

'He was already involved in crime as a Lloyd's man; breaking a trust with his fellow underwriters was for him a more dastardly act than murder,' noted Thadeus.

'What put you on to the Daphne Dennington – Edward Mannings connection?' asked Jackson.

'The file at Pearson & Salter's office,' replied Thadeus.

'From the note about ringing 901?' stated Jackson.

'I recognized Daphne Dennington's office telephone number, from her visiting card that she had given me at Tattersalls, Newmarket 901, but I thought at that time that it was the office used by her husband, Percy, built into one of the stables. Later, after we had studied the files, when I used the number to ask about a book that I knew was in

Percy's stable office she told me that she was at that time within the house, confirming my suspicion that she also ran an office herself upstairs in the main building. Also, of course, I recognized Edward Mannings' handwriting of the telephone number on the Pearson & Salter claim's file,'

'Why did Mannings write the number down on that file?' asked Jackson.

'He didn't,' said Thadeus. 'He jotted down a note that would make sense to him later, probably on one of those pieces of note paper that many boxes have hanging on a wire hook ready for quotes or memos, and the imprint of the writing was left on the file that happened to be in front of him at the time. Then when Percy obtained the files from Pearson & Salter for his investigation into the fraudulent claims, he noticed the indentations and thinking that they might be relevant to his scrutiny, used the same trick as us and shaded the area with a soft lead pencil, then erased the markings, smudging the paper as we later observed. Imagine his surprise to find his boss having made a note to ring his wife in her office in his own house.'

'And he challenged her about the connection?' suggested James.

'Yes, and got a full confession about the illegal credit insurance operation that she was running from home.'

'Then she went away for the weekend on the prearranged visit to her sister. It is no wonder that she was convinced that her husband had committed suicide,' said Jackson,

'Unfortunately she did not leave that night before telephoning Mannings and giving him the bad news that his dubious unlawful underwriting enterprise had been exposed to one of his staff and a fellow member of Lloyd's,' said Thadeus, downing his last drink of the afternoon. 'Home, Jackson,' he ordered. 'We have a meeting with Mr Sturge tomorrow morning.'

Three men sat in the Committee Rooms at Lloyd's with cups of coffee. Thadeus and Jackson relayed the events of the past week and the investigation over the last seven months; the ex-chairman listened attentively, making occasional notes.

'I think that I shall call you two the Lloyd's Investigation Department,' said Mr Sturge.

'Is there a subtle mnemonic in that title?' asked Thadeus.

'There could well be Mr Burke, there could well be.'

It had been decided that the fraudulent bloodstock claims should be left unrevealed. The money involved was substantial but had simply gone round in a circle, or off to a charity, and the perpetrator was dead. Off the record Thadeus would have a quiet word with Gussie, and with the help of Lady Daphne's charity books, some recovery could be made without the force of the law being used. The credit insurance profits would be returned to the syndicate, and the books fully investigated and audited. Mr Mannings would not appear in court but make a guilty plea before a magistrate, his barrister presenting medical evidence of the man's insanity and consequent diminished responsibility and the need of hospitalisation, a verdict with which Jackson was not entirely happy. Daphne Dennington would probably remarry one day; she was a wealthy, good-looking woman. The good name of Lloyd's would be unsullied.

Mr Sturge expressed his thanks for the full briefing and was grateful that the matter had been kept within the Lloyd's community, Thadeus having apologized to Howard Carter, the journalist, for being unable to deliver the promised coup, having considered the whole matter too delicate for the public eye and ear.

They shook hands and went to their separate next appointments.

The next week Inspector Jackson came into the Burke & Co office for a cup of coffee and wandered into Thadeus' room to generally make a nuisance of himself.

Thadeus was deep in study, pouring over stud books and old sales catalogues, writing names down on a foolscap sheet of paper.

'Working on a new case of pedigree fraud?' asked Jackson.

'A dastardly situation,' said Thadeus, looking up. 'There are over a thousand suspects.'

'Murder?' questioned Jackson.

'Worse!' said Thadeus.

'A massacre?' suggested the inspector.

'Close, but even more horrendous,' smiled Thadeus.

'I give up,' surrendered Jackson.

'I am seeking the winner of the Derby. If I can just find his mum this year and his dad next year, I'll book you in for the first Wednesday in June 1931.'